The Strollers

By
Frederic Stewart Isham

Double 9
BOOKS

The Strollers

by Frederic Stewart Isham

Copyright © 2024

ISBN: 978-93-56562-93-6

Published by

DOUBLE 9 BOOKS

2/13-B, Ansari Road
Daryaganj, New Delhi - 110002
info@double9books.com
www.double9books.com
Tel. 011-40042856

Printed in India.

About the Author

F rederic Stewart Isham was an American author and dramatist who composed mostly verifiable sentiments and experience books.

Isham was brought into the world in Detroit, Michigan, the child of Charles Storrs Isham and Lucy B. (Mott) Isham. He learned at the Royal Academy of Music in London for a considerable length of time. In 1895 he wedded Helen Margaret Frue He kicked the bucket in New York.

Isham started as a writer and later went to books, composing principally verifiable sentiments and experience books set in different periods. The shopping extravaganza following Thanksgiving, for instance, focuses on the American monetary emergency of 1869, while Under the Rose is set in sixteenth century Europe. His encounters in venue illuminated his most memorable novel, The Strollers. Mencken composed of his clever Half a Chance that it was "an energetic and engaging story, with not an excess of reality in it," which well sums up the overall tenor of Isham's work.

Contents

BOOK III:
THE FINAL CUE

PROLOGUE

THE MARQUIS' HONEYMOON

Old Drury Lane rang with applause for the performance of Madame Carew. Of British-French parentage, she was a recognized peer among the favorite actresses on the English stage and a woman whose attractions of face and manner were of a high order. She came naturally by her talents, being a descendant of Madame de Panilnac, famed as an actress, confidante of Louise-Benedicte, Duchess du Maine, who originated the celebrated nuits blanches at Sceaux during the close of Louis XIV's reign.

The bill for the evening under consideration was "Adrienne Lecouvreur" and in no part had the actress been more natural and effective. Her triumph was secure, for as the prologue says:

"Your judgment given--your sentence must remain; No writ of error lies--to Drury Lane."

She was the talk of the day and her praises or deficiencies were discussed by the scandal-carriers of the town; the worn-out dowagers, the superannuated maidens, the "tabernacle gallants," the male members of the tea tables and all the coxcombs, sparks and beaux who haunted the stage door.

The player had every stimulus to appear at her best on this particular evening, for the audience, frivolous, volatile, taking its character from the loose, weak king, was unusually complaisant through the presence of the first gentleman of Europe. As the last of the Georges declared himself in good-humor, so every toady grinned and every courtly flunkey swore in the Billingsgate of that profanely eloquent period that the actress was a "monstrous fine woman."

With rare discretion and spirit had the latter played, a queenly figure in that ribald, gross gathering. She had reached the scene where the actress turns upon her tormentors, those noble ladies of rank and position, and launches the curse of a soul lashed beyond endurance. Sweeping forward to confront her adversaries, about to face them, her troubled glance chanced to fall into one of the side boxes where were seated a certain foreign marquis, somewhat notorious, and a lady of insolent, patrician bearing. The anticipated action was arrested, for at sight of the nobleman and his companion, Adrienne swayed slightly, as though moved by a new overpowering emotion. Only for a moment she hesitated, then fixing her blazing eyes upon the two and lifting her arm threateningly, the bitter words flowed from her lips with an earnestness that thrilled the audience. A pallor overspread the face of the marquis, while the lady drew back behind the draperies, almost as if in fear. At the conclusion of that effort the walls echoed with plaudits; the actress stood as in a trance; her face was pale, her figure seemed changed to stone and the light went out of her eyes.

She fainted and fell and the curtain descended quickly. The woman by the marquis' side, who had trembled at first, now forced a laugh, as she said: "The trollop can curse! Let us go." Together they left the box, the marquis regretting the temerity which had led him to bring his companion to the theater. He, too, was secretly unnerved, and, when they entered the carriage, they seated themselves as far apart as possible, the marquis detesting the lady and she for her part disliking him just as cordially.

Next day the critics referred to the scene with glowing words, while in the coffee houses they discussed the proposition: Should an actress feel the emotion she portrays? With a cynical smile the marquis read the different accounts of the performance, when he and his companion found themselves in the old stage coach en route for Brighton. He felt no regret for his action--had not the Prince of Wales taught the gentlemen of his kingdom that it was fashionable to desert actresses? Had he not left the "divine Perdita" to languish, after snubbing her right royally in Hyde Park?

Disdainfully the lady in the coach regarded her husband and it was evident that the ties of affection which bound these two travelers together on life's road were neither strong nor enduring. Yet they were traveling together; their way was the same; their destination--but that belongs to the future. The marquis had been relieved in his mind after a consultation with a distinguished barrister, and, moreover, was pleased at the prospect of leaving this island of fogs for the sunny shores of France. The times were exciting; the country, on the verge of proposed electoral reforms. But in France the new social system had sprung into existence and--lamentable fact!--duty towards one's country had assumed an empire superior to ancient devotion toward kings.

To stem this tide and attach himself closely to King Charles X was the marquis' ambitious purpose. For this he had espoused a party in marrying a relative of the royal princess, thus enhancing the ties that bound him to the throne, and throwing to the winds his Perdita whose charms had once held him in folly's chains. Did he regret the step? Has ravening aspiration any compunction; any contrite visitings of nature? What did the player expect; that he would violate precedence; overthrow the fashionable maxims of good George IV; become a slave to a tragi-comic performer and cast his high destiny to the winds? Had ever a gentleman entertained such a project? Vows? Witness the agreeable perjuries of lovers; the pleasing pastime of fond hearts! Every titled rascallion lied to his mistress; every noble blackguard professed to be a Darby for constancy and was a Jonathan Wild by instinct. If her ideals were raised so high, the worse for her; if a farce of a ceremony was regarded as tying an indissoluble knot--let her take example by the lady who thought herself the king's spouse; pish! there are ceremonies and ceremonies, and wives and wives; those of the hedge-concealed cottage and those of palace and chateau!

As the coach sped over the road, the lady by his side smiled disagreeably from time to time, and my lord, when he became aware of it, winced beneath her glance. Had she fathomed his secret? Else why that eminently superior air; that manner which said as plainly as spoken words: "Now I have learned what to do if he should play the tyrant. Now I see a way to liberty, equality, fraternity!" And beneath the baneful gleam of that look of enlightenment, my lord cursed under his breath roundly. The only imperturbable person of the party was François, the marquis' valet, whose impassive countenance was that of a stoic, apathetic to the foibles of his betters; a philosopher of the wardrobe, to whom a wig awry or a loosened buckle seemed of more moment than the derangement of the marriage tie or the disorder of conjugal affection.

Not long thereafter the player left for America, where she procured an engagement in New York City, and, so far as London was concerned, she might have found rest and retiredness in the waters of Lethe. Of her reception in the old New York Theater; the verdict of the phalanx of critics assembled in the Shakespeare box which, according to tradition, held more than two hundred souls; the gossip over confections or tea in the coffee room of the theater--it is unnecessary to dwell upon. But had not the player become a voluntary exile; had she not foregone her former life for the new; had she not found that joy sometimes begets the bitterest grief, there would have been no occasion for this chronicle.

BOOK I:
ON THE CIRCUIT IN
THE WILDERNESS

CHAPTER I:
THE TRAVELERS' FRIEND

I t was a drizzly day in the Shadengo Valley. A mist had settled down upon the old inn; lost to view was the landscape with its varied foliage. Only the immediate foreground was visible to a teamster who came down the road--the trees with dripping branches, and the inn from the eaves of which water fell to the ground with depressing monotony; the well with its pail for watering the horses and the log trough in whose limpid waters a number of speckled trout were swimming. The driver drew up his horses before the Travelers' Friend--as the place was named--and called out imperatively:

"Hullo there!"

No one appearing, he leaned over and impatiently rapped on the door with the heavy oak butt-end of his whip. Still there was no response. Again he knocked, this time louder than before, and was preparing for an even more vigorous assault upon the unhospitable entrance, when the door swung back and the landlord, a tall, gaunt individual, confronted the driver.

"Well, I heard ye," he said testily. "Are ye coming in or shall I bring it out?"

"Bring it out," was the gruff response of the disgruntled teamster.

Shortly afterwards mine host reappeared with a tankard of generous dimensions. The teamster raised it; slowly drained it to the bottom; dropped a coin into the landlord's hand; cracked his whip in a lively manner and moved on. The steam from his horses mingled with the mist and he was soon swallowed up, although the cheerful snap of his whip could yet be heard. Then that became inaudible and the boniface who had stood for a brief space in the doorway, empty tankard in hand, re-entered the house satisfied that no more transient patronage would be forthcoming at present.

Going through an outer room, called by courtesy a parlor, the landlord passed into an apartment which served as dining-room, sitting-room and bar. Here the glow of a wood fire from the well swept hearth and the aspect of the varied assortment of bottles, glasses and tankards, gave more proof of the fitness of the appellation on the creaking sign of the road-house than appeared from a superficial survey of its exterior and far from neat stable yard, or from that chilly, forbidding room, so common especially in American residences in those days, the parlor. Any doubt regarding the contents of the hospitable looking bottles was dispelled by such prominent inscriptions in gilt letters as "Whisky," "Brandy" and "Rum." To add to the effect, between the decanters were ranged glass jars of striped peppermint and winter-green candies, while a few lemons suggested pleasing possibilities of a hot sling, spiced rum flip or Tom and Jerry. The ceiling of this dining-room was blackened somewhat and the huge beams overhead gave an idea of the substantial character of the construction of the place. That fuel was plentiful, appeared in evidence in the open fireplace where were burning two great logs, while piled up against the wall were many other good-sized sections of hickory.

Seated at a respectful distance from this cheerful conflagration was a young man of perhaps five-and-twenty, whose travel-stained attire indicated he had but recently been on the road. Upon a chair near by were a riding-whip and hat, the latter spotted with mud and testifying to the rough character of the road over which he had come. He held a short pipe to his lips and blew clouds of smoke toward the fire, while upon a table, within arm's length, rested a glass of some hot mixture. But in spite of his comfortable surroundings, the expression of his face was not that of a person in harmony with the Johnsonian conclusion, "A chair in an inn is a throne of felicity." His countenance, well bronzed as a weather-tried trooper's, was harsh, gloomy, almost morose; not an unhandsome face, but set in such a severe cast the observer involuntarily wondered what experience had indited that scroll. Tall, large of limb, muscular, as was apparent even in a restful pose, he looked an athlete of the most approved type, active and powerful.

Mine host, having found his guest taciturn, had himself become genial, and now remarked as he entered: "How do you find the punch? Is it to your liking?"

"Yes," shortly answered the stranger, without raising his eyes from a moody regard of the fire.

"You're from France, I guess?" continued the landlord, as he seated himself on the opposite side of the fireplace. "Been here long? Where you going?" Without waiting for an answer to his first question he exercised his time-honored privilege of demanding any and all information from wayfarers at the Travelers' Friend.

"I say, where you going?" he repeated, turning over a log and sending a shower of sparks up the flue.

With no change of countenance the guest silently reached for his punch, swallowed a portion of it, replaced the glass on the table and resumed his smoking as though oblivious of the other's presence. Momentarily disconcerted, the landlord devoted himself once more to the fire. After readjusting a trunk of old hickory on the great andirons and gazing absently for a moment at the huge crane supporting an iron kettle of boiling water, mine host tipped back in his chair, braced his feet against the wall, lighted a vile-smelling pipe and again returned valiantly to the attack, resolved to learn more about his guest.

"I hear things are kind of onsettled in France?" he observed diplomatically, emitting a cloud of smoke. "I see in a Syracuse paper that Louis Philippe is no longer king; that he and the queen have fled to England. Perhaps, now,"--inwardly congratulating himself on his shrewdness--"you left Paris for political reasons?"

The stranger deliberately emptied his pipe and thrust it into his pocket, while the landlord impatiently awaited the response to his pointed query. When it came, however, it was not calculated to allay the curiosity of his questioner.

"Is it your practice," said the young man coldly, in slow but excellent English, "to bark continuously at the heels of your guests?"

"Oh, no offense meant! No offense! Hope none'll be taken," stammered the landlord.

Then he recovered himself and his dignity by drawing forth a huge wine-colored silk handkerchief, set with white polka-dots, and ostentatiously and vigorously using it. This ear-splitting operation having once more set him up in his own esteem, he resumed his attentions to the stranger.

"I didn't know," he added with an outburst of honesty, "but what you might be some nobleman in disguise."

"A nobleman!" said the other with ill-concealed contempt. "My name is Saint-Prosper; plain Ernest Saint-Prosper. I was a soldier. Now I'm an adventurer. There you have it all in a nut-shell."

The inn-keeper surveyed his guest's figure with undisguised admiration.

"Well, you look like a soldier," he remarked. "You are like one of those soldiers who came over from France to help us in the Revolution."

This tribute being silently accepted, the landlord grew voluble as his guest continued reserved.

"We have our own troubles with lords, too, right here in New York State," he said confidentially. "We have our land barons, descendants of the patroons and holders of thousands of acres. And we have our bolters, too, who are making a big stand against feudalism."

Thereupon he proceeded to present the subject in all its details to the soldier; how the tenants were protesting against the enforcement of what they now deemed unjust claims and were demanding the abolition of permanent leaseholds; how they openly resisted the collection of rents and had inaugurated an aggressive anti-rent war against tyrannical landlordism. His lengthy and rambling dissertation was finally broken in upon by a rumbling on the road, as of carriage wheels drawing near, and the sound of voices. The noise sent the boniface to the window, and, looking out, he discovered a lumbering coach, drawn by two heavy horses, which came dashing up with a great semblance of animation for a vehicle of its weight, followed by a wagon, loaded with diversified and gaudy paraphernalia.

"Some troopers, I guess," commented the landlord in a tone which indicated the coming of these guests was not entirely welcome to him. "Yes," he added, discontentedly, "they're stage-folk, sure enough."

The wagon, which contained several persons, was driven into the stable yard, where it was unloaded of "drops" and "wings," representing a street, a forest, a prison, and so on, while the stage coach, with a rattle and a jerk, and a final flourish of the driver's whip, stopped at the front door. Springing to the ground, the driver opened the door of the vehicle, and at the same time two other men, with their heads muffled against the wind and rain, leisurely descended from the top. The landlord now stood at the entrance of the inn, a sour expression on his face. Certainly, if the travelers had expected in him the traditional glowing countenance, with the apostolic injunction to "use hospitality without grudging" writ upon it, they were doomed to disappointment.

A rustle of skirts, and there emerged from the interior of the coach, first, a little, dried-up old lady whose feet were enclosed in prunella boots, with Indian embroidered moccasins for outside protection; second, a young woman who hastily made her way into the hostelry, displaying a trim pair of ankles; third, a lady resembling the second and who the landlord afterwards learned was her sister; fourth, a graceful girl above medium height, wearing one of those provoking, quilted silk hoods of the day, with cherry-colored lining, known as "Kiss-me-if-you-dare" hoods.

Then followed a dark melancholy individual, the utility man, whose waistcoat of figured worsted was much frayed and whose "tooth-pick" collar was the worse for the journey. He preceded a more natty person in a bottle-green, "shad-belly" coat, who strove to carry himself as though he were fashionably dressed, instead of wearing clothes which no longer could conceal their shabbiness. The driver, called in theatrical parlance "the old man," was a portly personage in a blue coat with velvet collar and gilt buttons, a few of which were missing; while the ruffles of his shirt were in sad plight, for instead of protruding elegantly a good three or even four inches, their glory had gone and they lay ignominiously flattened upon the bosom of the wearer. A white choker rivaled in hue the tooth-pick collar of the melancholy individual.

The tavern's stable boy immediately began to remove the trunks into the main hallway. This overgrown, husky lad evidently did not share his employer's disapproval of the guests, for he gazed in open-eyed wonder at the sisters, and then, with increasing awe, his glance strayed to the young girl. To his juvenile imagination an actress appeared in the glamour of a veritable goddess. But she had obviously that tender consideration for others which belongs to humanity, for she turned to the old man with an affectionate smile, removing from his shoulders the wet Petersham overcoat, and, placing it on a chair, regarded him with a look of filial anxiety. Yet their appearance belied the assumption of such relationship; he was hearty, florid and sturdy, of English type, while she seemed a daughter of the South, a figure more fitting for groves of orange and cypress, than for this rugged northern wilderness.

The emotion of the stable boy as he gazed at her, and the forbidding mood of the landlord were broken in upon by the tiny old lady, who, in a large voice, remarked:

"A haven at last! Are you the landlord?"

"Yes, ma'am," testily replied that person.

"I am pleased to meet you, sir," exclaimed the melancholy individual, as he extended a hand so cold and clammy that shivers ran up and down the back of the host when he took it gingerly. "We are having fine tragedy weather, sir!"

"A fire at once, landlord!" commanded the would-be beau.

"Refreshments will be in order!" exclaimed she of the trim ankles.

"And show me the best room in the house," remarked her sister.

Mine host, bewildered by this shower of requests, stared from one to the other in helpless confusion, but finally collected his wits sufficiently to usher the company into the tap-room with:

"Here you'll find a fire, but as for the best room, this gentleman"--indicating the reticent guest--"already occupies it."

The young man at the fire, thus forced prominently into notice, arose slowly.

"You are mistaken, landlord," he said curtly, hardly glancing at the players. "I no longer occupy it since these ladies have come."

"Your complaisance does credit to your good nature, sir," exclaimed the old man. "But we can not take advantage of it."

"It is too good of you," remarked the elder sister with a glance replete with more gratitude than the occasion demanded. "Really, though, we could not think of it."

"Thank you; thank you," joined in the wiry old lady, bobbing up and down like a miniature figure moved by the unseen hand of the showman. "Allow me, sir!" And she gravely tendered him a huge snuff-box of tortoise shell, which he declined; whereupon she continued:

"You do not use it? New fashions; new habits! Though whether for the better is not for me to say."

She helped herself to a liberal portion and passed the box to the portly old gentleman. Here the landlord, in a surly tone, told the stable boy to remove the gentleman's things and show the ladies to their rooms. Before going, the girl in the provoking hood--now unfastened, and freeing sundry rebellious brown curls where the moisture yet sparkled like dew--turned to the old man:

"You are coming up directly? Your stock wants changing, while your ruffles"--laughing--"are disgraceful!"

"Presently, my dear; presently!" he returned.

The members of the company mounted the broad stairway, save the driver of the coach--he of the disordered ruffles--who wiped his heavy boots on a door mat and made his way to the fire, where he stood in English fashion with his coat-tails under his arms, rubbing his hands and drying himself before the flames.

"A disagreeable time of year, sir," he observed to the soldier, who had returned to his seat before the table. "Twice on the road we nearly broke down, and once the wagon dumped our properties in the ditch. Meanwhile, to make matters worse, the ladies heaped reproaches upon these gray hairs. This, sir, to the man who was considered one of the best whips in old Devonshire county."

The other did not answer immediately, but regarded the speaker with the look of one not readily disposed to make acquaintances. His conclusions were apparently satisfactory, however, for he presently vouchsafed the remark:

"You are the manager, I presume?"

"I enjoy that honor," returned the loquacious stranger. "But my duties are manifold. As driver of the chariot, I endure the constant apprehension of wrecking my company by the wayside. As assistant carpenter, when we can not find a stage it is my task to erect one. As bill-poster and license-procurer, treasurer and stage manager, my time is not so taken up, sir, as to preclude my going on and assuming a character."

"A life of variety," observed the young man, politely if indifferently.

"Yes; full of ups and downs, as the driver of the property wagon said when we entered this hilly district," replied the manager, with the contentment of a man who has found a snug haven after a hard ride in a comparatively unbroken country. "Affluence we may know, but poverty is apt to be our companion."

To this the other deemed no response necessary and a silence fell between them, broken only by the simmering water in the iron kettle, the sputtering of the sap in the burning logs and the creaking without of the long balancing pole that suspended the moss-covered bucket. The wind sighed in the chimney and the wooing flames sprang to meet it, while the heart of the fire glowed in a mass of coals between the andirons.

The old gentleman before the blaze began to outrival the kettle in steaming; from his coat-tails a thin veil of mist ascended, his face beaming through the vapor with benign felicity. Then he turned and toasted the other side and the kettle reigned supreme until he thawed once more and the clouds ascended, surrounding him like Jupiter on the celestial mount. At that the kettle hummed more angrily and the old gentleman's face beamed with satisfaction.

"A snug company, sir," he said, finally, glowing upon the impassive face before him, "like a tight ship, can weather a little bad weather. Perhaps you noticed our troupe? The old lady is Mrs. Adams. She is nearly seventy, but can dance a horn-pipe or a reel with the best of them. The two sisters are Kate and Susan Duran, both coquettes of the first water. Our juvenile man is a young Irishman who thinks much of his dress and little of the cultivation of mind and manners. Then," added the old man tenderly, "there is my Constance."

He paused abruptly. "Landlord, a pot of ale. My throat is hoarse from the mist. Fancy being for hours on a road not knowing where you are! Your good-fortune, sir!" Lifting the mug. "More than once we lurched like a cockle-shell."

The conversation at this point was interrupted by the appearance of the juvenile man.

"Mr. Barnes, the ladies desire your company immediately."

The manager hurriedly left the room and the newcomer regarded his retiring figure with a twinkle in his eye. Then he took a turn around the room in stilted fashion--like one who "carried about with him his pits, boxes and galleries"--and observed:

"Faith, Mr. Barnes' couch is not a bed of roses. It is better to have the fair ones dangling after you, than to be running at their every beck and call."

Here he twisted his mustache upward.

"A woman is a strange creature," he resumed. "If she calls and you come once, your legs will be busy for the rest of your natural days."

He seemed about to continue his observations along this philosophical line, when the manager appeared in much perturbation, approaching the landlord, who, at the same time, had entered the room from the kitchen.

"The ladies insist that their sheets are damp," began the manager in his most plausible manner.

A dangerous light appeared in the other's eyes.

"It's the weather, you understand. Not your fault; bless you, no!"

The landlord's face became a shade less acrimonious.

"Now, if there was a fire in the room--it is such a comfortable, cheery room--"

"Sandy!" interrupted the host, calling to the long-armed, red-handed stable boy, who thrust a shock of hair through the kitchen door. "Build a fire upstairs."

Mr. Barnes heaved a sigh of relief and drawing a chair to the blaze prepared once more to enjoy a well-earned rest.

By this time the shadows had begun to lengthen in the room as the first traces of early twilight filled the valley. The gurgling still continued down the water pipe; the old sign before the front door moaned monotonously. An occasional gust of wind, which mysteriously penetrated the mist without sweeping it aside, rattled the windows and waved wildly in mid-air a venturesome rose which had clambered to the second story of the old inn. The barn-yard appeared even more dismal because of the coming darkness and the hens presented a pathetic picture of discomfort as they tucked their heads under their wet feathers for the night, while his lordship, the rooster, was but a sorry figure upon his high perch, with the moisture regularly and unceasingly dripping through the roof of the hen-house upon his unprotected back.

An aroma from the kitchen which penetrated the room seemed especially grateful to the manager who smiled with satisfaction as he conjured up visions of the forthcoming repast. By his Falstaffian girth, he appeared a man not averse to good living, nor one to deny himself plentiful libations of American home-brewed ale.

"Next to actual dining," observed this past-master in the art, "are the anticipations of the table. The pleasure consists in speculation regarding this or that aroma, in classifying the viands and separating this combination of culinary odors into courses of which you will in due time partake. Alas for the poor stroller when the tavern ceases to be! Already it is almost extinct on account of the Erie Canal. Only a short time ago this room would have been crowded with teamsters of the broad-tired Pennsylvania wagons, drawn by six or eight horses."

Again the appetizing aroma from the kitchen turned the current of his reflections into its original channel, for he concluded with: "An excellent dinner is in progress, if my diagnosis of these penetrating fragrances be correct."

And it was soon demonstrated that the manager's discernment was not in error. There was not only abundance but quality, and the landlord's daughter waited on the guests, thereby subjecting herself to the very open advances of the Celtic Adonis. The large table was laden with heavy crockery, old-fashioned and quaint; an enormous rotary castor occupied the center of the table, while the forks and spoons were--an unusual circumstance!--of silver.

When the company had seated themselves around the board the waitress brought in a sucking pig, done to a turn, well stuffed, and with an apple in its mouth. The manager heaved a sigh.

"The lovely little monster," said Kate, admiringly.

"Monster!" cried Susan. "Say cherub!"

"So young and tender for such a fate!" exclaimed Hawkes, the melancholy individual, with knife and fork held in mid-air.

"But worthy of the bearer of the dish!" remarked Adonis, so pointedly that the landlord's daughter, overwhelmed with confusion, nearly dropped the platter, miniature porker and all. Whereupon Kate cast an angry glance at the offender whom "she could not abide," yet regarded in a certain proprietary way, and Adonis henceforth became less open in his advances.

Those other aromas which the manager had mentally classified took form and substance and were arranged in tempting variety around the appetizing and well-browned suckling. There were boiled and baked hams, speckled with cloves, plates of doughnuts and pound cake, beet root and apple sauce. Before each of the guests stood a foaming mug of home-brewed ale that carried with it a palpable taste of the hops.

"There is nothing of the stage repast about this," commented the manager.

To which Kate, having often partaken of the conventional banquet of the theater, waved her hand in a serio-comic manner toward the pièce de résistance and observed:

"Suppose, now, by some necromancy our young and tender friend here on the platter should be changed to a cleverly fashioned block of wood, painted in imitation of a roasted porker, with a wooden apple in his mouth?"

The manager, poising the carving knife, replied:

"Your suggestion is startling. We will obviate the possibility of any such transformation."

And he cut the "ambrosian fat and lean" with a firm hand, eying the suckling steadfastly the while as if to preclude any exhibition of Hindoo mysticism, while the buxom lass, the daughter of the boniface, with round arms bared, bore sundry other dishes from place to place until the plates were heaped with an assortment of viands.

"Well, my dear, how are you getting on?" said the manager to the young actress, Constance, as he helped himself to the crackle. "Have you everything you want?"

She nodded brightly, and the stranger who was seated some distance from her glanced up; his gaze rested on her for a moment and then returned in cold contemplation to the fare set before him.

Yet was she worthy of more than passing scrutiny. The gleam of the lamp fell upon her well-turned figure and the glistening of her eyes could be seen in the shadow that rested on her brow beneath the crown of hair. She wore a dark lavender dress, striped with silk, a small "jacquette," after the style of the day, the sleeves being finished with lace and the skirt full and flowing. Her heavy brown tresses were arranged in a coiffure in the fashion then prevailing, a portion of the hair falling in curls on the neck, the remainder brought forward in plaits and fastened at the top of the forehead with a simple pearl ornament.

If the young girl felt any interest in the presence of the taciturn guest she concealed it, scarcely looking at him and joining but rarely in the conversation. Susan, on the other hand, resorted to sundry coquetries.

"I fear, sir, that you find our poor company intrusive, since we have forced you to become one of us?" she said, toying with her fork, and thereby displaying a white and shapely hand.

His impassive blue eyes met her sparkling ones.

"I am honored in being admitted to your fellowship," he returned perfunctorily.

"Only poor players, sir!" exclaimed Hawkes deprecatingly, with the regal gesture a stage monarch might use in setting forth the perplexities of royal pre-eminence.

"The landlord does not seem to share your opinion?" continued Susan, looking once more at the stranger.

"As a host he believes in brave deeds, not fair words," said Kate, indicating the remains of the repast.

"Peace to his bones!" exclaimed the manager, extending a hand over the remnants of the suckling.

Here the dark-haired girl arose, the dinner being concluded. There was none of his usual brusqueness of manner, as the manager, leaning back in his chair and taking her hand, said:

"You are going to retire, my dear? That is right. We have had a hard day's traveling."

She bent her head, and her lips pressed softly the old man's cheek, after which she turned from the rest of the company with a grave bow. But as she passed through the doorway her flowing gown caught upon a nail in the wall. Pre-occupied though he seemed, her low exclamation did not escape the ear of the stranger, and, quitting his place, he knelt at her feet, and she, with half turned head and figure gracefully poised, looked down upon him.

With awkward fingers, he released the dress, and she bowed her acknowledgment, which he returned with formal deference. Then she passed on and he raised his head, his glance following her through the bleak-looking hall, up the broad, ill-lighted staircase, into the mysterious shadows which prevailed above.

Shortly afterward the tired company dispersed, and the soldier also sought his room. There he found the landlord's daughter before him with the warming-pan. She had spread open the sheets of his bed and was applying the old-fashioned contrivance for the prevention of rheumatism, but it was evident her mind was not on this commendable housewifely task, for she sighed softly and then observed:

"It must be lovely to be an actress!"

Dreamily she patted the pillows, until they were round and smooth, and absently adjusted the bed, until there was not a wrinkle in the snow-white counterpane, after which, like a good private in domestic service, she shouldered the warming pan with its long handle, murmured "good-night" and departed, not to dream of milking, churning or cheese-making, but of a balcony and of taking poison in a tomb.

Absently the stranger gazed at the books on the table: "Nutting's Grammar," "Adams' Arithmetic," "David's Tears" and the "New England Primer and Catechism"--all useful books undoubtedly, but not calculated long to engross the attention of the traveler. Turning from these prosaic volumes, the occupant of the chamber drew aside the curtain of the window and looked out.

Now the mists were swept away; the stars were shining and the gurgling had grown fainter in the pipes that descended from the roof to the ground. Not far was the dark fringe which marked the forest and the liquid note of a whippoorwill arose out of the solitary depths, a melancholy tone in the stillness of the night. The little owl, too, was heard, his note now sounding like the filing of a saw and again changing in character to the tinkling of a bell. A dog howled for a moment in the barn-yard, and then, apparently satisfied with having given this evidence of watchfulness, re-entered his house of one room and curled himself upon the straw in his parlor, after which nothing more was heard from him.

Drawing the curtains of his own couch, a large, four-posted affair, sleep soon overpowered the stranger; but sleep, broken and fitful! Nor did he dream only of France and of kings running away, of American land barons and of "bolters." More intrusive than these, the faces of the strollers crept in and disturbed his slumbers, not least among which were the features of the dark-eyed girl whose gown had caught as she passed through the doorway.

CHAPTER II:
A NEW ARRIVAL

The crowing of the cock awakened the French traveler, and, going to the window, he saw that daylight had thrown its first shafts upon the unromantic barn-yard scene, while in the east above the hill-tops spread the early flush of morning. The watch-dog had left his one-roomed cottage and was promenading before it in stately fashion with all the pomp of a satisfied land-holder, his great undershot jaw and the extraordinary outward curve of his legs proclaiming an untarnished pedigree. The hens were happily engaged in scratching the earth for their breakfast; the rooster, no longer crestfallen, was strutting in the sunshine, while next to the barn several grunting, squealing pigs struggled for supremacy in the trough. From the cow-shed came an occasional low and soon a slip-shod maid, yawning mightily, appeared, pail in hand, and moved across the yard to her early morning task.

Descending the stairs and making his way to the barn, the soldier called to Sandy, the stable boy, who was performing his ablutions by passing wet fingers through a shock of red hair, to saddle his horse. The sleepy lad led forth a large but shapely animal, and soon the stranger was galloping across the country, away from the village, now down a gentle declivity, with the virgin forest on either side, then through a tract of land where was apparent the husbandry of the people.

After a brisk pace for some miles, he reined in his horse, and, leisurely riding in a circuit, returned on the road that crossed the farming country back of the tavern. Around him lay fields of rye and buckwheat sweet with the odor of the bee-hive; Indian corn, whose silken tassels waved as high as those of Frederick's grenadiers', and yellow pumpkins nestling to the ground like gluttons that had partaken too abundantly of mother earth's nourishment. Intermingling with these great oblong and ovoid gourds, squashes, shaped like turbans and many-cornered hats, appeared in fantastic profusion.

The rider was rapidly approaching the inn, when a sudden turn in the highway, as the road swept around a wind-break of willows, brought him upon a young woman who was walking slowly in the same direction. So fast was the pace of his horse, and so unexpected the meeting, she was almost under the trampling feet before he saw her. Taken by surprise, she stood as if transfixed, when, with a quick, decisive effort, the rider swerved his animal, and, of necessity, rode full tilt at the fence and willows. She felt the rush of air; saw the powerful animal lift itself, clear the rail-fence and crash through the bulwark of branches. She gazed at the wind-break; a little to the right, or the left, where the heavy boughs were thickly interlaced, and the rider's expedient had proved serious for himself, but chance--he had no time for choice--had directed him to a vulnerable point of leaves and twigs. Before she had fairly recovered herself he reappeared at an opening on the other side of the willow-screen, and, after removing a number of rails, led his horse back to the road.

With quivering nostrils, the animal appeared possessed of unquenchable spirit, but his master's bearing was less assured as he approached, with an expression of mingled anxiety and concern on his face, the young girl whom the manager had addressed as Constance.

"I beg your pardon for having alarmed you!" he said. "It was careless, inexcusable!"

"It was a little startling," she admitted, with a faint smile.

"Only a little!" he broke in gravely. "If I had not seen you just when I did--"

"You would not have turned your horse--at such a risk to yourself!" she added.

"Risk to myself! From what?" A whimsical light encroached on the set look in his blue eyes. "Jumping a rail fence? But you have not yet said you have pardoned me?"

The smile brightened. "Oh, I think you deserve that."

"I am not so sure," he returned, glancing down at her.

Slanting between the lower branches of the trees the sunshine touched the young girl's hair in flickering spots and crept down her dress like caressing hands of light, until her figure, passing into a solid shadow, left these glimmerings prone upon the dusty road behind her. The "brides," or strings of her little muslin cap, flaunted in the breeze and a shawl of China crape fluttered from her shoulders. So much of her dusky hair as defied concealment contrasted strongly with the calm translucent pallor of her face. The eyes, alone, belittled the tranquillity of countenance; against the rare repose of features, they were the more eloquent, shining beneath brows, delicately defined but strongly marked, and shaded by long upturned lashes, deep in tone as a sloe.

"You are an early riser," he resumed.

"Not always," she replied. "But after yesterday it seemed so bright outdoors and the country so lovely!"

His gaze, following hers, traversed one of the hollows. Below yet rested deep shadows, but upon the hillside a glory celestial enlivened and animated the surrounding scene. Scattered houses, constituting the little hamlet, lay in the partial shade of the swelling land, the smoke, with its odor of burning pine, rising lazily on the languid air. In the neighboring field a farm hand was breaking up the ground with an old-fashioned, pug-nosed "dirt-rooter;" soil as rich as that of Egypt, or the land, Gerar, where Isaac reaped an hundred fold and every Israelite sat under the shadow of his own vine.

Pausing, the husbandman leaned on the handle of his plow and deliberately surveyed the couple on the road. Having at the same time satisfied his curiosity and rested his arms, he grasped the handles once more and the horses pulled and tugged at the primitive implement.

While the soldier and the young girl were thus occupied in surveying the valley and the adjacent mounds and hummocks, the horse, considering doubtlessly that there had been enough inaction, tapped the ground with rebellious energy and tossed his head in mutiny against such procrastination.

"Your horse wants to go on," she said, observing this equine by-play.

"He usually does," replied the rider. "Perhaps, though, I am interrupting you? I see you have a play in your hand."

"I was looking over a part--but I know it very well," she added, moving slowly from the border of willows. Leading his horse, he followed.

His features, stern and obdurate in repose, relaxed in severity, while the deep-set blue eyes grew less searching and guarded. This alleviation became him well, a tide of youth softening his expression as a wave smoothes the sands.

"What is the part?"

"Juliana, in 'The Honeymoon'! It is one of our stock pieces."

"And you like it?"

"Oh, yes." Lingering where a bit of sward was set with field flowers.

"And who plays the duke?" he continued.

"Mr. O'Flariaty," she answered, a suggestion of amusement in her glance. Beneath the shading of straight, black brows, her eyes were deceptively dark, until scrutinized closely, they resolved themselves into a clear gray.

"Ah," he said, recalling Adonis, O'Flariaty's, appearance, and, as he spoke, a smile of singular sweetness lightened his face. "A Spanish grandee with a touch of the brogue! But I must not decry your noble lord!" he added.

"No lord of mine!" she replied gaily. "My lord must have a velvet robe, not frayed, and a sword not tin, and its most sanguinary purpose must not be to get between his legs and trip him up! Of course, when we act in barns--"

"In barns!"

"Oh, yes, when we can find them to act in!"

She glanced at him half-mockingly.

"I suppose you think of a barn as only a place for a horse."

The sound of carriage wheels interrupted his reply, and, looking in the direction from whence it came, they observed a coach doubling the curve before the willows and approaching at a rapid pace. It was a handsome and imposing equipage, with dark crimson body and wheels, preserving much of the grace of ancient outline with the utility of modern springs.

As they drew aside to permit it to pass the features of its occupant were seen, who, perceiving the young girl on the road--the shawl, half-fallen from her shoulder revealing the plastic grace of an erect figure--gazed at her with surprise, then thrust his head from the window and bowed with smiling, if somewhat exaggerated, politeness. The next moment carriage and traveler vanished down the road in a cloud of dust, but an alert observer might have noticed an eye at the rear port-hole, as though the person within was supplementing his brief observation from the side with a longer, if diminishing, view from behind.

The countenance of the young girl's companion retrograded from its new-found favor to a more inexorable cast.

"A friend of yours?" he said, briefly.

"I never saw him before," she answered with flashing eyes. "Perhaps he is the lord of the manor and thought I was one of his subjects."

"There are lords in this country, then?"

"Lords or patroons, they are called," she replied, her face still flushed.

At this moment, across the meadows, beyond the fence of stumps--poor remains of primeval monarchs!--a woman appeared at the back door of the inn with a tin horn upon which she blew vigorously, the harsh blasts echoing over hill and valley. The startled swallows and martins arose from the eaves and fluttered above the roof. The farm hand at the plow released the handle, and the slip-shod maid appeared in the door of the cow-shed, spry and nimble enough at meal time.

From the window of her room Susan saw them returning and looked surprised as well as a bit annoyed. Truth to tell, Mistress Susan, with her capacity for admiring and being admired, had conceived a momentary interest in the stranger, a fancy as light as it was ephemeral. That touch of melancholy when his face was in repose inspired a transitory desire for investigation in this past-mistress of emotional analysis. But the arrival of the coach which had passed the couple soon diverted Susan's thoughts to a new channel.

The equipage drew up, and a young man, dressed in a style novel in that locality, sprang out. He wore a silk hat with scarcely any brim, trousers extremely wide at the ankle, a waistcoat of the dimensions of 1745, and large watch ribbons, sustaining ponderous bunches of seals.

The gallant fop touched the narrow brim of his hat to Kate, who was peeping from one window, and waved a kiss to Susan, who was surreptitiously glancing from another, whereupon both being detected, drew back hastily. Overwhelmed by the appearance of a guest of such manifest distinction, the landlord bowed obsequiously as the other entered the tavern with a supercilious nod.

To Mistress Susan this incident was exciting while it lasted, but when the dandy had disappeared her attention was again attracted to Constance and Saint-Prosper, who slowly approached. He paused with his horse before the front door and she stood a moment near the little porch, on either side of which grew sweet-williams, four-o'clocks and larkspur. But the few conventional words were scanty crumbs for the fair eavesdropper above, the young girl soon entering the house and the soldier leading his horse in the direction of the stable. As the latter disappeared around the corner of the tavern, Susan left the window and turned to the mirror.

"La!" she said, holding a mass of blond hair in one hand and deftly coiling it upon her little head, "I believe she got up early to meet him." But Kate only yawned lazily.

Retracing his steps from the barn, the soldier crossed the back-yard, where already on the clothes' line evidences of early matutinal industry, a pair of blue over-alls, with sundry white and red stockings, were dancing in the breeze. First the over-alls performed wildly, then the white stockings responded with vim, while the red ones outdid themselves by their shocking abandonment, vaunting skyward as though impelled by the phantom limbs of some Parisian danseuse.

Making his way by this dizzy saturnalia and avoiding the pranks of animated hosiery and the more ponderous frolics of over-alls, sheets and tablecloths, Saint-Prosper entered the kitchen. Here the farm hand and maid of all work were eating, and the landlord's rotund and energetic wife was bustling before the fireplace. An old iron crane, with various sized pothooks and links of chain, swung from the jambs at the will of the housewife. Boneset, wormwood and catnip had their places on the wall, together with ears of corn and strings of dried apples.

Bustling and active, with arms bared to the elbow and white with flour, the spouse of mine host realized the scriptural injunction: "She looketh well to the ways of her household." Deftly she spread the dough in the baking pan; smoothly leveled it with her palm; with nice mathematical precision distributed bits of apple on top in parallel rows; lightly sprinkled it with sugar, and, lo and behold, was fashioned an honest, wholesome, Dutch apple cake, ready for the baking!

In the tap-room the soldier encountered the newcomer, seated not far from the fire as though his blood flowed sluggishly after his long ride in the chill morning air. Upon the table lay his hat, and he was playing with the seals on his watch ribbon, his legs indolently stretched out straight before him. Occasionally he coughed when the smoke, exuding from the damp wood, was not entirely expelled up the chimney, but curled around the top of the fireplace and diffused itself into the atmosphere. Well-built, although somewhat slender of figure, this latest arrival had a complexion of tawny brown, a living russet, as warm and glowing as the most vivid of Vandyke pigments.

He raised his eyes slowly as the soldier entered and surveyed him deliberately. From a scrutiny of mere physical attributes he passed on to the more important details of clothes, noting that his sack coat was properly loose at the waist and that the buttons were sufficiently large to pass muster, but also detecting that the trousers lacked breadth at the ankles and that the hat had a high crown and a broad brim, from which he complacently concluded the other was somewhat behind the shifting changes of fashion.

"Curse me, if this isn't a beastly fire!" he exclaimed, stretching himself still more, yawning and passing a hand through his black hair. "Hang them, they might as well shut up their guests in the smoke-house with the bacons and hams! I feel as cured as a side of pig, ready to be hung to a dirty rafter."

With which he pulled himself together, went to the window, raised it and placed a stick under the frame.

"They tell me there's a theatrical troupe here," he resumed, returning to his chair and relapsing into its depths. "Perhaps you are one of them?"

"I have not that honor."

"Honor!" repeated the new arrival with a laugh. "That's good! That was one of them on the road with you, I'll be bound. You have good taste! Heigho!" he yawned again. "I'm anchored here awhile on account of a lame horse. Perhaps though"--brightening--"it may not be so bad after all. These players promise some diversion." At that moment his face wore an expression of airy, jocund assurance which faded to visible annoyance as he continued: "Where can that landlord be? He placed me in this kennel, vanished, and left me to my fate. Ah, here he is at last!" As the host approached, respectfully inquiring:

"Is there anything more I can do for you?"

"More?" exclaimed this latest guest, ironically. "Well, better late than never! See that my servant has help with the trunks."

"Very well, sir; I'll have Sandy look after them. You are going to stay then?" Shifting several bottles on the bar with apparent industry.

"How can I tell?" returned the newcomer lightly. "Fate is a Sphynx, and I am not OEdipus to answer her questions!"

The landlord looked startled, paused in his feigned employment, but slowly recovering himself, began to dust a jar of peppermint candy.

"How far is it to Meadtown?" continued the guest.

"Forty odd miles! Perhaps you are seeking the old patroon manor there? They say the heir is expected any day"--gazing fixedly at the young man--"at least, the anti-renters have received information he is coming and are preparing--"

The sprightly guest threw up his hands.

"The trunks! the trunks!" he exclaimed in accents of despair. "Look at the disorder of my attire! The pride of these ruffles leveled by the dew; my wristbands in disarray; the odor of the road pervading my person! The trunks, I pray you!"

"Yes, sir; at once, sir! But first let me introduce you to Mr. Saint-Prosper, of Paris, France. Make yourselves at home, gentlemen!"

With which the speaker hurriedly vanished and soon the bumping and thumping in the hall gave cheering assurance of instructions fulfilled.

"That porter is a prince among his kind," observed the guest satirically, wincing as an unusual bang overhead shook the ceiling. "But I'll warrant my man won't have to open my luggage after he gets through."

Then as quiet followed the racket above--"So you're from Paris, France?" he asked half-quizzically. "Well, it's a pleasure to meet somebody from somewhere. As I, too, have lived--not in vain!--in Paris, France, we may have mutual friends?"

"It is unlikely," said the soldier, who meanwhile had drawn off his riding gloves, placed them on the mantel, and stood facing the fire, with his back to the other guest. As he spoke he turned deliberately and bent his penetrating glance on his questioner.

"Really? Allow me to be skeptical, as I have considerable acquaintance there. In the army there's that fire-eating conqueror of the ladies, Gen--"

"My rank was not so important," interrupted the other, "that I numbered commanders among my personal friends."

"As you please," said the last guest carelessly. "I had thought to exchange a little gossip with you, but--n'importe! In my own veins flows some of the blood of your country."

For the time his light manner forsook him.

"Her tumults have, in a measure, been mine," he continued. "Now she is without a king, I am well-nigh without a mother-land. True; I was not born there--but it is the nurse the child turns to. Paris was my bonne--a merry abigail! Alas, her vicious brood have turned on her and cast her ribbons in the mire! Untroubled by her own brats, she could extend her estates to the Eldorado of the southwestern seas." He had arisen and, with hands behind his back, was striding to and fro. Coming suddenly to a pause, he asked abruptly:

"Do you know the Abbé Moneau?"

At the mention of that one-time subtle confidant of the deposed king, now the patron of republicanism, Saint-Prosper once more regarded his companion attentively.

"By reputation, certainly," he answered, slowly.

"He was my tutor and is now my frequent correspondent. Not a bad sort of mentor, either!" The new arrival paused and smiled reflectively. "Only recently I received a letter from him, with private details of the flight of the king and vague intimations of a scandal in the army, lately come to light."

His listener half-started from his seat and had the speaker not been more absorbed in his own easy flow of conversation than in the attitude of the other, he would have noticed that quick change of manner. Not perceiving it, however, he resumed irrelevantly:

"You see I am a sociable animal. After being cramped in that miserable coach for hours, it is a relief to loosen one's tongue as well as one's legs. Even this smoky hovel suggests good-fellowship and jollity beyond a dish of tea. Will you not join me in a bottle of wine? I carry some choice brands to obviate the necessity of drinking the home-brewed concoctions of the inn-keepers of this district."

"Thank you," said the soldier, at the same time rising from his chair. "I have no inclination so early in the day."

"Early?" queried the newcomer. "A half-pint of Chateau Cheval Blanc or Cru du Chevalier, high and vinous, paves a possible way for Brother Jonathan's déjeuner--fried pork, potatoes and chicory!" And turning to his servant who had meanwhile entered, he addressed a few words to him, and, as the door closed on the soldier, exclaimed with a shrug of the shoulders:

"An unsociable fellow! I wonder what he is doing here."

CHAPTER III:
AN INCOMPREHENSIBLE VENTURE

P ancakes, grits, home-made sausage, and, before each guest, an egg that had been proudly heralded by the clucking hen but a few hours before--truly a bountiful breakfast, discrediting the latest guest's anticipations! The manager, in high spirits, mercurial as the weather, came down from his room, a bundle of posters under his arm, boisterously greeting Saint-Prosper, whom he encountered in the hall:

"Read the bill! 'That incomparable comedy, The Honeymoon, by a peerless company.' How does that sound?"

"Attractive, certainly," said the other.

"Do you think it strong enough? How would 'unparagoned' do?"

"It would be too provincial, my dear; too provincial!" interrupted the querulous voice of the old lady.

"Very well, Madam!" the manager replied quickly. "You shall be 'peerless' if you wish. Every fence shall proclaim it; every post become loquacious with it."

"I was going to the village myself," said the soldier, "and will join you, if you don't mind?" he added suddenly.

"Mind? Not a bit. Come along, and you shall learn of the duties of manager, bill-poster, press-agent and license-procurer."

An hour or so later found the two walking down the road at a brisk pace, soon leaving the tavern behind them and beginning to descend a hill that commanded a view to eastward.

"How do you advertise your performances?" asked the younger man, opening the conversation.

"By posters, written announcements in the taverns, or a notice in the country paper, if we happen along just before it goes to press," answered Barnes. "In the old times we had the boy and the bell."

"The boy and the bell?"

"Yes," assented Barnes, a retrospective smile overspreading his good-natured face; "when I was a lad in Devonshire the manager announced the performance in the town market-place. I rang a cow-bell to attract attention and he talked to the people: Ding-a-ling!--'Good people, to-night will be given "Love in a Wood";' ding-a-long!--'to-morrow night, "The Beaux' Strategem'";' ding!--'Wednesday, "The Provoked Wife";' ling!--'Thursday, "The Way of the World."' So I made my début in a noisy part and have since played no rôle more effectively than that of the small boy with the big bell. Incidentally, I had to clean the lamps and fetch small beer to the leading lady, which duties were perfunctorily performed. My art, however, I threw into the bell," concluded the manager with a laugh.

"Do you find many theaters hereabouts?" asked the other, thoughtfully.

Barnes shook his head. "No; although there are plenty of them upon the Atlantic and Southern circuits. Still we can usually rent a hall, erect a stage and construct tiers of seats. Even a barn at a pinch makes an acceptable temple of art. But our principal difficulty is procuring licenses to perform."

"You have to get permission to play?"

"That we do!" sighed the manager. "From obdurate trustees in villages and stubborn supervisors or justices of the peace in the hamlets."

"But their reason for this opposition?" asked his companion.

They were now entering the little hamlet, exchanging the grassy path for a sidewalk of planks laid lengthwise, and the peace of nature for such signs of civilization as a troop of geese, noisily promenading across the thoroughfare, and a peacock--in its pride of pomp as a favored bird of old King Solomon--crying from the top of the shed and proudly displaying its gorgeous train. Barnes wiped the perspiration from his brow, as he answered:

"Well, a temperance and anti-theatrical agitation has preceded us in the Shadengo Valley, a movement originated in Baltimore by seven men who had been drunkards and are now lecturing throughout the country. This is known as the 'Washington' movement, and among the most formidable leaders of the crusade is an old actor, John B.

Gough. But here we are at the supervisor's office. I'll run in and get the license, if you'll wait a moment."

Saint-Prosper assented, and Barnes disappeared through the door of a one-story wooden building which boasted little in its architectural appearance and whose principal decorations consisted of a small window-garden containing faded geraniums, and a sign with sundry inverted letters. The neighborhood of this far from imposing structure was a rendezvous for many of the young men of the place who had much leisure, and, to judge from the sidewalk, an ample supply of Lone Jack or some other equally popular plug tobacco. As Saint-Prosper surveyed his surroundings, the Lone Jack, or other delectable brand, was unceremoniously passed from mouth to mouth with immediate and surprising results so far as the sidewalk was concerned. Regarding these village yokels with some curiosity, the soldier saw in them a possible type of the audiences to which the strollers must appeal for favor. To such hobnails must the fair Rosalind say: "I would kiss as many of you as had beards that pleased me." And the churls would applaud with their cowhide boots, devour her with eager eyes and--at this point the soldier found himself unconsciously frowning at his village neighbors until, with an impatient laugh, he recalled his wandering fancies. What was it to him whether the players appeared in city or hamlet? Why should he concern himself in possible conjectures on the fortunes of these strollers? Moreover--

Here Barnes reappeared with dejection in his manner, and, treading his way absent-mindedly past the Lone Jack contingent with no word of explanation to his companion, began to retrace his steps toward the hostelry on the hill.

"Going back so soon?" asked the young man in surprise.

"There is nothing to be done here! The temperance lecturer has just gone; the people are set against plays and players. The supervisor refuses the license."

With which the manager relapsed into silence, rueful and melancholy. Their road ran steadily upward from the sleepy valley, skirting a wood where the luxuriance of the overhanging foliage and the bright autumnal tint of the leaves were like a scene of a spectacular play. Out of breath from the steepness of the ascent, and, with his hand pressed to his side, Barnes suddenly called a halt, seated himself on a stump, his face somewhat drawn, and spoke for the first time since he left the hamlet.

"Let's rest a moment. Something catches me occasionally here," tapping his heart. "Ah, that's better! The pain has left. No; it's nothing. The machinery is getting old, that's all! Let me see--Ah, yes!" And he drew a cigar from his pocket. "Perhaps there lies a crumb of comfort in the weed!"

The manager smoked contemplatively, like a man pushed to the verge of disaster, weighing the slender chances of mending his broken fortunes. But as he pondered his face gradually lightened with a faint glimmer of satisfaction. His mind, seeking for a straw, caught at a possible way out of this labyrinth of difficulties and in a moment he had straightened up, puffing veritable optimistic wreaths. He arose buoyantly; before he reached the inn the crumb of comfort had become a loaf of assurance.

At the tavern the manager immediately sought mine host, stating his desire to give a number of free performances in the dining-room of the hotel. The landlord demurred stoutly; he was an inn-keeper, not the proprietor of a play-house. Were not tavern and theater inseparable, retorted Barnes? The country host had always been a patron of the histrionic art. Beneath his windows the masque and interlude were born. The mystery, harlequinade and divertissement found shelter in a pot-house.

In a word, so indefatigably did he ply arguments, appealing alike to clemency and cupidity--the custom following such a course--that the landlord at length reluctantly consented, and soon after the dining-room was transformed into a temple of art; stinted, it is true, for flats, drops, flies and screens, but at least more tenable than the roofless theaters of other days, when a downpour drenched the players and washed out the public, causing rainy tears to drip from Ophelia's nose and rivulets of rouge to trickle down my Lady Slipaway's marble neck and shoulders. In this labor of converting the dining-room into an auditory, they found an attentive observer in the landlord's daughter who left her pans, plates and platters to watch these preparations with round-eyed admiration. To her that temporary stage was surrounded by glamour and romance; a world remote from cook, scullion and maid of all work, and peopled with well-born dames, courtly ladies and exalted princesses.

Possibly interested in what seemed an incomprehensible venture--for how could the manager's coffers be replenished by free performances?--Saint-Prosper that afternoon reminded Barnes he had returned from the village without fulfilling his errand.

"Dear me!" exclaimed Barnes, his face wrinkling in perplexity. "What have I been thinking about? I don't see how I can go now. Hawkes or O'Flariaty can't be spared, what with lamps to polish and costumes to get in order! Hum!" he mused dubiously.

"If I can be of any use, command me," said the soldier, unexpectedly.

"You!"--exclaimed the manager. "I could not think--"

"Oh, it's a notable occupation," said the other with a satirical smile. "Was it not the bill-posters who caused the downfall of the French dynasty?" he added.

"In that case," laughed Barnes, with a sigh of relief, "go ahead and spread the inflammable dodgers! Paste them everywhere, except on the tombstones in the graveyard."

Conspicuously before the postoffice, grocery store, on the town pump and the fence of the village church, some time later, the soldier accordingly nailed the posters, followed by an inquisitive group, who read the following announcement: "Tuesday, 'The Honeymoon'; Wednesday, 'The School for Scandal'; Thursday, 'The Stranger,' with diverting specialties; Friday, 'Romeo and Juliet'; Saturday, 'Hamlet,' with a Jig by Kate Duran. At the Travelers' Friend. Entrance Free."

"They're going to play after all," commented the blacksmith's wife.

"I don't see much harm in 'Hamlet,'" said the supervisor's yokemate. "It certainly ain't frivolous."

"Let's go to 'The Honeymoon'?" suggested an amorous carl to his slip-slop Sal.

"Go 'long!" she retorted with barn-yard bashfulness.

"Did you ever see 'The School for Scandal'?" asked the smithy's good wife.

"Once," confessed the town official's faded consort, her worn face lighting dreamily. "It was on our wedding trip to New York. Silas warn't so strict then."

Amid chit-chat, so diverting, Saint-Prosper finished "posting" the town. It had been late in the afternoon before he had altered the posters and set out on his paradoxical mission; the sun was declining when he returned homeward. Pausing at a cross-road, he selected a tree for one of his remaining announcements. It was already adorned with a dodger, citing the escape of a negro slave and offering a reward for his apprehension; not an uncommon document in the North in those days.

As the traveler read the bill his expression became clouded, cheerless. Around him the fallen leaves gave forth a pleasant fragrance; caught in the currents of the air, they danced in a circle and then broke away, hurrying helter-skelter in all directions.

"Poor devil!" he muttered. "A fugitive--in hiding--"

And he nailed one of his own bills over the dodger. As he stood there reflectively the lights began to twinkle in the village below like stars winking upwards; the ascending smoke from a chimney seemed a film of lace drawn slowly through the air; from the village forge came a brighter glow as the sparks danced from the hammers on the anvils.

Shaking the reins on his horse's neck, the soldier continued his way, while the sun, out of its city of clouds, sent beams like a searchlight to the church spire; the fields, marked by the plow; the gaunt stumps in a clearing, displaying their giant sinews. Then the resplendent rays vanished, the battlements crumbled away and night, with its army of shadows, invaded the earth. As Saint-Prosper approached the tavern, set prominently on the brow of the hill, all was solemnly restful save the sign which now creaked in doleful doldrums and again complained wildly as the wind struck it a vigorous blow. The windows were bright from the fireplace and lamp; above the door the light streamed through the open transom upon the swaying sign and the fluttering leaves of the vine that clambered around the entrance.

In the parlor, near a deteriorated piano whose yellow keys were cracked and broken--in almost the seventh stage of pianodum, sans teeth, sans wire, sans everything--he saw the dark-eyed girl and reined his horse. As he did so, she seated herself upon the hair-cloth stool, pressed a white finger to a discolored key and smiled at the not unexpected result--the squeak of decrepitude. While her hand still rested on the board and her features shone strongly in relief against the fire like a cameo profile set in bloodstone, a figure approached, and, leaning gracefully upon the palsied instrument, bent over her with smiling lips. It was the grand seignior, he of the equipage with silver trimmings. If the horseman's gaze rested, not without interest, on the pleasing picture of the young actress, it was now turned with sudden and greater intentness to that of the dashing stranger, a swift interrogation glancing from that look.

How had he made his peace with her? Certainly her manner now betrayed no resentment. While motionless the rider yet sat in his saddle, an invisible hand grasped the reins.

"Shall I put up your horse?" said a small voice, and the soldier quickly dismounted, the animal vanishing with the speaker, as Saint-Prosper entered the inn. Gay, animated, conscious of his attractions, the fop hovered over the young girl, an all-pervading Hyperion, with faultless ruffles, white hands, and voice softly modulated. That evening the soldier played piquet with the wiry old lady, losing four shillings to that antiquated gamester, and, when he had paid the stakes, the young girl was gone and the buoyant beau had sought diversion in his cups.

"Strike me," muttered the last named personage, "the little stroller has spirit. How her eyes flashed when I first approached her! It required some tact and acting to make her believe I took her for some one else on the road. Not such an easy conquest as I thought, although I imagine I have put that adventurer's nose out of joint. But why should I waste time here? Curse it, just to cut that fellow out! Landlord!"

"Yes, sir," answered the host behind the bar, where he had been quietly dozing on a stool with his back against the wall.

"Do you think my horse will be fit for use to-morrow morning?"

"The swelling has gone down, sir, and perhaps, with care--"

"Perhaps! I'll take no chances. Hang the nag, but I must make the best of it! See that my bed is well warmed, and"--rising--"don't call me in the morning. I'll get up when I please. Tell my man to come up at once--I suppose he's out with the kitchen wenches. I have some orders to give him for the morning. Stay--send up a lamp, and--well, I believe that's all for now!"

The Strollers

CHAPTER IV:

"GREEN GROW THE RUSHES, O!"

So well advertised in the village had been the theatrical company and so greatly had the crusade against the play and players whetted public curiosity that on the evening of the first performance every bench in the dining-room--auditorium--of the tavern had an occupant, while in the rear the standing room was filled by the overflow. Upon the counter of the bar were seated a dozen or more men, including the schoolmaster, an itinerant pedagogue who "boarded around" and received his pay in farm products, and the village lawyer, attired in a claret-colored frock coat, who often was given a pig for a retainer, or knotty wood, unfit for rails.

From his place, well to the front, the owner of the private equipage surveyed the audience with considerable amusement and complacency. He was fastidiously dressed in double-breasted waistcoat of figured silk, loosely fitting trousers, fawn-colored kid gloves, light pumps and silk hose. Narrow ruffles edged his wristbands which were fastened with link buttons, while the lining of his evening coat was of immaculate white satin. As he gazed around upon a scene at once novel and incongruous, he took from his pocket a little gold case, bearing an ivory miniature, and, with the eyes of his neighbors bent expectantly upon him, extracted therefrom a small, white cylinder.

"What may that be, mister?" inquired an inquisitive rustic, placing his hand on the other's shoulder.

The latter drew back as if resenting that familiar touch, and, by way of answer, poised the cylinder in a tiny holder and deliberately lighted it, to the amazement of his questioner. Cigarettes were then unknown in that part of the state and the owner of the coach enjoyed the dubious distinction of being the first to introduce them there.

"Since which time," says Chronicler Barnes in his memoirs, "their use and abuse has, I believe, extended."

The lighting of the aboriginal American cigarette drew general attention to the smoker and the doctor, not a man of modern small pills, but a liberal dispenser of calomel, jalap, castor-oil and quinine, whispered to the landlord:

"Azeriah, who might he be?"

"The heir of the patroon estate, Ezekiel. I found the name on his trunks: 'Edward Mauville.'"

"Sho! Going to take possession at the manor?"

"He cal'lates to, I guess, ef he can!"

"Yes; ef he can!" significantly repeated the doctor. "So this is the foreign heir? He's got wristbands like a woman and hands just as small. Wears gloves like my darter when she goes to meeting-house! And silk socks! Why, the old patroon didn't wear none at all, and corduroy was good enough for him, they say. Wonder how the barn-burners will take to the silk socks? Who's the other stranger, Azeriah?" Indicating with his thumb the soldier, who, standing against a window casement in the rear of the room, was by his height a conspicuous figure in the gathering.

"I don't exactly know, Ezekiel," replied the landlord, regretfully. "Not that I didn't try to find out," he added honestly, "but he was so close, I couldn't get nothing from him. He's from Paris, France; may be Louis Philippe himself, for all I know."

"No; he ain't Louis Philippe," returned the doctor with decision, "'cause I seen his likeness in the magazine."

"Might be the dolphin then," suggested the boniface. "He's so mighty mysterious."

"Dolphin!" retorted the other contemptuously. "There ain't no dolphin. There hasn't been no dolphin since the French Revolution."

"Oh, I didn't know but there might a been," said the landlord vaguely.

From mouth to mouth the information, gleaned by the village doctor, was circulated; speculation had been rife ever since the demise of the last patroon regarding his successor, and, although the locality was beyond the furthermost reach of that land-holder, their interest was none the less keen. The old master of the manor had been like a myth, much spoken of, never seen without the boundaries of his acres; but the new lord was a reality, a creditable creation of tailor, hatter, hosier, cobbler--which trades had not flourished under the old master who bought his clothes, cap and boots at a country store, owned by himself. Anticipation of the theatrical performance was thus relieved in a measure by the presence of the heir, but the delay, incident to a first night on an improvised stage, was so unusual that the audience at length began to evince signs of restlessness.

Finally, however, when the landlord's daughter had gazed what seemed to her an interminable period upon the lady and the swan, the lake and the greyhound, painted on the curtain, this picture vanished by degrees, with an exhilarating creaking of the rollers, and was succeeded by the representation of a room in a cottage. The scenery, painted in distemper and not susceptible to wind or weather, had manifold uses, reappearing later in the performance as a nobleman's palace, supplemented, it is true, by a well-worn carpet to indicate ducal luxury.

Some trifling changes--concessions to public opinion--were made in the play, notably in the scene where the duke, with ready hospitality, offers wine to the rustic Lopez. In Barnes' expurgated, "Washingtonian" version (be not shocked, O spirit of good Master Tobin!) the countryman responded reprovingly: "Fie, my noble Duke! Have you no water from the well?" An answer diametrically opposed to the tendencies of the sack-guzzling, roistering, madcap playwrights of that early period!

On the whole the representation was well-balanced, with few weak spots in the acting for fault finding, even from a more captious gathering. In the costumes, it is true, the carping observer might have detected some flaws; notably in Adonis, a composite fashion plate, who strutted about in the large boots of the Low Countries, topped with English trunk hose of 1550; his hand upon the long rapier of Charles II, while a periwig and hat of William III crowned his empty pate!

Kate was Volante; not Tobin's Volante, but one fashioned out of her own characteristics; supine, but shapely; heavy, but handsome; slow, but specious. Susan, with hair escaping in roguish curls beneath her little cap; her taper waist encompassed by a page's tunic; the trim contour of her figure frankly revealed by her vestment, was truly a lad "dressed up to cozen" any lover who preferred his friend and his bottle to his mistress. Merry as a sand-boy she danced about in russet boots that came to the knee; lithe and lissome in the full swing of immunity from skirts, mantle and petticoats!

Conscious that his identity had been divined, and relishing, perhaps, the effect of its discovery, the young patroon gazed languidly at the players, until the entrance of Constance as Juliana, when he forgot the pleasing sensations of self-thought, in contemplation of the actress. He remarked a girlish form of much grace, attired in an attractive gown of white satin and silver, as became a bride, with train and low shimmering bodice, revealing the round arms and shoulders which arose ivory-like in whiteness. Instead of the customary feathers and other ornaments of the period, specified in the text of the play, roses alone softened the effect of her dark hair. Very different she appeared in this picturesque Spanish attire from the lady of the lane, with the coquettish cap of muslin and its "brides," or strings.

The light that burned within shone from her eyes, proud yet gay; it lurked in the corners of her mouth, where gravity followed merriment, as silence follows laughter when the brook sweeps from the purling stones to the deeper pools. Her art was unconscious of itself and scene succeeded scene with a natural charm, revealing unexpected resources, from pathos to sorrow; from vanity to humility; from scorn to love awakened. And, when the transition did come, every pose spoke of the quickening heart; her movements proclaimed the golden fetters; passion shone in her glances, defiant though willing, lofty though humble, joyous though shy.

Was it the heat from the lamps?--but Mauville's brow became flushed; his buoyancy seemed gross and brutal; desire lurked in his lively glances; Pan gleamed from the curls of Hyperion!

The play jogged on its blithesome course to its wonted end; the duke delivered the excellent homily,

"A gentle wife Is still the sterling comfort of a man's life,"

and the well-pleased audience were preparing to leave when Barnes, in a drab jacket and trunks, trimmed with green ribbon bows, came forward like the clown in the circus and addressed the "good people."

"In the golden age," said the father of Juliana, "great men treated actors like servants, and, if they offended, their ears were cut off. Are we, in brave America, returning to the days when they tossed an actor in a blanket or gave a poet a hiding? Shall we stifle an art which is the purest inspiration of Athenian genius? The law prohibits our performing and charging admission, but it does not debar us from taking a collection, if"--with a bow in which dignity and humility were admirably mingled--"you deem the laborer worthy of his hire?"

This novel epilogue was received with laughter and applause, but the audience, although good-natured, contained its proportion of timid souls who retreat before the passing plate. The rear guard began to show faint signs of demoralization, when Mauville sprang to his feet. Pan had disappeared behind his leafy covert; it was the careless, self-possessed man of the world who arose.

"I am not concerned about the ethics of art," he said lightly, "but the ladies of the company may count me among their devout admirers. I am sure," he added, bowing to the manager with ready grace, "if they were as charming in the old days, after the lords tossed the men, they made love to the women."

"There were no actresses in those days, sir," corrected Barnes, resenting the flippancy of his aristocratic auditor.

"No actresses?" retorted the heir. "Then why did people go to the theater? However, without further argument, let me be the first contributor."

"The prodigal!" said the doctor in an aside to the landlord. "He's holding up a piece of gold. It's the first time ever patroon was a spendthrift!"

But Mauville's words, on the whole, furthered the manager's project, and the audience remained in its integrity, while Balthazar, a property helmet in hand, descended from his palace and trod the aisles in his drab trunk-hose and purple cloak, a royal mendicant, in whose pot soon jingled the pieces of silver. No one shirked his admission fee and some even gave in excess; the helmet teemed with riches; once it had saved broken heads, now it repaired broken fortunes, its properties magical, like the armor of Pallas.

"How did you like the play, Mr. Saint-Prosper?" said Barnes, as he approached that person.

"Much; and as for the players"--a gleam of humor stealing over his dark features--"'peerless' was not too strong."

"'Your approbation likes me most, my lord,'" quoted the manager, and passed quickly on with his tin pot, in a futile effort to evade the outstretched hand of his whilom helper.

Thanking the audience for their generosity and complimenting them on their intelligence, the self-constituted lord of the treasury vanished once more behind the curtain. The orchestra of two struck up a negro melody; the audience rose again, the women lingering to exchange their last innocent gossip about prayer-meeting, or about the minister who "knocked the theologic dust from the pulpit cushions in the good old orthodox way," when some renegade exclaimed: "Clear the room for a dance!"

Jerusha's shawl straightway fell from her shoulders; Hannah's bonnet was whipped from her head; Nathaniel paused on his way to the stable yard to bring out the team and a score of willing hands obeyed the injunction amid laughing encouragement from the young women whose feet already were tapping the floor in anticipation of the Virginia Reel, Two Sisters, Hull's Victory, or even the waltz, "lately imported from the Rhine." A battered Cremona appeared like magic and

"In his shirt of check and tallowed hair The fiddler sat in his bull-rush chair,"

while "'Twas Monnie Musk in busy feet and Monnie Musk by heart"--old-fashioned "Monnie Musk" with "first couple join right hands and swing," "forward six" and "across the set"; an honest dance for country folk that only left regrets when it came to "Good Night for aye to Monnie Musk," although followed by the singing of "Old Hundred" or "Come, ye Sinners, Poor and Needy," on the homeward journey.

In the parlor the younger lads and lasses were playing "snap and catch 'em" and similar games. The portly Dutch clock gazed down benignly on the scene, its face shining good-humoredly like the round visage of some comfortable burgher. "Green grow the rushes, O!" came from many merry-makers. "Kiss her quick and let her go" was followed by scampering of feet and laughter which implied a doubt whether the lad had obeyed the next injunction, "But don't you muss her ruffle, O!" Forming a moving ring around a young girl, they sang: "There's a rose in the garden for you, young man." A rose, indeed, or a rose-bud, rather, with ruffles he was commanded not to "muss," but which, nevertheless, suffered sadly!

Among these boys and girls, the patroon discovered Constance, no longer "to the life a duchess," with gown in keeping with the "pride and pomp of exalted station," but attired in the simple dress of lavender she usually wore, though the roses still adorned her hair. Shunning the entrancing waltz, the inspiring "Monnie Musk" and the cotillion, lively when set to Christy's melodies, she had sought the more juvenile element, and, when seen by the land baron, was circling around with fluttering skirts. Joyous, merry, there was no hint now in her natural, girlish ways of the capacity that lay within for varied impersonations, from the lightness of coquetry to the thrill of tragedy.

He did not know how it happened, as he stood there watching her, but the next moment he was imprisoned by the group and voices were singing:

"There he stands, the booby; who will have him for his beauty?"

Who? His eye swept the group; the merry, scornful glances fixed upon him; the joyous, half-inviting glances; the red lips parted as in kindly invitation; shy lips, willing lips!

Who? His look kindled; he had made his selection, and the next moment his arm was impetuously thrown around the actress's waist.

"Kiss her quick and let her go!"

Amid the mad confusion he strove to obey the command, but a panting voice murmured "no, no!" a pair of dark eyes gazed into his for an instant, defiantly, and the pliant waist slipped from his impassioned grasp; his eager lips, instead of touching that glowing cheek, only grazed a curl that had become loosened, and, before he could repeat the attempt, she had passed from his arms, with laughing lips and eyes.

"Play fair!" shouted the lads. "He should 'kiss her quick and let her go.'"

"Oh, he let her go first!" said the others.

"'Kiss her quick,'" reiterated the boys.

"He can't now," answered the girls.

The voices took up the refrain: "Don't you muss the ruffles, O!" and the game went on. The old clock gossiped gleefully, its tongue repeating as plainly as words:

"Let-her-go!--ho!--ho!--one--two--three!"

Three o'clock! Admonishingly rang out the hour, the jovial face of the clock looking sterner than was its wont. It glowered now like a preacher in his pulpit upon a sinful congregation. Enough of "snatch-and-catch'em;" enough of Hull's Victory or the Opera Reel; let the weary fiddler descend from his bull-rush chair, for soon the touch of dawn will be seen in the eastern sky! The merry-making began to wane and already the sound of wagon-wheels rattled over the log road away from the tavern. Yes, they were singing, and, as Hepsibeth leaned her head on Josiah's shoulder, they uplifted their voices in the good old orthodox hymn, "Come, Ye Sinners," for thus they courted and worshiped in olden times.

"Good-night, every one!" said a sweet voice, as Constance passed calmly on, with not a ruffle mussed.

"Good-night," answered the patroon, a sparkle in his eyes. "I was truly a booby."

"What can you mean?" she laughed.

"There's many a slip 'twixt--lip and lip!" exclaimed Susan.

With heightened color the young girl turned, and as she did so her look rested on the soldier. His glance was cold, almost strange, and, meeting it, she half-started and then smiled, slowly mounting the stairs. He looked away, but the patroon never took his eyes from her until she had vanished. Afar, rising and falling on the clear air, sounded the voices of the singers:

"Praise God from whom all blessings flow; Praise Him all creatures here below;"

and finally, softer and softer, until the melody melted into silence:

"Praise Him above, ye Heavenly H-o-s-t--"

"One good turn deserves another," said Barnes to Saint-Prosper, when Susan and Kate had likewise retired. "Follow me, sir--to the kitchen! No questions; but come!"

CHAPTER V:
A CONFERENCE IN THE KITCHEN

A keen observer might have noticed that the door of the inn kitchen had been kept swinging to and fro as certain ones in the audience had stolen cautiously, but repeatedly, in and out of the culinary apartment while the dancing and other festivities were in progress. The itinerant pedagogue was prominent in these mysterious movements which possibly accounted for his white choker's being askew and his disposition to cut a dash, not by declining Greek verbs, but by inclining too amorously toward Miss Abigail, a maiden lady with a pronounced aversion for frivolity.

The cause of the schoolmaster's frolicsome deportment was apparent to the soldier when he followed Barnes into the kitchen, where, in a secluded corner, near the hospitable oven, in the dim light of a tallow dip, stood a steaming punch bowl. A log smoldered in the fireplace, casting on the floor the long shadows of the andirons, while a swinging pot was reflected on the ceiling like a mighty eclipse. Numerous recesses, containing pans and plates that gleamed by day, were wrapped in vague mystery. Three dark figures around the bowl suggested a scene of incantation, especially when one of them threw some bark from the walnut log on the coals and the flames sprang up as from a pine knot and the eclipse danced among the rafters overhead while the pot swung to and fro.

As the manager approached the bowl, the trio, moved by some vague impelling impulse, locked arms, walked toward the side door, crossed its threshold in some confusion, owing to a unanimous determination to pass out at one and the same time, and went forth into the tranquil night, leaving Barnes and Saint-Prosper the sole occupants of the kitchen. The manager now helped himself and his companion to the beverage, standing with his back to the tiny forks of flame from the shagbark. His face expanded with good-fellowship;

joviality shone from his eyes beaming upon the soldier whom he unconsciously regarded as an auxiliary.

"Here's to our better acquaintance," he said, placing his hand with little ceremony on the other's shoulder. "The Bill-Poster!" Raising his cup. "You gathered them in--"

"And you certainly gathered in the contents of their pockets!"

"A fair robbery!" laughed Barnes, "as Dick Turpin said when he robbed the minister who robbed the king who robbed the people! A happy thought that, turning the helmet into a collection box! It tided us over; it tided us over!"

Saint-Prosper returned the manager's glance in kind; Barnes' candor and simplicity were apparent antidotes to the other's taciturnity and constraint. During the country dance the soldier had remained a passive spectator, displaying little interest in the rustic merry-making or the open glances cast upon him by bonny lasses, burned in the sunlit fields, buxom serving maids, as clean as the pans in the kitchen, and hearty matrons, not averse to frisk and frolic in wholesome rural fashion.

But now, in the face of the manager's buoyancy at the success of a mere expedient--a hopefulness ill-warranted by his short purse and the long future before him!--the young man's manner changed from one of indifference to friendliness, if not sympathy, for the over-sanguine custodian of players. Would the helmet, like the wonderful pitcher, replenish itself as fast as it was emptied? Or was it but a make-shift? The manager's next remark seemed a reply to these queries, denoting that Barnes himself, although temporarily elated, was not oblivious to the precarious character of "free performances," with voluntary offerings.

"What we need," continued the manager, "is a temperance drama. With what intemperate eagerness would the people flock to see it! But where is it to be found? Plays don't grow on bushes, even in this agricultural district. And I have yet to discover any dramatists hereabouts, unless"--jocularly--"you are a Tom Taylor or a Tom Robertson in disguise. Are you sure you have never courted the divine muse? Men of position have frequently been guilty of that folly, sir."

"But once," answered the other in the same tone. "At college; a political satire."

The Strollers

"Was it successful?"

"Quite so--I was expelled for writing it!"

"Well," retorted Barnes, irrelevantly, "you have at least mildly coquetted with the muse. Besides, I dare say, you have been behind the scenes a good deal. The green room is a fashionable rendezvous. Where are you going? And what--if I may ask--is your business?"

"I am on my way to New Orleans," said the traveler, after a moment's hesitation. "My business, fortune-getting. In sugar, tobacco, or indigo-culture!"

"New Orleans!" exclaimed the manager, poising the ladle in mid air. "That, too, is our destination. We have an engagement to play there. Why not join our band? Write or adapt a play for us. Make a temperance drama of your play!"

"You are a whimsical fellow," said the stranger, smiling. "Why don't you write the play yourself?"

"I? An unread, illiterate dotard! Why, I never had so much as a day's schooling. As a lad I slept with the rats, held horses, swept crossings and lived like a mudlark! Me write a play! I might let fall a suggestion here and there; how to set a flat, or where to drop a fly; to plan an entrance, or to arrange an exit! No, no; let the shoemaker stick to his last! It takes"--with deference--"a scholar to write a drama."

"Thus you disqualify me," laughed the other, drawing out a pipe which he filled; and lighted with a coal held in the iron grip of the antique tongs. "If it were only to help plant a battery or stand in a gap!" he said grimly, replacing the tongs against the old brick oven at one side of the grate. "But to beset King Bacchus in three acts! To storm his castle in the first; scale the walls in the second, and blow up all the king's horses and all the king's men in the last--that is, indeed, serious warfare!"

"True, it will be a roundabout way to New Orleans," continued the manager, disregarding his companion's response, "but there is no better way of seeing the New World--that is, if you do not disdain the company of strolling players. You gain in knowledge what you lose in time. If you are a philosopher, you can study human nature through the buffoon and the mummer. If you are a naturalist, here are grand forests to contemplate. If you are not a recluse, here is free, though humble, comradeship."

His listener gazed thoughtfully into the fire. Was the prospect of sharing this gipsy-like life attractive to him? An adventurer himself, was he drawn toward these homeless strollers, for whom the illusions of dramatic art shone with enticing luster in the comparative solitude of the circuit on the wilderness?

As he sat before the glow, the light of the burning shagbark, playing elfishly above the dying embers, outlined the stalwart, yet active figure and the impenetrable, musing features. But when, with an upward shower of sparks, the backlog fell asunder and the waning flame cast yet more gloomy shadows behind them, he leaned back in his heavy, hewn chair and again bent an attentive look upon the loquacious speaker.

"Or, if you desire," resumed the manager after some hesitation, "it might become a business venture as well as a pleasure jaunt. Here is a sinking ship. Will the salvage warrant helping us into port; that is, New Orleans? There hope tells a flattering tale. The company is well equipped; has a varied repertoire, while Constance"--tenderly--"is a host in herself. If you knew her as I do; had watched her art grow"--his voice trembled--"and to think, sometimes I do not know where the next day's sustenance may come from! That she"--

He broke off abruptly, gazing at his companion half-apologetically. "We players, sir," he resumed, "present a jovial front, but"--tapping his breast--"few know what is going on here!"

"Therein," said the younger man, emptying his pipe, "you have stated a universal truth." He pushed a smoldering log with his foot toward the remnants of the embers. "Suppose I were so minded to venture"--and he mentioned a modest sum--"in this hazard and we patched up the play together?"

"You don't mean it?" cried the manager, eagerly. Then he regarded the other suspiciously: "Your proposal is not inspired through sympathy?"

"Why not through the golden prospects you have so eloquently depicted?" replied Saint-Prosper, coldly.

"Why not indeed!" exclaimed the reassured manager. "Success will come; it must come. You have seen Constance but once. She lives in every character to her heart's core. How does she do it? Who can tell? It's inborn. A heritage to her!"

His voice sank low with emotion. "Yes," he murmured, shaking his head thoughtfully, as though another image arose in his mind; "a heritage! a divine heritage!" But soon he looked up. "She's a brave girl!" he said. "When times were dark, she would always smile encouragingly, and, in the light of her clear eyes, I felt anew the Lord would temper the wind to the shorn lamb."

"One--two--three--four," rang the great clock through the silent hall, and, at its harsh clangor, Barnes started.

"Bless my soul, the maids'll be up and doing and find us here!" he exclaimed. "One last cup! To the success of the temperance drama!"

In a few moments they had parted for their respective chambers and only the landlord was left down-stairs. Now as he came from behind the bar, where he had been apparently dozing and secretly listening through the half-opened door leading into the kitchen, he had much difficulty to restrain his laughter.

"That's a good one to tell Ezekiel," he muttered, turning out the lights and sweeping the ashes on the hearth to the back of the grate. "To the temperance drama!"

CHAPTER VI:
THE DEPARTURE OF THE CHARIOT

D own the hill, facing the tavern, the shadows of night were slowly
withdrawn, ushering in the day of the players' leaving. A single
tree, at the very top, isolated from its sylvan neighbors, was bathed in
the warm sunshine, receiving the earliest benediction of day. Down,
down, came the dark shade, pursued by the light, until the entire
slope of the hill was radiant and the sad colored foliage flaunted in
new-born gaiety.

Returning from the stable, where he had been looking after his
horse, the soldier stood for a moment before the inn, when a flower
fell at his feet, and, glancing over his shoulder, he perceived Susan,
who was leaning from her window. The venturesome rose, which had
clambered as high as the second story, was gone; plucked, alas, by the
wayward hand of a coquette. Saint-Prosper bowed, and stooped for
the aspiring but now hapless flower which lay in the dust.

"You have joined the chariot, I hear?" said Susan.

"For the present," he replied.

"And what parts will you play?" she continued, with smiling
inquisitiveness.

"None."

"What a pity! You would make a handsome lover." Then she
blushed. "Lud! What am I saying? Besides"--maliciously--"I believe
you have eyes for some one else. But remember,"--shaking her finger
and with a coquettish turn of the head--"I am an actress and therefore
vain. I must have the best part in the new piece. Don't forget that, or
I'll not travel in the same chariot with you." And Susan disappeared.

"Ah, Kate," she said, a moment later, "what a fine-looking young
man he is!"

"Who?" drawled her sister.

"Mr. Saint-Prosper, of course."

"He is large enough," retorted Kate, leisurely.

"Large enough! O, Kate, what a phlegmatic creature you are!"

"Fudge!" said the other as she left the chamber.

Entering the tavern, the soldier was met by the wiry old lady who bobbed into the breakfast room and explained the kind of part that fitted her like a glove, her prejudices being strong against modern plays.

"Give me dramas like 'Oriana,' 'The Rival Queens' or Webster's pieces," she exclaimed, quoting with much fire for her years:

"'We are only like dead walls or vaulted graves!'"

"And do not forget the 'heavy' in your piece!" called out Hawkes across the table. "Something you can dig your teeth in!"

"Nor the 'juvenile lead,'" chimed in the Celtic Adonis.

"Adonis makes a great hit in a small part," laughed Kate, appearing at the door. "'My lord, the carriage is waiting!'"

"My lady, your tongue is too sharp!" exclaimed Adonis, nettled.

"And put in a love scene for Adonis and myself," she continued, lazily floating into the room. "He is so fond of me, it would not be like acting!"

This bantering was at length interrupted by the appearance of the chariot and the property wagon at the front door, ready for the journey. The rumbling of the vehicles, the resounding hoofs and the resonant voice of the stable boy awakened the young lord of the manor in his chamber above. He stretched himself sleepily, swore and again composed himself for slumber, when the noise of a property trunk, thumping its way down the front stairs a step at a time, galvanized him into life and consciousness.

"Has the world come to an end?" he muttered. "No; I remember; it's only the players taking their departure!"

But, although he spoke carelessly, the bumping of boxes and slamming and banging of portable goods annoyed him more than he would confess. With the "crazy-quilt"--a patch-work of heptagons of different hues and patterns--around his shoulders, clothing him with all the colors of the rainbow, he sat up in bed, wincing at each concussion.

"I might as well get up!" he exclaimed. "I'll see her once more--the perverse beauty!" And tossing the kaleidoscopic covering viciously from him, he began to dress.

Meanwhile, as the time for their going drew near, mine host down-stairs sped the parting guest with good cheer, having fared profitably by the patronage the players had brought to the inn; but his daughter, Arabella, looked sad and pensive. How weary, flat and stale appeared her existence now! With a lump in her throat and a pang in her heart, she recklessly wiped her eyes upon the best parlor curtains, when Barnes mounted to the box, as robust a stage-driver as ever extricated a coach from a quagmire. The team, playful through long confinement, tugged at the reins, and Sandy, who was at the bits, occasionally shot through space like an erratic meteor.

The manager was flourishing his whip impatiently when Constance and Susan appeared, the former in a traveling costume of blue silk; a paletot of dark cloth, and, after the fashion of the day, a bonnet of satin and velvet. Susan was attired in a jupe sweeping and immensely full--to be in style!--and jacquette with sleeves of the pagoda form. The party seemed in high spirits, as from his dormer window Mauville, adjusting his attire, peered through the lattice over the edge of the moss-grown roof and leaf-clogged gutters and surveyed their preparations for departure. How well the rich color of her gown became the young girl! He had told himself white was her best adornment, but his opinion veered on the moment now, and he thought he had never seen her to better advantage, with the blue of her dress reappearing in the lighter shade, above the dark paletot, in the lining of the bonnet and the bow of ribbons beneath her chin.

"On my word, but she looks handsome!" muttered the patroon. "Might sit for a Gainsborough or a Reynolds! What dignity! What coldness! All except the eyes! How they can lighten! But there's that adventurer with her," as the figure of the soldier crossed the yard to the property wagon. "No getting rid of him until the last moment!" And he opened the shutters wider, listening and watching more closely.

"Are you going to ride in the property wagon?" he heard Saint-Prosper ask.

"Yes; when I have a part to study I sometimes retire to the stage throne," she answered lightly. "I suppose you will ride your horse?"

Of his reply the listener caught only the words, "wind-break" and "lame." He observed the soldier assist her to the throne, and then, to Mauville's surprise, spring into the wagon himself.

"Why, the fellow is going with them!" exclaimed the land baron. "Or, at any rate, he is going with her. What can it mean?" And hurriedly quitting his post, his toilet now being complete, he hastened to the door and quickly made his way down-stairs.

During the past week his own addresses had miscarried and his gallantry had been love's labor lost. At first he had fancied he was making progress, but soon acknowledged to himself he had underestimated the enterprise. Play had succeeded play--he could not have told what part favored her most! Ophelia sighed and died; Susan danced on her grave between acts, according to the program, and turned tears into smiles; the farewell night had come and gone--and yet Constance had made no sign of compliance to reward the patient wooer. Now, at the sight of these preparations for departure, and the presence of the stalwart stranger in the property wagon, he experienced a sudden sensation of pique, almost akin to jealousy.

Stepping from the tavern, it was with an effort he suppressed his chagrin and vexation and assumed that air of nonchalance which became him well. Smilingly he bade Susan and the other occupants of the chariot farewell, shook Barnes by the hand, and turned to the property wagon.

"The noise of your departure awakened me," he said to the young girl. "So I have come to claim my compensation--the pleasure of seeing you--"

"Depart!" she laughed quickly.

Momentarily disconcerted, he turned to the soldier. "You ride early."

"As you see," returned the other, immovably.

"A habit contracted in the army, no doubt!" retorted Mauville, recovering his easy self-possession. "Well, a bumping trunk is as efficacious as a bugle call! But au revoir, Miss Carew; for we may meet again. The world is broad--yet its highways are narrow! There is no need wishing you a pleasant journey."

His glance rested on Saint-Prosper for a moment, but told nothing beyond the slight touch of irony in his words and then shifting to the young girl, it lingered upon each detail of costume and outline of feature. Before she could reply, Barnes cracked his whip, the horses sprang forward, and the stable boy, a confused tangle of legs and arms, was shot as from a catapult among the sweet-williams. The abrupt departure of the chariot was the cue for the property wagon, which followed with some labor and jolting, like a convoy struggling in the wake of a pretentious ship. From the door Mauville watched it until it reached a toll-gate, passed beneath the portcullis and disappeared into the broad province of the wilderness.

CHAPTER VII:
SOJOURNING IN ARCADIA

Calm and still was the morning; the wandering air just stirred the pendulous branches of the elms and maples, and, in the clear atmosphere, the russet hills were sharply outlined. As they swung out into the road, with Hans, the musician, at the reins, the young girl removed her bonnet and leaned back in the chair of state, where kings had fretted and queens had lolled.

The throne, imposing on the stage, now appeared but a flimsy article of furniture, with frayed and torn upholstering, and carving which had long since lost its gilded magnificence. Seated amid the jumble of theatrical appliances and accoutrements--scenery, rolled up rug-fashion, property trunks, stage clock, lamps and draperies-- she accepted the situation gracefully, even finding nothing strange in the presence of the soldier. New faces had come and gone in the company before, and, when Barnes had complacently informed her Saint-Prosper would journey with the players to New Orleans in a semi-business capacity, the arrangement appeared conformable to precedent. The manager's satisfaction augured well for the importance of the semi-business rôle assumed by the stranger, and Barnes' friendliness was perhaps in some degree unconsciously reflected in her manner; an attitude the soldier's own reserve, or taciturnity, had not tended to dispel. So, his being in the property wagon seemed no more singular than Hans' occupancy of the front seat, or if Adonis, Hawkes, or Susan had been there with her. She was accustomed to free and easy comradeship; indeed, knew no other life, and it was only assiduous attentions, like those of the land baron's, that startled and disquieted her.

As comfortably as might be, she settled back in the capacious, threadbare throne, a slender figure in its depths--more adapted to accommodate a corpulent Henry VIII!--and smiled gaily, as the wagon, in avoiding one rut, ran into another and lurched somewhat violently. Saint-Prosper, lodged on a neighboring trunk, quickly extended a steadying hand.

"You see how precarious thrones are!" he said.

"There isn't room for it to more than totter," she replied lightly, removing her bonnet and lazily swinging it from the arm of the chair.

"Then it's safer than real thrones," he answered, watching the swaying bonnet, or perhaps, contrasting the muscular, bronzed hand he had placed on the chair with the smooth, white one which held the blue ribbons; a small, though firm, hand to grapple with the minotaur, Life!

She slowly wound the ribbons around her fingers.

"Oh, you mean France," she said, and he looked away with sudden disquietude. "Poor monarchs! Their road is rougher than this one."

"Rougher truly!"

"You love France?" she asked suddenly, after studying, with secret, sidelong glances his reserved, impenetrable face.

His gaze returned to her--to the bonnet now resting in her lap--to the hand beside it.

"It is my native land," he replied.

"Then why did you leave it--in its trouble?" she asked impulsively.

"Why?" he repeated, regarding her keenly; but in a moment he added: "For several reasons. I returned from Africa, from serving under Bugeaud, to find the red flag waving in Paris; the king fled!"

"Oh," she said, quickly, "a king should--"

"What?" he asked, as she paused.

"I was going to say it was better to die like a king than--"

"Than live an outcast!" he concluded for her, a shadow on his brow.

She nodded. "At any rate, that is the way they always do in the plays," she added brightly. "But you were saying you found your real king fled?"

His heavy brows contracted, though he answered readily enough: "Yes, the king had fled. A kinsman in whose house I had been reared then bade me head a movement for the restoration of the royal fugitive. For what object? The regency was doomed. The king, a May-fly!"

"And so you refused?"

"We quarreled; he swore like a Gascon. His little puppet should yet sit in the chair where Louis XIV had lorded it! I, who owed my commission to his noble name, was a republican, a deserter! The best way out of the difficulty was out of the country. First it was England, then it was here. To-morrow--where?" he added, in a lower tone, half to himself.

"Where?" she repeated, lightly. "That is our case, too."

He looked at her with sudden interest. "Yours is an eventful life, Miss Carew."

"I have never known any other," she said, simply, adding after a pause: "My earliest recollections are associated with my mother and the stage. As a child I watched her from the wings. I remember a grand voice and majestic presence. When the audience broke into applause, my heart throbbed with pride."

But as her thoughts reverted to times past, the touch of melancholy, invoked by the memory of her mother, was gradually dispelled, as fancy conjured other scenes, and a flickering smile hovered over the lips whose parting displaced that graver mood.

"Once or twice I played with her, too," she added. "I thought it nice to be one of the little princes in Richard III and wear white satin clothes. One night after the play an old gentleman took me on his knee and said: I had to come, my child, and see if the wicked old uncle hadn't really smothered you!' When he had gone, my mother told me he was Mr. Washington Irving. I thought him very kind, for he brought me a bag of bonbons from the coffee-room."

"It's the first time I ever heard of a great critic laden with sweetmeats!" said the soldier. "And were you not flattered by his honeyed regard?"

"Oh, yes; I devoured it and wanted more," she laughed.

Hans' flourishing whip put an end to further conversation. "Der stage goach!" he said, turning a lumpish countenance upon them and pointing down the road.

Approaching at a lively gait was one of the coaches of the regular line, a vehicle of ancient type, hung on bands of leather and curtained with painted canvas, not unlike the typical French diligence, except for its absence of springs. The stage was spattered with mud from roof to wheel-tire, but as the mire was not fresh and the road fair, the presumption followed that custom and practice precluded the cleaning of the coach. The passengers, among whom were several ladies, wearing coquettish bonnets with ribbons or beau-catchers attached, were too weary even to view with wonder the odd-looking theatrical caravan. Only the driver, a diminutive person with puckered face the color of dried apples, so venerable as to be known as Old Hundred, seemed as spry and cheery as when he started.

"Morning," he said, briskly, drawing in his horses. "Come back, have ye, with yer troupe? What's the neuws from Alban-y?"

"Nothing, except Texas has been admitted as a State," answered Barnes.

"Sho! We air coming on!" commented the Methuselah of the road.

"Coming on!" groaned a voice in the vehicle, and the florid face of an English traveler appeared at the door. "I say, do you call this 'coming on!' I'm nearly gone, don't you know!"

"Hi!--ge' long!--steady there!" And Old Hundred again whipped up his team, precipitating a lady into the lap of the gentleman who was "nearly gone," and well-nigh completing his annihilation.

In less time than when a friendly sail is lost in the mist, Old Hundred's bulky land-wherry passed from view, and the soldier again turned to his companion. But she was now intent on some part in a play which she was quietly studying and he contented himself with lighting that staple luxury of the early commonwealth, a Virginia stogie, observing her from time to time over the glowing end. With the book upon her knee, her head downcast and partly turned from him, he could, nevertheless, through the mazy convolutions and dreamy spirals of the Indian weed, detect the changing emotions which swept over her, as in fancy she assumed a rôle in the drama. Now the faintest shadow of a smile, coming and going; again beneath the curve of her long lashes, a softer gleaming in the dark eyes, adding new charm to the pale, proud face. Around them nature seemed fraught with forgetfulness; the Libyan peace that knows not where or wherefore. Rocked in the cradle of ruts and furrows, Hans, portly as a carboy, half-dozed on the front seat.

Shortly before noon they approached an ancient hostelry, set well back from the road. To the manager's dismay, however, the door was locked and boards were nailed across the windows. Even the water pail, hospitably placed for man or beast, had been removed from its customary proximity to the wooden pump. Abandoned to decay, the tenantless inn was but another evidence of traffic diverted from the old stage roads by the Erie Canal Company. Cold was the fireplace before which had once rested the sheep-skin slippers for the guests; empty was the larder where at this season was wont to be game in abundance, sweet corn, luscious melons--the trophies of the hunt, the fruits of the field; missing the neat, compact little keg whose spigot had run with consolation for the wanderer!

Confronted by the deserted house, where they had expected convivial cheer, there was no alternative but to proceed, and their journey was resumed with some discomfiture to the occupants of the coach which now labored like a portly Spanish galleon, struck by a squall. They had advanced in this manner for some distance through furrow and groove, when the vehicle gave a sharper lurch down a deeper rut; a crash was followed by cries of affright and the chariot abruptly settled on one side. Barnes held the plunging horses in control, while the gentlemen scrambled to the ground and assisted the ladies to dismount.

"Any one hurt?" asked the manager from his box.

"No damage done--except to the coach," said Hawkes.

By this time the horses had become quiet and Barnes, now that the passengers were rescued, like a good skipper, left the quarter deck.

"We couldn't have chosen a better place for our lunch," he remarked philosophically. "How fortunate we should have broken down where we did!"

"Very fortunate!" echoed the old lady ironically.

The accident had happened upon a slight plateau, of which they accordingly took possession, tethering the horses to graze. From the branches overhead the squirrels surveyed them as if asking what manner of people were these, and the busy woodpecker ceased his drumming, cocking his head inquisitively at the intruders; then shyly drew away, mounting spirally the trunk of the tree to the hole, chiseled by his strong beak for a nest. As Barnes gazed around upon the pleasing prospect, he straightway became the duke in the comedy of the forest.

"Ha, my brothers in exile," he exclaimed, "are not these woods more free from peril than the envious court?"

"All it wants," said the tragedian, hungrily, "is mutton, greens and a foaming pot."

"I can't promise the foaming pot," answered the manager. "But, at least, we have a well-filled hamper."

Soon the coffee was simmering and such viands as they had brought with them--for Barnes was a far-sighted and provident manager--were spread out in tempting profusion. Near them a swift-flowing stream chattered about the stones like one of nature's busiest gossips; it whispered to the flowers, murmured to the rushes and was voluble to the overhanging branch that dragged upon the surface of the water. The flowers on its brim nodded, the rushes waved and the branch bent as if in assent to the mad gossip of the blithesome brook. And it seemed as though all this animated conversation was caused by the encampment of the band of players by the wayside.

The repast finished, they turned their attention to the injured chariot, but fortunately the damage was not beyond repair, and Barnes, actor, manager, bill-poster, license-procurer, added to his already extensive repertoire the part of joiner and wheelwright. The skilled artisans in coachmaking and coach-repairing might not have regarded the manager as a master-workman, but the fractured parts were finally set after a fashion. By that time, however, the sun had sunk to rest upon a pillow of clouds; the squirrels, law-abiding citizens, had sought their homes; the woodpecker had vanished in his snug chamber, and only forest dwellers of nocturnal habits were now abroad, their name legion like the gad-abouts of a populous city.

"There!" exclaimed the manager, surveying his handiwork. "The 'bus is ready! But there is little use going on to-night. I am not sure of the road and here is a likely spot to pass the night."

"Likely to be devoured by wild beasts," said Kate, with a shudder.

"I am sure I see two glistening eyes!" exclaimed Susan.

"Fudge!" observed the elastic old lady. "That's the first time you have been afraid of two-glistening eyes."

"There's a vast difference between wolves and men," murmured Susan.

"I'm not so sure of that," returned the aged cynic.

But as the light of day was withdrawn a great fire sprang up, illumining the immediate foreground. The flames were cheering, drawing the party more closely together. Even Hawkes partly discarded his tragedy face; the old lady threw a bundle of fifty odd years from her shoulders as easily as a wood-carrier would cast aside his miserable stack of fagots, while Barnes forgot his troubles in narrating the harrowing experience of a company which had penetrated the west at a period antedating the settlement of the Michigan and Ohio boundary dispute.

The soldier alone was silent, curiously watching the play of light and shade on the faces of the strollers, his gaze resting longest, perhaps, on the features of the young girl. Leaning against an ancient oak, so old the heart of it was gone and it towered but a mighty shell, the slender figure of the actress was clearly outlined, but against that dark and roughly-furrowed background she seemed too slight and delicate to buffet with storms and hardships. That day's experience was a forerunner of the unexpected in this wandering life, but another time the mishap might not be turned to diversion. The coach would not always traverse sunny byways; the dry leaf floating from the majestic arm of the oak, the sound of an acorn as it struck the earth presaged days less halcyon to come.

"How do you enjoy being a stroller?" asked a voice, interrupting the soldier's reverie. "It has its bitters and its sweets, hasn't it? Especially its sweets!" Susan added, glancing meaningly at the young girl. "But after all, it doesn't much matter what happens to you if you are in good company." The semi-gloom permitted her to gaze steadfastly into his eyes. He ignored the opportunity for a compliment, and Susan stifled a little yawn, real or imaginary.

"Positively one could die of ennui in this wilderness," she continued. "Do you know you are a welcome addition to our band? But you will have to make yourself very agreeable. I suppose"-- archly--"you were very agreeable in the property wagon?"

"Miss Carew had a part to study," he returned, coldly.

"A part to study!" In mock consternation. "How I hate studying parts! They say what you wouldn't, and don't say what you would! But I'm off to bed," rising impatiently. "I'm getting sleepy!"

"Sleepy!" echoed Barnes. "Take your choice! The Hotel du Omnibus"--indicating the chariot--"or the Villa Italienne?"--with a gesture toward a tent made of the drop curtain upon the walls of which was the picture of an Italian scene.

"The chariot for me," answered Susan. "It is more high and dry and does not suggest spiders and other crawling things."

"Good-night, then, and remember a good conscience makes a hard bed soft."

"Then I shall sleep on down. I haven't had a chance"--with a sigh--"to damage my conscience lately. But when I strike civilization again"--and Susan shook her head eloquently to conclude her sentence. "Oh, yes; if beds depend on conscience, boughs would be feathers for me to-night." With which half-laughing, half-defiant conclusion, Susan tripped to the chariot, pausing a moment, however, to cast a reproachful glance over her shoulder at Saint-Prosper before vanishing in the cavernous depths of the vehicle of the muses.

Her departure was the signal for the dispersing of the party to their respective couches. Now the fire sank lower, the stars came out brighter and the moon arose and traveled majestically up the heavens, taking a brief but comprehensive survey of the habitations of mortals, and then, as if satisfied with her scrutiny, sailed back to the horizon and dropped out of sight.

CHAPTER VIII:
FLIPPING THE SHILLING

S hortly after the departure of the strolling players from the tavern, Mauville summoned his servant and ordered his equipage. While waiting he strode impatiently to and fro in the dining-room, which, dismantled of the stage, by very contrast to the temporary temple of art, turned his thoughts to the players. The barrenness of the room smote him acutely with the memory of those performances, and he laughed ironically to himself that he should thus revert to them. But as he scoffed inwardly, his eyes gleamed with vivacity, and the sensations with which he had viewed the young girl night after night were reawakened. What was one woman lost to him, his egotism whispered; he had parted from many, as a gourmand leaves one meal for another. Yes; but she had not been his, insinuated vanity; another had whipped her off before his eyes.

"Why the devil didn't you tell me he was going with them?" he demanded of the landlord while settling his account.

"He--who?" asked the surprised inn-keeper.

"That adventurer you have been harboring here. How far's he going with them?"

"I don't know. The night after the performance I heard the manager ask him to join the company; to write a temperance play."

"Temperance play!" sneered Mauville. "The fool's gone with them on account of a woman."

"I did think he was mighty attentive to one of the actresses," said the landlord, reflectively. "The one with them melting eyes. Purty good-looking! Quiet and lady-like, too! So he's gallivanting after her? Well, well, I guess actresses be all alike."

"I guess they are," added the heir savagely. "And this one took me in," he thought to himself. "Holding me off and playing with him, the jade!" Then he continued aloud: "Where are they going?"

"Didn't hear 'em say," answered the other, "and I didn't like to appear too curious."

"You didn't?" returned Mauville, ironically. "You must have changed lately."

"I don't know as I understand you quite," replied the landlord with sudden dignity. "But here's your carriage and your things are all on. I guess your tenants will be glad to see you," he continued, not resisting a parting shot.

"Curse the tenants!" muttered the guest in ill-humor, as he strode from the tavern without more ado.

He was soon on his way, partly forgetting his vexation in new anticipations, and traveling with spirit to his destination, which he reached late that afternoon. The residence of the old patroons, a lordly manor where once lavish hospitality had been displayed, was approached through great gates of hammered iron in which the family arms were interwoven, leading into a fine avenue of trees. The branches of the more majestic met overhead, forming a sylvan arch that almost obscured the blue sky by day and the stars by night. Gazing through this vista, a stately portico appeared, with Corinthian columns, affording an inviting termination of the view. The grounds bore evidence of neglect in the grass growing knee-high and rank with weeds; the flower beds almost obliterated; a corn-crib sunk to one side like a quadruped gone weak-kneed; and the stream that struggled vainly through the leaves and rubbish barring its passage across the estate. The fence resembled the "company front" of an awkward squad, each picket being more or less independent of its neighbor, with here and there a break or gap in the ranks.

Passing through the leafy archway over a noiseless road and drawing near the manor, the heir could see that the broad windows, with their quaint squares of glass, were unwashed, the portico unswept and the brass finishings of the front door unpolished. At the right of the steps leading to the portico, moss-covered and almost concealed by a rose-bush, stood a huge block of granite upon which rested the "lifting-stone," as it was called, of one of the early masters. This not inconsiderable weight the new retainers had been required to lift in days of old, or failing, the patroon would have none of their services, for he wanted only lusty, broad-backed varlets for farmers or--when need were--soldiers.

In answer to repeated summons from the ponderous knocker, shuffling footsteps were finally heard within, the door was opened a few inches and the gleaming teeth of a great, gaunt dog were thrust into the opening, followed by an ominous growling. Mauville sprang back a step; the snarling resolved itself into a yelp, as some one unceremoniously dragged the canine back; the door was opened wider and a brawny figure, smoking a long-stemmed pipe, barred the way. The dog, but partly appeased, peered from behind the man's sturdy legs, awaiting hostilities. The latter, an imperturbable Dutchman, eyed the intruder askance, smoking as impassively in his face as one of his ancestors before William the Testy. From his point of vantage on the threshold the care-taker looked down upon the master so indifferently, while the dog glared so viciously that the land baron cried angrily:

"Why the devil don't you get out of the way and call off that beast?"

The man pondered. "No one but the heir would give orders like that," he said, so accustomed to speaking his thoughts in the solitude of the great rooms, that he gave way to the habit now. "This must be the heir."

Slowly the care-taker moved aside, the hound shifting his position accordingly, and Mauville entered, gazing around with some interest, for the interior of the manor realized the pretensions of its outward aspect. The floor of the hall was of satinwood and rosewood, and the mahogany wainscoting, extending almost to the ceiling, was black with age. With its rich carvings, the stairway suggested woody rioting in balustrades lifting up to the support of the heavy beams in the ceiling. The furnishings were in keeping, but dust obscured the mirror-like surface of the mahogany tables, the heavy draperies were in need of renovation, while a housewife would have viewed with despair the condition of brass and ebony inlaid cabinets, ancient tapestries, and pictures, well-nigh defaced, but worthy, even in their faded aspect, of the brush of Sir Godfrey Kneller, Benjamin West and the elder Peale.

Having casually surveyed his new home, the heir was reminded of the need for refreshment after his long journey, and, turning to the care-taker, asked him what there was in the house? The servant smoked silently as though deeply considering this momentous question, while the rear guard maintained unabated hostility between the man's firmly-planted feet. Then abruptly, without removing his pipe, the guardian of the manor ejaculated:

"Short-cakes and oly-koeks."

The other laughed, struck his knee with his light cane and demanded to be shown to the library, where he would have these outlandish dishes served.

"And bring with them, Mynheer Oly-koeks, a bottle of wine," he continued. "At the same time, chain up the dog. He eyes me with such hungry hostility that, gad! I believe he's an anti-renter!"

Mauville was ushered into a large room, where great leather-bound volumes filled the oak shelves to the ceiling. The care-taker turned, and, with echoing footsteps, slowly departed, followed by his faithful four-footed retainer. It is true the latter paused, swung half-around and regarded the land-owner with the look of a sulky and rebellious tenant, but, summoned by a stern "Oloffe!" from his master, the dog reluctantly pattered across the hard-wood floor.

In surveying his surroundings, the land baron's attention was attracted by a coat-of-arms deeply carved in the massive wood of the book-case--on a saltire sable, a fleur-de-lys or. This head of heraldic flowers appeared to interest Mauville, who smiled grimly. "From what I know of my worthy ancestors," he muttered, "and their propensities to prey on their fellow-men, I should say a more fitting device would be that of Lovett of Astwell: Gules, three wolves passant sable, in pale."

Pleased with his own humor, he threw himself upon a couch near the window, stretching himself luxuriously. Soon the man reappeared with the refreshments and a bottle of old-fashioned, substantial girth, which he uncorked with marked solicitude.

"Where are the oly-koeks?" exclaimed the heir.

The watchman pointed to a great dish of dark blue willow-ware pattern.

"Oh, doughnuts!" said Mauville. "You know where the family lawyer lives? Have my man drive you to his house and bring him here at once."

As the care-taker again disappeared the heir bent over the curiously shaped bottle in delight, for when the cork was drawn a fragrance filled the musty apartment as from a bouquet.

"Blessings on the ancestor who laid down this wine!" he muttered. "May his ghost wander in to sniff it! These oly-koeks are not bad. I suppose this man, Ten Breecheses, or whatever he is called, is at once cook and housekeeper. Although I don't think much of his housekeeping," ruminated Mauville, as he observed a herculean spider weaving a web from an old volume of Giraldus Cambrensis, antiquary, to the classical works of one Joseph of Exeter. There is a strong sympathy between wine and cobwebs, and Mauville watched with increasing interest the uses to which these ponderous tomes had sunk--but serving the bloodthirsty purpose of the nimble architect, evolving its delicate engineering problem in mid air.

A great blundering fly had just bobbed into the net and the spider, with hideous, carnivorous zest, was scrambling for it, when the guardian of the manor returned with the family solicitor, a little man who bore in his arms a bundle of papers which, after the customary greetings, he spread upon the table. He helped himself to a glass of burgundy and proceeded forthwith to enter into the history of his trust.

Mynheer, the patroon, Mauville's predecessor, a lonely, arrogant man, had held tenaciously to the immense tracts of land acquired in the colonial days by nominal purchase. He had never married, his desire for an heir being discounted by his aversion for the other sex, until as the days dragged on, he found himself bed-ridden and childless in his old age. Unfortunately the miser can not take his acres into Paradise, and the patroon, with many an inward groan, cast about him for some remote relative to whom he would reluctantly transfer his earthly hereditaments. These were two: one a man of piety, who prayed with the tenants when they complained of their lot; the other, Mauville, upon whom he had never set eyes.

When the earliest patroons had made known to the West India Company their intention of planting colonies in New Netherland, they had issued attractive maps to promote their colonization projects. Among those who had been lured to America by these enticing advertisements was an ancestor of Edward Mauville. Incurring the displeasure of the governor for his godless views, this Frenchman was sent to the pillory, or whipping post, and his neighbors were about to cast out the devil of irreverence in good old-fashioned manner, when one of Mynheer's daughters interceded, carried off the handsome miscreant, and--such was her imperious way!--married him! He was heard in after years to aver that the whipping would have been the milder punishment, but, be that as it may, a child was born unto them who inherited the father's adventuresome and graceless character, deserted his home, joined hands with some ocean-rovers and sailed for that pasture-ground of buccaneers, the Caribbean sea. Of his subsequent history various stories may be found in the chronicles of New Orleans and Louisiana.

The only other person who might have any pretensions to the estate was a reverend gentleman who had been a missionary among the Indians, preaching from a stump, and called "Little Thunder" by the red men because of his powerful voice; a lineal descendant of the Rev. Doctor Johannes Vanderklonk, the first dominie of the patroons, who served for one thousand guilders, payable in meat or drink, twenty-two bushels of wheat and two firkins of butter. He saved the souls of the savages, while the white men cheated their bodies. Now and then, in those early days, the children of the forest protested against this evangelizing process and carried off the good dominie to the torture stake, where they plucked out his finger nails; but he returned with as much zest to his task of landing these simple souls in Paradise as those who employed him displayed in making an earthly Paradise out of the lands the red men left behind them.

When by this shrewd system the savages were gradually saved, and incidentally exterminated, Little Thunder's occupation was gone and he became a pensioner of Mynheer the Patroon, earning his bread by an occasional sermon to the tenants, exhorting them to thrift and industry, to be faithful and multiply, and to pay their rents promptly. As Mynheer's time drew near he sent for his attorney and commanded him to look up the life, deeds and character of Edward Mauville.

"This I did," said the lawyer, "and here it is." Waving a roll of papers before his interested listener.

"A nauseating mess, no doubt," carelessly remarked the land baron.

"Oh, sir!" deprecated the lawyer, opening the roll. "'Item: Religion; pupil of the brilliant Jesuit, Abbé Moneau. Item: Morals; Exhibit A,

the affair with Countess ---- in Paris, where he was sent to be educated after the fashion of French families in New Orleans; Exhibit B--'"

"Spare me," exclaimed Mauville. "Life is wearisome enough, but a biography--" He shrugged his shoulders. "Come to your point."

"Of course, sir, I was only trying to carry out his instructions. The same, sir, as I would carry out yours!" With an ingratiating smile. Whereupon the attorney told how he had furnished the patroon this roll and fastened it to his bed, so that he might wind and unwind it, perusing it at his pleasure. This the dying man did, sternly noting the damaging facts; thinking doubtlessly how traits will endure for generations--aye, for ages, in spite of the pillory!--the while Little Thunder was roaring petitions to divinity by his bedside, as though to bluster and bully the Almighty into granting his supplications. The patroon glanced from his pensioner to the roll; from the kneeling man to that prodigious list of peccadillos, and then he called for a shilling, a coin still somewhat in use in America. This he flipped thrice.

"Roué or sham," he said the first time.

"Rake or hypocrite," he exclaimed the second time.

"Devil or Pharisee," he cried the third time.

He peered over the coin and sent for his attorney. His soul passed away, mourned by Little Thunder until the will was read, when his lamentations ceased; he soundly berated Mynheer, the Patroon, in his coffin and refused to go to his burying. Then he became an ardent anti-renter, a leader of "bolters," a thunderer of the people's cause, the devoted enemy of land barons in general, and one patroon in particular, the foreign heir of the manor.

"But let him thunder away, sir," said Scroggs, soothingly. "The estate's yours now, for the old patroon can't come back to change his mind. He's buried sure enough in the grove, a dark and sombrous spot as befitted his disposition, but restful withal. Aye, and the marble slab's above him, which reminds me that only a month before he took to his bed he was smoking his pipe on the porch, when his glance fell upon the lifting-stone. Suddenly he strode towards it, bent his back and raised it a full two inches. 'So much for age!' said he, scoffing-like. But age heard him and now he lies with a stone on him he can not lift, while you, sir"--to his listener, deferentially--"are sole heir to the estate and to the feud."

"A feud goes with the property?" remarked Mauville carelessly.

"The tenants object to paying rent," replied Scroggs, sadly. "They're a sorry lot!"

"Evade their debts, do they?" said the land baron languidly. "What presumption to imitate their betters! That won't do; I need the money."

"They claim the rights of the landlord originated in fraud--"

"No doubt!" Yawning. "My ancestors were rogues!"

"Oh, sir"--deprecatorily.

"If the tenants don't pay, turn them out," interrupted Mauville, listlessly, "if you have to depopulate the country."

Having come to an understanding with his client, the lawyer arose to take his departure.

"By the way," he said, obsequiously, selecting a yellow, well-worn bit of paper from his bundle of documents, "it may interest you to keep this yourself. It is the original deed for all these lands from the squaw Pewasch. You can see they were acquired for a few shillings' worth of 'wet and dry goods' and seventeen and a half ells of duffels."

"The old patroons could strike a rare bargain," muttered the heir, as he casually surveyed the ancient deed, and then, folding it, placed it in his breast pocket. "For a mere song was acquired--"

"A vast principality," added the solicitor, waving his hand toward the fields and meadows far in the distance.

CHAPTER IX:
SAMPLING THE VINTAGES

Having started the wheels of justice fairly moving, with Scroggs at the throttle, the new land baron soon discovered that he was not in consonance with the great commoner who said he was savage enough to prefer the woods and wilds of Monticello to all the pleasures of Paris. In other words, those rural delights of his forefathers, the pleasures of a closer intimacy with nature, awoke no responsive chord in Mauville's breast, and he began to tire before long of a patriarchal existence and crullers and oly-koeks and playing the fine lord in solitary grandeur.

The very extent of the deserted manor carried an overwhelming sense of loneliness, especially at this season when nature was dying and triumphal tints of decay were replacing the vernal freshness of the forests, flaunting gaudy vestments that could not, however, conceal the sadness of the transition. The days were growing shorter and the leaden-colored vapors, driven by the whip of that taskmaster, the wind, replaced the snow-white clouds becalmed in the tender depths of ether. Soon would the hoar frost crystallize on grass and fence, or the autumn rains descend, dripping mournfully from the water spouts and bubbling over the tubs. Already the character of the dawn was changed to an almost sullen awakening of the day, denoting a seeming uneasiness of the hidden forces, while an angry passing of the glowing orb replaced the Paphian sunset.

In nook and cranny, through the balustrades and woody screens of the ancient house, penetrated the wandering currents of air. The draperies waved mysteriously, as by a hidden hand, and, at nightfall, the floor of satin and rosewood creaked ominously as if beneath the restless footsteps of former inmates, moving from the somber hangings of the windows to the pearl-inlaid harpsichord whose melody was gone, and thence up the broad staircase, pausing naturally at the landing, beneath which had assembled gay gatherings in the colonial days. And such a heedless phantom group--fine gentlemen in embroidered coats, bright breeches, silk stockings and peruke, and, peeping through ethereal lace wristbands, a white hand fit for no sterner toil than to flourish with airy grace a gold-headed cane; ladies with gleaming bare shoulders, dressed in "cumbrous silk that with its rustling made proud the flesh that bore it!" The imaginative listener could almost distinguish these footfalls, as the blind will recognize the tread of an unseen person.

To further add to the land baron's dissatisfaction over his heritage, "rent-day"--that all-important day in the olden times; when my lord's door had been besieged by the willing lease-holders, cheerful in rendering unto Caesar what was due Caesar!--seemed to have been dropped from the modern calendar, as many an ancient holiday has gradually been lost in the whirligig of time. No long procession now awaited the patroon's pleasure, when it should suit him to receive the tribute of guilders, corn or meal; the day might have been as obsolete as an Hellenic festival day to Zeus, for all the observance it was accorded.

"Your notices, Scroggs, were wasted on the desert air," said the patroon, grimly, to that disappointed worthy. "What's the use of tenants who don't pay? Playing at feudal lord in modern times is a farce, Scroggs. I wish we had lived about four hundred years ago."

"Yes, if four hundred years ago were now," assented the parasite, "I'd begin with Dick, the tollman! He's a regular Goliath and,"--his face becoming purple--"when I threatened him with the law, threw me out of the barn on an obnoxious heap of refuse."

"You weren't exactly a David, then?" laughed the patroon, in spite of his bad humor.

"I'll throw the stone yet," said the little man, viciously showing his yellow teeth. "The law's the sling."

That evening, when the broad meadows were inundated by the shadow of the forest that crept over it like an incoming tide, the land baron ordered lights for every room. The manor shone in isolated grandeur amid the gloomy fields, with the forest-wall around it; radiant as of old, when strains of music had been heard within and many figures passed the windows. But now there was light, and not life, and a solitary anti-renter on the lonely road regarded with surprise the unusual illumination.

"What does it mean?" asked Little Thunder--for it was he--waiting and watching, as without the gates of Paradise.

Well might he ask, for the late Mynheer, the Patroon, had been a veritable bat for darkness; a few candles answered his purpose in the spacious rooms; he played the prowler, not the grand lord; a recluse who hovered over his wine butts in the cellar and gloated over them, while he touched them not; a hermit who lived half his time in the kitchen, bending over the smoky fireplace, and not a lavender-scented gentleman who aired himself in the drawing-room, a fine fop with nothing but the mirrors to pay him homage. Little Thunder, standing with folded arms in the dark road, gloomy as Lucifer, almost expected to see the brilliant fabric vanish like one of those palaces of joy built by the poets.

Hour after hour passed, midnight had come and gone, and still the lights glowed. Seated in the library, with the curtains drawn, were the land baron and Scroggs, a surveyor's map between them and a dozen bottles around them. Before Mauville stood several glasses, containing wines of various vintages which the land baron compared and sipped, held to the light and inhaled after the manner of a connoisseur sampling a cellar. He was unduly dignified and stately, but the attorney appeared decidedly groggy. The latter's ideas clashed against one another like pebbles in a child's rattle, and, if the round table may be supposed to represent the earth, as the ancient geographers imagined it, Scrogg's face was surely the glowing moon shining upon it.

Readily had the attorney lent himself to the new order of procedure. With him it was: "The king is dead! Long live the king!" He, who had found but poor pickings under the former master--dry crust fees for pleadings, demurrers or rejoinders--now anticipated generous booty and spoil. Alert for such crumbs as might fall from a bountiful table; keen of scent for scraps and bits, but capable of a mighty mouthful, he paid a courtier's price for it all; wheedling, pandering, ready for any service, ripe for any revelry. With an adulator's tact, he still strove strenuously to hold the thread of his companion's conversation, as Mauville said:

"Too old, Scroggs; too old!" Setting down a glass of burgundy in which fine particles floated through the magenta-hued liquid. "It has lost its luster, like a woman's eyes when she has passed the meridian. Good wine, like a woman, has its life. First, sweetly innocent, delicately palatable, its blush like a maiden of sixteen; then glowing with a riper development, more passionate in hue, a siren vintage; finally, thin, waning and watery, with only memories of the deeper, rosy-hued days. Now here, my good, but muddled friend, is your youthful maiden!" Holding toward the lamp a glass, clear as crystal, with luster like a gem. "Dancing eyes; a figure upright as a reed; the bearing of a nymph; the soul of a water lily before it has opened its leaves to the wooing moonlight!"

"Lord! How you go on!" exclaimed Scroggs. "What with a sampling this and sampling that, my head's going round like a top. If there's anything in the cellar the old patroons put down we haven't tried, sir, I beg to defer the sampling. I am of the sage's mind--'Of all men who take wine, the moderate only enjoy it,' says Master Bacon, or some one else."

"Pass the bottle!" answered the other. "Gently, man! Don't disturb its repose, and remember it disdains the perpendicular."

"So will I soon," muttered Scroggs. "I hope you'll excuse me, sir, but that last drop of Veuve Cliquot was the whip-cord that started the top going, and, on my word"--raising his hands to his head--"I feel like holding it on to keep it from spinning off."

"Spinning or not, you shall try this vintage"--the young man's eyes gleamed with such fire as shone in the glass--"and drink to Constance Carew!"

"Constance Carew!" stammered the other, desperately swallowing the toast.

Mauville slowly emptied the glass. "A balsamic taste, slightly piquant but agreeable," he observed. "A dangerous wine, Scroggs! It carries no warning; your older kind is like a world-worn coquette whose glances at once place you on the defensive. This maiden vintage, just springing into glorious womanhood, comes over you like a springtime dream."

"Who--who is she?" muttered Scroggs.

"She is not in the scroll you prepared for my lamented kinsman, eh? They are, for the most part, deep red, dark scarlet--that list of fair dames! She doesn't belong to them--yet! No title, man; not even a society lady. A stroller, which is next door to a vagrant."

"Well, sir, she's a woman and that's enough," replied the lawyer. "And my opinion is, it's better to have nothing to do with 'em."

This sententious remark seemed to arouse Scroggs to momentary vivacity.

"Now there was my Lord Hamerton, whose picture is upstairs," he went on quickly, like a man who is bent on grasping certain ideas before they escape him. "He brought a beautiful woman here--carried her off, they say from England--and installed her as mistress of the manor. I have heard my father say that his great-grandfather, who was my lord's solicitor, said that before his death my lord desired to make her his wife, having been brought to a sense of the sinful life he had led by a Puritan preacher. But at that, this woman straightened herself up, surveyed him with scorn, and, laughing like a witch, answered: 'They say marriages are made in heaven, my lord--and you are the devil!' So my lord died without having atoned, and, as for my lady who refused to become an honest woman, I am sure she was damned!" concluded Scroggs triumphantly.

"No doubt! So this wicked lord abducted her, Scroggs?" he added thoughtfully. "A man of spirit, until the Puritans got after him and showed him the burning pit and frightened him to that virtue which was foreign to his inclinations. My lady was right in refusing to honor such a paltry scoundrel with her hand. But it takes courage, Scroggs, to face everlasting damnation."

"They say, too, there was a spice of revenge about her unwillingness to give her hand to my lord," resumed the narrator, unmindful of the interruption. "This Puritan father said nothing but marriage with her would save Hamerton from the sulphurous flames and so my lady refused to sanctify their relations and rescue her lord from perdition!"

"A pleasant revenge!" laughed the land baron. "He made life a hell for her and she gave him an eternity of it. But take a little of this white wine, man. We've drunk to the roses of desire, and now should drink to the sanctified lilies. Her neck, Scroggs, is like a lily, and her hand and her brow! Beneath that whiteness, her eyes shine with a tenderness inviting rays of passion to kindle them. Drink!"

But the other gave a sudden lurch forward. "My lady--refused--perdition!" he muttered, and his head dropped to the board.

"Wake up, man, and drink!" commanded the master.

"Jush same--they ought to have been married," said his companion drowsily. "They lived together so--so ill!" And then to place himself beyond reach of further temptation from the bottle, he quietly and naturally slid under the table.

The patroon arose, strode to the window, which he lifted, and the night air entered, fanning his hot brow. The leaves, on high, rustled like falling rain. The elms tossed their branches, striking one another in blind confusion. The long grass whispered as the breeze stirred it like the surface of an inland lake. Withering flowers gave up their last perfume, while a storm-cloud fled wildly across the heavens. Some of the restlessness of the external world disturbed that silent dark figure at the window; within him, conflicting passions jarred like the boughs of the trees and his fancies surged like the eddying leaves.

"The roses of desire--the sanctified lilies!" he muttered.

As he stood there the stars grew pale; the sky trembled and quivered before the advent of morn. A heavy footstep fell behind him, and, turning, he beheld the care-taker.

"Not in bed yet, Oly-koeks?" cheerfully said the land baron.

"I am just up."

"In that case, it is time for me to retire," returned the master, with a yawn. "This is a dull place, Oly-koeks; no life; no variety. Nothing going on!"

The servant glanced at the formidable array of bottles. "And he calls this a quiet life!" thought the care-taker, losing his impassiveness and viewing the table with round-eyed wonder.

"Nothing going on?" he said aloud. "Mynheer, the Patroon, complained of too much life here, with people taking farms all around. But, if you are dull, a farmer told me last night there was a company of strolling players in Vanderdonkville--"

"Strollers!" exclaimed Mauville, wheeling around. "What are they called?"

"Lord; I don't know, sir. They're show-folks, and that's all--"

"Do many strolling players come this way?"

"Not for weeks and months, sometimes! The old patroon ordered the schout to arrest them if they entered the wyck."

"Is Vanderdonkville in the wyck?" asked the land baron quickly.

"No. It was separated from the wyck when Rickert Jacobus married--"

"Never mind the family genealogy! Have the coach ready at nine--"

"To-night?"

"This morning," replied Mauville, lightly. "And, meanwhile, put this to bed," indicating Scroggs, who was now snoring like a bag-pipe with one arm lovingly wound around a leg of the library table.

The care-taker hoisted the attorney on his broad shoulders, his burden still piping as they crossed the hall and mounted the stairway. Having deposited his load within the amazing depths of a Dutch feather mattress, where he lay well-nigh lost to sight, but not unheard, the wacht-meester of the steyn left him to well-earned slumber and descended to the kitchen.

At the appointed hour, the land baron, freshly shaven, not a jaded line in his face, and elastic in step, appeared on the front porch before which his carriage was waiting.

"When shall I expect you back?" asked Oly-koeks, who had reappeared at the sound of his master's footsteps.

"Any time or never!" laughed the patroon, springing into the vehicle.

But as he drove through a bit of wood, wrapped in pleasing reflections, he received startling proof that the warfare between landlord and tenants had indeed begun in earnest, for a great stone suddenly crashed through the window of the vehicle, without, however, injuring the occupant. Springing from his carriage, Mauville dashed through the fringe of wood, discharging his revolver at what he fancied was a fleeing figure. But a fluttering in the trees from the startled birds was the only result.

Little Thunder was too spry to be caught by even a pursuing bullet.

The Strollers

CHAPTER X:

SEALING THE COMPACT

"The show troupe has come to town," said the tall, lank postmaster to every one who called, and the words passed from mouth to mouth, so that those who did not witness the arrival were soon aware of it. Punchinello and his companions never attracted more attention from the old country peasants than did the chariot and its occupants, as on the day after their night in the woods they passed through the main thoroughfare of the village where they were soon to appear.

Children in woolen dresses of red retinet, or in calico vandykes and aprons, ran after the ponderous vehicle with cries of delight; the staid, mature contingent of the population shook their heads disapprovingly, while viewing with wonder the great lumbering coach, its passengers inside and out, and, behind, the large wagon with its load of miscellaneous trappings. Now on the stage throne lolled the bass viol player, even as Jacques assumed the raiment of the Duke of Aranza, reclining the while in his chair of state. Contentment was written upon his face, and he was as much a duke or a king, as Jacques when he swelled like a shirt bleaching in a high wind and looked burly as a Sunday beadle.

The principal avenue of the village boasted but few prosperous-looking business establishments. In the general "mixed store," farmers' implements, groceries, West India goods and even drugs were dispensed. But the apothecary's trade then had its limitations, homeopathy being unknown, while calomel, castor oil and rhubarb were mainly in demand, as well as senna, manna and other bitter concoctions with which both young and old were freely dosed. The grocer, haberdasher, and druggist, all rolled into one substantial personage, so blocked the doorway of his own establishment, while gazing at the strollers, it would have puzzled a customer, though but a "sketch and outline" of a man, to have slipped in or out. Dashing as in review before the rank and file of the village, the coach, with an extra flourish, rattled up to the hotel, a low but generous-sized edifice, with a wide, comfortable veranda, upon the railing of which was an array of boots, and behind them a number of disconsolate-looking teamsters.

"You want to register, do you?" said the landlord in answer to Barnes' inquiry, as the latter entered the office, the walls of which were covered with advertisements of elections, auctions, sales of stock, lands and quack medicines.

"We don't keep no register," continued the landlord, "but I guess we can accommodate you, although the house is rather full with the fellers from the ark. Or," he added, by way of explanation in answer to the manager's look of surprise, "Philadelphia freight wagons, I suppose you would call them. But we speak of them as arks, because they take in all creation. Them's the occupants, making a Mount Ararat of the porch. They're down-hearted, because they used to liquor up here and now they can't, for the town's temperance."

"I trust, nevertheless, you are prepared for a season of legitimate drama," suggested Barnes.

The other shook his head dubiously. "The town's for lectures clear through," he answered. "They've been making a big fuss about show folks."

The manager's countenance did not fall, however, upon hearing this announcement; on the contrary, it shed forth inscrutable satisfaction.

No sooner were they settled in far from commodious quarters than preparations for the future were seriously begun; and now the drama proceeded apace, with Barnes, the moving spirit. Despite his assertion that he was no scholar, the manager's mind was the storehouse of a hundred plays, and in that depository were many bags of gold and many bags of chaff. From this accumulation he drew freely, frankly, in the light-fingered fashion of master playwrights and lesser theatrical thimble-riggers.

Before the manager was a table--the stage!--upon which were scattered miscellaneous articles, symbols of life and character. A stately salt-cellar represented the leading lady; a pepper box, the irascible father; a rotund mustard pot, the old woman; a long, slim cruet, the ingenue; and a pewter spoon, the lover.

Barnes gravely demonstrated the action of the scene to Saint-Prosper, and the soldier became collaborator, "abandoning, as it were," wrote the manager in his autobiographical date-book and diary, "the sword for the pen, and the glow of the Champ de Mars for the glimmer of a kerosene lamp." And yet not with the inclination of Burgoyne, or other military gentlemen who have courted the buskin and sock! On the contrary, so foreign was the occupation to his leaning, that often a whimsical light in his eye betrayed his disinclination and modest disbelief in his own fitness for the task. "He said the way I laid out an act reminded him of planning a campaign, with the outriders and skirmishers before; the cavalry arrayed for swift service, and the infantry marching steadily on, carrying with them the main plot, or strength of the movement."

No sooner were the Salt Cellar and Pepper Box reunited, and the Pewter Spoon clasped in the arms of the loving Cruet, with the curtain descending, than Barnes, who like the immortal Alcibiades Triplet could turn his hand to almost anything, became furiously engaged in painting scenery. A market-place, with a huge wagon, containing porkers and poultry, was dashed off with a celerity that would have made a royal academician turn green with envy. The Tiddly Wink Inn was so faithfully reproduced that the painted bottles were a real temptation, while on the pastoral green of a rural landscape grazed sheep so life-like that, as Hawkes observed, it actually seemed "they would eat the scenery all up." But finally sets and play were alike finished, and results demonstrated that the manager was correct in his estimate of such a drama, which became a forerunner of other pieces of this kind, "The Bottle," "Fruits of the Wine Cup," "Aunt Dinah's Pledge," and "Ten Nights in a Bar Room."

In due time the drama was given in the town hall, after the rehearsals had been witnessed by a committee from the temperance league, who reported that the play "could not but exercise a good influence and was entertaining withal ... We recommend the license to be issued and commend the drama to all Good Templars." Therefore, the production was not only well attended, but play and players were warmly received. The town hall boasted a fairly commodious platform which now served the purpose of a stage, and--noteworthy circumstance!--there were gas jets for footlights, the illuminating fluid having at that early date been introduced in several of the more progressive villages. Between the acts, these yellow lights were turned low, and--running with the current of popular desire--the orchestra, enlarged to four, played, by special request, "The Old Oaken Bucket."

The song had just sprung into popularity, and, in a moment, men, women and children had added their voices to the instruments. It was not the thrill of temperance fanaticism that stirred their hearts, but it was the memories of the old pioneer home in the wilderness; the rail-splitting, road-building days; the ancient rites of "raisings" and other neighborly ceremonies; when the farmer cut rye with a cradle, and threshed it out with his flail; when "butter and eggs were pin money" and wheat paid the store-keeper.

"How solemnly they take their amusements in the North, Mr. Barnes!" exclaimed a voice in one of the entrances. "What a contrast to the South--the wicked South!"

The manager turned sharply.

"We are mere servants of the public, Mr. Mauville."

"And the public is master, Mr. Barnes! How the dramatic muse is whipped around! In Greece, she was a goddess; in Rome, a hussy; in England, a sprightly dame; now, a straight-laced Priscilla. But you have a recruit, I see?"

"You mean Saint-Prosper?"

"Yes, and I can hardly blame him--under the circumstances!" murmured the land baron, at the same time glancing around as though seeking some one.

"Circumstances! What circumstances?" demanded the manager.

"Why, the pleasant company he finds himself in, of course," said the visitor, easily. "Ah, I see Miss Carew," he added, his eye immediately lightening, "and must congratulate her on her performance. Cursed dusty hole, isn't it?" Brushing himself with his handkerchief as he moved away.

"What business has he behind the scenes anyway?" grumbled the manager. "Dusty hole, indeed! Confound his impudence!" But his attention being drawn to the pressing exigencies of a first night,

Barnes soon forgot his irritation over this unwarranted intrusion in lowering a drop, hoisting a fly or readjusting a flat to his liking.

The land baron meanwhile crossed to the semi-darkness at the rear of the stage behind the boxed scene, where he had observed the young girl waiting for the curtain to rise on the last act. A single light on each side served partly to relieve the gloom; to indicate the frame-work of the set scene and throw in shadow various articles designed for use in the play. As she approached Mauville, who stood motionless in an unlighted spot, the pale glow played upon her a moment, white on her neck, in sheen on the folds of her gown, and then she stepped into the shadow, where she was met by a tall figure, with hand eagerly outstretched.

"Mr. Mauville!" she exclaimed, drawing back at the suddenness of the encounter.

His restless eyes held hers, but his greeting was conventional.

"Did I not say the world was small and that we might meet again?"

"Of course, we are always meeting people and parting from them," she replied unconcernedly.

He laughed. "With what delightful indifference you say that! You did not think to see me again?"

"I hadn't thought about it," she answered, frankly, annoyed by his persistence.

"I am unfortunate!" he said.

Beneath his free gaze she changed color, as though the shadow of a rose had touched her face.

"You are well?" he continued.

"Yes."

"I need not have asked." His expression conveyed more--so much more, she bit her lip impatiently. "How do you like the new part?"

"It is hard to tell yet," she answered evasively.

"You would do justice to any rôle, but I prefer you in a historical or romantic play, with the picturesque old costumes. If it were in my domains, you should appear in those dramas, if I had to hang every justice of the peace in the district."

Her only response was a restless movement and he hastened to add: "I fear, however, I am detaining you."

He drew aside with such deference to permit her to pass that her conscience smote her and she was half-minded to turn and leave him more graciously, but this impulse was succeeded by another feeling, ill-defined, the prevailing second thought. Had she looked, she would have seen that her fluttering shawl touched his hand and he quickly raised it to his lips, releasing it immediately. As it was, she moved on, unaware of the gesture. The orchestra, or rather string quartet, had ceased; Hans, a host in himself, a mountain of melody, bowed his acknowledgments; the footlights glared, the din of voices subsiding; and the curtain rose.

Remaining in the background, the land baron watched the young girl approach the entrance to the stage, where she stood, intent, one hand resting against the scenery, her dress upheld with the other; the glimmer from the footlights, reflected through the opening, touching her face; suddenly, with a graceful movement, she vanished, and her laughing voice seemed to come from afar.

Was it for this he had made his hasty journey? To be treated with indifference by a wandering player; he, the patroon, the unsuccessful suitor of a stroller! She, who appeared in taverns, in barns, perhaps, was as cold and proud as any fine lady, untroubled about the morrow, and, as he weighed this phase of the matter, the land baron knew not whether he loved her most for her beauty or hated her for the slight she put upon him. But love or hate, it was all one, and he told himself he would see the adventure to the end.

"How do you do, Mr. Mauville?" said a gay but hushed voice, interrupting his ruminations, and Susan, in a short skirt and bright stockings, greeted him.

"The better for seeing you, Mistress Susan." Nonchalantly surveying her from head to foot.

She bore his glance with the assurance of a pretty woman who knows she is looking her best.

"Pooh!" Curtesying disdainfully. "I don't believe you! You came to see some one else. Well"--lightly--"she is already engrossed."

"Really?" said the land baron.

"Yes. You understand? He follows her with his every glance," she added roguishly. Susan was never averse to straining the truth a little when it served her purpose.

"I should infer he was following her with more than his eyes," retorted the master of the manor dryly.

Susan tapped the stage viciously with a little foot. "She's a lovely girl," she continued, drawing cabalistic figures with the provoking slipper.

"You are piqued?" he said, watching her skeptically.

"Not at all." Quickly, startled by his blunt accusation.

"Not a little jealous?" he persisted playfully.

"Jealous?" Then with a frown, hesitatingly: "Well, she is given prominence in the plays and--"

"--You would not be subordinated, if she were not in the company? Apart from this, you are fond of her?"

The foot ceased its tracing and rested firmly on the floor.

"I hate her!" snapped Susan, angered by this baiting. No sooner had she spoken than she regretted her outburst. "How you draw one out! I was only joking--though she does have the best parts and we take what we can get!"

"But she's a lovely girl!" concluded the land baron. Susan's eyes flashed angrily.

"How clever of you! You twist and turn one's words about and give them a different meaning from what was intended. If I wanted to catch you up--"

"A truce!" he exclaimed. "Let us take each other seriously, hereafter. Is it agreed?" She nodded. "Well, seriously, you can help me and help yourself."

"How?" doubtfully.

"Why not be allies?"

"What for?"

"Mutual service."

"Oh!" dubiously.

"A woman's 'yes'!"

"No," with affirmative answer in her eyes.

He believed the latter.

"We will seal the compact then."

And he bent over and saluted Mistress Susan on the lips. She became as rosy as the flowers she carried and tapped him playfully with them.

"For shame! La! What must you think of me?"

"That you are an angel."

"How lovely! But I must go."

"May I see you after the play?"

"Yes."

"Do not fail me, or the soldier will not transfer his affections to you!"

"If he dared!" And she shook her head defiantly as she tripped away.

"Little fool!" murmured Mauville, his lips curling scornfully. "The one is a pastime; the other"--he paused and caught his breath--"a passion!"

But he kept his appointment with Susan, escorting her to the hotel, where he bade her good-night with a lingering pressure of the hand, and--ordered his equipage to the door!

"Hadn't you better wait until morning?" asked the surprised landlord, when the young patroon announced his intention of taking an immediate departure. "There are the barn-burners and--traveling at night--"

"Have they turned footpads?" was the light reply. "Can't I drive through my own lands? Let me see one of their thieving faces--" And he made a significant gesture. "Not ride at night! These Jacobins shall not prevent me."

Barring the possible danger from the lease-holders who were undoubtedly ripe for any mischief, the journey did not promise such discomfiture as might have been expected, the coach being especially constructed for night traveling. On such occasions, between the seats the space was filled by a large cushion, adapted to the purpose, which in this way converted the interior of the vehicle into a sleeping-room of limited dimensions. With pillows to neutralize the jarring, the land baron stretched himself indolently upon his couch, and gazed through the window at the crystalline lights of the heavens, while thoughts of lease-holders and barn-burners faded into thin air.

At dawn, when he opened his eyes, the morning star yet gleamed with a last pale luster. Raising himself on his elbow and looking out over the country to learn his whereabouts, his eye fell upon a tree, blood-red, a maple amid evergreens. Behind this somber community of pines, stiff as a band of Puritan elders, surrounding the bright-hued maple, a Hester in that austere congregation, appeared the glazed tile roof of Little Thunder's habitation, a two-story abode of modest proportions and olden type. As the land baron passed, a brindle cow in the side yard saluted the morn, calling the sluggard from his couch, but at the manor, which the patroon shortly reached, the ever wakeful Oly-koeks was already engaged in chopping wood near the kitchen door. The growling of the hound at his feet called the care-taker's attention to the master's coming, and, driving the ax into an obstinate stick of hickory, he donned his coat, drawing near the vehicle, where he stood in stupid wonderment as the land baron alighted.

"Any callers, Oly-koeks?" carelessly asked the master.

"A committee of barn-burners, Mynheer, to ask you not to serve any more writs."

"And so give them time to fight me with the lawmakers! But there; carry my portmanteau into the library and"--as Oloffe's upper lip drew back--"teach your dog to know me."

"He belonged to the old master, Mynheer. When he died, the dog lay near his grave day and night."

"I dare say; like master, like dog! But fetch the portmanteau, you Dutch varlet!" Entering the house, while the coachman drove the tired horses toward the barn. "There's something in it I want. Bring it here." As he passed into the library. "Yes; I put it in there, I am sure.

Ah, here we have it!" And unpacking the valise, he took therefrom a handsome French writing case.

"Thou Wily Limb of the Law," wrote the patroon, "be it known by these presents, thou art summoned to appear before me! I have work for you--not to serve any one with a writ; assign; bring an action, or any of your rascally, pettifogging tricks! Send me no demurrer, but your own intemperate self."

Which epistle the patroon addressed to his legal satellite and despatched by messenger.

CHAPTER XI:
THE QUEST OF THE SOLDIER

Several bleak days were followed by a little June weather in October. A somnolent influence rested everywhere. Above the undulation of land on the horizon were the clouds, like heavenly hills, reflecting their radiance on those earthly elevations. The celestial mountains and valleys gave wondrous perspective to the outlook, and around them lay an atmosphere, unreal and idyllic.

On such a morning Susan stood at a turn in the road, gazing after a departing vehicle with ill-concealed satisfaction and yet withal some dubiousness. Now that the plan, suggested by Mauville, had not miscarried, certain misgivings arose, for there is a conscience in the culmination wanting in the conception of an act. As the partial realization of the situation swept over her, she gave a gasp, and then, the vehicle having meanwhile vanished, a desperate spirit of bravado replaced her momentary apprehension. She even laughed nervously as she waved her handkerchief in the direction the coach had taken: "Bon voyage!"

But as the words fell from the smiling lips, her eyes became thoughtful and her hand fell to her side; it occurred to Susan she would be obliged to divert suspicion from herself. The curling lips straightened; she turned abruptly and hastened toward the town. But her footsteps soon lagged and she paused thoughtfully.

"If I reach the hotel too soon," she murmured, "they may overtake him."

So she stopped at the wayside, attracted by the brilliant cardinal flowers, humming as she plucked them, but ever and anon glancing around guiltily. The absurd thought came to her that the bright autumn blossoms were red, the hue of sin, and she threw them on the sward, and unconsciously rubbed her hands on her dress.

Still she lingered, however, vaguely mindful she was adding to her burden of ill-doing, but finally again started slowly toward the village, hurrying as she approached the hotel, where she encountered the soldier on the veranda. Her distressed countenance and haste proclaimed her a messenger of disaster.

"Oh, dear! Oh, dear!" she exclaimed excitedly. "Where is Mr. Barnes?"

"What is the matter, Miss Duran?" Suspecting very little was the matter, for Susan was nothing, if not all of a twitter.

"Constance has been carried off!"

"Carried off!" He regarded her as if he thought she had lost her senses.

"Yes; abducted!"

"Abducted! By whom?"

"I--I did not see his face!" she gasped. "And it is all my fault! I asked her to take a walk! Oh, what shall I do?" Wringing her hands in anguish that was half real. "We kept on and on--it was so pleasant!--until we had passed far beyond the outskirts of the village. At a turn in the road stood a coach--a cloak was thrown over my head by some one behind--I must have fainted, and, when I recovered, she was gone. Oh, dear! Oh, dear!"

"When did it happen?" As he spoke the young man left the veranda. Grazing contentedly near the porch was his horse and Saint-Prosper's hand now rested on the bridle.

"I can't tell how long I was unconscious," said the seemingly hysterical young woman, "but I hurried here as soon as I recovered myself."

"Where did it occur? Down the road you came?"

"Ye-es."

Saint-Prosper vaulted into the saddle. "Tell the manager to see a magistrate," he said.

"But you're not going to follow them alone?" began Susan. "Oh dear, I feel quite faint again! If you would please help me into the--"

By way of answer, the other touched his horse deeply with the spur and the mettlesome animal reared and plunged, then, recalled by the sharp voice of the rider, galloped wildly down the road. Susan observed the sudden departure with mingled emotions.

"How quixotic!" she thought discontentedly. "But he won't catch them," came the consoling afterthought, as she turned to seek the manager.

Soon the soldier, whose spirited dash down the main thoroughfare had awakened some misgivings in the little town, was beyond the precincts of village scrutiny. The country road was hard, although marked by deep cuts from traffic during a rainy spell, and the horse's hoofs rang out with exhilarating rhythm. Regardless of all save the distance traversed, the rider yet forbore to press the pace, relaxing only when, after a considerable interval, he came to another road and drew rein at the fork. One way to the right ran gently through the valley, apparently terminating in the luxuriant foliage, while the other, like a winding, murky stream, stretched out over a more level tract of land.

Which thoroughfare had the coach taken? Dismounting, the young man hastily examined the ground, but the earth was so dry and firm, and the tracks of wheels so many, it was impossible to distinguish the old marks from the new. Even sign-post there was none; the roads diverged, and the soldier could but blindly surmise their destination, selecting after some hesitation the thoroughfare running into the gorgeous, autumnal painted forest.

He had gone no inconsiderable distance when his doubts were abruptly confirmed. Reaching an opening, bright as the chapel of a darkened monastery, he discerned a farmer in a buckboard approaching from the opposite direction. The swift pace of the rider and the leisurely jog of the team soon brought them together.

"Did you pass a coach down the road?" asked the soldier.

"No-a," said the farmer, deliberately, as his fat horses instinctively stood stock still; "didn't pass nobody."

"Have you come far?"

"A good ways."

"You would have met a coach, if it had passed here an hour ago?"

"I guess I would," said the man. "This road leads straight across the country."

"Where does the other road at the fork go?"

"To the patroon village. There's a reform orator there to-day and a barn-burners' camp-fire."

Without waiting to thank his informant, Saint-Prosper pulled his horse quickly around, while the man in the buckboard gradually got under way, until he had once more attained a comfortable, slow gait. Indeed, by the time his team had settled down to a sleepy jog, in keeping with the dreamy haze, hanging upon the upland, his questioner was far down the road.

When, however, the soldier once more reached the fork, and took the winding way across a more level country, he moderated his pace, realizing the need of husbanding his horse's powers of endurance. The country seemed at peace, as though no dissension nor heated passions could exist within that pastoral province. And yet, not far distant, lay the domains of the patroons, the hot-bed of the two opposing branches of the Democratic party: The "hunkers," or conservative-minded men, and the "barn-burners," or progressive reformers, who sympathized with the anti-renters.

After impatiently riding an hour or more through this delectable region, the horseman drew near the patroon village, a cluster of houses amid the hills and meadows. Here the land barons had originally built for the tenants comfortable houses and ample barns, saw and grist mills. But the old homes had crumbled away, and that rugged ancestry of dwellings had been replaced by a new generation of houses, with clapboards, staring green blinds and flimsy verandas.

In the historic market place, as Saint-Prosper rode down the street, were assembled a number of lease-holders of both sexes and all ages, from the puny babe in arms to the decrepit crone and hoary grand-sire, listening to the flowing tongue of a rustic speech-maker. This forum of the people was shaded by a sextette of well-grown elms. The platform of the local Demosthenes stood in a corner near the street.

"'Woe to thee, O Moab! Thou art undone, O people of Chemosh,' if you light not the torch of equal rights!" exclaimed the platform patterer as Saint-Prosper drew near. "Awake, sons of the free soil!

Now is the time to make a stand! Forswear all allegiance to the new patroon; this Southern libertine and despot from the land of slavery!"

The grandam wagged her head approvingly; the patriarch stroked his beard with acquiescence and strong men clenched their fists as the spokesman mouthed their real or fancied wrongs. It was an earnest, implacable crowd; men with lowering brows merely glanced at the soldier as he rode forward; women gazed more intently, but were quickly lured back by the tripping phrases of the mellifluous speaker.

On the outskirts of the gathering, near the road, stood a tall, beetling individual whom Saint-Prosper addressed, reining in his horse near the wooden rail, which answered for a fence.

"Dinna ye ken I'm listening?" impatiently retorted the other, with a fierce frown. "Gang your way, mon," he added, churlishly, as he turned his back.

Judging from the wrathful faces directed toward him, the lease-holders esteemed Saint-Prosper a political disturber, affiliating with the other faction of the Democratic party, and bent, perhaps, on creating dissension at the tenants' camp-fire. The soldier's impatience and anger were ready to leap forth at a word; he wheeled fiercely upon the weedy Scot, to demand peremptorily the information so uncivilly withheld, when a gust of wind blowing something light down the road caused his horse to shy suddenly and the rider to glance at what had frightened the animal. After a brief scrutiny, he dismounted quickly and examined more attentively the object,--a pamphlet with a red cover, upon which appeared the printed design of the conventional Greek masks of Tragedy and Comedy, and beneath, the title, "The Honeymoon." The bright binding, albeit soiled by the dusty road, and the fluttering of the leaves in the breeze had startled the horse and incidentally attracted the attention of his master. Across the somber mask of melancholy was traced in buoyant hand the name of the young actress.

But the soldier needed not the confirmation, for had he not noticed this same prompt book in her lap on the journey of the chariot? It was a mute, but eloquent message. Could she have spoken more plainly if she had written with ink and posted the missive with one of those new bronze-hued portraits of Franklin, called stamps by the government and "sticking plaster" by the people? Undoubtedly she had hoped the manager was following her when she intrusted the message to that erratic postman, Chance, who plied his vocation long before the black Washington or the bronze Franklin was a talisman of more or less uncertain delivery.

The soldier, without a moment's hesitation, thrust the pamphlet inside his coat, flung himself on his horse, and, turning from the market-place, dashed down the road.

CHAPTER XII:

AN ECCENTRIC JAILER

"For a man who can't abide the sex, this is a predicament," muttered the patroon's jackal, as the coach in which he found himself sped rapidly along the highway. "Here am I as much an abductor as my lord who whipped his lady from England to the colonies!" Gloomily regarding a motionless figure on the seat opposite, and a face like ivory against the dark cushions. "Curse the story; telling it led to this! How white she is; like driven snow; almost as if--"

And Scroggs, whose countenance lost a shade of its natural flush, going from flame-color to salmon hue, bent with sudden apprehension over a small hand which hung from the seat.

"No; it's only a swoon," he continued, relieved, feeling her wrist with his knobby fingers. "How she struggled! If it hadn't been for smothering her with the cloak--but the job's done and that's the end of it."

Settling back in his seat he watched her discontentedly, alternately protesting against the adventure, and consoling himself weakly with the remembrance of the retainer; weighing the risks, and the patroon's ability to gloss over the matter; now finding the former unduly obtrusive, again comforted with the assurance of the power pre-empted by the land barons. Moreover, the task was half-accomplished, and it would be idle to recede now.

"Why couldn't the patroon have remained content with his bottle?" he grumbled. "But his mind must needs run to this frivolous and irrational proceeding! There's something reasonable in pilfering a purse, but carrying off a woman--Yet she's a handsome baggage."

Over the half-recumbent figure swept his glance, pausing as he surveyed her face, across which flowed a tress of hair loosened in the struggle. Save for the unusual pallor of her cheek, she might have been sleeping, but as he watched her the lashes slowly lifted, and he sullenly nerved himself for the encounter. At the aspect of those bead-like eyes, resolute although ill at ease, like a snake striving to charm an adversary, a tremor of half-recollection shone in her gaze and the color flooded her face. Mechanically, sweeping back the straggling lock of hair, she raised herself without removing her eyes. He who had expected a tempest of tears shifted uneasily, even irritably, from that steady stare, until, finding the silence intolerable, he burst out:

"Well, ma'am, am I a bugbear?"

In her dazed condition she probably did not hear his words; or, if she did, set no meaning to them, Her glance, however, strayed to the narrow window, and then wandered back to the well-worn interior of the coach. Suddenly, as the startling realization of her position came to her, she uttered a loud cry, sprang toward the door, and, with nervous fingers, strove to open it. The man's face became more rubicund as he placed a detaining hand on her shoulder, and roughly thrust her toward the seat.

"Make the best of it!" he exclaimed peremptorily. "You'd better, for I'm not to be trifled with."

Recoiling from his touch, she held herself aloof with such aversion, a sneer crossed his face, and he observed glumly:

"Oh, I'm not a viper! If you're put out, so am I."

"Who are you?" she demanded, breathlessly.

"That's an incriminating question, Ma'am," he replied. "In this case, though, the witness has no objection to answering. I'm your humble servant."

His forced drollery was more obnoxious than his ill-humor, and, awakening her impatience, restored in a measure her courage. He was but a pitiful object, after all, with his flame-colored visage, and short, crouching figure; and, as her thoughts passed from the brutal part he had played on the road to her present situation, she exclaimed with more anger than apprehension:

"Perhaps you will tell me the meaning of this outrage--your smothering me--forcing me into this coach--and driving away--where?"

His face became once more downcast and moody. Driven into a corner by her swift words, his glance met hers fairly; he drummed his fingers together.

"There's no occasion to show your temper, Miss," he said reflectively. "I'm a bit touchy myself to-day; 'sudden and quick in quarrel.' You see I know my Shakespeare, Ma'am. Let us talk about that great poet and the parts you, as an actress, prefer--"

"Can I get an answer from you?" she cried, subduing her dread.

"What is it you asked?"

"As if you did not know!" she returned, her lip trembling with impatience and loathing.

"Yes; I remember." Sharply. "You asked where we were driving? Across the country. What is the meaning of this--outrage, I believe you called it? All actions spring from two sources--Cupid and cupidity. The rest of the riddle you'll have to guess." Gazing insolently into her face, with his hands on his knees.

"But you have told me nothing," she replied, striving to remain mistress of herself and to hide her apprehension.

"Do you call that nothing? You have the approximate cause-- causa causans. Was it Cupid? No, for like Bacon, your sex's 'fantastical' charms move me not."

This sally put him in better temper with himself. She was helpless, and he experienced a churlish satisfaction in her condition.

"What was it, then? Cupidity. Do you know what poverty is like in this barren region?" he cried harshly. "The weapons of education only unfit you for the plow. You stint, pinch, live on nothing!" He rubbed his dry hands together. "It was crumbs and scraps under the parsimonious régime; but now the prodigal has come into his own and believes in honest wages and a merry life."

Wonderingly she listened, the scene like a grotesque dream, with the ever-moving coach, the lonely road, the dark woods, and--so near, she could almost place her hand upon him--this man, muttering and mumbling. He had offered her the key of the mystery, but she had failed to use it. His ambiguous, loose talk, only perplexed and alarmed her; the explanation was none at all.

As he watched her out of the corner of his eye, weighing doubt and uncertainty, new ideas assailed him. After all she had spirit, courage! Moreover, she was an actress, and the patroon was madly in love with her.

"If we were only leagued together, how we could strip him!" he thought.

His head dropped contemplatively to his breast, and for a long interval he remained silent, abstracted, while the old springless coach, with many a jolt and jar, covered mile after mile; up the hills, crowned with bush and timber; across the table land; over the plank bridges spanning the brooks and rivulets. More reconciled to his part and her presence, his lips once or twice parted as if he were about to speak, but closed again. He even smiled, showing his amber-hued teeth, nodding his head in a friendly fashion, as to say: "It'll come out all right, Madam; all right for both of us!" Which, indeed, was his thought. She believed him unsettled, bereft of reason, and, although, he was manifestly growing less hostile, his surveillance became almost unbearable. At every moment she felt him regarding her like a lynx, and endeavored therefore to keep perfectly still. What would her strange warder do next? It was not an alarming act, however. He consulted a massive watch, remarking:

"It's lunch time and over! With your permission, I'll take a bite and a drop. Will you join me?"

She turned her head away, and, not disconcerted by her curt refusal, he drew a wicker box from beneath a seat and opened it. His reference to a "bite and a drop" was obviously figurative, especially the "drop," which grew to the dimensions of a pint, which he swallowed quickly. Perhaps the flavor of the wine made him less attentive to his prisoner, for as he lifted the receptacle to his lips, she thrust her arms through the window and a play book dropped from her hand, a possible clue for any one who might follow the coach. For some time she had been awaiting this opportunity and when it came, the carriage was entering a village.

Scroggs finished his cup. "You see, we're provided for," he began. Here the bottle fell from his hand.

"The patroon village!" he exclaimed in consternation. "I'd forgotten we were so close! And they're all gathered in the square, too!"

He cast a quick glance at her. "You're all ready to call for help," he sneered, "but I'm not ready to part company yet."

Hastily drawing up one of the wooden shutters, he placed himself near the other window, observing fiercely; "I don't propose you shall undo what's being done for you. Let me hear from you"--jerking his finger toward the square--"and I'll not answer for what I'll do." But in spite of his admonition he read such determination in her eyes, he felt himself baffled.

"You intend to make trouble!" he cried. And putting his head suddenly through the window, he called to the driver: "Whip the horses through the market place!"

As the affrighted animals sprang forward he blocked the window, placing one hand on her shoulder. He felt her escape from his grasp, but not daring to leave his post, he leaned out of the window when they were opposite the square, and shook his fist at the anti-renters, exclaiming:

"I'll arrest every mother's son of you! I'll evict you--jail you for stealing rent!"

Drowned by the answering uproar, "The patroon's dog!" "Bullets for deputies!" the emissary of the land baron continued to threaten the throng with his fist, until well out of ear-shot, and, thanks to the level road, beyond reach of their resentment. Not that they strove to follow him far, for they thought the jackal had taken leave of his senses. Laughter mingled with their jeers at the absurd figure he presented, fulminating and flying at the same time. But there was no defiance left in him when they were beyond the village, and he fell back into his seat, his face now ash-colored.

"If they'd stopped us my life wouldn't have been worth the asking," he muttered hoarsely. "But I did it!" Triumphantly gazing at the young girl who, trembling with excitement, leaned against the side of the coach. "I see you managed to get down the shutter. I hope you heard your own voice. I didn't; and, what's more, I'm sure they didn't!"

With fingers he could hardly control he opened a second bottle, dispensed with the formality of a glass, and set the neck to his lips, repeating the operation until it was empty, when he tossed it out of the window to be shattered against a rock, after which he sank again into a semblance of meditation.

Disappointed over her ineffectual efforts, overcome by the strain, the young girl for the time relaxed all further attempt. Unseen, unheard, she had stood at her window! She had tried to open the door, but it resisted her frantic efforts, and then the din had died away and left her weak, powerless, hardly conscious of the hateful voice of her companion from time to time addressing her.

But fortunately he preferred the gross practice of draining the cup to the fine art of conversation. Left to the poor company of her thoughts, she dwelt upon the miscarriage of her design, and the slender chance of assistance. They would probably pass through no more villages and if they did, he would undoubtedly find means to prevent her making herself known. Unless--and a glimmer of hope flickered through her thoughts!--her warder carried his potations to a point where vigilance ceased to be a virtue. Inconsiderately he stopped at the crucial juncture, with all the signs of contentment and none of drowsiness.

So minutes resolved themselves into hours and the day wore on. Watching the sun-rays bathe the top of the forest below them, she noted how fast the silver disk was descending. The day which had seemed interminable now appeared but too short, and she would gladly have recalled those fleeting hours. Ignorant of the direction in which they had been traveling, she realized that the driver had been unsparing and the distance covered not inconsiderable. The mystery of the assault, the obscurity of the purpose and the vagueness of their destination were unknown quantities which, added to the declining of the day and the brewing terrors of the night, were well calculated to terrify and crush her.

Despairingly, she observed how the sun dipped, and ever dipped toward the west, when suddenly a sound afar rekindled her fainting spirits. Listening more attentively, she was assured imagination had not deceived her; it was the faint patter of a horse's hoofs. Nearer it drew; quicker beat her pulses. Moreover, it was the rat-a-tat of galloping. Some one was pursuing the coach on horseback. Impatient to glance behind, she only refrained for prudential reasons.

Immersed in his own grape-vine castle her jailer was unmindful of the approaching rider, and she turned her face from him that he might not read her exultation. Closer resounded the beating hoofs, but her impatience outstripped the pursuer, and she was almost impelled to rush to the window.

Who was the horseman? Was it Barnes? Saint-Prosper? The latter's name had quickly suggested itself to her.

Although the rider, whoever he might be, continued to gain ground, to her companion, the approaching clatter was inseparable from the noise of the vehicle, and it was not until the horseman was nearly abreast, and the cadence of the galloping resolved itself into clangor, that the dreamer awoke with an imprecation. As he sprang to his feet, thus rudely disturbed, a figure on horseback dashed by and a stern voice called to the driver:

"Stop the coach!"

Probably the command was given over the persuasive point of a weapon, for the animals were drawn up with a quick jerk and came to a standstill in the middle of the road. Menacing and abusive, as the vehicle stopped, the warder's hand sought one of his pockets, when the young girl impetuously caught his arm, clinging to it tenaciously.

"Quick!--Mr. Saint-Prosper!" she cried, recognizing, as she thought, the voice of the soldier.

"You wild-cat!" her jailer exclaimed, struggling to throw her off.

Not succeeding, he raised his free arm in a flurry of invective.

"Curse you, will you let go!"

"Quick! Quick!" she called out, holding him more tightly.

A flood of Billingsgate flowed from his lips. "Let go, or--"

But before he could in his blind passion strike her or otherwise vent his rage, a revolver was clapped to his face through the window, and, with a look of surprise and terror, his valor oozing from him, he crouched back on the cushions. At the same time the carriage door was thrown open, and Edward Mauville, the patroon, stood in the entrance!

Only an instant his eyes swept her, observing the flushed cheeks and disordered attire, leading her wonder at his unexpected appearance, and--to his satisfaction!--her relief as well; only an instant, during which the warder stared at him open-mouthed--and then his glance rested on the now thoroughly sober limb of the law.

"Get out!" he said, briefly and harshly.

"But," began the other with a sickly grin, intended to be ingratiating, "I don't understand--this unexpected manner--this forcible departure from--"

Coolly raising his weapon, the patroon deliberately covered the hapless jailer, who unceremoniously scrambled out of the door. The land baron laughed, replaced his revolver and, turning to the young girl, removed his hat.

"It was fortunate, Miss Carew, I happened along," he said gravely. "With your permission, I will get in. You can tell me what has happened as we drive along. The manor house, my temporary home, is not far from here. If I can be of any service, command me!"

The jackal saw the patroon spring into the carriage, having fastened his horse behind, and drive off. Until the vehicle had disappeared, he stood motionless in the road, but when it had passed from sight, he seated himself on a stone.

"That comes from mixing the breed!" he muttered. "Dramatic effect, à la France!" He wiped the perspiration from his brow. "Well, I'm three miles from my humble habitation, but I'd rather walk than ride--under some circumstances!"

CHAPTER XIII:
THE COMING OF LITTLE THUNDER

The afternoon was waning; against the golden western sky the old manor house loomed in solemn majesty, the fields and forests emphasizing its isolation in the darkening hour of sunset, as a coach, with jaded horses, passed through the avenue of trees and approached the broad portico. A great string of trailing vine had been torn from the walls by the wind and now waved mournfully to and fro with no hand to adjust it. In the rear was a huge-timbered barn, the door of which was unfastened, swinging on its rusty hinges with a creaking and moaning sound.

As gaily as in the days when the periwigged coachman had driven the elaborate equipage of the early patroons through the wrought-iron gate this modern descendant entered the historic portals, not to be met, however, by servitors in knee breeches at the front door, but by the solitary care-taker who appeared on the portico in considerable disorder and evident state of excitement, accompanied by the shaggy dog, Oloffe.

"The deputies shot two of the tenants to-day," hurriedly exclaimed the guardian of the place, without noticing Mauville's companion. "The farmers fired upon them; they replied, and one of the tenants is dead."

"A good lesson for them, since they were the aggressors," cried the heir, as he sprang from the coach. "But you have startled the lady."

An exclamation from the vehicle in an unmistakably feminine voice caused the "wacht-meester" now to observe the occupant for the first time and the servant threw up his hands in consternation. Here was a master who drank all night, shot his tenants by proxy, visited strollers, and now brought one of them to the steyn. That the strange lady was a player, Oly-koeks immediately made up his mind, and he viewed her with mingled aversion and fear, as the early settlers regarded sorcerers and witches. She was very beautiful, he observed in that quick glance, but therefore the more dangerous; she appeared distressed, but he attributed her apparent grief to artfulness. He at once saw a new source of trouble in her presence; as though the threads were not already sufficiently entangled, without the introduction of a woman--and she a public performer!--into the complicated mesh!

"Fasten the iron shutters of the house," briefly commanded Mauville, breaking in upon the servant's painful reverie. "Then help this man change the horses and put in the grays."

Oly-koeks, with a final deprecatory glance at the coach, expressive of his estimate of his master's light conduct and his apprehension of the outcome, disappeared to obey this order.

"May I assist you, Miss Carew?" said the land baron deferentially, offering his arm to the young girl, whose pale but observant face disclosed new demur and inquiry.

"But you said we would go right on?" she returned, drawing back with implied dissent.

"When the horses are changed! If you will step out, the carriage will be driven to the barn."

Reluctantly she obeyed, and as she did so, the patroon and the coachman exchanged pithy glances.

"Look sharp!" commanded the master, sternly. "Oh, he won't run away," added Mauville quickly, in answer to her look of surprise. "He knows I could find him, and"--fingering his revolver--"will not disoblige me. Later we'll hear the rogue's story."

The man's averted countenance smothered a clandestine smile, as he touched the horses with his whip and turned them toward the barn, leaving the patroon and his companion alone on the broad portico. Sweeping from a distant grove of slender poplars and snowy birch a breeze bore down upon them, suddenly bleak and frosty, and she shivered in the nipping air.

"You are chilled!" he cried. "If you would but go into the house while we are waiting! Indeed, if you do not, I shall wonder how I have offended you! It will be something to remember"--half lightly, half seriously--"that you have crossed my threshold!"

He stood at the door, with such an undissembled smile, his accents so regretful, that after a moment's hesitation, Constance entered, followed by the patron. Sweeping aside the heavy draperies from the window, he permitted the golden shafts of the ebbing day to enter the hall, gleaming on the polished floors, the wainscoting and the furniture, faintly illuminating the faded pictures and weirdly revealing the turnings of the massive stairway. No wonder a half-shudder of apprehension seized the young actress in spite of her self-reliance and courage, as she entered the solemn and mournful place, where past grandeur offered nothing save morbid memories and where the frailty of existence was significantly written! After that Indian summer day the sun was sinking, angry and fiery, as though presaging a speedy reform in the vagaries of the season and an immediate return to the legitimate surroundings of October.

Involuntarily the girl moved to the window, where the light rested on her brown tresses, and as Mauville watched that radiance, shifting and changing, her hair alight with mystic color, the passion that had prompted him to this end was stirred anew, dissipating any intrusive doubts. The veering and flickering sheen seemed but a web of entangling irradiation. A span of silence became an interminable period to her, with no sight of fresh horses nor sign of preparation for the home journey.

"What takes him so long?" she said, finally, with impatience. "It is getting so late!"

"It is late," he answered. "Almost too late to go on! You are weary and worn. Why not rest here to-night?"

"Rest here?" she repeated, with a start of surprise.

"You are not fit to drive farther. To-morrow we can return."

"To-morrow!" she cried. "But--what do you mean?"

"That I must insist upon your sparing yourself!" he said, firmly, although a red spot flushed his cheek.

"No; no! We must leave at once!" she answered.

He smiled reassuringly. "Why will you not have confidence in me?" he asked. "You have not the strength to travel all night--over a rough road--after such a trying day. For your own sake, I beg you to give up the idea. Here you are perfectly safe and may rest undisturbed."

"Please call the horses at once!"

An impatient expression furrowed his brow. He had relied on easily prevailing upon her through her gratitude; continuing in his disinterested rôle for yet some time; resuming the journey on the morrow, carrying her farther away under pretext of mistaking the road, until--Here his plans had faded into a vague perspective, dominated by unreasoning self-confidence and egotism.

But her words threatened a rupture at the outset that would seriously alter the status of the adventure.

"It is a mistake to go on to-night," he said, with a dissenting gesture. "However, if you are determined--" And Mauville stepped to the window. "Why, the carriage is not there!" he exclaimed, looking out.

"Not there!" she repeated, incredulously. "You told them to change the horses. Why--"

"I don't understand," returned the land baron, with an effort to make his voice surprised and concerned. "He may--Hello-a, there! You!--Oly-koeks!" he called out, interrupting his own explanation.

Not Oly-koeks, but the driver's face, appeared from behind the barn door, and, gazing through the window, the young girl, with a start, suddenly realized that she had seen him not for the first time that day--but where?--when? Through the growing perplexity of her thoughts she heard the voice of her companion

"Why don't you hitch up the grays?"

"There are no horses in the barn," came the answer.

"Strange, the care-taker did not tell me they had been taken away!" commented the other, hastily, stepping from the window as the driver vanished once more into the barn. "I am sorry, but there seems no alternative but to wait--at least, until I can send for others."

She continued to gaze toward the door through which the man had disappeared. She could place him now, although his livery had been discarded for shabby clothes; she recalled him distinctly in spite of this changed appearance.

"Why not make the best of it?" said Mauville, softly, but with glance sparkling in spite of himself. "After all, are you not giving yourself needless apprehensions? You are at home here. Anything you wish shall be yours. Consider yourself mistress; me, one of your servants!"

Almost imperceptibly his manner had changed. Instinctive misgivings which had assailed her in the coach with him now resolved themselves into assured fears. Something she could not explain had aroused her suspicions before they reached the manor, but his words had glossed these inward qualms, and a feeling of obligation suggested trust, not shrinking; but, with his last words, a full light illumined her faculties; an association of ideas revealed his intent and performance.

"It was you, then," she said, slowly, studying him with steady, penetrating glance.

"You!" she repeated, with such contempt that he was momentarily disconcerted. "The man in the carriage--he was hired by you. The driver--his face is familiar. I remember now where I saw him--in the Shadengo Valley. He is your coachman. Your rescue was planned to deceive me. It deceived even your man. He had not expected that. Your reassuring me was false; the plan to change horses a trick to get me here--"

"If you would but listen--"

"When"--her eyes ablaze--"will this farce end?"

Her words took him unawares. Not that he dreaded the betrayal of his actual purpose. On the contrary, his reckless temper, chafing under her unexpected obduracy, now welcomed the opportunity of discarding the disinterested and chivalrous part he had assumed.

"When it ends in a honeymoon, ma belle Constance!" he said, swiftly.

His sudden words, removing all doubts as to his purpose, awoke such repugnance in her that for a moment aversion was paramount to every other feeling. Again she looked without, but only the solitude of the fields and forests met her glance.

The remoteness of the situation gave the very boldness of his plan feasibility. Was he not his own magistrate in his own province? Why, then, he had thought, waste the golden moments? He had but one heed now; a study of physical beauty, against a crimson background.

"To think of such loveliness lost in the wilderness!" he said, softly. "The gates of art should all open to you. Why should you play to rustic bumpkins, when the world of fashion would gladly receive you? I am a poor prophet if you would not be a success in town. It is not always easy to get a hearing, to procure an audience, but means could be found. Soon your name would be on every one's lips. Your art is fresh. The jaded world likes freshness. The cynical town runs to artless art as an antidote to its own poison. Most of the players are wrinkled and worn. A young face will seem like a new-grown white rose."

She did not answer; unresponsive as a statue, she did not move. The sun shot beneath an obstructing branch, and long, searching shafts found access to the room. Mauville moved forward impetuously, until he stood on the verge of the sunlight on the satinwood floor.

"May I not devote myself to this cause, Constance?" he continued. "You are naturally resentful toward me now. But can I not show you that I have your welfare at heart? If you were as ambitious as you are attractive, what might you not do? Art is long; our days are short; youth flies like a summer day."

His glance sought hers questioningly; still no reply; only a wave of blood surged over her neck and brow, while her eyes fell. Then the glow receded, leaving her white as a snow image.

"Come," he urged. "May I not find for you those opportunities?"

He put out his eager hand as if to touch her. Then suddenly the figure in the window came to life and shrank back, with widely opened eyes fixed upon his face. His gaze could not withstand hers, man of the world though he was, and his free manner was replaced by something resembling momentary embarrassment. Conscious of this new and annoying feeling, his egotism rose in arms, as if protesting against the novel sensation, and his next words were correspondingly violent.

"Put off your stage manners!" he exclaimed. "You are here at my pleasure. It was no whim, my carrying you off. After you left I went to the manor, where I tried to forget you. But nights of revelry--why should I not confess it?--could not efface your memory." His voice unconsciously sank to unreserved candor. "Your presence filled these halls. I could no longer say: Why should I trouble myself about one who has no thought for me?"

Breathing hard, he paused, gazing beyond her, as though renewing the memories of that period.

"Learning you were in the neighboring town," he continued, "I went there, with no further purpose than to see you. On the journey perhaps I indulged in foolish fancies. How would you receive me? Would you be pleased; annoyed? So I tempted my fancy with air-castles like the most unsophisticated lover. But you had no word of welcome; scarcely listened to me, and hurried away! I could not win you as I desired; the next best way was this."

He concluded with an impassioned gesture, his gaze eagerly seeking the first sign of lenity or favor on her part, but his confession seemed futile. Her eyes, suggestive of tender possibilities, expressed now but coldness and obduracy. In a revulsion of feeling he forgot the distance separating the buskined from the fashionable world; the tragic scatterlings from the conventions of Vanity Fair! He forgot all save that she was to him now the one unparagoned entirety, overriding other memories.

"Will not a life of devotion atone for this day, Constance?" he cried. "Do you know how far-reaching are these lands? All the afternoon you drove through them, and they extend as wide in the other direction. These--my name--are yours!"

A shade of color swept over her brow.

"Answer me," he urged.

"Drive back and I will answer you."

"Drive back and you will laugh at me," he retorted, moodily. "You would make a woman's bargain with me."

"Is yours a man's with me?" Contemptuously.

"What more can I do?"

"Undo what you have done. Take me back!"

"I would cut a nice figure doing that! No; you shall stay here."

He spoke angrily; her disdain at his proposal not only injured his pride but awoke his animosity. On the other hand, his words demonstrated she had not improved her own position. If he meant to keep her there he could do so, and opposition made him only more obstinate, more determined to press his advantage. Had she been more politic--Juliana off the stage as well as on--she, whose artifice was glossed by artlessness--

Her lashes drooped; her attitude became less aggressive; her eyes, from beneath their dark curtains, rested on him for a moment. What it was in that glance so effective is not susceptible to analysis. Was it the appeal that awakened the quixotic sense of honor; the helplessness arousing compassion; the irresistible quality of a brimming eye so fatal to masculine calculation and positiveness? Whatever it was, it dispelled the contraction on the land baron's face, and--despite his threats, vows!--he was swayed by a look.

"Forgive me," he said, tenderly.

"You will drive back?"

"Yes; I will win you in your own way, fairly and honestly! I will take you back, though the whole country laughs at me. Win or lose, back we go, for--I love you!" And impetuously he threw his arm around her waist.

Simulation could not stand the test; it was no longer acting, but reality; she had set herself to a rôle she could not perform. Hating him for that free touch, she forcibly extricated herself with an exclamation and an expression of countenance there was no mistaking. From Mauville's face the glad light died; he regarded her once more cruelly, vindictively.

"You dropped the mask too soon," he said, coldly. "I was not prepared for rehearsal, although you were perfect. You are even a better actress than I thought you, than which"--mockingly--"I can pay you no better compliment."

She looked at him with such scorn he laughed, though his eyes flashed.

"Bravo!" he exclaimed.

While thus confronting each other a footfall sounded without, the door burst open, and the driver of the coach, with features drawn by fear, unceremoniously entered the room. The patroon turned on him enraged, but the latter without noticing his master's displeasure, exclaimed hurriedly:

"The anti-renters are coming!"

The actress uttered a slight cry and stepped toward the window, when she was drawn back by an irresistible force.

"Pardon me," said a hard voice, from which all passing compunction had vanished. "Be kind enough to come with me."

"I will follow you, but--" Her face expressed the rest.

"This way then!"

He released her and together they mounted the stairway. For a long time a gentle footfall had not passed those various landings; not since the ladies in hoops, with powdered hair, had ascended or descended, with attendant cavaliers, bewigged, beruffled, bedizened. The land baron conducted his companion to a distant room up stairs, the door of which he threw open.

"Go in there," he said curtly.

She hesitated on the threshold. So remote was it from the main part of the great manor, the apartment had all the requirements of a prison.

"You needn't fear," he continued, reading her thoughts. "I'm not going to be separated from you--yet! But we can see what is going on here."

Again she mutely obeyed him, and entered the room. It was a commodious apartment, where an excellent view was offered of the surrounding country on three sides. But looking from the window to discern his assailants, Mauville could see nothing save the fields and openings, fringed by the dark groves. The out-houses and barns were but dimly outlined, while scattered trees here and there dotted the open spaces with small, dark patches. A single streak of red yet lingered in the west. A tiny spot, moving through the obscurity, proved to be a cow, peacefully wandering over the dewy grass. The whirring sound of a diving night-hawk gave evidence that a thing of life was inspecting the scene from a higher point of vantage.

From that narrow, dark crimson ribbon, left behind by the flaunting sun, a faint reflection entered the great open windows of the chamber and revealed Mauville gazing without, pistol in hand; Constance leaning against the curtains and the driver of the coach standing in the center of the room, quaking inwardly and shaking outwardly. This last-named had found an old blunderbuss somewhere, useful once undoubtedly, but of questionable service now.

Meanwhile Oly-koeks had not returned. Having faithfully closed and locked all the iron shutters, he had crept out of a cellar window and voluntarily resigned as care-taker of the manor, with its burden of dangers and vexations. With characteristic prudence, he had timed the period of his departure with the beginning of the end in the fortunes of the old patroon principality. The storm-cloud, gathering during the life of Mauville's predecessor, was now ready to burst, the impending catastrophe hastened by the heir's want of discretion and his failure to adjust difficulties amicably. That small shadow, followed by a smaller shadow, passing through the field, were none other than Oly-koeks and Oloffe, who grew more and more imperceptible until they were finally swallowed up and seemingly lost forever in the darkness of the fringe of the forest.

A branch of a tree grated against the window as Mauville looked out over the peaceful vale to the ribbon of red that was being slowly withdrawn as by some mysterious hand. Gradually this adornment, growing shorter and shorter, was wound up while the shadows of the out-houses became deeper and the meadow lands appeared to recede in the distance. As he scanned the surrounding garden, the land baron's eye fell upon an indistinct figure stealing slowly across the sward in the partial darkness. This object was immediately followed by another and yet another. To the observer's surprise they wore the headgear of Indians.

Suddenly the patroon heard the note of the whippoorwill, the nocturnal songster that mourns unseen. It was succeeded by the sharp tones of a saw-whet and the distinct mew of a cat-bird. A wild pigeon began to coo softly in another direction and was answered by a thrush. The listener vaguely realized that all this unexpected melody came from the Indians, who had by this time surrounded the house and who took this method of communicating with one another.

An interval of portentous silence was followed by a loud knocking at the front door, which din reverberated through the hall, echoing and re-echoing the vigorous summons. Mauville at this leaned from the window and as he did so, there arose a hooting from the sward as though bedlam had broken loose. Maintaining his post, the heir called out:

"What do you want, men?"

At these words the demonstration became more turbulent, and, amid the threatening hubbub, voices arose, showing too well the purpose of the gathering. Aroused to a fever of excitement by the shooting of the tenants, they were no longer skulking, stealthy Indians, but a riotous assemblage of anti-renters, expressing their determination in an ominous chorus:

"Hang the land baron!"

In the midst of this far from reassuring uproar a voice arose like a trumpet:

"We are the messengers of the Lord, made strong by His wrath!"

"You are the messenger of the devil, Little Thunder," Mauville shouted derisively.

A crack of a rifle admonished the land baron that the jest might have cost him dear.

CHAPTER XIV:
THE ATTACK ON THE MANOR

After this brief hostile outbreak in the garden below the right wing, Mauville prepared to make as effective defense as lay in his power and looked around for his aid, the driver of the coach. But that quaking individual had taken advantage of the excitement to disappear. Upon hearing the threats, followed by the singing of bullets, and doubting not the same treatment accorded the master would be meted out to the servant, the coachman's fealty so oozed from him that he dropped his blunderbuss, groping his way through the long halls to the cellar, where he concealed himself in an out-of-the-way corner beneath a heap of potato sacks. In that vast subterranean place he congratulated himself he would escape with a whole skin, his only regret being certain unpaid wages which he considered as good as lost, together with the master who owed them.

Mauville, however, would have little regretted the disappearance of this poor-spirited aid, on the theory a craven follower is worse than none at all, had not this discovery been followed quickly by the realization that the young girl, too, had availed herself of the opportunity while he was at the window and vanished.

"Why, the slippery jade's gone!" he exclaimed, staring around the room, confounded for the moment. Then recovering himself, he hurriedly left the chamber, more apprehensive lest she should get out of the manor than that the tenants should get in.

"She can't be far off," he thought, pausing doubtfully in the hall.

For the moment he almost forgot the anti-renters and determined to find her at all hazard. He hastily traversed the upper hall, but was rewarded with no sight of her. He gazed down the stairs eagerly, with no better result; the front door was still closed, as he had left it. Evidently she had fled toward the rear of the house and made good her escape from one of the back or side entrances.

"Yes; she's gone," he repeated. "What a fool I was to have trusted her to herself for a moment!"

A new misgiving arose, and he started. What if she had succeeded in leaving the manor? He knew and distrusted Little Thunder and his cohorts. What respect would they have for her? For all he had done, it was, nevertheless, intolerable to think she might be in possible danger--from others save himself! A wave of compunction swept over him. After all, he loved her, and, loving her, could not bear to think of any calamity befalling her. He hated her for tricking him; feared for her, for the pass to which he had brought her; cared for her beyond the point his liking had reached for any other woman. A mirthless laugh escaped him as he stood at the stairway looking down the empty hall.

"Surely I've gone daft over the stroller!" he thought, as his own position recurred to him in all its seriousness. "Well, what's done is done! Let them come!" His eyes gleamed.

With no definite purpose of searching further, he nevertheless walked mechanically down the corridor toward the other side of the manor and suddenly, to his surprise and satisfaction, discerned Constance in a blind passage, where she had inadvertently fled.

At the end of this narrow hall a window looked almost directly out upon the circular, brick dove-cote, now an indistinct outline, and on both sides were doors, one of which she was vainly endeavoring to open when he approached. Immediately she desisted in her efforts; flushed and panting, she stood in the dim light of the passage. Quiet, unbroken save for the cooing in the cote, had succeeded the first noisy demonstration; the anti-renters were evidently arranging their forces to prevent the land baron's escape or planning an assault on the manor.

In his momentary satisfaction at finding her, Mauville overlooked the near prospect of a more lengthy, if not final, separation, and surveyed the young girl with a sudden, swift joyousness, but the fear and distrust written on her features dissipated his concern for her; his best impulses were smothered by harsher feelings.

"Unfortunately, the door is locked," he said, ironically. "Meanwhile, as this spot has no strategic advantages, suppose we change our base of defense?"

Realizing how futile would be resistance, she accompanied him once more to the chamber in the wing, where he had determined to make his last defense. After closing and locking the door, he lighted one of many candles on the mantel. The uncertain glow from the great candelabra, covered with dust, like the white marble itself, and evidently placed there many years before, revealed faded decorations and a ceiling, water-stained as from a defective roof. Between the windows, with flowery gilt details, an ancient mirror extended from floor to ceiling. A musty smell pervaded the apartment, for Mynheer, the Patroon, had lived so closely to himself that he had shut out both air and sunlight from his rooms.

The flickering glare fell upon the young actress standing, hand upon her heart, listening with bated breath, and Mauville, with ominous expression, brooding over that chance which sent the lease-holders to the manor on that night of nights. It was intolerable that no sooner had she crossed his threshold than they should appear, ripe for any mischief, not only seeking his life, but wresting happiness from his very lips. For, of the outcome he could have little doubt, although determined to sell dearly that which they sought.

The violent crash of a heavy body at the front of the house and a tumult of voices on the porch, succeeded by a din in the hall, announced that the first barrier had been overcome and the anti-renters were in possession of the lower floor of the manor. Mauville had started toward the door, when the anticipation in the young girl's eyes held him to the spot. Inaccessible, she was the more desired; her reserve was fuel to his flame, and, at that moment, while his life hung in the balance, he forgot the rebuff he had received and how she had nearly played upon him.

Words fell from his lips, unpremeditated, eloquent, voicing those desires which had grown in the solitude of the manor. Passionately he addressed her, knowing the climax to his difficulties was at hand. Once near her, he could not be at peace without her, he vowed, and this outcome had been inevitable. All this he uttered impetuously, at times incoherently, but as he concluded, she only clasped her hands helplessly, solely conscious of the uproar below which spread from the main hall to the adjoining rooms.

"They are coming--they are coming!" she said, and Mauville stopped short.

But while anger and resentment were at strife within him, some one tried the door of the chamber and finding it locked, set up a shout. Immediately the prowlers in the wings, the searchers in the kitchen and all the stragglers below congregated in the main hall; footsteps were heard ascending rapidly, pausing in doubt at the head of the stairway, not knowing whether to turn to the right or to the left.

"Here they are!" called out the man at the door.

"You meddlesome fool!" exclaimed Mauville, lifting a revolver and discharging it in the direction of the voice. Evidently the bullet, passing through the panel of the door, found its mark, for the report was followed by a cry of pain.

This plaint was answered from the distance and soon a number of anti-renters hastened to the spot. Mauville, in vicious humor, moved toward the threshold. One of the panels was already broken and an arm thrust into the opening. The land baron bent forward and coolly clapped his weapon to the member, the loud discharge being succeeded by a howl from the wounded lease-holder. Mauville again raised his weapon when an exclamation from the actress caused him to turn quickly, in time to see a figure spring unexpectedly into the room from the balcony. The land baron stood in amazement, eying the intruder who had appeared so suddenly from an unguarded quarter, but before he could recover his self-possession, his hand was struck heavily and the revolver fell with a clatter to the floor.

His assailant quickly grasped the weapon, presenting it to the breast of the surprised land-owner, who looked, not into the face of an unknown anti-renter, but into the stern, familiar countenance of Saint-Prosper.

CHAPTER XV:
A HASTY EXIT

The afternoon following the soldier's departure from the patroon village went by all too slowly, his jaded horse's feet as heavy as the leaden moments. That he had not long since overtaken the coach was inexplicable, unless Susan had been a most tardy messenger. True, at the fork of the road he had been misled, but should before this have regained what he had lost, unless he was once more on the wrong thoroughfare. As night fell, the vastness of the new world impressed the soldier as never before; not a creature had he met since leaving the patroon village; she whom he sought might have been swallowed up in the immensity of the wilderness. For the first time his task seemed as if it might be to no purpose; his confidence of the morning had gradually been replaced by consuming anxiety. He reproached himself that he had not pressed his inquiries further at the patroon village, but realized it was now too late for regrets; go on he must and should.

Along the darkening road horse and rider continued their way. Only at times the young man pulled at the reins sharply, as the animal stumbled from sheer weariness. With one hand he stroked encouragingly the foam-flecked arch of the horse's neck; the other, holding the reins, was clenched like a steel glove. Leaving the brow of a hill, the horseman expectantly fixed his gaze ahead, when suddenly on his right, a side thoroughfare lay before him. As he drew rein indecisively at the turn, peering before him through the gathering darkness, a voice from the trees called out unexpectedly:

"Hitch up in here!"

At this peremptory summons the soldier gazed quickly in the direction of the speaker. Through the grove, where the trees were so slender and sparsely planted the eye could penetrate the thicket, he saw a band of horsemen dismounting and tying their animals.

There was something unreal, grotesque even, in their appearance, but it was not until one of their number stepped from the shadow of the trees into the clearer light of the road that he discerned their head-dress and garb to be that of Indians. Recalling all he had heard of the masquerading, marauding excursions of the anti-renters, the soldier at once concluded he had encountered a party of them, bent upon some nefarious expedition. That he was taken for one of their number seemed equally evident.

"Come!" called out the voice again, impatiently. "The patroon is at the manor with his city trollop. It's time we were moving."

An exclamation fell from the soldier's lips. The patroon!--his ill-disguised admiration for the actress!--his abrupt reappearance the night of the temperance drama! Any uncertainty Saint-Prosper might have felt regarding the identity of him he sought, or the reason for that day's work, now became compelling certitude. But for the tenants, he might have ridden by the old patroon house. As it was, congratulating himself upon this accidental meeting rather than his own shrewdness, he quickly dismounted. A moment's thought, and he followed the lease-holders.

In the attack on the manor, his purpose, apart from theirs, led him to anticipate the general movement of the anti-renters in front of the house and to make his way alone, aided by fortuitous circumstances, to the room where the land baron had taken refuge. As he sprang into this chamber the young girl's exclamation of fear was but the prelude to an expression of gladness, while Mauville's consternation when he found himself disarmed and powerless, was as great as his surprise. For a moment, therefore, in his bearing bravado was tempered with hesitancy.

"You here?" stammered the land baron, as he involuntarily recoiled from his own weapon.

The soldier contemptuously thrust the revolver into his pocket. "As you see," he said coldly, "and in a moment, they"--indicating the door--"will be here!"

"You think to turn me over to them!" exclaimed the other violently. "But you do not know me! This is no quarrel of yours. Give me my weapon, and let me fight it out with them!"

The soldier's glance rested for a moment on the young girl and his face grew stern and menacing.

"By heaven, I am half-minded to take you at your word! But you shall have one chance--a slender one! There is the window; it opens on the portico!"

"And if I refuse?"

"They have brought a rope with them. Go, or hang!"

The heir hesitated, but as he pondered, the anti-renters were effectually shattering the heavy door, regaling themselves with threats taught them by the politicians who had advocated their cause on the stump, preached it in the legislature, or grown eloquent over it in the constitutional assembly.

"The serfs are here! The drawers of water and hewers of wood have arisen! Hang the land baron! Hang the feudal lord!"

A braver man than Mauville might have been cowed by that chorus. But after pausing irresolutely, weighing the chances of life and death, gazing jealously upon the face of the apprehensive girl, and venomously at the intruder, the heir finally made a virtue of necessity and strode to the window. With conflicting emotions struggling in his mind--fury toward the lease-holders, hatred for the impassive mediator--he yet regained, in a measure, an outwardly calm bearing.

"It's a poor alternative," he said, shortly, flashing a last glance at the actress. "But it's the best that offers!"

So saying, he sprang upon the balcony--none too soon, for a moment later the door burst open and an incongruous element rushed into the room. Many were attired in outlandish head-dresses, embroidered moccasins and fringed jackets, their faces painted in various hues, but others, of a bolder spirit, had disdained all subterfuge of disguise. Not until then did the soldier discover that he had overlooked the possible unpleasantness of remaining in the land baron's stead, for the anti-renters promptly threw themselves upon him, regardless of his companion. The first to grapple with him was a herculean, thick-ribbed man, of extraordinary stature, taller than the soldier, if not so well-knit; a Goliath, indeed, as Scroggs had deemed him, with arms long as windmills.

"Stand back, lads," he roared, "and let me throw him!" And Dick, the tollman, rushed at Saint-Prosper with furious attack; soon they were chest to chest, each with his chin on his opponent's right shoulder, and each grasping the other around the body with joined hands.

Dick's muscles grew taut, like mighty whip-cords; his chest expanded with power; he girded his loins for a great effort, and it seemed as if he would make good his boast. Held in the grasp of those arms, tight as iron bands, the soldier staggered. Once more the other heaved and again Saint-Prosper nearly fell, his superior agility alone saving him.

Then slowly, almost imperceptibly, the soldier managed to face to the right, twisting so as to place his left hip against his adversary--his only chance; a trick of wrestling unknown to his herculean, but clumsy opponent. Gathering all his strength in a last determined effort, he stooped forward suddenly and lifted in his turn. One portentous moment--a moment of doubt and suspense--and the proud representative of the barn-burners was hurled over the shoulder of the soldier, landing with a crash on the floor where he lay, dazed and immovable.

Breathing hard, his chest rising and falling with labored effort, Saint-Prosper fell back against the wall. The anti-renters quickly recovering from their surprise, gave him no time to regain his strength, and the contest promised a speedy and disastrous conclusion for the soldier, when suddenly a white figure flashed before him, confronting the tenants with pale face and shining eyes. A slender obstacle; only a girlish form, yet the fearlessness of her manner, the eloquence of her glance--for her lips were silent!--kept them back for the instant.

But fiercer passions were at work among them, the desire for retaliation and bitter hatred of the patroon, which speedily dissipated any feeling of compunction or any tendency to waver,

"Kill him before his lady love!" cried a piercing voice from behind. "Did they not murder my husband before me? Kill him, if you are men!"

And pressing irresistibly to the front appeared the woman whose husband had been shot by the deputies. Her features, once soft and matronly, flamed with uncontrollable passions.

"Are only the poor to suffer?" she continued, as her, burning eyes fell on the young girl. "Shall she not feel what I did?"

"Back woman!" exclaimed one of the barn-burners, sternly. "This is no place for you."

"Who has a better right to be here?" retorted the woman.

"But this is not woman's work!"

"Woman's work!" Fiercely. "As much woman's work as for his trull to try to save him! Oh? let me see him!"

Gently the soldier, now partly recovering his strength, thrust the young girl behind him, as pushing to the foreground the woman regarded him vengefully. But in her eyes the hatred and bitter aversion faded slowly, to be replaced by perplexity, which in turn gave way to wonder, while the uplifted arm, raised threateningly against him, fell passively to her side. At first, astonished, doubting, she did not speak, then her lips moved mechanically.

"That is not the land baron," she cried, staring at him in disappointment that knew no language.

"The woman is right," added a masquerader. "I know Mauville, too, for he told me to go to the devil when I asked him to wait for his rent."

At this unexpected announcement, imprecations and murmurs of incredulity were heard on all sides.

"Woman, would you shield your husband's murderer?" exclaimed an over-zealous barn-burner.

"Shield him!" she retorted, as if aroused from a trance. "No, no! I'm not here for that! But this is not the patroon. His every feature is burned into my heart! I tell you it is not he. Yet he should be here. Did I not see him driving toward the manor?" And she gazed wildly around.

For a moment, following this impassioned outburst, their rough glances sought one another's, and the soldier quickly took advantage of this cessation of hostilities.

"No; I am not the land baron," he interposed.

"You aren't?" growled a disappointed lease-holder. "Then who the devil are you? An anti-renter?" he added, suspiciously.

"He must be an enemy of the land baron," interrupted the woman, passing her hand across her brow. "He was with us in the grove. I saw him ride up and took him to be a barn-burner. He crossed the meadow with us. I saw his face; distinctly as I see it now! He asked me about the patroon--yes, I remember now!--and what was she like, the woman who was with him!"

"I am no friend of his," continued the soldier in a firm voice. "You had one purpose in seeking him; I, another! He carried off this lady. I was following him, when I met you in the grove."

"Then how came you here--in this room?"

"By the way of a tree, the branch of which reaches to the window."

"The land baron was in this room a moment ago. Where is he now?"

For answer Saint-Prosper pointed to the window.

"Then you let him--"

"We're wasting time," impatiently shouted the barn-burner who had disclaimed the soldier's identity to the patroon. "Come!" With an oath. "Do you want to lose him after all? He can't be far away. And this one, damn him! isn't our man!"

For a second the crowd wavered, then with a vengeful shout they shot from the room, disappearing as quickly as they had come. Led by Little Thunder, who, being a man of peace, had discreetly remained without, they had reached the gate in their headlong pursuit when they were met by a body of horsemen, about to turn into the yard as the anti-renters were hurrying out. At sight of this formidable band, the lease-holders immediately scattered. Taken equally by surprise, the others made little effort to intercept them and soon they had vanished over field and down dell. Then the horsemen turned, rode through the avenue of trees, and drew up noisily before the portico.

From their window the soldier and his companion observed the abrupt encounter at the entrance of the manor grounds and the dispersion of the lease-holders like leaves before the autumn gusts. Constance, who had breathlessly watched the flight of the erstwhile assailants, felt her doubts reawakened as the horsemen drew up before the door.

"Are they coming back?" she asked, involuntarily clasping the arm of her companion.

She who had been so courageous and self-controlled throughout that long, trying day, on a sudden felt strangely weak and dependent. He leaned from the narrow casement to command the view below, striving to pierce the gloom, and she, following his example, gazed over his shoulder. Either a gust of air had extinguished the light in the candelabra on the mantel, or the tallow dip had burnt itself out, for the room was now in total darkness so that they could dimly see, without being seen.

"These men are not the ones who just fled," he replied.

"Then who are they?" she half-whispered, drawing unconsciously closer in that moment of jeopardy, her face distant but a curl's length.

Below the men were dismounting, tying their horses among the trees. Like a noisy band of troopers they were talking excitedly, but their words were indistinguishable.

"Why do you suppose they fled from them?" she continued.

Was it a tendril of the vine that touched his cheek gently? He started, his face toward the haze in the open borderland.

"Clearly these men are not the lease-holders. They may be seeking you."

She turned eagerly from the window. In the darkness their hands met. Momentary compunction made her pause.

"I haven't yet thanked you!" And he felt the cold, nervous pressure of her hands on his. "You must have ridden very hard and very far!"

His hand closed suddenly upon one of hers. He was not thinking of the ride, but of how she had placed herself beside him in his moment of peril; how she had held them--not long--but a moment--yet long enough!

"They're coming in! They're down stairs!" she exclaimed excitedly.

A flickering light below suddenly threw dim moving shadows upon the ceiling of the hall. As she spoke she stepped forward and stumbled over the debris at the door. His arm was about her, almost before the startled exclamation had fallen from her lips; for a moment her shapely, young figure rested against him. But quickly she extricated herself, and they picked their way cautiously over the bestrewn threshold out into the hall.

At the balustrade, they paused. Reconnoitering at the turn, they were afforded full survey of the lower hall where the latest comers had taken possession. Few in numbers, the gathering had come to a dead stop, regarding in surprise the broken door, and the furniture wantonly demolished. But amid this scene of rack and ruin, an object of especial wonder to the newcomers was the great lifting-stone lying in the hall amid the havoc it had wrought.

"No one but Dick, the tollman, could have thrown that against the door!" said a little man who seemed a person of authority. "I wonder where the patroon can be?"

With unusual pallor of face the young girl stepped from behind the sheltering post. Her hand, resting doubtfully upon the balustrade, sought in unconscious appeal her companion's arm, as they descended together the broad steps. In the partial darkness the little man ill discerned the figures, but divined their bearing in the relation of outlines limned against the obscure background.

"Why," he muttered in surprise, "this is not the patroon! And here, if I am not mistaken, is the lady Mr. Barnes is so anxious about."

"Mr. Barnes--he is with you?"

It was Constance that spoke.

"Yes; but--"

"Where is he?"

"We left him a ways down the road and--"

The sound of a horse's hoof beats in front of the manor, breaking in on this explanation, was followed by hurried footsteps upon the porch. The newcomer paused on the threshold, when, with an exclamation of joy, Constance rushed to him, and in a moment was clasped in the arms of the now jubilant Barnes.

CHAPTER XVI:
THE COUNCIL AT THE TOWN PUMP

N ext morning the sun had made but little progress in the heavens and the dew was not yet off the grass when the party, an imposing cavalcade, issued from the manor on the return journey. Their homecoming was uneventful. The barn-burners had disappeared like rabbits in their holes; the manor whose master had fled, deserted even by the faithful Oly-koeks, was seen for the last time from the brow of the hill, and then, with its gables and extensive wings, vanished from sight.

"Well," remarked Barnes as they sped down the road, "it was a happy coincidence for me that led the anti-renters to the patroon's house last night."

And he proceeded to explain how when he had sought the magistrate, he found that official organizing a posse comitatus for the purpose of quelling an anticipated uprising of lease-holders. In answer to the manager's complaint the custodian of the law had asserted his first duty was generally to preserve the peace; afterward, he would attend to Barnes' particular grievance. Obliged to content himself as best he might with this meager assurance, the manager, at his wit's end, had accompanied the party whose way had led them in the direction the carriage had taken, and whose final destination-- an unhoped-for consummation!--had proved the ultimate goal of his own desires.

On reaching, that afternoon, the town where they were playing, Susan was the first of the company to greet Constance.

"Now that it's all over," she laughed, "I rather envy you that you were rescued by such a handsome cavalier."

"Really," drawled Kate, "I should have preferred not being rescued. The owner of a coach, a coat of arms, silver harness, and the best horses in the country! I could drive on forever."

But later, alone with Susan, she looked hard at her:

"So you fainted yesterday?"

"Oh, I'm a perfect coward," returned the other, frankly.

Kate's mind rapidly swept the rough and troubled past; the haphazard sea upon which they had embarked so long ago--

"Dear me!" she remarked quietly, and Susan turned to conceal a blush.

Owing to the magistrate's zeal in relating the story of the rescue, the players' success that night was great.

"The hall was filled to overflowing," says the manager in his date book. "At the end of the second act, the little girl was called out, and much to her inward discomfiture the magistrate presented her with a bouquet and the audience with a written speech. Taking advantage of the occasion, he pointed a political moral from the tale, and referred to his own candidacy to the legislature, where he would look after the interests of the rank and file. It was time the land-owners were taught their places--not by violence--Oh, no--no French methods for Americans!--by ballot, not by bullet! Let the people vote for an amendment to the constitution!

"As we were preparing to leave the theater, the magistrate appeared behind the scenes. 'Of course, Mr. Barnes, you will appear against the patroon?' he said. 'His prosecution will do much to fortify the issue.'

"'That is all very fine,' I returned, satirically. 'But will the Lord provide while we are trying the case? Shall we find miraculous sustenance? We live by moving on, sir. One or two nights in a place; sometimes, a little longer! No, no; 'tis necessary to forget, if not to forgive. You'll have to fortify your issue without us.'

"'Well, well,' he said, good-naturedly, 'if it's against your interests, I have no wish to press the matter.' Whereupon we shook hands heartily and parted. I looked around for Constance, but she had left the hall with Saint-Prosper. Have I been wise in asking him to join the chariot? I sometimes half regret we are beholden to him--"

From the Shadengo Valley Barnes' company proceeded by easy stages to Ohio, where the roads were more difficult than any the chariot had yet encountered. On every hand, as they crossed the country, sounded the refrains of that memorable song-campaign which gave to the state the fixed sobriquet of "Buckeye." Drawing near the capital, where the convention was to be held, a log cabin, on an enormous wagon, passed the chariot. A dozen horses fancifully adorned were harnessed to this novel vehicle; flowers over-ran the cabin-home, hewn from the buckeye logs of the forest near Marysville. In every window appeared the faces of merry lads and lasses, and, as they journeyed on, their chorus echoed over field and through forest. The wood-cutter leaned on his ax to listen; the plowman waved his coonskin cap, his wife, a red handkerchief from the doorway of their log cabin.

"Oh, tell me where the Buckeye cabin was made? 'Twas built among the boys who wield the plow and spade, Where the log-cabin stands in the bonnie Buckeye shade."

From lip to lip the song had been carried, until the entire country was singing it, and the log-cabin had become a part of the armorial bearings of good citizenship, especially applicable to the crests of presidents. Well might the people ask:

"Oh, what has caused this great commotion All the country through?"

which the ready chorus answered:

"It is a ball a-rolling on For Tippecanoe and Tyler, too!"

The least of the strollers' troubles at this crucial period of their wanderings were the bad roads or the effects of song and log-cabin upon the "amusement world," the greatest being a temperance orator who thundered forth denunciations of rum and the theater with the bitterness of a Juvenal inveighing profligate Rome. The people crowded the orator's hall, upon the walls of which hung the customary banners: a serpent springing from the top of a barrel; the steamboat, Alcohol, bursting her boiler and going to pieces, and the staunch craft, Temperance, safe and sound, sailing away before a fair wind. With perfect self-command, gift of mimicry and dramatic gestures, the lecturer swayed his audience; now bubbling over with witty anecdotes, again exercising his power of graphic portraiture. His elixir vitae--animal spirits--humanized his effort, and, as Sir Robert Peel played upon the House of Commons "as on an old fiddle," so John B. Gough (for it was the versatile comic singer, actor and speaker) sounded the chords of that homely gathering.

Whatever he was, "poet, orator and dramatist, an English Gavazzi," or, "mountebank," "humbug," or "backslider," Mr. Gough was, even at that early period, an antagonist not to be despised. He had been out of pocket and out at the elbows--indeed, his wardrobe now was mean and scanty; want and privation had been his companions, and, from his grievous experiences, he had become a sensational story-teller of low life and penury. Certainly Barnes had reason to lament the coincidence which brought players and lecturer into town at the same time, especially as the latter was heralded under the auspices of the Band of Hope.

The temperance lectures and a heavy rain combined to the undoing of the strollers. Majestically the dark clouds rolled up, outspread like a pall, and the land lay beneath the ban of a persistent downpour. People remained indoors, for the most part, and the only signs of life Barnes saw from the windows of the hotel were the landlord's Holderness breed of cattle, mournfully chewing their monotonous cuds, and some Leicester sheep, wofully wandering in the pasture, or huddled together like balls of stained cotton beneath the indifferent protection of a tree amid field.

Exceptional inducements could not tempt the villagers to the theater. Even an epilogue gained for them none of Mr. Gough's adherents. "The Temperance Doctor" failed miserably; "Drunkard's Warning" admonished pitiably few; while as for "Drunkard's Doom," no one cared what it might be and left him to it.

After such a disastrous engagement the manager not only found himself at the end of his resources, but hopelessly indebted, and, with much reluctance, laid the matter before the soldier who had already advanced Barnes a certain sum after their conversation on the night of the country dance and had also come to his assistance on an occasion when box-office receipts and expenses had failed to meet. Moreover, he had been a free, even careless, giver, not looking after his business concerns with the prudent anxiety of a merchant whose ventures are ships at the rude mercy of a troubled sea. To this third application, however, he did not answer immediately.

"Is it as bad as that?" he said at length, thoughtfully.

"Yes; it's hard to speak about it to you," replied the manager, with some embarrassment, "but at New Orleans--"

The soldier encountered his troubled gaze. "See if you can sell my horse," he answered.

"You mean--" began the other surprised.

"Yes."

"Hanged if I will!" exclaimed the manager. Then he put out his hand impulsively. "I beg your pardon. If I had known--but if we're ever out of this mess, I may give a better account of my stewardship."

Nevertheless, his plight now was comparable to that of the strollers of old, hunted by beadles from towns and villages, and classed as gypsies, vagabonds and professed itinerants by the constables. He was no better served than the mummers, clowns, jugglers, and petty chapmen who, wandering abroad, were deemed rogues and sturdy beggars. Yet no king's censor could have found aught "unchaste, seditious or unmete" in Barnes' plays; no cause for frays or quarrels, arising from pieces given in the old inn-yards; no immoral matter, "whatsoever any light and fantastical head listeth to invent or devise;" no riotous actors of rollicking interludes, to be named in common with fencers, bearwards and vagrants.

"Better give it up, Mr. Barnes," said a remarkably sweet and sympathetic voice, as the manager was standing in the hotel office, turning the situation over and over in his mind.

Barnes, looking around quickly to see who had read his inmost thoughts, met the firm glance of his antagonist.

"Mr. Gough, it is an honor to meet one of your talents," replied the manager, "but"--with an attempt to hide his concern--"I shall not be sorry, if we do not meet again."

"An inhospitable wish!" answered the speaker, fixing his luminous eyes upon the manager. "However, we shall probably see each other frequently."

"The Fates forbid, sir!" said Barnes, earnestly. "If you'll tell me your route, we'll--go the other way!"

"It won't do, Mr. Barnes! The devil and the flesh must be fairly fought. 'Where thou goest'--You know the scriptural saying?"

"You'll follow us!" exclaimed the manager with sudden consternation.

The other nodded.

"Why, this is tyranny! You are a Frankenstein; an Old-Man-of-the Sea!"

"Give it up," said the orator, with a smile that singularly illumined his thin, but powerful features. "As I gave it up! Into what dregs of vice, what a sink of iniquity was I plunged! The very cleansing of my soul was an Augean task. Knavery, profligacy, laxity of morals, looseness of principles--that was what the stage did for me; that was the labor of Hercules to be cleared away! Give it up, Mr. Barnes!" And with a last penetrating look, he strode out of the office.

In spite of Barnes' refusal, the soldier offered to sell his horse to the landlord, but the latter curtly declined, having horses enough to "eat their heads off" during the winter, as he expressed it. His Jeremy Collier aversion to players was probably at the bottom of this point-blank rebuff, however. He was a stubborn man, czar in his own domains, a small principality bounded by four inhospitable walls. His guests--having no other place to go--were his subjects, or prisoners, and distress could not find a more unfitting tribunal before which to lay its case. There was something so malevolent in his vigilance, so unfriendly in his scrutiny, that to the players he seemed an emissary of disaster, inseparable from their cruel plight.

Thus it was that the strollers perforce reached a desperate conclusion when making their way from the theater on the last evening. By remaining longer, they would become the more hopelessly involved; in going--without their host's permission--they would be taking the shortest route toward an honorable settlement in the near future; a paradoxical flight from the brunt of their troubles, to meet them squarely! This, to Barnes, ample reason for unceremonious departure was heartily approved by the company in council assembled around the town pump.

"Stay and become a county burden, indeed!" exclaimed Mrs. Adams, tragically.

"As well be buried alive as anchored here!" fretfully added Susan.

"The council is dissolved," said the manager, promptly, "with no one the wiser--except the town pump."

"An ally of Mr. Gough!" suggested Adonis.

Thus more merrily than could have been expected, with such a distasteful enterprise before them, they resumed their way. It was disagreeable under foot and they presented an odd appearance, each one with a light. Mrs. Adams, old campaigner that she was, led the way for the ladies, elastic and chatty as though promenading down Broadway on a spring morning. With their lanterns and the purpose they had in view, they likened themselves to a band of conspirators. As Barnes marched ahead with his light, Susan playfully called him Guy Fawkes, of gun-powder fame, whereupon his mind almost misgave him concerning the grave adventure upon which they were embarked.

The wind was blowing furiously, doors and windows creaked, and all the demons of unrest were moaning that night in the hubbub of sounds. Save for a flickering candle in the hall, the tavern was dark, and landlord and maids had long since retired to rest. Amid the noise of the rain and the sobbing of the wind, trunks were lowered from the window; the chariot and property wagon were drawn from the stable yard and the horses led from their stalls. In a trice they were ready and the ladies, wrapped in their cloaks, were in the coach. But the clatter of hoofs, the neighing of a horse, or some other untoward circumstance, aroused the landlord; a window in the second story shot up and out popped a head in a night-cap.

"Here!--What are you about?" cried the man.

"Leaving!" said the manager, laconically.

The landlord threw up his arms like Shylock at the loss of his money-bags.

"The reckoning!" he exclaimed. "What about the reckoning?"

"Your pound of flesh, sir!" replied Barnes.

"My score! My score!" shouted the other. "You would not leave without settling it!"

"Go to bed, sir," was the answer, "and let honest people depart without hindrance. You will be paid out of our first profits."

But the man was not so easily appeased. "Robbers! Constable!" he screamed.

Conceiving it was better to be gone without further parley, having assured him of their honorable intentions, Barnes was about to lash the horses, when Kate suddenly exclaimed:

"Where's Constance?"

"Isn't she inside?" asked the manager quickly.

"No; she isn't here."

"Oh, I sent her back to get something for me I had forgotten," spoke up Mrs. Adams, "and she hasn't returned yet."

"Sent her back! Madam, you have ruined everything!" burst out Barnes, bitterly.

"Mr. Barnes, I won't be spoken to like a child!"

"Child, indeed--"

But the querulous words were not uttered, for, as the manager was about to leave the box in considerable perturbation, there-- gazing down upon them at a window next to that occupied by the landlord--stood Constance!

For a tippet, or a ruff, or some equally wretched frippery, carelessly left by the old lady, all their plans for deliverance appeared likely to miscarry. Presumably, Constance, turned from her original purpose by the noisy altercation, had hurried to the window, where now the landlord perceived her and immediately availed himself of the advantage offered.

"So one of you is left behind," he shouted exultantly. "And it's the leading lady, too! I'll take care she stays here, until after a settlement. I'll stop you yet! Stealing away in the middle of the night, you--you vagabonds!"

His voice, growing louder and louder, ended in a shrieking crescendo. Disheartened, there seemed no alternative for the players save to turn back and surrender unconditionally. Barnes breathed a deep sigh; so much for a tippet!--their dash for freedom had been but a sorry attempt!--now he saw visions of prison bars, and uttered a groan, when the soldier who was riding his own horse dashed forward beneath the window and stood upright in his stirrups.

"Do not be afraid, Miss Carew," he said.

Fortunately the window was low and the distance inconsiderable, but Barnes held his breath, hoping the hazard would deter her.

"Do not, my dear!" he began.

But she did not hesitate; the sight of the stalwart figure and the strong arms, apparently reassured her, and she stepped upon the sill.

"Quick!" he exclaimed, and, at the word, she dropped into his upstretched arms. Scarcely had she escaped, however, before the landlord was seen at the same window. So astonished was he to find her gone, surprise at first held him speechless; then he burst into a volley of oaths that would have shamed a whaler's master.

"Come back!" he cried. "Come back, or--" The alternative was lost in vengeful imprecation.

Holding Constance before him, the soldier resumed his saddle. "Drive on!" he cried to Barnes, as past the chariot sped his horse, with its double burden.

CHAPTER XVII:
THE HAND FERRY

At a lively gait down the road toward the river galloped the horse bearing Saint-Prosper and Constance. The thoroughfare was deserted and the dwelling houses as well as the principal buildings of the town were absolutely dark. At one place a dog ran out to the front gate, disturbed by the unusual noise on the road, and barked furiously, but they moved rapidly on. Now the steeple of the old church loomed weirdly against the dark background of the sky and then vanished.

On; on, they went, past the churchyard, with its marble slabs indistinctly outlined in the darkness, like a phantom graveyard, as immaterial and ghostlike itself as the spirits of the earliest settlers at rest there beneath the sod. This was the last indication of the presence of the town, the final impression to carry away into the wide country, where the road ran through field and forest. As they sped along, they plunged into a chasm of blackness, caused by the trees on both sides of the road which appeared to be constantly closing upon them. In the darkness of that stygian tunnel, dashing blindly through threatening obscurity, she yet felt no terrors, for a band of steel seemed to hold her above some pit of "visible night."

Out of the tunnel into the comparatively open space, the wind boomed with all its force, and like an enraged monster, drove the storm-clouds, now rainless, across the sky. Occasionally the moon appeared through some aperture, serene, peace-inspiring, momentarily gilding the dark vapor, and again was swallowed up by another mass of clouds. A brood of shadows leaped around them, like things of life, now dancing in the road or pursuing through the tufts of grass, then vanishing over the meadows or disappearing in murky nooks. But a moment were they gone and then, marshaled in new numbers, menacing before and behind, under the very feet of the horse, bidding defiance to the clattering hoofs. With mane tossed in the angry wind, and nostrils dilated, the animal neighed with affright, suddenly leaping aside, as a little nest of unknown dangers lurked and rustled in the ambush of a drift of animated brush.

At that abrupt start, the rider swayed; his grasp tightened about the actress' waist; her arms involuntarily held him closer. Loosened by the wind and the mad motion, her hair brushed his cheek and fell over his shoulder, whipped sharply in the breeze. A fiercer gust, sweeping upon them uproariously, sent all the tresses free, and scudded by with an exultant shriek. For a time they rode in this wise, her face cold in the rush of wind; his gaze fixed ahead, striving to pierce the gloom, and then he drew rein, holding the horse with some difficulty at a standstill in the center of the thoroughfare.

With senses numbed by the stirring flight, the young girl had been oblivious to the firmness of the soldier's sustaining grasp, but now as they paused in the silent, deserted spot, she became suddenly conscious of it. The pain--so fast he held her!--made her wince. She turned her face to his. A glint of light fell on his brow and any lines that had appeared there were erased in the magical glimmer; eagerness, youth, passion alone shone upon his features.

His arm clasped her even yet more closely, as if in the wildness of the moment he would fiercely draw her to him regardless of all. Did she understand--that with her face so near his, her hair surrounding him, her figure pressed in that close embrace--he must needs speak to her; had, indeed, spoken to her. She was conscious her hand on his shoulder trembled. Her cheek was no longer cold; abruptly the warm glow mantled it. Was it but that a momentary calm fell around them; the temporary hush of the boisterous wind? And yet, when again the squall swept by with renewed turmoil, her face remained unchilled. She seemed but a child in his arms. How light her own hand-touch compared to that compelling grasp with which he held her! She remembered he had but spoken to her standing in the window, and she had obeyed without a question--without thought of fear. She longed to spring to the ground now, to draw herself from him.

"You can hear the chariot down the road, Miss Carew."

Quickly her glance returned to his face; his gaze was bent down the thoroughfare. He spoke so quietly she wondered at her momentary fears; his voice reassured her.

A gleam of light shot through a rift in the clouds.

"Hello-a!" came a welcome voice from the distance.

"Hello-a!" answered the soldier.

"You'd better ride on!" shouted the manager. "They're after us!"

For answer the soldier touched his horse, and now began a race for the river and the ferry, which were in plain sight, Luna fortunately at this critical moment sailing from between the vapors and shining from a clear lake in the sky. The chaste light, out of the angry convulsions of the heavens, showed the fugitives the road and the river, winding like a broad band of silver across the darkness of the earth, its surface rippled into waves by the northern wind. Behind them the soldier and Constance could hear the coach creaking and groaning. It seemed to career on its beams' end, but some special providence was watching over the players and no catastrophe occurred.

Nearer came the men on horseback down the hill; now the foremost shouted. Closer was the river; Saint-Prosper reached its bank; the gang-plank was in position and he dashed aboard. With a mighty tossing and rolling, the chariot approached, rattled safely across the gangway, followed by the property wagon, and eager hands grasped the rope, extending from shore to shore above the large, flat craft. These hand ferries, found in various sections of the country, were strongly, although crudely, constructed, their sole means of locomotion in the stationary rope, by means of which the passengers, providing their own power for transportation, drew themselves to the opposite shore.

The energy now applied to the hempen strand sent the ferry many feet from the shore out into the river, where the current was much swifter than usual, owing to the heavy rainfalls. The horses on the great cumbersome craft were snorting with terror.

Crack! pish! One of the men on the shore used his revolver.

"An illogical and foolish way to collect debts, that!" grumbled the manager, tugging at the rope. "If they kill us, how can we requite them for our obligations?"

The river was unusually high and the current set the boat, heavily loaded, tugging at the rope. However, it resisted the strain and soon the craft grated on the sand and the party disembarked, safe from constable and bailiff in the brave, blue grass country. Only one mishap occurred, and that to Adonis, who, in his haste, fell into the shallow water. He was as disconsolate as the young hero Minerva threw into the sea to wrest him from the love of Eucharis. But in this case, Eucharis (Kate) laughed immoderately at his discomfiture.

As Barnes was not sure of the road, the strollers camped upon the bank. The river murmured a seductive cradle-song to the rushes, and, on the shore, from the dark and ominous background, came the deeper voice of the pines.

Constance, who had been unusually quiet and thoughtful, gradually recovered her spirits.

"Here, Mrs. Adams, is your tippet," she said with a merry smile, taking a bit of lace from her dress.

"Thank you, my dear; I wouldn't have lost it for anything!" said the old lady, effusively, while Barnes muttered something beneath his breath.

The soldier, who had dismissed the manager's thanks somewhat abruptly, occupied himself arranging the cushions from the chariot on the grass. Suddenly Mrs. Adams noticed a crimson stain on his shoulder.

"Sir!" she exclaimed, in the voice of the heroine of "Oriana," "you are wounded!"

"It is nothing, Madam!" he replied.

Stripping off his coat, Barnes found the wound was, indeed, but slight, the flesh having just been pierced.

"How romantic!" gushed Susan. "He stood in front of Constance when the firing began. Now, no one thought of poor me. On the contrary, if I am not mistaken, Mr. Hawkes discreetly stood behind me."

"Jokes reflecting upon one's honor are in bad taste," gravely retorted the melancholy actor.

"Indeed, I thought it no jest at the time!" replied the other.

"Mistress Susan, your tongue is dangerous!"

"Mr. Hawkes, your courage will never lead you into danger!"

"Nay," he began, angrily, "this is a serious offense--"

"On the contrary," she said, laughing, "it is a question of defense."

"There is no arguing with a woman," he grumbled. "She always takes refuge in her tongue."

"While you, Mr. Hawkes, take refuge--"

But the other arose indignantly and strode into the gloom. Meanwhile Barnes, while dressing the injury, discovered near the cut an old scar thoroughly healed, but so large and jagged it attracted his attention.

"That hurt was another matter," said he, touching it.

Was it the manager's fingers or his words caused Saint-Prosper to wince? "Yes, it was another matter," he replied, hurriedly. "An Arab spear--or something of the kind!"

"Tell us about it," prattled Susan. "You have never told us anything about Africa. It seems a forbidden subject."

"Perhaps he has a wife in Tangiers, or Cairo," laughed Kate.

"He was wed in Amsterdam, Again in far Siam, And after this Sought triple bliss And married in Hindustan,"

sang Susan.

The soldier made some evasive response to this raillery and then became silent. Soon quiet prevailed in the encampment; only out of the recesses of the forest came the menacing howl of a vagabond wolf.

"Such," says Barnes in his notebook, "is the true history of an adventure which created some talk at the time. A perilous, regrettable business at best, but we acted according to our light and were enabled thereafter to requite our obligations, which could not have been done had they seized the properties, poor garments of players' pomp; tools whereby we earned our meager livelihood. If, after this explanation, anyone still has aught of criticism, I must needs be silent, not controverting his censure.

"With some amusement I learned that our notable belligerent, Mr. Gough, was well-nigh reduced to the same predicament as that in which we found ourselves. He could not complain of his audiences, and the Band of Hope gained many recruits by his coming, but, through some misapprehension, the customary collections were overlooked. The last night of the lecture, the chairman of the evening, at the conclusion of the address, arose and said: 'I move we thank Mr. Gough for his eloquent effort and then adjourn.'

"The motion prevailed, and the gathering was about to disperse when the platform bludgeon-man held them with a gesture. 'Will you kindly put your thanks in writing, that I may offer it for my hotel bill,' said he.

"But for this quick wit and the gathering's response to the appeal he would have been in the same boat with us, or rather, on the same boat--the old hand ferry! Subsequently, he became a speaker of foreign and national repute, but at that time he might have traveled from Scarboro' to Land's End without attracting a passing glance."

BOOK II:
DESTINY AND
THE MARIONETTES

CHAPTER I:
THE FASTIDIOUS MARQUIS

Through the land of the strapping, thick-ribbed pioneers of Kentucky the strollers bent their course--a country where towns and hamlets were rapidly springing up in the smiling valleys or on the fertile hillsides; where new families dropping in, and old ones obeying the injunction to be "fruitful and multiply" had so swelled the population that the region, but a short time before sparsely settled, now teemed with a sturdy people. To Barnes' satisfaction, many of the roads were all that could have been wished for, the turnpike system of the center of the state reflecting unbounded credit upon its builders.

If a people may be judged by its highways, Kentucky, thus early, with its macadamized roads deserved a prominent place in the sisterhood of states. Moreover, while mindful always of her own internal advancement, she persistently maintained an ever-watchful eye and closest scrutiny on the parental government and the acts of congress. "Give a Kentuckian a plug of tobacco and a political antagonist and he will spend a comfortable day where'er he may be," has been happily said. It was this hardy, horse-raising, tobacco-growing community which had given the peerless Clay to the administrative councils of the country; it was this rugged cattle-breeding, whisky-distilling people which had offered the fearless Zach Taylor to spread the country's renown on the martial field.

What sunny memories were woven in that pilgrimage for the strollers! Remembrance of the corn-husking festivities, and the lads who, having found the red ears, kissed the lasses of their choice; of the dancing that followed--double-shuffle, Kentucky heel-tap, pigeon wing or Arkansas hoe-down! And mingling with the remembrance of such pleasing diversions were the yet more satisfying recollections of large audiences, generous-minded people and substantial rewards, well-won; rewards which enabled them shortly afterward to pay by post the landlord from whom they had fled.

Down the Father of Waters a month or so after their flight into the blue grass country steamed the packet bearing the company of players, leaving behind them the Chariot of the Muses.

At the time of their voyage down the Mississippi "the science of piloting was not a thing of the dead and pathetic past," and wonderful accounts were written of the autocrats of the wheel and the characteristics of the ever-changing, ever-capricious river. "Accidents!" says an early steamboat captain. "Oh, sometimes we run foul of a snag or sawyer, occasionally collapse a boiler and blow up sky-high. We get used to these little matters and don't mind them."

None of these trifling incidents was experienced by the players, however, who thereby lost, according to the Munchausens of the period, half of the pleasure and excitement of the trip. In fact, nothing more stirring than taking on wood from a flatboat alongside, or throwing a plank ashore for a passenger, varied the monotony of the hour, and, approaching their destination, the last day on the "floating palace" dawned serenely, uneventfully.

The gray of early morn became suffused with red, like the flush of life on a pallid cheek. Arrows of light shot out above the trees; an expectant hush pervaded the forest. Inside the cabin a sleepy negro began the formidable task of sweeping. This duty completed, he shook a bell, which feature of his daily occupation the darky entered into with diabolical energy, and soon the ear-rending discord brought the passengers on deck. But hot cornbread, steaks and steaming coffee speedily restored that equanimity of temper disturbed by the morning's clangorous summons.

Breakfast over, some of the gentlemen repaired to the boiler deck for the enjoyment of cigars, the ladies surrounded the piano in the cabin, while a gambler busied himself in getting into the good graces of a young fellow who was seeing the world. Less lonely became the shores, as the boat, panting as if from long exertion, steamed on. Carrolton and Lafayette were left behind. Now along the banks stretched the showy houses and slave plantations of the sugar planters; and soon, from the deck of the boat, the dome of the St. Charles and the cathedral towers loomed against the sky.

Beyond a mile or so of muddy water and a formidable fleet of old hulks, disreputable barges and "small fry broad-horns," lay Algiers, graceless itself as the uninviting foreground; looking out contemplatively from its squalor at the inspiring view of Nouvelle Orleans, with the freighters, granaries and steamboats, three stories high, floating past; comparing its own inertia--if a city can be presumed capable of such edifying consciousness!--with the aspect of the busy levee, where cotton bales, sugar hogsheads, molasses casks, tobacco, hemp and other staple articles of the South, formed, as it were, a bulwark, or fortification of peace, for the habitations behind it. Such was the external appearance--suggestive of commerce--of that little center whose social and bohemian life was yet more interesting than its mercantile features.

At that period the city boasted of its Addison of letters--since forgotten; its Feu-de-joie, the peerless dancer, whose beauty had fired the Duke Gambade to that extravagant conduct which made the recipient of those marked attentions the talk of the town; its Roscius of the drama; its irresistible ingenue, the lovely, little Fantoccini; and its theatrical carpet-knight, M. Grimacier, whose intrigue with the stately and, heretofore, saintly Madame Etalage had, it was said later, much to do with the unhappy taking-off of that ostentatious and haughty lady. It had Mlle. Affettuoso, songstress, with, it is true, an occasional break in her trill; and, last, but not least, that general friend of mankind, more puissant, powerful and necessary than all the nightingales, butterflies, or men of letters--who, nevertheless, are well enough in their places!--Tortier, the only Tortier, who carried the art de cuisine to ravishing perfection, whose ragouts were sonnets in sauce and whose fricassees nothing less than idyls!

Following the strollers' experiences with short engagements and improvised theaters, there was solace in the appearance of the city of cream and honey, and the players, assembled on the boiler deck,

---

regarded the thriving port with mingled feelings as they drew nearer. Susan began forthwith to dream of conquests--a swarthy Mexican, the owner of an opal mine; a prince from Brazil; a hidalgo, exile, or any other notable among the cosmopolitan people. Adonis bethought himself of dusky beauties, waiting in their carriages at the stage entrance; sighing for him, languishing for him; whirling him away to a supper room--and Paradise! Regretfully the wiry old lady reverted to the time when she and her first husband had visited this Paris of the South, and, with a deep sigh, paid brief tribute to the memory of conjugal felicity.

Constance's eyes were grave as they rested upon the city where she would either triumph or fail, and the seriousness of her task came over her, leaning with clasped hands against the railing of the boat. Among that busy host what place would be made for her? How easy it seemed to be lost in the legion of workers; to be crushed in the swaying crowd! It was as though she were entering a room filled with strangers, and stood hesitating on the threshold. But youth's assurance soon set aside this gloomy picture; the shadow of a smile lighted her face and her glance grew bright. At twenty the world is rosy and in the perspective are many castles.

Near by the soldier also leaned against the rail, looking not, however, at New Orleans but at her, while all unconscious of his regard she continued to gaze cityward. His face, too, was thoughtful. The haphazard journey was approaching its end, and with it, in all likelihood, the bond of union, the alliance of close comradeship associated with the wilderness. She was keenly alive to honor, fame, renown. What meaning had those words to him--save for her? He smiled bitterly, as a sudden revulsion of dark thoughts crowded upon him. He had had his bout; the sands of the arena that once had shone golden now were dust.

Drawing up to the levee, they became a part of the general bustle and confusion; hurriedly disembarked, rushed about for their luggage, because every one else was rushing; hastily entered carriages of which there was a limited supply, and were whisked off over the rough cobblestones which constituted the principal pavements of the city; catching momentary glimpses, between oscillations, of oyster saloons, fruit and old clothes' shops, and coffee stands, where the people ate in the open air. In every block were cafés or restaurants, and the sign "Furnished Rooms" appearing at frequent intervals along the thoroughfare through which they drove at headlong pace, bore evidence to the fact that the city harbored many strangers.

The hotel was finally reached--and what a unique hostelry it was! "Set the St. Charles down in St. Petersburg," commented a chronicler in 1846, "and you would think it a palace; in Boston, and ten to one, you would christen it a college; in London, and it would remind you of an exchange." It represented at that day the evolution of the American tavern, the primitive inn, instituted for passengers and wayfaring men; the development of the pot-house to the metropolitan hotel, of the rural ale-room to the palatial saloon.

"What a change from country hostelries!" soliloquized the manager, after the company were installed in commodious rooms. "No more inns where soap and towels are common property, and a comb, without its full complement of teeth, does service for all comers!" he continued, gazing around the apartment in which he found himself. "Think of real gas in your room, Barnes, and great chairs, easy as the arms of Morpheus! Are you comfortable, my dear?" he called out.

Constance's voice in an adjoining room replied affirmatively, and he added: "I'm going down stairs to look around a bit."

Beneath the porch and reception hall extended the large bar-room, where several score of men were enjoying their liquors and lunches, and the hum of conversation, the clinking of glasses and the noise made by the skilful mixer of drinks were as sweet music to the manager, when shortly after he strode to the bar. Wearing neither coat nor vest, the bartender's ruffled shirt displayed a glistening stone; the sleeves were ornamented with gold buttons and the lace collar had a Byronic roll.

"What will you have, sir?" he said in a well-modulated voice to a big Virginian, who had preceded Barnes into the room.

"A julep," was the reply, "and, while you are making it, a little whisky straight."

A bottle of bourbon was set before him, and he wasted no valuable time while the bartender manipulated the more complicated drink. Experiencing the felicity of a man who has entered a higher civilization, the manager ordered a bottle of iced ale, drank it with gusto, and, seating himself, was soon partaking of a palatable dish. By this time the Virginian, joined by a friend, had ordered another julep for the near future and a little "straight" for the immediate present.

"Happy days!" said the former.

"And yours happier!" replied the newcomer.

"Why, it's Utopia," thought Barnes. "Every one is happy!"

But even as he thus ruminated, his glance fell upon an old man at the next table whom the waiters treated with such deference the manager concluded he must be some one of no slight importance. This gentleman was thin, wrinkled and worn, with a face Voltairian in type, his hair scanty, his dress elegant, and his satirical smile like the "flash of a dagger in the sunlight." He was inspecting his bouillon with manifest distrust, adjusting his eye-glass and thrusting his head close to the plate. The look of suspicion deepened and finally a grimace of triumph illumined his countenance, as he rapped excitedly on the table.

"Waiter, waiter, do you see that soup?" he almost shouted.

"Yes, Monsieur le Marquis," was the humble response.

"Look at it well!" thundered the old gentleman. "Do you find nothing extraordinary about it?"

Again the bouillon was examined, to the amusement of the manager.

"I am sorry, Monsieur le Marquis; I can detect nothing unusual," politely responded the waiter, when he had concluded a pains-taking scrutiny with all the gravity and seriousness attending so momentous an investigation.

"You are blind!" exclaimed the old man. "See there; a spot of grease floating in the bouillon, and there, another and another! In fact, here is an 'Archipelago of Greece!'" This witticism was relieved by an ironical smile. "Take it away!"

The waiter hurried off with the offending dish and the old man looked immensely satisfied over the disturbance he had created.

"Well has it been said," thought the manager, "that the destiny of a nation depends upon the digestion of its first minister! I wonder what he'll do next?"

Course after course that followed was rejected, the guest keeping up a running comment:

"This sauce is not properly prepared. This salad is not well mixed. I shall starve in this place. These truffles; spoiled in the importation!"

"Oh, Monsieur le Marquis,"--clasping his hands in despair--"they were preserved in melted paraffin."

"What do I care about your paraffin? Never mind anything more, waiter. I could not eat a mouthful. What is the bill? Very well; and there is something for yourself, blockhead."

"Thank you, Monsieur le Marquis." Deferentially.

"The worst meal I've ever had! And I've been in Europe, Asia and Africa. Abominable--abominable--idiot of a waiter--miserable place, miserable--and this dyspepsia--"

Thus running on, with snatches of caustic criticism, the old gentleman shambled out, the waiter holding the door open for him and bowing obsequiously.

"An amiable individual!" observed Barnes to the waiter. "Is he stopping at the hotel?"

"No, Monsieur. He has an elegant house near by. The last time he was here he complimented the cook and praised the sauces. He is a little--what you call it?--whimsical!"

"Yes; slightly inclined that way. But is he here alone?"

"He is, Monsieur. He loses great sums in the gambling rooms. He keeps a box at the theater for the season. He is a prince--a great lord-?"

"Even if he calls you 'liar' and 'blockhead'?"

"Oh, Monsieur,"--displaying a silver dollar with an expressive shrug of the shoulders--"this is the--what you call it?--balm."

"And very good balm, too," said Barnes, heartily.

Still grumbling to himself, the marquis reached the main corridor, where the scene was almost as animated as in the bar and where the principal topic of conversation seemed to be horses and races that had been or were about to be run. "I'd put Uncle Rastus' mule against that hoss!" "That four-year-old's quick as a runaway nigger!" "Five hundred, the gelding beats the runaway nigger!" "Any takers on Jolly Rogers?" were among the snatches of talk which lent life and zest to the various groups.

Sitting moodily in a corner, with legs crossed and hat upon his knee, was a young man whose careless glance wandered from time to time from his cigar to the passing figures. As the marquis slowly hobbled along, with an effort to appear alert, the young man arose quickly and came forward with a conventional smile, intercepting the old nobleman near the door.

"My dear Monsieur le Marquis," he exclaimed, effusively, "it is with pleasure I see you recovered from your recent indisposition."

"Recovered!" almost shrieked the marquis. "I'm far from recovered; I'm worse than ever. I detest congratulations, Monsieur! It's what a lying world always does when you are on the verge of dissolution."

"You are as discerning as ever," murmured the land baron--for it was Edward Mauville.

"I'm not fit to be around; I only came out"--with a sardonic chuckle--"because the doctors said it would be fatal."

"Surely you do not desire--"

"To show them they are impostors? Yes."

"And does New Orleans continue to please you?" asked the other, with some of that pride Southerners entertained in those days for their queen city.

"How does the exile like the forced land of his adoption?" returned the nobleman, irritably. "My king is in exile. Why should I not be also? Should I stay there, herd with the cattle, call every shipjack 'Citizen' and every clod 'Brother'; treat every scrub as though she were a duchess?"

"There is, indeed, a regrettable tendency to deify common clay nowadays," assented the patroon, soothingly.

"Why, your 'Citizen' regards it as condescension to notice a man of condition!" said the marquis, violently. "When my king was driven away by the rabble the ocean was not too broad to separate me from a swinish civilization. I will never go back; I will live there no more!"

"That is good news for us," returned the land baron.

"Your politeness almost reconciles me to staying," said the old man, more affably. "But I am on my way to the club. What do you say to a rubber?"

The Strollers

The patroon readily assented. In front of the hotel waited the marquis' carriage, on the door of which was his coat-of-arms--argent, three mounts vert, on each a sable bird. Entering this conveyance, they were soon being driven over the stones at a pace which jarred every bone in the marquis' body and threatened to shake the breath of life from his trembling and attenuated figure. He jumped about like a parched pea, and when finally they drew up with a jerk and a jolt, the marquis was fairly gasping. After an interval to recover himself, he took his companion's arm, and, with his assistance, mounted the broad steps leading to the handsome and commodious club house.

"At least," said the nobleman, dryly, as he paused on the stairs, "our pavements are so well-kept in Paris that a drive there in a tumbril to the scaffold is preferable to a coach in New Orleans!"

CHAPTER II:

"ONLY AN INCIDENT"

To the scattering of the anti-renters by the rescue party that memorable night at the manor the land baron undoubtedly owed his safety. Beyond reach of personal violence in a neighboring town, without his own domains, from which he was practically exiled, he had sought redress in the courts, only to find his hands tied, with no convincing clue to the perpetrators of these outrages. On the patroon lay the burden of proof, and he found it more difficult than he had anticipated to establish satisfactorily any kind of a case, for alibis blocked his progress at every turn.

At war with his neighbors, and with little taste for the monotony of a northern winter, he bethought him of his native city, determined to leave the locality and at a distance wait for the turmoil to subside. His brief dream of the rehabilitation of the commonwealth brought only memories stirring him to restlessness. He made inquiries about the strollers, but to no purpose. The theatrical band had come and gone like gipsies.

Saying nothing to any one, except Scroggs, to whom he entrusted a load of litigation, he at length quietly departed in the regular stage, until he reached a point where two strap rails proclaimed the new method of conveyance. Wedged in the small compartment of a little car directly behind a smoking monster, with an enormous chimney, fed with cord-wood, he was borne over the land, and another puffing marvel of different construction carried him over the water. Reaching the Crescent City some time before the strollers--his progress expedited by a locomotive that ran full twenty miles an hour!--the land baron found among the latest floating population, comprised of all sorts and conditions, the Marquis de Ligne. The blood of the patroons flowed sluggishly through the land baron's veins, but his French extraction danced in every fiber of his being. After learning the more important and not altogether discreditable circumstances about the land baron's ancestors--for if every gentleman were whipped for godlessness, how many striped backs would there be!--the marquis, who declined intimacy with Tom, Dick and Harry, and their honest butchers, bakers and candlestick-makers of forefathers, permitted an acquaintance that accorded with his views governing social intercourse.

"This is a genuine pleasure, Monsieur le Marquis," observed the land baron suavely, when the two found themselves seated in a card room with brandy and soda before them. "To meet a nobleman of the old school is indeed welcome in these days when New Orleans harbors the refugees of the world, for, strive as we will, outsiders are creeping in and corrupting our best circles."

"Soon we shall all be corrupt," croaked the old man. "France--but what can you expect of a nation that exiles kings!"

"Ah, Louis Philippe! My father once entertained him here in New Orleans," said Mauville.

"Indeed?" remarked the marquis with interest.

"It was when he visited the city in 1798 with his brothers, the Duke of Montpensier and the Count of Beaujolais. New Orleans then did not belong to America. France was not so eager to sell her fair possessions in those days. I remember my father often speaking of the royal visit. The king even borrowed money, which"--laughing--"he forgot to pay!"

The marquis' face was a study, as he returned stiffly: "Sir, it is a king's privilege to borrow."

"It is his immortal prerogative," answered Mauville easily. "I only mentioned it to show how highly he honored my father."

The nobleman lifted his eyebrows, steadily regarding his companion.

"It was a great honor," he said softly. "One does not lend to a king. When Louis Philippe borrowed from your father he lent luster to your ancestry."

"Yes; I doubt not my father regarded himself as the debtor. Again, we had another distinguished compatriot of yours at our house--General Lafayette."

"Lafayette!" repeated the marquis. "Ah, that's another matter! A man, born to rank and condition, voluntarily sinking to the level of the commonalty! A person of breeding choosing the cause of the rout and rabble! How was he received?"

"Like a king!" laughed Mauville. "A vast concourse of people assembled before the river when he embarked on the 'Natchez' for St. Louis."

Muttering something about "bourgeoisie!--épicier!" the nobleman partook of the liquid consolation before him, which seemed to brighten his spirits.

"If my doctors could see me now! Dolts! Quacks!"

"It's a good joke on them," said Mauville, ironically.

"Isn't it? They forbid me touching stimulants. Said they would be fatal! Impostors! Frauds! They haven't killed me yet, have they?"

"If so, you are a most agreeable and amiable ghost," returned Mauville.

"An amiable ghost!" cackled the old man. "Ha! Ha! you must have your joke! But don't let me have such a ghastly one again. I don't like"--in a lower tone--"jests about the spirits of the other world."

"What! A well-seasoned materialist like you!"

"An idle prejudice!" answered the marquis. "Only when you compared me to a ghost"--in a half whisper--"it seemed as though I were one, a ghost of myself looking back through years of pleasure--years of pleasure!"

"A pleasant perspective such memories make, I am sure," observed the land baron.

"Memories," repeated the marquis, wagging his head. "Existence is first a memory and then a blank. But you have been absent from New Orleans, Monsieur?"

"I have been north to look after certain properties left me by a distant relative--peace to his ashes!"

"Only on business?" leered the marquis. "No affair of the heart? You know the saying: 'Love makes time pass--'"

"'And time makes love pass,'" laughed Mauville, somewhat unnaturally, his cynicism fraught with a twinge. "Nothing of the kind, I assure you! But you, Marquis, are not the only exile."

The nobleman raised his brows interrogatively.

"You fled from France; I fled from the ancestral manor. The tenants claimed the farms were theirs. I attempted to turn them out and--they turned me out! I might as well have inherited a hornet's nest. It was a legacy-of hate! The old patroon must have chuckled in his grave! One night they called with the intention of hanging me."

"My dear sir, I congratulate you!" exclaimed the nobleman enthusiastically.

"Thanks!" Dryly.

"It is the test of gentility. They only hang or cut off the heads of people of distinction nowadays."

"Gad! then I came near joining the ranks of the well-born angels. But for an accident I should now be a cherub of quality."

"And how, Monsieur, did you escape such a felicitous fate?"

The land baron's face clouded. "Through a stranger--a Frenchman--a silent, taciturn fellow--more or less an adventurer, I take it. He called himself Saint-Prosper--"

"Saint-Prosper!"

The marquis gazed at Mauville with amazement and incredulity. He might even have flushed or turned pale, but such a possible exhibition of emotion was lost beneath an artificial bloom, painted by his valet. His eyes, however, gleamed like candles in a death's head.

"This Saint-Prosper you met was a soldier?" he asked, and his voice trembled. "Ernest Saint-Prosper?"

"Yes; he was a soldier; served in Africa, I believe. You knew him?" Turning to the marquis in surprise.

"Knew him! He was my ward, the rascal!" cried the other violently. "He was, but now--ingrate!--traitor!--better if he were dead!"

"You speak bitterly, Monsieur le Marquis?" said the patroon curiously.

"Bitterly!--after his conduct!--he is no longer anything to me! He is dead to me--dead!"

"How did he deviate from the line of duty?" asked Mauville, with increasing interest, and an eagerness his light manner did not disguise. "A sin of omission or commission?"

"Eh? What?" mumbled the old nobleman, staring at his questioner, and, on a sudden, becoming taciturn. "A family affair!" he added finally, with dignity. "Not worth repeating! But what was he doing there?"

"He had joined a strolling band of players," said the other, concealing his disappointment as best he might at his companion's evasive reply.

"A Saint-Prosper become an actor!" shouted the marquis, his anger again breaking forth. "Has he not already dragged an honored name in the dust? A stroller! A player!" The marquis fairly gasped at the enormity of the offense; for a moment he was speechless, and then asked feebly: "What caused him to take such a humiliating step?"

"He is playing the hero of a romance," said the land baron, moodily. "I confess he has excellent taste, though! The figure of a Juno--eyes like stars on an August night--features proud as Diana--the voice of a siren--in a word, picture to yourself your fairest conquest, Monsieur le Marquis, and you will have a worthy counterpart of this rose of the wilderness!"

"My fairest conquest!" piped the listener. With lack-luster eyes he remained motionless like a traveler in the desert who gazes upon a mirage. "You have described her well. The features of Diana! It was at a revival of Vanbrugh's 'Relapse' I first met her, dressed after the fashion of the Countess of Ossory. Who would not worship before the figures of Lely?"

He half closed his eyes, as though gazing in fancy upon the glossy draperies and rosy flesh of those voluptuous court beauties.

"The wooing, begun in the wings, ended in an ivy-covered villa--a retired nook--solitary walks by day--nightingales and moonshine by night. It was a pleasing romance while it lasted, but joy palls on one. Nature abhors sameness. The heart is like Mother Earth--ever varying. I wearied of this surfeit of Paradise and--left her!"

"A mere incident in an eventful life," said his companion, thoughtfully.

"Yes; only an incident!" repeated the marquis. "Only an incident! I had almost forgotten it, but your conversation about players and your description of the actress brought it to mind. It had quite passed away; it had quite passed away! But the cards, Monsieur Mauville; the cards!"

CHAPTER III:
AT THE RACES

For several days, after rehearsals were over, the strollers were free to amuse themselves as they pleased. Their engagement at the theater did not begin for about a week, and meanwhile they managed to combine recreation with labor in nearly equal proportions. Assiduously they devoted themselves to a round of drives and rambles: through pastures and wood-land to Carrolton; along the shell road to Lake Pontchartrain; to Biloxi, the first settlement of the French; and to the battle grounds, once known as the plains of Chalmette, where volunteer soldiers were now encamped, awaiting orders to go to the front in the Mexican campaign. For those who craved greater excitement, the three race-courses--the Louisiana, the Metairie and the Carrolton offered stimulating diversion.

Within sight of the Metairie were the old dueling grounds, under the oaks, where, it is related, on one Sunday in '39 ten duels occurred; where the contestants frequently fought on horseback with sabers; and, where the cowherds, says a chronicler, became so accustomed to seeing honor satisfied in this manner that they paid little attention to these meetings, pursuing their own humble duties, indifferent to the follies of fashionable society. The fencing schools flourished--what memories cluster around that odd, strange master of the blade, Spedella, a melancholy enigma of a man, whose art embodied much of the finest shading and phrasing peculiar to himself; from whom even many of Bonaparte's discarded veterans were not above acquiring new technique and temperament! Men in those days were most punctilious about reputation, but permitted a sufficiently wide latitude in its interpretation not to hamper themselves or seriously interfere with their desires or pleasures. Thus, virtue did not become a burden, nor honor a millstone. Both, like epaulets or tassels, were worn lightly and befittingly.

Shortly after the players' arrival began the celebrated Leduc matches, attracting noted men and women from all over the South. The hotels were crowded, the lodging-houses filled, while many of the large homes hospitably opened their doors to visiting friends. The afternoons found the city almost deserted; the bartenders discontentedly smoked in solitude; the legion of waiters in the hotels and resorts became reduced to a thinly scattered array; while even the street venders had "folded their tents" and silently stolen to the races. On one such memorable occasion most of the members of Barnes' company repaired to the Metairie.

Below the grand stand, brilliant with color, strutted the dandies attending to their bets; above they played a winning or losing game with the fair sex. Intrigue and love-making were the order of the hour, and these daughters of the South beguiled time--and mortals!-- in a heyday of pleasure. In that mixed gathering burly cotton planters from the country rubbed elbows with aristocratic creoles, whose attire was distinguishable by enormous ruffles and light boots of cloth. The professional follower of these events, the importunate tout, also mingled with the crowd, plainly in evidence by the pronounced character of his dress, the size of his diamond studs or cravat pin, and the massive dimensions of his finger rings. No paltry, scrubby track cadger was this resplendent gentleman, but a picturesque rogue, with impudence as pronounced as his jewels!

Surrounded by a bevy of admirers, Susan, sprightly and sparkling, was an example of that "frippery one of her sex is made up with, a pasticcio of gauzes, pins and ribbons that go to compound that multifarious thing, a well-dressed woman." Ever ready with a quick retort, she bestowed her favors generously, to the evident discomfiture of a young officer in her retinue whom she had met several days before, and who, ever since, had coveted a full harvest of smiles, liking not a little the first sample he had gathered. However, it was not Susan's way to entrust herself fully to any one; it was all very interesting to play one against another; to intercept angry gleams; to hold in check clashing suitors--this was exciting and diverting--but she exercised care not to transgress those bounds where she ceased to be mistress of the situation. Perhaps her limits in coquetry were further set than most women would have ventured to place them, but without this temerity and daring, the pastime would have lost its charm for her. She might play with edged tools, but she also knew how to use them.

Near her was seated Kate, indolent as of yore, now watching her sister with an indulgent, enigmatic expression, anon permitting a scornful glance to stray toward Adonis, who, for his part, had eyes only for his companion, a distinct change from country hoidens, tavern demoiselles and dainty wenches, with their rough hands and rosy cheeks. This lady's hands were like milk; her cheeks, ivory, and Adonis in bestowing his attentions upon her, had a two-fold purpose: to return tit for tat for Kate's flaunting ways, and to gratify his own ever-fleeting fancy.

In a box, half the length of the grand stand removed, some distance back and to the left of Susan's gay party, Constance, Mrs. Adams and the soldier were also observers of this scene of animation.

Since the manager's successful flight from the landlord and the constables, the relations of the young girl and Saint-Prosper had undergone little change. At first, it is true, with the memory of the wild ride to the river fresh in her mind, and the more or less disturbing recollections of that strange, dark night, a certain reticence had marked her manner toward the soldier; but, as time went by, this touch of reserve wore off, and was succeeded by her usual frankness or gaiety. In her eyes appeared, at times, a new thoughtfulness, but for no longer period than the quick passing of a summer cloud over a sunny meadow. This half-light of brief conjecture or vague retrospection only mellowed the depths of her gaze, and Barnes alone noted and wondered.

But to-day no partial shadows lay under the black, shading lashes; the exhilarating scene, the rapidly succeeding events, the turbulence and flutter around her, were calculated to dispel the most pronounced abstraction. Beneath a protecting parasol--for the sunlight shot below the roof at the back and touched that part of the grand stand--a faint glow warmed her cheeks, while her eyes shone with the gladness of the moment. Many of the dandies, regarding her with marked persistency, asked who she was, and none knew, until finally Editor-Rhymster Straws was appealed to. Straws, informed on all matters, was able to satisfy his questioners.

"She is an actress," said Straws. "So we are told. We shall find out next week. She is a beauty. We can tell that now."

"You're right, Straws!" exclaimed a pitch-and-toss youngster. "If she shows as well at the wire--"

"You'd take a long chance on her winning?" laughed the philosopher.

"I'll play you odds on it!" cried the juvenile. "Four to one, damme! I'll risk that on her eyes."

"Four to one on a lady's eyes, child! Say forty to one, and take the hazard of the die."

Standing near the rhymster, story-writer and journalist, was a tall young man, dressed in creole fashion. He followed the glances of Straws' questioners and a pallor overspread his dark complexion as he looked at the object of their attention.

"The stroller!" he exclaimed half audibly. "Her counterpart doesn't exist."

He stepped back where he could see her more plainly. In that sea of faces, her features alone shone before him, clearly, insistently.

"Do you know her, Mr. Mauville?" asked the rhymster, observing that steadfast glance.

"Know her?" repeated the land baron, starting. "Oh, I've seen her act."

"Tip me off her points and I'll tip my readers."

"She is going to play here then?" said the patroon.

"Yes. What is she like? Does tragedy or comedy favor her most? You see," he added apologetically, "when people begin to talk about anybody, we Grubstreet hacks thrive on the gossip. It is deplorable"--with regret--"but small talk and tattle bring more than a choice lyric or sonnet. And, heaven help us!"--shaking his head--"what a vendible article a fine scandal is! It sells fast, like goods at a Dutch auction. Penny a line? More nearly six pence! If I could only bring myself to deal in such merchandise! If I were only a good rag picker, instead of a bad poet!" And Straws walked away, forgetting the questions he had asked in his own more interesting cogitations.

Without definite purpose, the patroon, who had listened with scant attention to the poet, began to move slowly toward the actress, and at that moment, the eyes of the soldier, turning to the saddling paddock, where the horses were being led out, fell upon the figure drawing near, recognizing in him the heir to the manor, Edward Mauville. Construing in his approach a deliberate intention, a flush of quick anger overspread Saint-Prosper's face and he glanced at the girl by his side. But her manner assured him she had not observed the land baron, for at that moment she was looking in the opposite direction, endeavoring to discover Barnes or the others of the company in the immense throng.

Murmuring some excuse to his unconscious companion and cutting short the wiry old lady's reminiscences of the first public trotting race in 1818, the soldier left the box, and, moving with some difficulty through the crowd, met Mauville in the aisle near the stairway. The latter's face expressed surprise, not altogether of an agreeable nature, at the encounter, but he immediately regained his composure.

"Ah, Monsieur Saint-Prosper," he observed easily, "I little thought to see you here."

"Nor I you!" said the other bluntly.

The patroon gazed in seeming carelessness from the soldier to the young girl. Saint-Prosper's presence in New Orleans could be accounted for; he had followed her from the Shadengo Valley across the continent; the drive begun at the country inn--he looking down from the dormer window to witness the start--had been a long one; very different from his own brief flight, with its wretched end. These thoughts coursed rapidly through the land baron's brain; her appearance rekindled the ashes of the past; the fire in his breast flamed from his eyes, but otherwise he made no display of feeling. He glanced out upon the many faces below them, bowing to one woman and smiling at another.

"Oh, I couldn't stand a winter in the North," resumed the patroon, turning once more to the soldier. "Although the barn-burners promised to make it warm for me!"

Offering no reply to this sally, Saint-Prosper's gaze continued to rest coldly and expectantly upon the other. Goaded by that arbitrary regard, an implied barrier between him and the young girl, the land baron sought to press forward; his glittering eyes met the other's; the glances they exchanged were like the thrust and parry of swords. Without wishing to address the actress--and thereby risk a public rebuff--it was, nevertheless, impossible for the hot-blooded Southerner to submit to peremptory restraint. Who had made the soldier his taskmaster? He read Saint-Prosper's purpose and was not slow to retaliate.

"If I am not mistaken, yonder is our divinity of the lane," said the patroon softly. "Permit me." And he strove to pass.

The soldier did not move.

"You are blocking my way, Monsieur," continued the other, sharply.

"Not if it lies the other way."

"This way, or that way, how does it concern you?" retorted the land baron.

"If you seek further to annoy a lady whom you have already sufficiently wronged, it is any man's concern."

"Especially if he has followed her across the country," sneered Mauville. "Besides, since when have actresses become so chary of their favors?" In his anger the land baron threw out intimations he would have challenged from other lips. "Has the stage then become a holy convent?"

"You stamped yourself a scoundrel some time ago," said the soldier slowly, as though weighing each word, "and now show yourself a coward when you malign a young girl, without father, brother--"

"Or lover!" interrupted the land baron. "Perhaps, however, you were only traveling to see the country! A grand tour, enlivened with studies of human nature, as well as glimpses of scenery!"

"Have you anything further with me?" interjected Saint-Prosper, curtly.

The patroon's blood coursed, burning, through his veins; the other's contemptuous manner stung him more fiercely than language.

"Yes," he said, meaningly, his eyes challenging Saint-Prosper's. "Have you been at Spedella's fencing rooms? Are you in practice?"

Saint-Prosper hesitated a moment and the land baron's face fell. Was it possible the other would refuse to meet him? But he would not let him off easily; there were ways to force--and suddenly the words of the marquis recurring to him, he surveyed the soldier, disdainfully.

"Gad! you must come of a family of cowards and traitors! But you shall fight or--the public becomes arbiter!" And he half raised his arm threateningly.

The soldier's tanned cheek was now as pale as a moment before it had been flushed; his mouth set resolutely, as though fighting back some weakness. With lowering brows and darkening glance he regarded the land baron.

"I was thinking," he said at length, with an effort, "that if I killed you, people would want to know the reason."

The patroon laughed. "How solicitous you are for her welfare-- and mine! Do you then measure skill only by inches? If so, I confess you would stand a fair chance of despatching me. But your address? The St. Charles, I presume." The soldier nodded curtly, and, having accomplished his purpose, Mauville had turned to leave, when loud voices, in a front box near the right aisle, attracted general attention from those occupying that part of the grand stand. The young officer who had accompanied Susan to the races was angrily confronting a thick-set man, the latest recruit to her corps of willing captives. The lad had assumed the arduous task of guarding the object of his fancy from all comers, simply because she had been kind. And why should she not have been?--he was only a boy--she was old enough to be--well, an adviser! When, after a brief but pointed altercation, he flung himself away with a last reproachful look in the direction of his enslaver, Susan looked hurt. That was her reward for being nice to a child!

"A fractious young cub!" said the thick-set man, complacently.

"Well, I like cubs better than bears!" retorted Susan, pointedly.

Not long, however, could the interest of the spectators be diverted from the amusement of the day and soon all eyes were drawn once more to the track where the horses' hoofs resounded with exciting patter, as they struggled toward the wire, urged by the stimulating voices of the jockeys.

But even when Leduc won the race, beating the best heat on record; when the ladies in the grand stand arose in a body, like a thousand butterflies, disturbed by a sudden footfall in a sunlit field; when the jockey became the hero of the hour; when the small boys outside nearly fell from the trees in their exuberance of ecstasy, and the men threw their hats in the air and shouted themselves hoarse--even these exhilarating circumstances failed to reawaken the land baron's concern in the scene around him. His efforts at indifference were chafing his inmost being; the cloak of insouciance was stifling him; the primeval man was struggling for expression, that brute-like rage whose only limits are its own fury and violence.

A quavering voice, near at hand, recalled him to himself, and turning, he beheld the marquis approaching with mincing manner, the paint and pigments cracked by the artificial smiles wreathing his wrinkled face. In that vast assemblage, amid all the energy, youth and surfeit of vitality, he seemed like a dried and crackling leaf, tossed helplessly, which any foot might crush to dust. The roar of the multitude subsided, a storm dying in the distance; the ladies sank in their seats--butterflies settling once more in the fields--and Leduc, with drooping head, was led to the paddock, followed by a few fair adorers.

"I placed the winner, Monsieur Mauville," piped the marquis. "Though the doctors told me the excitement would kill me! What folly! Every new sensation adds a day to life."

"In your case, certainly, Marquis, for I never saw you looking younger," answered the land baron, with an effort.

"You are too amiable, my dear friend! The ladies would not think so," he added, mournfully wagging his head with anile melancholy.

"Nonsense!" protested the other. "With your spirit, animation--"

"If I thought you were right," interrupted the delighted marquis, taking his young friend's arm, "I would ask you to present me to the lady over there--the one you just bowed to."

"The deuce!" said Mauville to himself. "The marquis is becoming a bore."

"You rascal! I saw the smile she gave you," continued the other playfully. "And you ran away from her. What are the young men made of nowadays? In the old days they were tinder; women sparks. But who is she?"

"You mean Susan Duran, the actress?"

"An actress!" exclaimed the nobleman. "A charming creature at any rate!"

"All froth; a bubble!" added Mauville impatiently.

"How entertaining! Any lovers?" leered the nobleman.

"A dozen; a baker's dozen, for all I know!"

"What is her history?" said the marquis eagerly.

"I never inquired."

"Sometimes it's just as well," murmured the other vaguely. "How old is she?"

"How can you tell?" answered Mauville.

"In Paris I kept a little book wherein was entered the passe-parole of every pretty woman; age; lovers platonic! When a woman became a grandmother, I put a black mark against her name, for I have always held," continued the nobleman, wagging his head, "that a woman who is a grandmother has no business to deceive a younger generation of men. But present me to Miss Susan at once, my dear friend. I am all impatience to meet her."

His eagerness permitted no refusal; besides, Mauville was not in the mood to enjoy the nobleman's society, and was but too pleased to turn him over to the tender care of Susan.

"How do you do, Miss Duran," he said, having made his way to her box.

"Where did you drop from?" she asked, in surprise, giving him her hand.

"The skies," he returned, with forced lightness.

"A fallen angel!" commented Susan.

"Good! Charming!" cried the marquis, clapping his withered hands.

"Miss Duran, the Marquis de Ligne has requested the pleasure of meeting you."

She flashed a smile at him. He bent over her hand; held it a moment in his icy grasp.

"The pleasure," said Susan, prettily, not shirking the ordeal, "is mine."

"In which case," added Mauville, half ironically, "I will leave you together to enjoy your happiness."

Eagerly availing himself of the place offered at her side, soon the marquis was cackling after the manner of a senile beau of the old school; relating spicy anecdotes of dames who had long departed this realm of scandal; and mingling witticism and wickedness in one continual flow, until like a panorama another age was revived in his words--an age when bedizened women wore patches and their perfumed gallants wrote verses on the demise of their lap-dogs; when "their virtue resembled a statesman's religion, the Quaker's word, the gamester's oath and the great man's honor--but to cheat those that trusted them!"

The day's events, however, were soon over; the city of pleasure finally capitulated; its people began rapidly to depart. That sudden movement resembled the migration of a swarm of bees to form a new colony, when, if the day be bright, the expedition issues forth with wondrous rapidity. So this human hive commenced to empty itself of queens, drones and workers. It was an outgoing wave of such life and animation as is apparent in the flight of a swarm of cell-dwellers, giving out a loud and sharp-toned hum from the action of their wings as they soar over the blooming heather and the "bright consummate flowers." And these human bees had their passions, too! their massacres; their tragedies; their "Rival Queens"; their combats; their sentinels; their dreams of that Utopian form of government realized in the communistic society of insects.

"How did you enjoy it, my dear?" asked Barnes, suddenly reappearing at Constance's box. "A grand heat, that! Though I did bet on the wrong horse! But don't wait for us, Saint-Prosper. Mrs. Adams and I will take our time getting through the crowd. I will see you at the hotel, my dear!" he added, as the soldier and Constance moved away.

Only the merry home-going remained, and the culmination, a dinner at Moreau's, Victor's, or Miguel's, the natural epilogue to the day's pastime, the tag to the comedy! In the returning throng were creoles with sky-blue costumes and palmetto hats; the Lafourche or Attakapas planter; representatives of the older régime and the varied newer populace. Superb equipages mingled in democratic confusion with carts and wagons; the broken-winded nag and spavined crowbait--veterans at the bugle call!--pricked up their ears and kicked up their heels like colts in pasture, while the delighted darkies thumped their bony shanks to encourage this brief rejuvenescence.

Those who had lost felt the money well spent; those who had won would be the more lavish in the spending. They had simply won a few more pleasures. "Quick come; quick go!" sang the whirling wheels. "The niggard in pound and pence is a usurer in happiness; a miser driving a hard bargain with pleasure. Better burn the candle at both ends than not burn it at all! In one case, you get light; in the other nothing but darkness. Laughter is cheap at any price. A castle in the air is almost as durable as Solomon's temple. How soon--how soon both fade away!"

Thus ran the song of the wheels before them and behind them, as the soldier and Constance joined the desultory fag-end of the procession. On either side of the road waved the mournful cypress, draped by the hoary tillandsia, and from the somber depths of foliage came the chirp of the tree-crickets and the note of the swamp owl. Faint music, in measured rhythm, a foil to disconnected wood-sound, was wafted from a distant plantation.

"Wait!" said Constance.

He drew in the horses and silently they listened. Or, was he listening? His glance seemed bent so moodily--almost!--on space she concluded he was not. She stole a sidelong look at him.

"A penny for your thoughts!" she said gaily.

He started. "I was thinking how soon I might leave New Orleans."

"Leave New Orleans!" she repeated in surprise. "But I thought you intended staying here. Why have you changed your mind?"

Did he detect a subtle accent of regret in her voice? A deep flush mounted to his brow. He bent over her suddenly, eagerly.

"Would it matter--if I went?"

She drew back at the abruptness of his words.

"How unfair to answer one question with another!" she said lightly.

A pause fell between them. Perhaps she, too, felt the sudden repulse of her own answer and the ensuing constraint. Perhaps some compunction moved her to add in a voice not entirely steady:

"And so you think--of going back to France?"

"To France!" he repeated, quickly. "No"--and stopped.

Looking up, a half-questioning light in her eyes took flight to his, until suddenly arrested by the hard, set expression of his features. Abruptly chilled by she knew not what, her lashes fell. The horses champed their bits and tugged at the reins, impatient of the prolonged pause.

"Let us go!" she said in a low, constrained voice.

At her words he turned, the harshness dropping from his face like a discarded mask; the lines of determination wavering.

"Let us go!" she said again, without looking up.

He made no motion to obey, until the sound of a vehicle behind them seemed to break the spell and mechanically he touched the horses with the whip.

CHAPTER IV:

LEAR AND JULIET

S usan dismissed her admirers at the races with some difficulty, especially the tenacious marquis, who tenderly squeezed her hand, saying:

"Were I twenty years younger, I would not thus be set aside."

"Fie, Marquis!" she returned. "These other people are dull, while you are charmingly wicked."

"You flatter me," he cackled, detaining her, to the impatience of the thick-set man who was waiting to escort the young woman back to town. "But do you notice the gentleman over there with the medals?"

"The distinguished-looking man?" asked Susan.

"Yes; that is the Count de Propriac. It was he who was one of the agents of Louis Philippe in the Spanish double marriage plot. It was arranged the queen should marry her cousin, and her sister the son of Louis Philippe. The queen and her cousin were not expected to have children--but had them, to spite us all, and Louis Philippe's projects for the throne of Spain failed disastrously."

"How inconsiderate of the queen! Good afternoon, marquis! I have been vastly entertained."

"And I"--kissing her hand--"enamored!" Then, chuckling: "A week ago my stupid doctors had me laid out in funereal dignity, and now I am making love to a fine woman. Pretty pouting lips!"--tapping her chin playfully--"Like rose-buds! Happy the lover who shall gather the dew! But we meet again, Mistress Susan?"

"That will depend upon you, marquis," answered Susan, coquettishly, as a thought flashed through her mind that it would not be unpleasant to be called "Marquise," or "Marchioness"--she did not quite know which would be the proper title. It was nearly vesper-time with the old nobleman; he seemed but a procrastinating presence in the evening of mortal life; a chateau and carriage--

"Then we will meet again," said the marquis, interrupting these new-born ambitions.

"In that case you would soon get tired of me," laughed Susan.

"Never!" Tenderly. "When may I see you?"

"How importunate you are! Call when you will."

"But if you are out"--he insisted.

"That will make it the more delightfully uncertain," she said gaily.

"So it will!" Rubbing his hands. "Delightfully uncertain!" he repeated. And he departed with many protestations, taking no more notice of the thick-set man than if he were a block of wood.

"What an old ape!" growled the latter, viciously, as the marquis ambled from their stall.

"Do you think so?" answered Susan, tossing her head. "He has that air of distinction which only persons of rank and title can command."

"Distinction!" said the other, who was but a well-to-do merchant. "I should call it bad manners."

"Because he never noticed you!" laughed Susan, spitefully. "But why are we standing here? I believe you expect to take me home, don't you?"

Although she chattered like a magpie on the road, he was silent and sullen, nursing his injured pride and wounded self-sufficiency. Susan, who was interested in him for the novel reason she disliked him so heartily, parted from him with the air of a duchess, and entered the hotel, holding her head so high that he swore under his breath as he drove away. And, as a result of the quarrel with the lad, he would probably have to risk being "pinked" for this jade! Susan, on the other hand, was as happy as a lark when she entered the dining-room of the St. Charles, that great eating-place and meeting-place of all classes of people.

As she seated herself at a table, a smile lurked around the corners of her mouth and flickered faintly upon the waiter who forthwith became a Mercury for expedition and a prodigal for variety. Her quarrel on the road with her companion had in nowise interfered with that appetite which the fresh air and the lateness of the hour had provoked, nor were her thoughts of a character to deter from the zest of eating.

From the present to the past was but an instant's flight of the mind--thus may the once august years swiftly and unceremoniously be marshaled by!--and she dwelt in not unpleasing retrospection on an endless field of investigation and discovery and the various experiences which had befallen her in arriving at the present period of mature knowledge; a proficiency which converted her chosen researches into an exact science.

Thus meditating and dining--counting on her fingers twice over the fair actresses who had become titled ladies, and enviously disbelieving she would join that triumphant company--Susan was still seated at the table some time later when the soldier glanced in. Imperatively she motioned him to her side and he obeyed with not entirely concealed reluctance, and was so preoccupied, she rallied him upon his reserve.

"I believe you and Constance had a quarrel on the road." Maliciously. "I hope you were more amiable than my companion. He hardly spoke a word, and, when I left him"--her voice sank to a whisper--"I heard him swear."

"He pleased you so much earlier in the day that a duel will probably be the outcome."

Susan laughed gaily.

"A duel! Then my fortune is made. All the newspapers will contain paragraphs. It is too good to be true." And she clapped her hands. "When is it to take place? Tell me about it!"

Then noting his manner, she continued with an assumption of plaintiveness: "Now you are cross with me! You think me heartless. Is it my fault? I care nothing for either of them and I am not to be blamed if they are so foolish. It might be different if either had touched my heart." And she assumed a coquettish demeanor, while Saint-Prosper coolly studied her through the wreaths of smoke from his weed.

"You are wondering what sort of a person I am!" she continued, merrily, raising her glass of wine with: "To unrequited passion!"

Her roguish face sparkled as he asked; "Whose?"

She drained the glass and set it down demurely. "Mine!"

The cigar was suspended; the veil cleared between them.

"For whom?" he said.

"You!" Offering him the limpid depths of her blue eyes. "Is my liking returned?"

"Liking? Perhaps!"

"My love?"

"Love? No." Coldly.

"You do not fear a woman scorned?" Her lips curved in a smile, displaying her faultless teeth.

"Not when the avenging angel is so charming and so heartless!" he added satirically.

Her lashes veiled the azure orbs.

"You think to disarm her with a compliment? How well you understand women!" And, as he rose, the pressure of the hand she gave him at parting was lingering.

* * * * *

Above in his room, Barnes, with plays and manuscripts scattered around him, was engaged in writing in his note and date book, wherein autobiography, ledger and journal accounts, and such miscellaneous matter mingled indiscriminately. "To-day she said to me: 'I am going to the races with Mr. Saint-Prosper.' What did I say? 'Yes,' of course. What can there be in common between Lear and Juliet? Naturally, she sometimes turns from an old fellow like me--now, if she were only a slip of a girl again--with her short frock--her disorder of long ringlets--running and romping--

"A thousand details pass through my mind, reminiscences of her girlhood, lightening a lonesome life like glimmerings of sunshine in a secluded wood; memories of her mother and the old days when she played in my New York theater--for Barnes, the stroller, was once a metropolitan manager! Her fame had preceded her and every admirer of histrionic art eagerly awaited her arrival.

"But the temple of art is a lottery. The town that had welcomed her so wildly now went Elssler-mad. The gossamer floatings of this French danseuse possessed everyone. People courted trash and trumpery. Greatness gave way to triviality. This pitiful condition preyed upon her. The flame of genius never for a moment became less dim, but her eyes grew larger, brighter, more melancholy. Sometimes she would fall into a painful reverie and I knew too well the subject of her thoughts. With tender solicitude she would regard her daughter, thinking, thinking! She was her only hope, her only joy!

"'The town wants dancers, not tragedians, Mr. Barnes,' she said sadly one day.

"'Nonsense,' I replied. 'The town wants a change of bill. We will put on a new piece next week.'

"'It will be but substituting one tragedy for another,' she retorted. 'One misfortune for a different one! You should import a rival dancer. You are going down; down hill! I will leave you; perhaps you will discover your dancer, and your fortune is made!'

"'And you? What would you do?' I demanded. 'And your child?'

"At this her eyes filled and she could not answer. 'And now, Madam,' I said firmly, 'I refuse once and for all to permit you to break your contract. Pooh! The tide will change. Men and women are sometimes fools; but they are not fools all the time. The dancer will have had her day. She will twirl her toes to the empty seats and throw her kisses into unresponsive space. Our patrons will gradually return; they will grow tired of wriggling and twisting, and look again for a more substantial diet.'

"Matters did, indeed, begin to mend somewhat, when to bring the whole fabric tumbling down on our heads, this incomparable woman fell ill.

"'You see? I have ruined you,' she said sadly.

"'I am honored, Madam,' was all I could reply.

"She placed her hand softly on mine and let her luminous eyes rest on me.

"'Dear old friend!' she murmured.

"Then she closed her eyes and I thought she was sleeping. Some time elapsed when she again opened them.

"'Death will break our contract, Mr. Barnes,' she said softly.

"I suppose my hand trembled, for she tightened her grasp and continued firmly: 'It is not so terrible, after all, or would not be, but for one thing.'

"'You will soon get well, Madam,' I managed to stammer.

"'No! Do you care? It is pleasant to have one true, kind friend in the world; one who makes a woman believe again in the nobility of human nature. My life has been sad as you know. I should not regret giving it up. Nor should I fear to die. I can not think that God will be unkind to one who has done her best; at least, has tried to. Yet there is one thing that makes me crave for life. My child--what will she do-- poor, motherless, fatherless girl--all alone, all alone--.

"'Madam, if I may--will you permit me to care for her? If I might regard her as my child!'

"How tightly she held my hand at that! Her eyes seemed to blaze with heavenly fire. But let me not dwell further upon the sad events that led to the end of her noble career. Something of her life I had heard; something, I surmised. Unhappy as a woman, she was majestic as an actress; the fire of her voice struck every ear; its sweetness had a charm, never to be forgotten. But only to those who knew her well were revealed the unvarying truth and simplicity of her nature. Even as I write, her spirit, tender and steadfast, seems standing by my side; I feel her eyes in the darkness of night, and, when the time comes--and often of late, it has seemed not far--to go from this mere dressing-room, the earth, into the higher life--"

A knock at the door rudely dispelled these memories. For a moment the manager looked startled, as one abruptly called back to his immediate surroundings; then the pen fell from his hand, and he pushed the book from him to the center of the table.

"Come in," he said.

The door opened and Saint-Prosper entered.

"Am I interrupting you?" asked the soldier, glancing at the littered table.

"Not at all," answered the manager, recovering himself, and settling back in his chair. "Make yourself at home. You'll find some cigars on the mantel, or if you prefer your pipe, there's a jar of tobacco on the trunk. Do you find it? I haven't had time yet to bring order out of chaos. A manager's trunks are like a junk-shop, with everything from a needle to an anchor."

Filling his pipe from the receptacle indicated, which lay among old costumes and wigs, the soldier seated himself near an open window that looked out upon a balcony. Through a door at the far end of the balcony a light streamed from a chandelier within, playing upon the balustrade. Once the figure of the young actress stepped for a moment out upon the balcony; she leaned upon the balustrade, looked across the city, breathed the perfume of the flowers, and then quickly vanished.

"Can you spare me a little time to-morrow morning--early--before rehearsal?" said Saint-Prosper, finally.

"Yes," returned the manager, in surprise. "What is it?"

"A foolish piece of business! The patroon is in New Orleans."

Barnes uttered an exclamation of annoyance and apprehension. "Here! What is he doing here?" he said. "I thought we had seen the last of him. Has he followed--Constance?"

"I don't know. We met yesterday at the races."

"It is strange she did not tell me about it," remarked the manager, without endeavoring to conceal the anxiety this unexpected information afforded him.

"She does not know he is here." And Saint-Prosper briefly related the circumstances of his meeting with the land baron, to which the manager listened attentively.

"And so she must be dragged into it?" exclaimed Barnes at length, resentfully. "Her name must become public property in a broil?"

A frown darkened the soldier's face, but he replied quickly: "Need any one know? The land baron has not been seen with her."

"No; but you have," returned the manager, suddenly pausing and looking down at the other.

The silence between them lasted for some moments. Barnes stood with his hands in his pockets, his face downcast and moody. He felt that events were happening over which he had no control, but which were shaping the destiny of all he loved best. In the dim light the rugged lines of his countenance were strongly, decisively outlined. Turning to the trunk, with a quick, nervous step, he filled a pipe himself. After he had lighted it, he once more contemplated the soldier, thinking deeply, reviewing the past.

"We have been together for some time, Mr. Saint-Prosper," he said, at length. "We have gone through fair and rough weather, and"-

-he paused a moment before continuing--"should understand each other. You asked me when you came in if you were interrupting me, and I told you that you were not. As a matter of fact, you were."

And, walking to a table, Barnes took up the notebook.

"A garrulous, single man must tell his little secrets somewhere," he continued. "Will you look at the pages I was writing when you came in?"

Saint-Prosper took the book, and, while he was turning the leaves that were hardly dry, the manager relighted his pipe, over which he glanced nervously from time to time at his companion. Finally, when the soldier had finished the perusal of the diary, Barnes turned to him expectantly, but the other silently laid down the little volume, and, after waiting some moments for him to speak, the manager, as though disappointed by his reticence, breathed a sigh. Then, clearing his throat, in a voice somewhat husky, he went on, simply:

"You will understand now why she is so much to me. I have always wanted to keep her from the world as much as possible; to have her world, her art! I have tried to keep the shadow of the past from her. An actress has a pretty face; and there's a hue and cry! It is not notoriety she seeks, but fame; fame, bright and pure as sunlight!"

"The land baron will not cry abroad the cause of the meeting," said the soldier, gravely. "These fashionable affairs need but flimsy pretexts."

"Flimsy pretexts!" cried Barnes. "A woman's reputation--her good name--"

"Hush!" said Saint-Prosper.

From the door at the far end of the balcony Constance had again emerged and now approached their room. A flowing gown of an early period surrounded her like a cloud as she paused before Barnes' apartment. At the throat a deep-falling collar was closely fastened; the sleeves were gathered in at elbow and wrist, and from a "coverchief," set upon the dusky hair, fell a long veil of ample proportions. With the light shimmering on the folds of her raiment, she stood looking through the open door, regarding the manager and Saint-Prosper.

"Oh, you are not alone?" she said to the former. "You look as though you were talking together very seriously?" she added, turning to Saint-Prosper.

"Nothing of consequence, Miss Carew!" he replied, flushing beneath her clear eyes.

"Only about some scenery!" interposed the manager, so hastily that she glanced, slightly surprised, from the one to the other. "Some sets that are--"

"'Flimsy pretexts!' I caught that much! I only wanted to ask you about this costume. Is it appropriate, do you think, for the part we were talking about?" Turning around slowly, with arms half-raised.

"Charming, my dear; charming!" he answered, enthusiastically.

"If I only thought that an unbiased criticism!" Her dark lashes lowered; she looked toward the soldier, half shyly, half mockingly. "What do you think, Mr. Saint-Prosper?"

At that moment her girlish grace was irresistible.

"I think it is not only appropriate, but"--looking at her and not at the costume--"beautiful!"

A gleam like laughter came into her eyes; nor did she shun his kindling gaze.

"Thank you!" she said, and courtesied low.

* * * * *

That same evening Spedella's fencing rooms were fairly thronged with devotees of the ancient art of puncturing. The master of the place was a tall Italian, lank and lean, all bone and muscle, with a Don Quixote visage, barring a certain villainous expression of the eyes, irreconcilable with the chivalrous knight-errant of distressed Dulcineas. But every man with a bad eye is not necessarily a rascallion, and Spedella, perhaps, was better than he looked. With a most melancholy glance he was now watching two combatants, novices in feats of arms. Dejection sat upon his brow; he yawned over a clumsy feinte seconde, when his sinister eyes fell on a figure that had just entered the hall. Immediately his melancholy vanished, and he advanced to meet the newcomer with stately cordiality.

"Well met, Mr. Mauville," he exclaimed, extending a bony hand that had fingers like the grip of death. "What good fortune brought you here?"

"An ill wind, Spedella, rather!"

"It's like a breath of the old days to see you; the old days before you began your wanderings!"

"Get the foils, Spedella; I'll have a bout with the master. Gad, you're as ill-looking as ever! It's some time since I've touched a foil. I want to test myself. I have a little affair to-morrow. Hark you, my old brigand; I wish to see if I can kill him!"

"A lad of spirit!" chuckled the master, a gleam of interest illumining his cavernous eyes. "Young!--frisky!--an affair of honor to-day is but nursery sport. Two children with tin swords are more diverting. The world goes backward! A counter-jumper thinks he can lunge, because he is spry, that he can touch a button because he sells them. And I am wasting my genius with ribbon-venders--"

"I see the wolf growls as much as ever!" said the patroon. "Here's a quiet corner. Come; tell me what I've forgotten."

"Good!" returned the other. "You can tell me about your travels as we fence."

"Hang my travels!" replied the patroon, as they leisurely engaged. "They've brought me nothing but regrets."

"Feinte flanconnade--well done!" murmured Spedella. "So it was not honey you brought home from your rambles? Feinte seconde and decisive tierce! It's long since I've touched a good blade. These glove-sellers and perfume-dealers--"

"You are bitter against trade, my bravo," remarked the land baron.

"I was spoiling with languor when you came. Not bad, that feint--but dangerous, because of the possibility of misjudging the attack. Learn the paroles he affects to-morrow by quick, simple thrusts, and then you will know what feints to attack him with. Time in octave--you quitted the blade in a dangerous position. Cluck; cluck, my game cock! Intemperance has befogged your judgment; high-living has dimmed your--"

"You have it!" laughed the land baron.

The button of his foil touched the old bravo's breast; the steel was bent like a bow.

Spedella forgot his English and swore in soft and liquid Italian. "I looked around to see how those ribbon-venders were getting on," he said after this euphonious, foreign prelude. "They pay me; I have to keep an eye on them. All the same," he added, generously, "there isn't another man in New Orleans could have stopped that stroke--except myself!"

"Will I do--for to-morrow?" asked the patroon, moodily.

The master cocked his head quizzically; his deep-set eyes were soft and friendly.

"The devil's with him, if you don't put your spur in him, my bantam!"

CHAPTER V:

THE MEETING BENEATH THE OAKS

The mist was lifting from the earth and nature lay wrapped in the rosy peace of daybreak as the sun's shafts of gold pierced the foliage, illumining the historic ground of the Oaks. Like shining lances, they gleamed from the interstices in the leafy roof to the dew-bejeweled sward. From this stronghold of glistening arms, however, the surrounding country stretched tranquil and serene. Upon a neighboring bank sheep were browsing; in the distance cow-bells tinkled, and the drowsy cowherds followed the cattle, faithful as the shepherds who tended their flocks on the Judean hills.

Beneath the spreading trees were assembled a group of persons variously disposed. A little dapper man was bending over a case of instruments, as merry a soul as ever adjusted a ligature or sewed a wound. Be-ribboned and be-medaled, the Count de Propriac, acting for the land baron, and Barnes, who had accompanied the soldier, were consulting over the weapons, a magnificent pair of rapiers with costly steel guards, set with initials and a coronet. Member of an ancient society of France which yet sought to perpetuate the memory of the old judicial combat and the more modern duel, the count was one of those persons who think they are in honor bound to bear a challenge, without questioning the cause, or asking the "color of a reason."

"A superb pair of weapons, count!" observed the doctor, rising.

"Yes," said the person addressed, holding the blade so that the sunlight ran along the steel; "the same Jacques Legres and I fought with!"

Here the count smiled in a melancholy manner, which left no doubt regarding the fate of the hapless Jacques. But after a moment he supplemented this indubitable assurance by adding specifically:

"The left artery of the left lung!"

"Bless my soul!" commented the medical man. "But what is this head in gold beneath the guard?"

"Saint Michael, the patron saint of duelists!" answered the count.

"Patron!" exclaimed the doctor. "Well, all I have to say is, it is a saintless business for Michael."

The count laughed and turned away with a business-like air.

"Are you ready, gentlemen?"

At his words the contestants immediately took their positions. The land baron, lithe and supple, presented a picture of insolent and conscious pride, his glance lighted by disdain, but smoldering with fiercer passions as he examined and tested his blade.

"Engage!" exclaimed the count.

With ill-concealed eagerness, Mauville began a vigorous, although guarded attack, as if asserting his supremacy, and at the same time testing his man. The buzzing switch of the steel became angrier; the weapons glinted and gleamed, intertwining silently and separating with a swish. The patroon's features glowed; his movements became quicker, and, executing a rapid parry, he lunged with a thrust so stealthy his blade was beaten down only as it touched the soldier's breast.

Mauville smiled, but Barnes groaned inwardly, feeling his courage and confidence fast oozing from him. Neither he nor the other spectators doubted the result. Strength would count but little against such agility; the land baron was an incomparable swordsman.

"Gad!" muttered the count to himself. "It promises to be short and sweet."

As if to demonstrate the verity of this assertion, Mauville suddenly followed his momentary advantage with a dangerous lunge from below. Involuntarily Barnes looked away, but his wandering attention was immediately recalled. From the lips of the land baron burst an exclamation of mingled pain and anger. Saint-Prosper had not only parried the thrust, but his own blade, by a rapid riposte, had grazed the shoulder of his foe.

Nor was the manager's surprise greater than that of the count. The latter, amazed this unusual strategem should have failed when directed by a wrist as trained and an eye as quick as Mauville's, now interposed.

"Enough!" he exclaimed, separating the contestants. "Demme! it was superb. Honor has been satisfied."

"It is nothing!" cried the land baron, fiercely. "His blade hardly touched me." In his exasperation and disappointment over his failure, Mauville was scarcely conscious of his wound. "I tell you it is nothing," he repeated.

"What do you say, Mr. Saint-Prosper?" asked the count.

"I am satisfied," returned the young man, coldly.

"But I'm not!" reiterated the patroon, restraining himself with difficulty. "It was understood we should continue until both were willing to stop!"

"No," interrupted the count, suavely; "it was understood you should continue, if both were willing!"

"And you're not!" exclaimed the land baron, wheeling on Saint-Prosper. "Did you leave the army because--"

"Gentlemen, gentlemen! let us observe the proprieties!" expostulated the count. "Is it your intention, sir"--to Saint-Prosper--"not to grant my principal's request?"

A fierce new anger gleamed from the soldier's eyes, completely transforming his expression and bearing. His glance quickly swept from the count to Mauville at the studied insult of the latter's words; on his cheek burned a dark red spot.

"Let it go on!"

The count stepped nimbly from his position between the two men. Again the swords crossed. The count's glance bent itself more closely on the figure of the soldier; noting now how superbly poised was his body; what reserves of strength were suggested by the white, muscular arm! His wrist moved like a machine, lightly brushing aside the thrusts. Had it been but accident that Mauville's unlooked-for expedient had failed?

"The devil!" thought the count, watching the soldier. "Here is a fellow who has deceived us all."

But the land baron's zest only appeared to grow in proportion to the resistance he encountered; the lust for fighting increased with the music of the blades. For some moments he feinted and lunged, seeking an opening, however slight. Again he appeared bent upon forcing a quick conclusion, for suddenly with a rush he sought to break over Saint-Prosper's guard, and succeeded in wounding the other slightly in the forehead. Now sure of his man, Mauville sprang at him savagely.

But dashing the blood from his eyes with his free hand, and without giving way, Saint-Prosper met the assault with a wrist of iron, and the land baron failed to profit by what had seemed a certain advantage. The wound had the effect of making the soldier more cautious, and eye, foot and hand were equally true. Mauville was breathing heavily from his exertions, but the appearance of both men, the supple movements of the one contrasting with the perfect precision of the other, would have delighted those members of the count's society, who regarded these matches as leading to a renaissance of chivalry.

In his fury that his chance had slipped away, after wounding, and, as he supposed, blinding his opponent, Mauville, throwing prudence to the winds, recklessly attempted to repeat his rash expedient, and this time the steel of his antagonist gleamed like quicksilver, passing beneath his arm and inflicting a slight flesh wound. Something resembling a look of apprehension crossed the land baron's face. "I have underestimated him!" he thought. "The next stroke will be driven nearer home."

He felt no fear, however; only mute, helpless rage. In the soldier's hand the dainty weapon was a thing of marvelous cunning; his vastly superior strength made him practically tireless in this play. Not only tireless; he suddenly accelerated the tempo of the exercise, but behind this unexpected, even passionate, awakening, the spectators felt an unvarying accuracy, a steely coldness of purpose. The blades clicked faster; they met and parted more viciously; the hard light in Saint-Prosper's eyes grew brighter as he slowly thrust back his antagonist.

Mauville became aware his own vigor was slowly failing him; instead of pressing the other he was now obliged to defend himself. He strove to throw off the lethargy irresistibly stealing over him; to shake the leaden movements from his limbs. He vainly endeavored to penetrate the mist falling before his eyes and to overcome the dizziness that made his foeman seem like a figure in a dream. Was it through loss of blood, or weariness, or both?--but he was cognizant his thrusts had lost force, his plunges vitality, and that even an element of chance prevailed in his parries. But he uttered no sound. When would that mist become dark, and the golden day fuse into inky night?

Before the mist totally eclipsed his sight he determined to make one more supreme effort, and again sprang forward, but was driven back with ease. The knowledge that he was continuing a futile struggle smote him to the soul. Gladly would he have welcomed the fatal thrust, if first he could have sent his blade through that breast which so far had been impervious to his efforts. Now the scene went round and round; the golden day became crimson, scarlet; then gray, leaden, somber. Incautiously he bent his arm to counter an imaginary lunge, and his antagonist thrust out his rapier like a thing of life, transfixing Mauville's sword arm. He stood his ground bravely for a moment, playing feebly into space, expecting the fatal stroke! When would it come? Then the slate-colored hues were swallowed in a black cloud. But while his mind passed into unconsciousness, his breast was openly presented to his antagonist, and even the count shuddered.

With his blade at guard, Saint-Prosper remained motionless; the land baron staggered feebly and then sank softly to the earth. That fatal look, the expression of a duelist, vanished from the soldier's face, and, allowing the point of his weapon to drop to the ground, he surveyed his prostrate antagonist.

"Done like a gentleman!" cried the count, breathing more freely. "You had him at your mercy, sir"--to Saint-Prosper--"and spared him."

A cold glance was the soldier's only response, as without a word he turned brusquely away. Meanwhile the doctor, hastening to Mauville's side, opened his shirt.

"He is badly hurt?" asked Barnes, anxiously, of the surgeon.

"No; only fainted from loss of blood," replied that gentleman, cheerfully. "He will be around again in a day or two."

The count put away his blades as carefully as a mother would deposit her babe in the cradle.

"Another page of history, my chicks!" he observed. "Worthy of the song of Pindar!"

"Why not Straws or Phazma?" queried the surgeon, looking up from his task.

"Would you have the press take up the affair? There are already people who talk of abolishing dueling. When they do they will abolish reputation with it. And what's a gentleman got but his honor--demme!" And the royal emissary carefully brushed a crimson stain from the bespattered saint.

By this time the land baron had regained consciousness, and, his wounds temporarily bandaged, walked, with the assistance of the count, to his carriage. As they were about to drive away the sound of a vehicle was heard drawing near, and soon it appeared followed by another equipage. Both stopped at the confines of the Oaks and the friends of the thick-set man--Susan's admirer--and the young lad, on whom she had smiled, alighted.

"Ha!" exclaimed the doctor, who had accompanied the count and his companion to the carriage. "Number two!"

"Yes," laughed the count, as he leaned back against the soft cushions, "it promises to be a busy day at the Oaks! Really"--as the equipage rolled on--"New Orleans is fast becoming a civilized center--demme!"

CHAPTER VI:
A BLOT IN THE 'SCUTCHEON

The land baron's injuries did not long keep him indoors, for it was his pride rather than his body that had received deep and bitter wounds. He chafed and fumed when he thought how, in all likelihood, the details of his defeat could not be suppressed in the clubs and cafés. This anticipated publicity he took in ill part, fanning his mental disorder with brandy, mellow and insidious with age. But beneath the dregs of indulgence lay an image which preyed upon his mind more than his defeat beneath the Oaks: a figure, on the crude stage of a country tavern; in the manor window, with an aureole around her from the sinking sun; in the grand stand at the races, the gay dandies singling her out in all that seraglio of beauty.

"I played him too freely," he groaned to the Count de Propriac, as the latter sat contemplatively nursing the ivory handle of his cane and offering the land baron such poor solace as his company afforded. "I misjudged the attack, besides exposing myself too much. If I could only meet him again!"

The visitor reflectively took the handle of the stick from his lips, thrust out his legs and yawned. The count was sleepy, having drowned dull care the night before, and had little sympathy with such spirited talk so early in the day. His lack-luster gaze wandered to the pictures on the wall, the duel between two court ladies for the possession of the Duc de Richelieu and an old print of the deadly public contest of François de Vivonne and Guy de Jarnac and then strayed languidly to the other paraphernalia of a high-spirited bachelor's rooms--foils, dueling pistols and masks--trappings that but served to recall to the land baron his defeat.

"It would be like running against a stone wall," said the count, finally; "demme if it wouldn't! He could have killed you!"

"Why didn't he do it, then?" demanded the land baron, fiercely.

The count shrugged his shoulders, drank his brandy, and handed the bottle to his companion, who helped himself, as though not averse to that sort of medicine for his physical and mental ailments.

"What's the news?" he asked abruptly, sinking back on his pillow.

"The levees are flooded."

"Hanged if I care if it's another deluge!" said Mauville. "I mean news of the town, not news of the river."

"There's a new beauty come to town--a brunette; all the bloods are talking about her. Where did she come from? Who is she? These are some of the questions asked. But she's a Peri, at any rate! shy, hard to get acquainted with--at first! An actress--Miss Carew!"

The glass trembled in the patroon's hand. "Do you know her?" he asked unsteadily.

Smiling, the visitor returned the cane to his lips and gazed into vacancy, as though communing with agreeable thoughts.

"I have met her," he said finally. "Yes; I may say I have met her. Ged! Next to a duel with rapiers is one with eyes. They thrust at you; you parry; they return, and, demme! you're stabbed! But don't ask me any more--discretion--you understand--between men of the world-- demme!"--and the count relapsed into a vacuous dream.

"What a precious liar he is!" commented the land baron to himself. But his mind soon reverted to the duel once more. "If I had only followed Spedella's advice and studied his favorite parades!" he muttered, regretfully.

"It would have been the same," retorted the count, brutally. "When you lost your temper, you lost your cause. Your work was brilliant; but he is one of the best swordsmen I ever saw. Who is he, anyway?"

"All I know is, he served in Algiers," said Mauville, moodily.

"A demmed adventurer, probably!" exclaimed the other.

"I'd give a good deal to know his record," remarked the patroon, contemplatively. "You should be pretty well acquainted with the personnel of the army?"

"It includes everybody nowadays," replied the diplomat. "I have a large acquaintance, but I am not a directory. A person who knows everybody usually knows nobody--worth knowing! But it seems to me I did know of a Saint-Prosper at the military college at Saumur; or was it at the Ecole d'application d'état-major? Demmed scapegrace, if I am not mistaken; sent to Algiers; must be the same. A hell-rake hole!--full of German and French outcasts! Knaves, adventureres, ready for plunder and loot!"

Here the count, after this outburst, closed his eyes and seemed almost on the point of dropping off, but suddenly straightened himself.

"Let's get the cards, or the dice, Mauville," he said, "or I'll fall into a doze. Such a demmed sleepy climate!"

Soon the count was shuffling and the land baron and he were playing bezique, but in spite of the latter's drowsiness, he won steadily from his inattentive companion, and, although the noble visitor had some difficulty in keeping his eyes open, what there was of his glance was vigilantly concentrated on his little pile of the coin of the realm. His watchfulness did not relax nor his success desert him, until Mauville finally threw down the cards in disgust, weary alike of such poor luck and the half-nodding automaton confronting him; whereupon the count thrust every piece of gold carefully away in his pocket, absently reached for his hat, drawled a perfunctory farewell and departed in a brown study.

The count's company, of which he had enjoyed a good deal during the past forty-eight hours, did not improve Mauville's temper, and he bore his own reflections so grudgingly that inaction became intolerable. Besides, certain words of his caller concerning Saint-Prosper had stimulated his curiosity, and, in casting about for a way to confirm his suspicions, he had suddenly determined in what wise to proceed. Accordingly, the next day he left his rooms, his first visit being to a spacious, substantial residence of stone and lime, with green veranda palings and windows that opened as doors, with a profusion of gauzy curtains hanging behind them. This house, the present home of the Marquis de Ligne, stood in the French quarter, contrasting architecturally with the newer brick buildings erected for the American population. The land baron was ushered into a large reception room, sending his card to the marquis by the neat-appearing colored maid who answered the door.

If surroundings indicate the man, the apartments in which the visitor stood spoke eloquently of the marquis' taste. Eschewing the stiff, affected classicalism of the Empire style, the furniture was the best work of André Boule and Riesener; tables, with fine marquetry of the last century, made of tulip wood and mahogany; mirrors from Tourlaville; couches with tapestry woven in fanciful designs after Fragonard, in the looms of Beauvais--couches that were made for conversation, not repose; cabinets exemplifying agreeable disposition of lines and masses in the inlaid adornment, containing tiny drawers that fitted with old-time exactness, and, without jamming, opened and shut at the touch. The marquis' character was stamped by these details; it was old, not new France, to which he belonged.

Soon the marquis' servant, a stolid, sober man, of virtuous deportment, came down stairs to inform the land baron his master had suffered a relapse and was unable to see any one.

"Last night his temperature was very high," said the valet. "My master is very ill; more so than I have known him to be in twenty years."

"You have served the marquis so long?" said the visitor, pausing as he was leaving the room. "Do you remember the Saint-Prosper family?"

"Well, Monsieur. General Saint-Prosper and my master were distant kinsmen and had adjoining lands."

"Surely the marquis did not pass his time in the country?" observed Mauville.

"He preferred it to Paris--when my lady was there!" added François, softly.

In spite of his ill-humor, the shadow of a smile gleamed in the land baron's gaze, and, encouraged by that questioning look, the man continued: "The marquis and General Saint-Prosper were always together. My lady had her own friends."

"So I've heard," commented the listener.

François' discreet eyes were downcast. Why did the visitor wish to learn about the Saint-Prosper family? Why, instead of going, did he linger and eye the man half-dubiously? François had sold so many of his master's secrets he scented his opportunities with a sixth sense.

"The marquis and General Saint-Prosper were warm friends?" asked the land baron at length.

"Yes, Monsieur; the death of the latter was a severe shock to the Marquis de Ligne, but, mon Dieu!"--lifting his eyes--"it was as well he did not live to witness the disgrace of his son."

"His son's disgrace," repeated the land baron, eagerly. "Oh, you mean running in debt--gaming--some such fashionable virtue?"

"If betraying his country is a fashionable virtue," replied the valet. "He is a traitor."

Incredulity overspread the land baron's features; then, coincident with the assertion, came remembrance of his conversation with the marquis.

"He certainly called him that," ruminated the visitor. Not only the words, but the expression of the old nobleman's face recurred to him. What did it mean unless it confirmed the deliberate charge of the valet? The land baron forgot his disappointment over his inability to see the marquis, and began to look with more favor on the man.

"He surrendered a French stronghold," continued the servant, softly. "Not through fear; oh, no; but for ambition, power, under Abd-el-Kader, the Moorish leader."

"How do you know this?" said the patroon, sharply.

"My master has the report of the military board of inquiry," replied the man, steadily.

"Why has the matter attracted no public attention, if a board of inquiry was appointed?"

"The board was a secret one, and the report was suppressed. Few have seen it, except the late King of France and my master."

"And yourself, François?" said the patroon, his manner changing.

"Oh, Monsieur!" Deprecatorily.

"Since it has been inspected by such good company, I confess curiosity to look at it myself. But your master is ill; I can not speak with him; perhaps you--"

"I, Monsieur!" Indignantly.

"For five hundred francs, François?"

Like oil upon the troubled waters, this assurance wrought a swift change in the valet's manner.

"To oblige Monsieur!" he answered, softly, but his eyes gleamed like a lynx's. His stateliness was a sham; his perfidy and hypocrisy surprised even the land baron.

"You have no compunctions about selling a reputation, François?"

"Reputation is that!" said the man, contemptuously snapping his fingers, emboldened by his compact with the caller. "Francs and sous are everything."

"Lord, how servants imbibe the ideas of their betters!" quoth the patroon, as he left the house and strode down the graveled walk, decapitating the begonias with his cane.

Furtively the valet watched his departing figure. "Why does he want it?" he thought.

Then he shrugged his shoulders. "What do I care!"

"François!" piped a shrill and querulous treble from above, dispelling the servant's conjectures.

"Coming, my lord!" And the valet slowly mounted the broad stairway amid a fusillade of epithets from the sick chamber. An hour before the marquis had ordered him out of his sight as vehemently as now he summoned him, all of which François endured with infinite patience and becoming humility.

Passing into the Rue Royale, the favorite promenade of the Creole-French, the land baron went on through various thoroughfares with French-English nomenclature into St. Charles Street, reaching his apartments, which adjoined a well-known club. He was glad to stretch himself once more on his couch, feeling fatigued from his efforts, and having rather overtaxed his strength.

But if his body was now inert, his mind was active. His thoughts dwelt upon the soldier's reticence, his disinclination to make acquaintances, and the coldness with which he had received his, Mauville's, advances in the Shadengo Valley. Why, asked Mauville, lying there and putting the pieces of the tale together, did not Saint-Prosper remain with his new-found friends, the enemies of his country? Because, came the answer, Abd-el-Kader, the patriot of Algerian independence, had been captured and the subjection of the country had followed. Since Algeria had become a French colony, where could Saint-Prosper have found a safer asylum than in America? Where more secure from "that chosen curse" for the man who owes his weal to his country's woe?

In his impatience to possess the promised proof, the day passed all too slowly. He even hoped the count would call, although that worthy brought with him all the "flattering devils, sweet poison and deadly sins" of inebriation. But the count, like a poor friend, was absent when wanted, and it was a distinct relief to the land baron when François appeared at his apartments in the evening with a buff-colored envelope, which he handed to him.

"The suppressed report?" asked the latter, weighing it in his hand.

"No, Monsieur; I could not find that. My master must have destroyed it."

The land baron made a gesture of disappointment and irritation.

"But this," François hastened to add, "is a letter from the Duc d'Aumale, governor of Algeria, to the Marquis de Ligne, describing the affair. Monsieur will find it equally as satisfactory, I am sure."

"How did you get it?" said the patroon, thoughtfully.

"My master left the keys on the dresser."

"And if he misses this letter--"

"Oh, Monsieur, I grieve my master is so ill he could not miss anything but his ailments! Those he would willingly dispense with. My poor master!"

"There! Take your long, hypocritical face out of my sight!" said Mauville, curtly, at the same time handing him the promised reward, which François calmly accepted. A moment later, however, he drew himself up.

"Monsieur has not paid for the right to libel my character," he said.

"Your character!"

"My character, Monsieur!" the valet replied firmly, and bowed in the stateliest fashion of the old school as he backed out of the room with grand obsequiousness. Deliberately, heavily and solidly, resounded the echoing footsteps of François upon the stairway, like the going of some substantial personage of unimpeachable rectitude.

As the front door closed sharply the land baron threw the envelope on the table and quietly surveyed it, the remnants of his pride rising in revolt.

"Have I then sunk so low as to read private communications or pry into family secrets? Is it a family secret, though? Should it not become common property? Why have they protected him? Did the marquis wish to spare the son of an old friend? Besides"--his glance again seeking the envelope--"it is my privilege to learn whether I have fought with a gentleman or a renegade." But even as he meditated, he felt the sophistry of this last argument, while through his brain ran the undercurrent: "He has wooed her--won her, perhaps!" Passion, rather than injured hauteur, stirred him. At the same time a great indignation filled his breast; how Saint-Prosper had tricked her and turned her from himself!

And moving from the mantel upon which he was leaning, Mauville strode to the table and untied the envelope.

CHAPTER VII:
A CYNICAL BARD

A dusty window looking out upon a dusty thoroughfare; a dusty room, lighted by the dusty window, and revealing a dusty chair, a dusty carpet and--probably--a dusty bed! Over the foot and the head of the bed the lodger's wardrobe lay carelessly thrown. He had but to reach up, and lo! his shirt was at hand; to reach down, and there were collar and necktie! Presto, he was dressed, without getting out of bed, running no risk from cold floors for cold feet, lurking tacks or stray needles and pins! On every side appeared evidence of confusion, or a bachelor's idea of order.

Fastened to the head-board of the bed was a box, wherein were stored various and divers articles and things. With as little inconvenience as might be imagined the lodger could plunge his hand into his cupboard and pull out a pipe, a box of matches, a bottle of ink, a bottle of something else, paper and pins, and, last but not least, his beloved tin whistle of three holes, variously dignified a fretiau, a frestele, or a galoubet, upon which he played ravishing tunes.

Oh, a wonderful box was Straws' little bedstead cupboard! As Phazma said of it, it contained everything it should not, and nothing it should contain. But that was why it was a poet's box. If it had held a Harpagon's Interest Computer, instead of a well-thumbed Virgil, or Oldcodger's Commercial Statistics for 184--, instead of an antique, leather-covered Montaigne, Straws would have had no use for the cupboard. It was at once his library--a scanty one, for the poet held tenaciously to but a few books--his sideboard, his secrétaire, his music cabinet--giving lodgment in this last capacity to a single work, "The Complete and Classical Preceptor for Galoubet, Containing Tunes, Polkas and Military Pieces."

Suspended from the ceiling hung a wooden cage, confining a mocking bird that had become acclimated to the death-dealing atmosphere of tobacco smoke, alcoholic fumes and poetry. All these the songster had endured and survived, nay, thriven upon, lifting up its voice in happy cadence and blithely hopping about its prison, the door of which Straws sometimes opened, permitting the feathered captive the dubious freedom of the room. Pasted on the foot-board of the bed was an old engraving of a wandering musician mountebank, playing a galoubet as an accompaniment to a dancing dog and a cock on stilts, a never-wearying picture for Straws, with his migratory, vagabond proclivities.

A bracket on the wall looked as though it might have been intended for a piece of statuary, or a bit of porcelain or china decoration, but had really been set there for his ink-pot, when he was mindful to work in bed, although how the Muse could be induced to set foot in that old nookery of a room could only be explained through the whims and crotchets of that odd young person's character.

Yet come she would and did, although she got dust on her flowing skirts when she swept across the threshold; dust on her snow-white gown--if the writers are to be believed in regard to its hue!--when she sat down in the only chair, and dust in her eyes when she flirted her fan. Fortunate was it for Straws that the Muse is a wayward, freakish gipsy; a straggler in attics; a vagrant of the streets; fortunately for him she is not at all the fine lady she has been depicted! Doubtless she has her own reasons for her vagaries; perhaps because it is so easy to soar from the hovel to fairy-land, but to soar from a palace--that is obviously impossible; it is a height in itself! So this itinerant maiden ever yawns amid scenes of splendor, and, from time immemorial, has sighed for lofts, garrets, and such humble places as Straws' earthly abode.

At the present time, however, Straws was alone. This eccentric but lovely young lady had not deigned to visit him that day. Once, indeed, she had just looked in, but whisked back again into the hall, slamming the door after her, and the pen, momentarily grasped, had fallen from Straws' hand. Instead of reaching for the ink-bottle he reached in the cupboard for the other bottle. Again she came near entering through the window--having many unconventional ways of coming into a room!--but after looking in for a moment, changed her mind after her fashion and floated away into thin space like the giddy, volatile mistress that she was. After that she appeared no more--probably making a friendly call on some one else!--and Straws resigned himself to her heartless perfidy, having become accustomed to her frivolous, fantastic moods.

Indeed, what else could he have done; what can any man do when his lady-love deserts him, save to make the best of it? But he found his consolation in a pipe; not a pipe of tobacco, nor yet a pipe of old madeira, which, figuratively, most disappointed lovers seek; but a pipe of melody, a pipe of flowing tunes and stirring marches; a pipe of three holes, vulgarly termed by those who know not its high classic origin from the Grecian reeds and its relation to the Pandian pipes, a tin whistle! Thus was Straws classic in his taste, affecting the instrument wherein Acis sighed his soul and breath away for fair Galatea!

It had been a lazy, purposeless day. He had awakened at noon; had coffee and rolls in bed; had dressed, got up, looked out, lain down again, read, and vainly essayed original composition. Now, lying on his back, with the Complete and Classic Preceptor before him, he soothed himself with such music "as washes the every-day dust from the soul." For a pipe of three holes, his instrument had a remarkable compass; melody followed melody--"The Harp that Once through Tara's Hall," "She is Far from the Land," "In Death I shall Calm Recline," and other popular pieces. When Straws missed a note he went back to find it; when he erred in a phrase, he patiently repeated it. The cadence in the last mournful selection, "Bid her not shed a tear of sorrow," was, on his first attempt, fraught with exceeding discord, and he was preparing once more to assault the citadel of grief, entrenched with bristling high notes, when an abrupt knocking at the door, followed by the appearance of a face marred by wrath and adorned with an enormous pair of whiskers, interrupted his attack.

"Sair," said this person, excitedly, with no more than his head in the room, like a Punch and Judy figure peering from behind a curtain, "you are ze one gran' nuisance! Eet is zat--what you call eet?--whistle! I am crazee--crazee!"

"Yes; you look it!" replied Straws, sympathetically. "Perhaps, if you had a keep--"

"I am not crazee!" vociferated the man.

"No? Perhaps I could tell better, if I could see more of you. Judging from the sample, I confess to curiosity for a full-length view. If you will step in--"

"I will not step in! I will step out! I will leave zis house! I will leave--forever!"

And the head vanished as suddenly as it had appeared, to be followed by hasty footsteps down the stairway.

"Now I can understand why Orpheus was torn to pieces," ruminated Straws, mournfully surveying the offending pipe. "He played on the lyre! Return to thy cupboard, O reed divine!"--putting the whistle back in the box--"a vile world, as Falstaff says! Heigho!"--yawning--"life is an empty void--which reminds me I have a most poetic appetite. What shall I do"--and Straws sat up relinquishing his lounging attitude--"go out, or have pot-luck in the room? Tortier's bouillabaisse would about tickle the jaded palate. A most poetic dish, that bouillabaisse! Containing all the fish that swim in the sea and all the herbs that grow on the land! Thus speaks gluttony! Get thee behind me, odoriferous temptation of garlic! succulent combination of broth and stew!"

So saying, Straws sprang from his bed, lighted a charcoal fire in his tiny grate; rummaged a bureau drawer and drew forth an end of bacon, a

potato or two, a few apples, an onion and the minor part of a loaf of bread, all of which, except the bread, he sliced and thrust indiscriminately into the frying-pan and placed over the blue flame. Next from behind the mirror he produced a diminutive coffee pot into which he measured, with extreme care, just so much of the ground berry, being rather over-nice about his demitasse. Having progressed thus far in his preparation for pot, or frying-pan luck--and indeed it seemed a matter of luck, or good fortune, how that mixture would turn out--he rapped on the floor with the heel of his boot, like the prince in the fairy tale, summoning his attendant good genii, and in a few moments a light tapping on the door announced the coming of a servitor.

Not a mighty wraith nor spook of Arabian fancy, but a very small girl, or child, with very black hair, very white skin and very dark, beautiful eyes. A daughter of mixed ancestry, yet with her dainty hands and little feet, she seemed descended from sprites or sylphs.

"Monsieur called," she said in her pretty dialect.

"Yes, my dear. Go to Monsieur Tortier's, Celestina, and tell him to give you a bottle of the kind Monsieur Straws always takes."

"At once, Monsieur," she answered, very gravely, very seriously. And Celestina vanished like a butterfly that flutters quickly away.

"Now this won't be bad after all," thought Straws, sniffing at the frying-pan which had begun to sputter bravely over the coals, while the coffee pot gave forth a fragrant steam. "A good bottle of wine will transform a snack into a collation; turn pot-luck into a feast!"

As thus he meditated the first of night's outriders, its fast-coming shadows, stole through the window; following these swift van-couriers, night's chariot came galloping across the heavens; in the sky several little clouds melted like Cleopatra's pearls. Musing before his fire the poet sat, not dreaming thoughts no mortal ever dreamed before, but turning the bacon and apples and stirring in a few herbs, for no other particular reason than that he had them and thought he might as well use them.

"Celestina is taking longer than usual," he mused. "Perhaps, though, Monsieur Tortier intends to surprise me with an unusually fine bottle. Yes; that is undoubtedly the reason for the delay. He is hunting about in the cellar for something a little out of the ordinary. But here is Celestina now!" as the child reappeared, with footsteps so noiseless the poet saw before he heard her. "Where is the bottle, my little Ariel? It must be an extra fine vintage. Bless old Tortier's noble heart!"

"There isn't any bottle," said the child. "Monsieur said that your account--"

"The miserable old hunks! His heart's no bigger than a pin-head!"

"Please, I'm so sorry!" spoke up Celestina, a suspicious moisture in her eyes.

"I know it, my dear," returned Straws. "Your heart is as big as his whole body. One of your tears is more precious than his most priceless nectar."

"I beg-ged him--that's why I--I stayed so--long!" half-sobbed Celestina.

"There! there!" said Straws, wiping her eyes. "Of course it's very tragic, but there's no use crying over spilled milk. Dear me, dear me; what can we do? It's terrible, but you know the proverb: 'Every cloud has a silver lining.' Perhaps this one has. I wish it had; or a golden one! Think of a cloud of gold, Celestina! Wouldn't we be rich? What would you do with it?"

"I'd go to--Monsieur Tortier's and--and get the bottle," said the child in an agony of distress.

He lifted her on his knee, soothed her and held her in his arms, stroking her dark hair.

"I believe you would," he said. "And now, as we haven't got the golden cloud, let us see how we can get on without it. How shall we conquer that ogre, Monsieur Tortier? What would you suggest, Celestina?"

The child looked into the fire, with eyes wide-open.

"Come, be a good fairy now," urged Straws, "and tell me."

"Why don't you write him a poem?" said Celestina, turning her eyes, bright with excitement, upon him.

"A poem! Non--by Jove, you're right! An inspiration, my dear! People like to be thought what they are not. They want to be praised for virtues foreign to themselves. The ass wants to masquerade as the lion. 'Tis the law of nature. Now Monsieur Tortier is a Jew; a scrimp; a usurer! Very well, we will celebrate the virtues he hath not in verse and publish the stanza in the Straws' column. After all, we are only following the example of the historians, and they're an eminently respectable lot of people. Celestina! You watch the coffee pot, and I'll grind out the panegyric!"

The child knelt before the fire, but her glance strayed from the steaming spout to the poet's face, as he sat on the edge of his bed and rapidly scribbled. By the time the bacon was fairly done and the other condiments in the frying-pan had turned to a dark hue, the production was finished and triumphantly waved in mid air by the now hopeful Straws.

"I'll just read you a part of it, my dear!" he said. "It's not half bad. But perhaps it would--bore you?" With exaggerated modesty.

"Oh, I just love your poetry!" cried the girl, enthusiastically.

"If everybody were only like you now! Isn't it too bad you've got to grow up and grow wiser? But here's the refrain. There are six stanzas, but I won't trouble you with all of them, my dear. One mustn't drive a willing horse, or a willing auditor."

And in a voice he endeavored to render melodious, with her rapt glance fixed upon him, Straws read:

"Sing, my Muse, the lay of the prodigal host! Who enters here leaveth behind not hope. Course follows course; entrée, relevé, ragoût, Ambrosial sauces, pungent, after luscious soup. The landlord spurs his guests to fresh attack, With fricassee, réchauffé and omelets; A toothsome feast that Apicius would fain have served, While wine, divine, new zeal in all begets. Who is this host, my Muse, pray say? Who but that prodigal, Tortier!

"There, my dear," concluded Straws, "those feet are pretty wobbly to walk, but flattery moves on lame legs faster than truth will travel on two good ones. Besides, I haven't time to polish them properly, or the mess in the frying-pan will spoil. Better spoil the poem than the contents of the flesh pots! Now if--dear me, Celestina, if you haven't let the coffee pot boil over!"

"Oh, Monsieur," cried the child, almost weeping again. "I forgot to watch it! I just couldn't while you were writing poetry."

"The excuse more than condones the offense," continued the other. "But as I was about to say, you take this poem to Monsieur Tortier, make your prettiest bow and courtesy--let me see you make a courtesy."

The girl bowed as dainty as a little duchess.

"That should melt a heart of stone in itself," commented Straws. "But Tortier's is flint! After that charming bow, you will give him my compliments; Mr. Straws' compliments, remember; and, would he be kind enough just to glance over this poem which Mr. Straws, with much mental effort, has prepared, and which, if it be acceptable to Monsieur Tortier, will appear in Mr. Straws' famous and much-talked-of column in the paper?"

"Oh, Monsieur, I can't remember all that!" said the girl.

"Do it your own way then. Besides, it will be better than mine."

With the poem hugged to her breast, the child fairly flew out of the room, leaving Straws a prey to conflicting emotions. He experienced in those moments of suspense all the doubts and fears of the nestling bard or the tadpole litterateur, awaiting the pleasure and sentence of the august editor or the puissant publisher. Tortier had been suddenly exalted to the judge's lofty pedestal. Would he forthwith be an imperial autocrat; turn tyrant or Thersites; or become critic, one of "those graminivorous animals which gain subsistence by gorging upon buds and leaves of the young shrubs of the forest, robbing them of their verdure and retarding their progress to maturity"?

Straws' anxiety was trouble's labor lost. Celestina appeared, the glad messenger of success, and now, as she came dancing into the room, bore in her arms the fruits of victory which she laid before the poet with sparkling eyes and laughing lips.

"So the poem was accepted?" murmured Straws. "Discerning Tortier! Excellent dilettante! Let him henceforth be known as a man of taste!" Here the poet critically examined the bottle. "Nothing vapid, thin or characterless there!" he added, holding it before the blaze in the grate. "Positively I'll dedicate my forthcoming book to him. 'To that worshipful master and patron, the tasteful Tortier!' What did he say, Celestina, when you tendered him the poem?"

"At first he frowned and then he looked thoughtful. And then he gave me some orange syrup. And then--O, I don't want to say!" A look of unutterable concern displacing the happiness on her features.

"Say on, my dear!" cried Straws.

"He--he said he--he didn't think much of it as--O, I can't tell you; I can't! I can't!"

"Celestina," said the poet sternly, "tell me at once. I command you."

"He said he didn't think much of it as poetry, but that people would read it and come to his café and--O dear, O dear!"

"Beast! Brute! Parvenu! But there, don't cry, my dear. We have much to be thankful for--we have the bottle."

"Oh, yes," she said with conviction, and brightening a bit. "We have the bottle." And as she spoke, "pop" it went, and Celestina laughed. "May I set your table?" she asked.

"After your inestimable service to me, my dear, I find it impossible to refuse," he replied gravely.

"How good you are!" she remarked, placing a rather soiled cloth, which she found somewhere, over a battered trunk.

"I try not to be, but I can't help it!" answered the poet modestly.

"No; that's it; you can't help it!" she returned, moving lightly around the room, emptying the contents of the frying-pan--now an aromatic jumble--on to a cracked blue platter, and setting knife and fork, and a plate, also blue, before him! "And may I wait on you, too?"

"Well, as a special favor--" He paused, appearing to ponder deeply and darkly.

Her eyes were bent upon his face with mute appeal, her suspense so great she stood stock-still in the middle of the floor, frying-pan in hand.

"Yes; you may wait on me," he said finally, after perplexed and weighty rumination.

At that her little feet fairly twinkled, but her hand was ever so careful as she took the coffee pot from the fire and put it near the blue plate. A glass--how well she knew where everything was!--she found in some mysterious corner and, sitting down on the floor, cross-legged like a little Turk, a mere mite almost lost in the semi-obscurity of the room, she polished it assiduously upon the corner of the table cloth until it shone free from specks of dust; all the time humming very lightly like a bird, or a housewife whose heart is in her work. A strange song, a curious bit of melody that seemed to spring from some dark past and to presage a future, equally sunless.

"Your supper is ready, Monsieur," she said, rising.

"And I am ready for it. Why, how nicely the table looks! Really, when we both grow up, I think we should take a silver ship and sail to some silver shore and live together there forever and evermore. How would you like it?"

Celestina's lips were mute, but her eyes were full of rapturous response, and then became suddenly shy, as though afraid of their own happiness.

"May I pour your wine?" she asked, with downcast lashes.

"Can you manage it and not spill a drop? Remember Cratinus wept and died of grief seeing his wine--no doubt, this same vintage--spilt!"

But Straws was not called upon to emulate this classic example. The feat of filling his glass was deftly accomplished, and a moment later the poet raised it with, "'Drink to me only with thine eyes!'" An appropriate sentiment for Celestina who had nothing else to drink to him with. "Won't you have some of this--what shall I call it?--hash, stew or ration?"

"Oh, I've had my supper," she answered.

"How fortunate for you, my dear! It isn't exactly a company bill of fare! But everything is what I call snug and cozy. Here we are high up in the world--right under the roof--all by ourselves, with nobody to disturb us--"

A heavy footfall without; rap, rap, rap, on the door; no timid, faltering knock, but a firm application of somebody's knuckles!

"It's that Jack-in-the-box Frenchman," muttered the writer. "Go to the devil!" he called out.

The door opened.

"You have an original way of receiving visitors!" drawled a languid voice, and the glance of the surprised poet fell upon Edward Mauville. "Really, I don't know whether to come in or not," continued the latter at the threshold.

"I beg your pardon," murmured Straws. "I thought it was a--"

"Creditor?" suggested Mauville, with an amused smile. "I know the class. Don't apologize! I am intruding. Quite a family party!" he went on, his gaze resting upon Celestina and the interrupted repast.

With his elegant attire, satin waistcoat and fine ruffles, he seemed out of place in the attic nook of the Muse; a lordling who had wandered by mistake into the wrong room. But he bore himself with the easy assurance of a man who could adapt himself to any surroundings; even to Calliope's shabby boudoir!

"My dear," remarked the disconcerted bard, "get a chair for Mr. Mauville. Or--I beg your pardon--would you mind sitting on the bed? Won't you have some wine? Celestina, bring another glass."

But the girl only stood and stared at the dark, courtly being who thus unexpectedly had burst in upon them.

"There isn't any more," she finally managed to say. "You've got the only glass there is, please!"

"Dear me; dear me!" exclaimed Straws. "How glasses do get broken! I have so few occasions to use them, too, for I don't very often have visitors."

"You are surprised to see me?" continued Mauville, pleasantly, seating himself on the edge of the bed. "Go on with your supper. You don't mind my smoking while you eat?"

"No; the odor of onions is a little strong, isn't it?" laughed the other. "Rather strange, by the by, some of nature's best restoratives should be rank and noisome, while her poisons, like the Upas tree, are often sweet-smelling and agreeable?"

"Yes," commented the land baron; "we make the worst faces over the medicines that do us the most good."

"I presume," said Straws, delighted at the prospect of an argument, and forgetting his curiosity over the other's visit in this brief interchange of words, "nature but calls our attention to the fact that we may know our truest friends are not those with the sweetest manners."

"Heaven forbid!" remarked Mauville. "But how are you getting on with your column? A surfeit of news and gossip, I presume? What a busy fellow you are, to be sure! Nothing escapes through your seine. Big fish or little fish, it is all one. You dress them up with alluring sauce."

The bard shook his head.

"The net has been coming in dry," he said gloomily. "But that's the way with the fish. Sometimes you catch a good haul, and then they all disappear. It's been bad luck lately."

"Perhaps I can make a cast for you," cried the patroon eagerly.

"And bring up what?" asked the hack.

"Something everybody will read; that will set the gossips talking."

"A woman's reputation?"

"No; a man's."

"That is to be regretted," said Straws. "If, now, it were only a woman's--.However, it's the next best thing to start the town a-gossiping. I am much obliged to you for taking the trouble of calling. All those stairs to climb, too!"

"I was sure you would be glad to hear of it," remarked the patroon, slowly, studying with his bright, insolent glance, the pale, intellectual face of the scribbler.

"Yes; there's only one thing stands in the way."

"And that?"

"I never publish anything I don't believe. Don't misunderstand me, please." Pouring out a glass of wine. "Unfortunately I am so incredulous! Isn't it a pity? I am such a carping cynic; a regular skeptic that follows the old adage, 'Believe that story false that ought not to be true.' It's such a detriment to my work, too! A pretty scandal at the top of my column would make me famous, while a sprinkling of libels and lampoons would enable me to move down a story or two. But, after all, I'd feel lost in the luxury of a first floor front chamber. So, you see, nature adjusts herself to our needs."

"Makes the shell to fit the snail, as it were," commented the land baron, patronizingly, gazing around the little cupboard of a room. "At any rate," he added, in an effort to hide his dissatisfaction, "it's a pleasure to become better acquainted with such a--what shall I say?--whimsical fellow as yourself?"

"That's it," returned the bard. "Whimsical!"

"I dare say you have had many a chance to turn an honest penny or two, if you had not been so skeptical, as you call it?" remarked the patroon, significantly. "People, I presume, have even offered to pay you for publishing the compliments of the season about their neighbors?"

"Well," answered the scribbler, laughing, "I may have Midas' longing for gold, but I also have his ears. And the ears predominate. I am such an ass I have even returned a fair petitioner's perfumed note! Such a dainty little hand! How good the paper smelt! How devilish it read! The world's idea about the devil always smelling of sulphur and brimstone is a slander on that much abused person. I can positively affirm that he smells of musk, attar, myrrh; as though he had lain somewhere with a lady's sachet or scent-bag."

"Really you should revise Milton," murmured the land baron, carelessly, his interest quite gone. "But I must be moving on." And he arose. "Good evening."

"Good night!" said Straws, going to the door after his departing guest. "Can you see your way down? Look out for the turn! And don't depend too much on the bannisters--they're rather shaky. Well, he's gone!" Returning once more to the room. "We're coming up in the world, my dear, when such fashionable callers visit us! What do you think of him?"

"He is very--handsome!" replied the child.

"Oh, the vanity of the sex! Is he--is he handsomer than I?"

"Are you--handsome?" she asked.

"Eh? Don't you think so?"

"No-o," she cried, in a passion of distressed truthfulness.

"Thank you, my dear! What a flattering creature you'll become, if you keep on as you've begun! How you'll wheedle the men, to be sure!"

"But mustn't I say what I think?"

"Always! I'm a bad adviser! Think of bringing up a young person, especially a girl, to speak the truth! What a time she'll have!"

"But I couldn't do anything else!" she continued, with absorbing and painful anxiety.

"Don't, then! I'm instructing you to your destruction, but--don't! I'm a philosopher in the School for Making Simpletons. What will you do when you go out into the broad world with truth for your banner and your heart on your sleeve?"

"How could I have my heart on my sleeve?" asked Celestina.

"Because you couldn't help it!"

"Really and truly on my sleeve?"

"Really and truly!" he affirmed, gravely.

"How funny!" answered the girl.

"No; tragic! But what shall we do now, Celestina?"

"Wash the dishes," said the child, practically.

"But, my dear, we won't need them until to-morrow," expostulated the poet. "Precipitancy is a bad fault. Now, if you had proposed a little music, or a fairy tale--"

"Oh, I could wash them while you played, or told me a story," suggested the child, eagerly.

"That isn't such a bad idea," commented Straws, reflectively.

"Then you will let me?" she asked.

"Go ahead!" said the bard, and he reached for the whistle.

CHAPTER VIII:

THE SWEETEST THING IN NATURE

The city, bustling and animated by day, like an energetic housewife, was at night a gay demoiselle, awakening to new life and excitement. The clerk betook himself to his bowling or billiards and the mechanic to the circus, while beauty and fashion repaired to the concert room or to the Opéra Français, to listen to Halévy or Donizetti. Restless Americans or Irishmen rubbed elbows with the hurrying Frenchman or Spaniard, and the dignified creole gentleman of leisure alone was wrapped in a plenitude of dignity, computing probably the interest he drew on money loaned these assiduous foreigners.

Soldiers who had been granted leave of absence or had slipped the guard at the camp on Andrew Jackson's battle-ground swaggered through the streets. The change from a diet of pork and beans and army hard tack was so marked that Uncle Sam's young men threw restraint to the winds, took the mask balls by storm and gallantly assailed and made willing prisoners of the fair sex. Eager to exchange their irksome life in camp for the active campaign in Mexico, it was small wonder they relieved their impatience by many a valiant dash into the hospitable town.

Carriages drove by with a rumble and a clatter, revealing a fleeting glimpse of some beauty with full, dark eye. Venders of flowers importuned the passers-by, doing a brisk business; the oyster and coffee stands reminded the spectator of a thoroughfare in London on a Saturday night, with the people congregating about the street stalls; but the brilliantly illumined places of amusement, with their careless patrons plainly apparent to all from without, resembled rather a boulevard scene in the metropolis of France. "Probably," says a skeptical chronicler, "here and there are quiet drawing-rooms, and tranquil firesides, where domestic love is a chaste, presiding goddess." But the writer merely presumes such might have been the case, and it is evident from his manner of expression, he offers the suggestion, or afterthought, charitably, with some doubts in his mind. Certainly he never personally encountered the chaste goddess of the hearth, or he would have qualified his words and made his statement more positive.

From the life of the streets, the land baron turned into a well-lighted entrance, passing into a large, luxuriously furnished saloon, at one end of which stood a table somewhat resembling a roulette board. Seated on one side was the phlegmatic cashier, and, opposite him, the dealer, equally impassive. Unlike faro--the popular New Orleans game--no deal box was needed, the dealer holding the cards in his hand, while a cavity in the center of the table contained a basket, where the cards, once used, were thrown. A large chandelier cast a brilliant light upon the scene.

"Messieurs, faites vos jeux," drawled the monotonous voice of the dealer, and expectation was keenly written on the faces of the double circle of players--variously disclosed, but, nevertheless, apparent in all; a transformation of the natural expression of the features; an obvious nervousness of manner, or where the countenance was impassive, controlled by a strong will, a peculiar glitter of the eyes, betokening the most insatiable species of the gambler. As the dealer began to shuffle together six packs of cards and place them in a row on the table, he called out:

"Nothing more goes, gentlemen!"

The rapidity with which the cashier counted the winnings at a distance and shoved them here and there with the long rake was amazing and bewildering to the novice risking a few gold pieces for the first time on the altar of chance. Sorting the gold pieces in even bunches, the cashier estimated them in a moment; shoved them together; counted an equal amount of fives with his fingers; made a little twirl in the pile on the table; pushed it toward the winning pieces and left them tumbled up together in pleasing confusion.

"Messieurs, faites vos--"

And the clinking went on, growing louder and louder, the clinking of gold, which has a particularly musical sound, penetrating, crystalline as the golden bells of Exodus, tinkling in the twilight of the temple on the priest's raiment. The clinking, clinking, that lingers in the brain long after, drawing the players to it night after night; an intoxicating murmur, singing the desires that dominate the world; the jingling that makes all men kin!

"Oh, dear!" said a light feminine voice, as the rapacious rake unceremoniously drew in a poor, diminutive pile of gold. "Why did I play? Isn't it provoking?"

"You have my sympathy, Mistress Susan," breathed a voice near her.

Looking around, she had the grace to blush becomingly, and approached Mauville with an expressive gesture, leaving Adonis and Kate at the table.

"Don't be shocked, Mr. Mauville," she began, hurriedly. "We were told it was among the sights, and, having natural curiosity--"

"I understand. Armed with righteousness, why should not one go anywhere?"

"Why, indeed?" she murmured.

"But I'm afraid I'm taking you from your play?"

"I'm not going to play any more to-night."

"Tired, already?"

"No; but--but I haven't a cent. That miserable table has robbed me of everything. All I have left"--piteously--"are the clothes on my back."

"Something must have been the matter with your 'system.' But if a temporary loan--"

Susan was tempted, gazing longingly at the table, with the fever burning in her.

"No," she said, finally. "I think I would win, but, of course, I might lose."

"A wise reservation! Never place your fortune on the hazard of the die."

"But I have! What's the use of making good resolutions now? It's like closing the barn-door after--"

"Just so!" he agreed. "But it might have been worse."

"How?" In dismay. "Didn't that stony-looking man rake in my last gold piece? He didn't even look sorry, either. But what is the matter with your arm?" The land baron's expression became ominous. "You shook hands with your left hand. Oh, I see; the duel!" Lightly.

"How did you hear about it?" asked Mauville, irritably.

"Oh, in a roundabout way. Murder will out! And Constance--she was so solicitous about Mr. Saint-Prosper, but rather proud, I believe, because he"--with a laugh--"came off victorious."

Susan's prattle, although accompanied by innocent glances from her blue eyes, was sometimes the most irritating thing in the world, and the land baron, goaded beyond endurance, now threw off his careless manner and swore in an undertone by "every devil in Satan's calendar."

"Can you not reserve your soliloquy until you leave me?" observed Susan, sweetly. "Otherwise--"

"I regret to have shocked your ladyship," he murmured, satirically.

"I forgive you." Raising her guileless eyes. "When I think of the provocation, I do not blame you--so much!"

"That is more than people do in your case," muttered the land baron savagely.

Susan's hand trembled. "What do you mean?" she asked, not without apprehension regarding his answer.

"Oh, that affair with the young officer--the lad who was killed in the duel, you know--"

Her composure forsook her for the moment and she bit her lip cruelly.

"Don't!" she whispered. "I am not to blame. I never dreamed it would go so far! Why should people--"

"Why?" he interposed, ironically.

Susan pulled herself together. "Yes, why?" she repeated, defiantly. "Can women prevent men from making fools of themselves any more than they can prevent them from amusing themselves as they will? To-day it is this toy; to-morrow, another. At length"--bitterly--"a woman comes to consider herself only a toy."

Her companion regarded her curiously. "Well, well!" he ejaculated, finally. "Losing at cards doesn't agree with your temper."

"Nor being worsted by Saint-Prosper with yours!" she retorted quickly.

Mauville looked virulent, but Susan, feeling that she had retaliated in ample measure, recovered her usual equanimity of temper and placed a conciliatory hand sympathetically on his arm.

"We have both had a good deal to try us, haven't we? But how stupid men are!" she added suddenly. "As if you could not find other consolation!"

He directed toward her an inquiring glance.

"Some time ago, while I was acting in London," resumed Susan, thoughtfully, "the leading lady refused to receive the attentions of a certain odious English lord. She was to make her appearance in a piece upon which her reputation was staked. Mark what happened! She was hissed! Hissed from the stage! My lord led this hostile demonstration and all his hired claqueurs joined in. She was ruined; ruined!" concluded Susan, smiling amiably.

"You are ingenious, Mistress Susan--not to say a trifle diabolical. Your plan--"

She opened her eyes widely. "I have suggested no plan," she interrupted, hurriedly.

"Well, let us sit down and I will tell you about a French officer who--But here is a quiet corner, Mistress Susan, and if you will promise not to repeat it, I will regale you with a bit of interesting gossip."

"I promise--they always do!" she laughed.

For such a frivolous lady, Susan was an excellent listener. She, who on occasions chattered like a magpie, was now silent as a mouse, drinking in the other's words with parted lips and sparkling eyes. First he showed her the letter François had brought him. Unmarked by postal indications, the missive had evidently been intrusted to a private messenger of the governor whose seal it bore. Dated about three years previously, it was written in a somewhat illegible, but not unintelligible, scrawl, the duke's own handwriting.

"I send you, my dear marquis," began the duke, "a copy of the secret report of the military tribunal appointed to investigate the charges against your kinsman, Lieut. Saint-Prosper, and regret the finding of the court should have been one of guilty of treason.

"Saint-Prosper and Abd-el-Kader met near the tomb of a marabout. From him the French officer received a famous ruby which he thrust beneath his zaboot--the first fee of their compact. That night when the town lay sleeping, a turbaned host, armed with yataghans, stole through the flowering cactuses. Sesame! The gate opened to them; they swarmed within! The soldiers, surprised, could render little resistance; the ruthless invaders cut them down while they were sleeping or before they could sound the alarm. The bravest blood of France flowed lavishly in the face of the treacherous onslaught; blood of men who had been his fastest friends, among whom he had been so popular for his dauntless courage and devil-may-care temerity! But a period, fearfully brief, and the beloved tri-color was trampled in the dust; the barbarian flag of the Emir floated in its place.

"All these particulars, and the part Saint-Prosper played in the terrible drama, Abd-el-Kader, who is now our prisoner, has himself confessed. The necessity for secrecy, you, my dear Marquis, will appreciate. The publicity of the affair now would work incalculable injury to the nation. It is imperative to preserve the army from the taint of scandal. The nation hangs on a thread. God knows there is iniquity abroad. I, who have labored for the honor of France and planted her flag in distant lands, look for defeat, not through want of bravery, but from internal causes. A matter like this might lead to a popular uprising against the army. Therefore, the king wills it shall be buried by his faithful servants."

As Mauville proceeded Susan remained motionless, her eyes growing larger and larger, until they shone like two lovely sapphires, but when he concluded she gave a little sigh of pleasure and leaned back with a pleased smile.

"Well?" he said, finally, after waiting some moments for her to speak.

"How piquantly wicked he is!" she exclaimed, softly.

"Piquantly, indeed!" repeated the land baron, dryly.

"And he carries it without a twinge! What a petrified conscience!"

"I believe you find him more interesting than ever?" said Mauville, impatiently.

"Possibly!" Languidly. "An exceptional moral ailment sometimes makes a man more attractive--like a--an interesting subject in a hospital, you know! But I have always felt," she continued, with sudden seriousness, "there was something wrong with him. When I first saw him, I was sure he had had no ordinary past, but I did not dream it was quite so--what shall we call it--"

"Unsavory?" suggested her companion.

"That accounts for his unwillingness to talk about Africa," went on Susan. "Soldiers, as a rule, you know, like to tell all about their sanguinary exploits. But the tented field was a forbidden topic with him. And once when I asked him about Algiers he was almost rudely evasive."

"He probably lives in constant fear his secret will become known," said Mauville, thoughtfully. "As a matter of fact, the law provides that no person is to be indicted for treason unless within three years after the offense. The tribunal did not return an indictment; the three years have just expired. Did he come to America to make sure of these three years?"

But Susan's thoughts had flitted to another feature of the story.

"How strange my marquis should be connected with the case! What an old compliment-monger he was! He vowed he was deeply smitten with me."

"And then went home and took to his bed!" added Mauville, grimly.

"You wretch!" said the young woman, playfully. "So that is the reason the dear old molly-coddle did not take me to any of the gay suppers he promised? Is it not strange Saint-Prosper has not met him?"

"You forget the marquis has been confined to his room since his brief, but disastrous, courtship of you. His infatuation seems to have brought him to the verge of dissolution."

"Was it not worth the price?" she retorted, rising. "But I see my sister and Adonis are going, so I must be off, too. So glad to have met you!"

"You are no longer angry with me?"

"No; you are very nice," she said. "And you have forgiven me?"

"Need you ask?" Pressing her hand. "Good evening, Mistress Susan!"

"Good evening. Oh, by the way, I have an appointment with Constance to rehearse a little scene together this evening. Would you mind loaning me that letter?"

"With pleasure; but remember your promise."

"Promise?" repeated the young woman.

"Not to tell."

"Oh, of course," said Susan.

"But if you shouldn't--"

"Then?"

"Then you might say the marquis, your friend and admirer, gave you the letter. It would, perhaps, be easier for you to account for it than for me."

"But if the marquis should learn--" began the other, half-dubiously.

"He is too ill for anything except the grave."

"Oh, the poor old dear!"

She looked at the gaming table with its indefatigable players and then turned to Kate and Adonis who approached at that moment. "How did you come out, Adonis?"

"Out," he said, curtly.

"Lucky in love, unlucky at"--began Kate.

"Then you must be very unlucky in love," he retorted, "for you were a good winner at cards."

"Oh, there are exceptions to that rule," said Kate lazily, with a yawn. "I'm lucky at both--in New Orleans!"

"I have perceived it," retorted Adonis, bitterly.

"Don't quarrel," Susan implored. Regarding the table once more, she sighed: "I'm so sorry I came!"

But her feet fairly danced as she flew towards the St. Charles. She entered, airy as a saucy craft, with "all sails in full chase, ribbons and gauzes streaming at the top," and, with a frou-frou of skirts, burst into Constance's room, brimful of news and importance. She remained there for some time, and when she left, it was noteworthy her spirits were still high. In crossing the hall, her red stockings became a fitting color accompaniment to her sprightly step, as she moved over the heavy carpet, skirts raised coquettishly, humming with the gaiety of a young girl who has just left boarding school.

"A blooming, innocent creature!" growled an up-the-river planter, surveying her from one of the landings. "Lord love me, if she were only a quadroon, I'd buy her!"

CHAPTER IX:
A DEBUT IN THE CRESCENT CITY

A versatile dramatic poet is grim Destiny, making with equal facility tragedy, farce, burletta, masque or mystery. The world is his inn, and, like the wandering master of interludes, he sets up his stage in the court-yard, beneath the windows of mortals, takes out his figures and evolves charming comedies, stirring melodramas, spirited harlequinades and moving divertissement. But it is in tragedy his constructive ability is especially apparent, and his characters, tripping along unsuspectingly in the sunny byways, are suddenly confronted by the terrifying mask and realize life is not all pleasant pastime and that the Greek philosophy of retribution is nature's law, preserving the unities. When the time comes, the Master of events, adjusting them in prescribed lines, reaches by stern obligation the avoidless conclusion.

Consulting no law but his own will, the Marquis de Ligne had lived as though he were the autocrat of fate itself instead of one of its servants, and therefore was surprised when the venerable playwright prepared the unexpected dénouement. In pursuance of this end, it was decreed by the imperious and incontrovertible dramatist of the human family that this crabbed, vicious, antiquated marionette should wend his way to the St. Charles on a particular evening. Since the day at the races, the eccentric nobleman had been ill and confined to his room, but now he was beginning to hobble around, and, immediately with returning strength, sought diversion.

"François," he said, "what is there at the theater to-night?"

"Comic opera, my lord?"

The marquis made a grimace. "Comic opera outside of Paris!" he exclaimed, with a shrug of the shoulders.

"A new actress makes her début at the St. Charles."

"Let it be the début, then! Perhaps she will fail, and that will amuse me."

"Yes, my lord."

"And, by the way, François, did you see anything of a large envelope, a buff-colored envelope, I thought I left in my secretary?"

"No, my lord." But François became just a shade paler.

"It is strange," said the marquis, half to himself, "what could have become of it! I destroyed other papers, but not that. You are sure, François, you did not steal it?"

By this time the servant's knees began to tremble, and, had the marquis' eyesight been better, he could not have failed to detect the other's agitation. But the valet assumed a bold front, as he asked:

"Why should I have stolen it?"

"True, why?" grumbled the marquis. "It would be of no service to you. No; you didn't take it. I believe you honest--in this case!"

"Thank you, my lord!"

"After all, what does it matter?" muttered the nobleman to himself. "What's in a good name to-day--with traitors within and traitors without? 'Tis love's labor lost to have protected it! We've fostered a military nest of traitors. The scorpions will be faithful to nothing but their own ends. They'll fight for any master."

Recalled to his purpose of attending the play by François' bringing from the wardrobe sundry articles of attire, the marquis underwent an elaborate toilet, recovering his good humor as this complicated operation proceeded. Indeed, by the time it had reached a triumphant end and the valet set the marquis before a mirror, the latter had forgotten his dissatisfaction at the government in his pleasure with himself.

"Too much excitement is dangerous, is it?" he mumbled. "I am afraid there will be none at all. A stage-struck young woman; a doll-like face, probably; a milk-and-water performance! Now, in the old days actors were artists. Yes, artists!" he repeated, as though he had struck a chord that vibrated in his memory.

Arriving at the theater, he was surprised at the scene of animation; the line of carriages; the crowd about the doors and in the entrance hall! Evidently the city eagerly sought novelty, and Barnes' company, offering new diversion after many weeks of opera, drew a fair proportion of pleasure-seekers to the portals of the drama. The noise of rattling wheels and the banging of carriage doors; the aspect of many fair ladies, irreproachably gowned; the confusion of voices from venders hovering near the gallery entrance--imparted a cosmopolitan atmosphere to the surroundings.

"You'd think some well-known player was going to appear, François!" grumbled the marquis, as he thrust his head out of his carriage. "Looks like a theater off the Strand! And there's an orange-girl! A dusky Peggy!"

The vehicle of the nobleman drew up before the brilliantly-lighted entrance. Mincingly, the marquis dismounted, assisted by the valet; within he was met by a loge director who, with the airs of a Chesterfield, bowed the people in and out.

"Your ticket, sir!" said this courteous individual, scraping unusually low.

The marquis waved his hand toward his man, and François produced the bits of pasteboard. Escorted to his box, the nobleman settled himself in an easy chair, after which he stared impudently and inquisitively around him.

And what a heterogeneous assemblage it was; of how many nationalities made up; gay bachelors, representatives of the western trade and eastern manufacturers; a fair sprinkling of the military element, seeking amusement before departing for the front, their brass buttons and striking new uniforms a grim reminder of the conflict waging between the United States and Mexico; cotton brokers, banking agents, sugar, tobacco and flour dealers; some evidently English with their rosy complexions, and others French by their gesticulations! And among the women, dashing belles from Saratoga, proud beauties from Louisville, "milliner-martyred" daughters of interior planters, and handsome creole matrons, in black gowns that set off their white shoulders!

In this stately assemblage--to particularize for a moment!-- was seated the (erstwhile!) saintly Madame Etalage, still proud in her bearing, although white as an angel, and by her side, her carpet knight, an extravagant, preposterous fop. A few seats in front of her prattled the lovely ingenue, little Fantoccini, a biting libeller of other actresses, with her pitiless tongue. To her left was a shaggy-looking gentleman, the Addison of New Orleans' letters, a most tolerant critic, who never spoke to a woman if he could avoid doing so, but who, from his philosophical stool, viewed the sex with a conviction it could do no wrong; a judgment in perspective, as it were!

The marquis paid little attention to the men; it was the feminine portion of the audience that interested him, and he regarded it with a gloating leer, the expression of a senile satyr. Albeit a little on the seamy side of life, his rank and wealth were such that he himself attracted a good deal of attention, matronly eyes being turned in his direction with not unkindly purport. The marquis perceived the stir his presence occasioned and was not at all displeased; on the contrary, his manner denoted gratification, smiling and smirking from bud to blossom and from blossom to bud!

How fascinating it was to revel in the sight of so much youth and beauty from the brink of the grave whereon he stood; how young it made him feel again! He rubbed his withered hands together in childish delight, while he contemplated the lively charms of Fantoccini or devoted himself to the no less diverting scrutiny of certain other dark-haired ladies.

While occupied in this agreeable pastime the nobleman became dimly conscious the debutante had appeared and was greeted with the moderate applause of an audience that is reserving its opinion. "Gad," said one of the dandies who was keenly observing the nobleman, "it's fashionable to look at the people and not at the actors!" And he straightway stared at the boxes, assuming a lackadaisical, languishing air. Having taken note of his surroundings to his satisfaction, the marquis at length condescended to turn his eye-glass deliberately and quizzically to the stage. His sight was not the best, and he gazed for some time before discerning a graceful figure and a pure, oval face, with dark hair and eyes.

"Humph, not a bad stage presence!" he thought. "Probably plenty of beauty, with a paucity of talent! That's the way nowadays. The voice--why, where have I heard it before? A beautiful voice! What melody, what power, what richness! And the face--" Here he wiped the moisture from his glasses--"if the face is equal to the voice, she has an unusual combination in an artist."

Again he elevated the glass. Suddenly his attenuated frame straightened, his hand shook violently and, the glasses fell from his nerveless fingers.

"Impossible!" he murmured. But the melody of those tones continued to fall upon his ears like a voice from the past.

When the curtain went down on the first act there was a storm of applause. In New Orleans nothing was done by halves, and Constance, as Adrienne Lecouvreur, radiant in youth and the knowledge of success, was called out several times. The creoles made a vigorous demonstration; the Americans were as pleased in their less impulsive way; and in the loges all the lattices were pushed up, "a compliment to any player," said Straws. To the marquis, the ladies in the loges were only reminiscent of the fashionable dames, with bare shoulders and glittering jewels, in the side boxes of old Drury Lane, leaning from their high tribunals to applaud the Adrienne of twenty years ago!

He did not sit in a theater in New Orleans now, but in London town, with a woman by his side who bent beneath the storm of words she knew were directed at her. As in a dream he lingered, plunged in thought, with no longer the cynical, carping expression on his face as he looked at the stage, but awed and wonder-stricken, transported to another scene through the lapse of years that folded their shadowy wings and made the past to-day. Two vivid pictures floated before him as though they belonged to the present: Adrienne, bright, smiling and happy, as she rushed into the green room, with the plaudits of the multitude heard outside; Adrienne, in her last moments, betrayed to death!

They were applauding now, or was it but the mocking echo of the past? The curtain had descended, but went up again, and the actress stood with flowers showered around her. Save that she was in the springtime of life, while the other had entered summer's season; that her art was tender and romantic, rather than overwhelming and tragic, she was the counterpart of the actress he had deserted in London; a faithful prototype, bearing the mother's eyes, brow and features; a moving, living picture of the dead, as though the grave had rolled back its stone and she had stepped forth, young once more, trusting and innocent.

The musical bell rang in the wine room, where the worshipers of Bacchus were assembled, the signal that the drop would rise again in five minutes. At the bar the imbibers were passing judgment.

"What elegance, deah boy! But cold--give me Fantoccini!" cried the carpet knight.

"Fantoccini's a doll to her!" retorted the worldly young spark addressed.

"A wicked French doll, then! What do you think?" Turning to the local Addison.

"Sir, she 'snatches a grace beyond the reach of art'!" replied that worthy.

"You ask for a criticism, and he answers in poetry!" retorted the first speaker.

"'Tis only the expression of the audience!" interposed another voice.

"Oh, of course, Mr. Mauville, if you, too, take her part, that is the end of it!"

The land baron's smile revealed withering contempt, as with eyes bright with suppressed excitement, and his face unusually sallow, he joined the group.

"The end of it!" he repeated, fixing his glance upon the captious dandy. "The beginning, you mean! The beginning of her triumphs!"

"Oh, have your own way!" answered the disconcerted critic.

Mauville deliberately turned his back. "And such dunces sit in judgment!" he muttered to the scholar.

"Curse me, Mauville's in a temper to-night!" said the spark in a low voice. "Been drinking, I reckon! But it's time for the next act!"

Punches and juleps were hastily disposed of, and the imbibers quickly sought their places. This sudden influx, with its accompanying laughter and chattering, aroused the marquis from his lethargy. He started and looked around him in bewilderment. The noise and the light conversation, however, soon recalled his mind to a sense of his surroundings, and he endeavored to recover his self-possession.

Could it be possible it was but a likeness his imagination had converted into such vivid resemblance? A sudden thought seized him and he looked around toward the door of the box.

"François!" he called, and the valet, who had been waiting his master's pleasure without, immediately appeared.

"Sit down, François!" commanded the marquis. "I am not feeling well. I may conclude to leave soon, and may need your arm."

The servant obeyed, and the nobleman, under pretense of finding more air near the door, drew back his chair, where he could furtively watch his man's face. The orchestra ceased; the curtain rose, and the valet gazed mechanically at the stage. In his way, François was as blasé as his master, only, of course, he understood his position too well to reveal that lassitude and ennui, the expression of which was the particular privilege of his betters. He had seen many great actresses and heard many peerless singers; he had delved after his fashion into sundry problems, and had earned as great a right as any of the nobility to satiety and defatigation in his old age, but unfortunately he was born in a class which may feel but not reveal, and mask alike content and discontent.

Again those tones floated out from the past; musical, soft! The marquis trembled. Did not the man notice? No; he was still looking gravely before him. Dolt; did he not remember? Could he not recall the times beyond number when he had heard that voice; in the ivy-covered cottage; in the garden of English roses?

Suddenly the valet uttered an exclamation; the stolid aspect of his face gave way to an obvious thrill of interest.

"My lord!" he cried.

"An excellent actress, François; an excellent actress!" said the marquis, rising. "Is that my coat? Get it for me. What are you standing there for? Your arm! Don't you see I am waiting?"

Overwrought and excitable, he did not dare remain for the latter portion of the drama; better leave before the last act, he told himself, and, dazed by the reappearance of that vision, the old man fairly staggered from the box.

The curtain fell for the last time, and Barnes, with exultation, stood watching in the wings. She had triumphed, his little girl; she had won the great, generous heart of New Orleans. He clapped his hands furiously, joining in the evidences of approval, and, when the ovation finally ceased and she approached, the old manager was so overcome he had not a word to say. She looked at him questioningly, and he who had always been her instructor folded her fondly to his breast.

"I owe it all to you," she whispered.

"Pooh!" he answered. "You stole fire from heaven. I am but a theatrical, bombastic, barnstorming Thespian."

"Would you spoil me?" she interrupted, tenderly.

"You are your mother over again, my dear! If she were only here now! But where is Saint-Prosper? He has not yet congratulated you? He, our good genius, whose generosity has made all this possible!" And Barnes half-turned, when she placed a detaining hand on his arm.

"No, no!"

"Why, my dear, have you and he--"

"Is it not enough that you are pleased?" replied Constance, hastily, with a glance so shining he forgot all further remonstrances.

"Pleased!" exclaimed Barnes. "Why, I feel as gay as Momus! But we'll sing Te Deum later at the festive board. Go now and get ready!"

CHAPTER X:
LAUGHTER AND TEARS

A supper was given the company after the performance by the manager, to which representatives of the press--artful Barnes!--had been invited. Of all the merry evenings in the bohemian world, that was one of the merriest. Next to the young girl sat the Count de Propriac, his breast covered with a double row of medals. Of the toasts drunk to Constance, the manager, poets Straws and Phazma, etc., unfortunately no record remains. Of the recollections of the wiry old lady; the impromptu verse of the rhymsters; the roaring speech of Mr. Barnes; the song and dainty flower dance by Susan and Kate--only the bare facts have descended to the chronicler.

So fancy must picture the wreaths of smoke; the superabundance of flowers, the fragrance of cigars mingling with the perfume of fading floral beauties; the pale dark-eyed girl presiding, upon her dusky hair a crown of laurel, set there, despite her protestations, by Phazma and Straws; the devotion of the count to his fair neighbor; the almost superhuman pride of noisy Barnes; the attention bestowed by Susan upon Saint-Prosper, while through his mind wandered the words of a French song:

"Adieu, la cour, adieu les dames; Adieu les filles et les femmes--"

Intermixed with this sad refrain the soldier's thoughts reverted to the performance, and amidst the chatter of Susan, he reviewed again and again the details of that evening. Was this the young girl who played in school-houses, inns or town halls, he had asked himself, seated in the rear of the theater? How coldly critical had been her auditors; some of the faces about him ironical; the bored, tired faces of men who had well-nigh drained life's novelties; the artificially vivacious faces of women who played at light-heartedness and gaiety! Yet how free from concern had she been, as natural and composed as though her future had not depended upon that night!

When she won an ovation, he had himself forgotten to applaud, but had sat there, looking from her to the auditors, to whom she was now bound by ties of admiration and friendliness.

"Don't you like her?" a voice next to him had asked.

Like her? He had looked at the man, blankly.

"Yes," he had replied.

Then the past had seemed to roll between them: the burning sands; the voices of the troops; the bugle call! In his brain wild thoughts had surged and flowed--as they were surging and flowing now.

"Is he not handsome, Constance's new admirer?" whispered Susan. "What can he be saying? She looks so pleased! He is very rich, isn't he?"

"I don't know," answered Saint-Prosper, brusquely.

Again the thoughts surged and surged, and the past intruded itself! Reaching for his glass, he drank quickly.

"Don't you ever feel the effects of wine?" asked the young woman.

His glance chilled her, it seemed so strange and steely!

"I believe you are so--so strong you don't even notice it," added Susan, with conviction. "But you don't have half as good a time!"

"Perhaps I enjoy myself in my way," he answered.

"What is your way?" she asked quickly. "You don't appear to be wildly hilarious in your pleasures." And Susan's bright eyes rested on him curiously. "But we were speaking about the count and Constance. Don't you think it would be a good match?" she continued with enthusiasm. "Alas, my titled admirer got no further than the beginning. But men are deceivers ever! When they do reach the Songs of Solomon, they pass on to Exodus!"

"And leave the fair ones to Lamentations," said Straws, who had caught her last remarks.

"Or Revelations!" added Phazma.

At the sound of their laughter, Constance looked coldly their way, until a remark from the count at her right, and, "As I was saying, my dear," from the old lady at her left, engrossed the young girl's attention once more. But finally the great enemy of joy--the grim guardian of human pleasure--the reaper whose iron hands move ever in a circle, symbolical of eternity--finally, Time reminded Barnes that the hour had surely arrived when the curtain should descend upon these festivities. So he roared out a last blithe farewell, and the guests departed one by one, taking with them flowers in memory of the occasion, until all had left save Constance, the count, Saint-Prosper and the manager. Barnes was talking somewhat incoherently, holding the soldier by the coat and plunging into successive anecdotes about stage folk, while Saint-Prosper, apparently listening, observed the diplomat and Constance, whose conversation he could overhear.

"As I said to the Royal Infanta of Spain, flattery flies before truth in your presence, Mademoiselle," sighed the count. And then raising her hand to his lips, "Ah, ma chere Mademoiselle, que je vous adore!" he whispered.

She withdrew it hastily, and, ogling and gesticulating, he bowed himself out, followed by the manager.

Leaning against the chair, her figure outlined by the glow from the crystal chandelier, her face in shadow, the hand the diplomat had pressed to his lips resting in the exposed light on the mahogany, the gaiety went out of her face, and the young girl wearily brushed the hair from her brow. As if unaware of the soldier's presence, she glanced absently at the table in its wrecked glory, and, throwing her lace wrap over her arm, was moving toward the door, when he spoke.

"Miss Carew!"

She paused, standing with clasped hands before him, while the scarf slipped from her arm and fell at her feet.

"May I not also tell you how glad I am--that you succeeded to-night?"

"I dislike congratulations!" she said, indifferently.

He looked at her quickly, but her eyes expressed only apathy. In his a sudden gleam of light appeared.

"From me, you mean?" The light became brighter.

She did not answer. His self-control was fast ebbing.

"You underestimate your favors, if you fancy they are easily forgotten!"

A crimson flush extended to her brow; the unconcern died out of her eyes.

"I do not understand," she answered, slowly.

"When a woman says 'I do not understand,' she means 'I wish to forget'."

Her wide-open glance flashed ominously to his; she clasped and unclasped her fingers.

"Forget what?" she said, coldly.

"Nameless nothings!" he returned. "A smile--a glance--nothing to you, perhaps, but"--the set expression of his face giving way to abrupt passion!--"everything to me! Perhaps I had not meant to say this, but it seems as though the words must come out to-night. It may be"--his voice vibrating with strange earnestness--"for once I want to be myself. For weeks we have been--friends--and then suddenly you begin to treat me--how? As though I no longer existed! Why did you deceive me--let me drift on? Because I was mute, did you think I was blind? Why did I join the strollers--the land baron accused me of following you across the country. He was right; I was following you. I would not confess it to myself before. But I confess it now! It was a fool's paradise," he ended, bitterly.

She shrank back before his vehement words; something within her appeared violated; as though his plea had penetrated the sanctity of her reserve.

"Would it not be well to say nothing about deception?" she replied, and her dark eyes swept his face. Then, turning from him abruptly, she stepped to the window, and, drawing aside the lace curtains mechanically, looked out.

The city below was yet teeming with life, lights gleaming everywhere and shadowy figures passing. Suddenly out of the darkness came a company of soldiers who had just landed, marching through the streets toward the camping ground and singing as they went.

The chorus, like a mighty breath of patriotism, filled her heart to overflowing. It seemed as though she had heard it for the first time; had never before felt its potency. All the tragedy of war swept before her; all that inspiring, strange affection for country, kith and kin, suddenly exalted her.

Above the tramping of feet, the melody rose and fell on the distant air, dying away as the figures vanished in the gloom. With its love of native land, its expression of the unity of comradeship and ties stronger than death, the song appeared to challenge an answer; and, when the music ceased, and only the drum-beats still seemed to make themselves heard, she raised her head without moving from her position and looked at him to see if he understood. But though she glanced at him, she hardly saw him. In her mind was another picture--the betrayed garrison; the soldiers slain!--and the horror of it threw such a film over her gaze that he became as a figure in some distressing dream.

An inkling of her meaning--the mute questioning of her eyes-- the dread evoked by that revolting vision of the past--were reflected in his glance.

"Deceived you?" he began, and his voice, to her, sounded as from afar. "How--what--"

"Must it be--could it be put into words?"

The deepest shadows dwelt in her eyes; shadows he could not penetrate, although he still doggedly, yet apprehensively, regarded her! Watching her, his brow grew darker.

"Why not?" he continued, stubbornly.

Why? The dimness that had obscured her vision lifted. Now she saw him very plainly, indeed; tall and powerful; his face, harsh, intense, as though by the vigor of physical and mental force he would override any charge or imputation.

Why? She drew herself up, as he quickly searched her eyes, bright with the passions that stirred her breast.

"You told me part of your story that day in the property wagon," she began, repugnance, scorn and anger all mingling in her tones. "Why did you not tell me the rest?"

His glance, too, flashed. Would he still profess not to understand her? His lips parted; he spoke with an effort.

"The rest?" he said, his brow lowering.

"Yes," she answered quickly; "the stain upon your name!--the garrison sold!--the soldiers killed!--murdered!--"

She had turned to him swiftly, fiercely, with her last words, but before the look of sudden shame and dread on his face, her eyes abruptly fell as though a portion of his dishonor had inexplicably touched her. He made no attempt to defend himself--motionless he stood an instant--then, without a word, he moved away. At the threshold he paused, but she did not look up--could not! A moment; an eternity!

"Why don't you go?" she cried. "Why don't you go?"

The door opened, closed; she was alone.

Pale as the dying lilies on the table, she stepped toward the threshold, when Barnes, chipper and still indefatigable, entered by another door. He was too inspired with festal intoxication to observe her agitation.

"What, my dear!" he exclaimed cheerily. "Has he gone? Did you make up your little differences? Did you settle your quarrel before he leaves for Mexico?"

"For Mexico!" she repeated, mechanically.

"Of course. He has his commission in the army and leaves early in the morning. But you look tired, my dear. I declare you are quite pale"--pinching her cheek--"rest will bring back the roses, though."

Impulsively she threw her arms around his neck.

"Why, why, what's this?" he said, patting her head.

"I only care for you," she whispered. "My dear! My dear!"

CHAPTER XI:
THE PASSING OF A FINE GENTLEMAN

"'Perhaps she will fail, and that will amuse me,'" ruminated François on his high seat next to the coachman, repeating the marquis' words, as they drove home after the nobleman's precipitous retreat from the theater. "Well, he didn't look as though he had been particularly amused. But no wonder he was startled! It even"-- reviewing the impression first made upon him at sight of the actress-- "sent a shiver through me!" Here the carriage drew up sharply before the marquis' home, and François, hastily alighting, threw open the door.

"Eh? What? Are we here?" muttered the marquis, starting from the corner where he had been reclining.

He arose with some difficulty; traversed the sidewalk and the shell-strewn path to the house which loomed darkly before them; paused at the foot of the stairs where he breathed heavily, complaining of the oppressiveness of the air; and finally, with the assistance of the valet, found himself once more in his room, the sick chamber he had grown to detest! Here alone--having dismissed the servant as soon as possible--he moved restlessly to and fro, pondering deeply. Since the moment when he had seen and recognized his daughter, all the buoyancy which had given his wasted figure a sort of galvanic vitality seemed to vanish. It was like the exhaustion of a battery, the collapse of the sustaining power.

"That resemblance can not be coincidence!" he thought. "Oh, errors of the past, you come home in our old age when the limbs are faltering and life is failing!"

Going to the secrétaire, he took out a box that had not been opened in years, and, with trembling fingers, turned over many papers. He shivered, and, thinking it was cold, stirred the fire. Returning to the secretary, he took from the box a package tied with a ribbon still, after the lapse of these many years, slightly fragrant, and he breathed that perfume, so faint, so subtle, while recollections smote him like a knife.

Its scent was familiar to him; it seemed to bring life to the dead, and for the moment in his mind's eye he saw her glowing figure, the love of his youth, with flashing, revengeful eyes and noble mien. He cowered over the desk, as if shrinking from an avenging spirit, while the perfume, like opium, filled his brain with strange fantasies. He strove to drown remembrance, but some force--it seemed not his own!--drove him irresistibly to untie that ribbon, to scrutinize many old theater programs and to gaze upon a miniature in ivory depicting a woman in the loveliness of her charms, but whose striking likeness to the young actress he had just seen filled his heart with strange fear. Some power--surely it could not have been his will which rebelled strenuously!--impelled him to open those letters and to read them word for word. The tenderness of the epistles fell on his heart as though to scorch it, and he quivered like a guilty wretch. His eyes were fascinated by these words in her last letter: "Should you desert me and your unborn child, your end will be miserable. As I believe in retribution, I am sure you will reap as you have sown."

Suddenly the reader in a frenzy threw the letter to the floor and trampled on it. He regarded the face in the miniature with fear and hatred, and dashing it into the drawer, called down maledictions on her. He ceased abruptly, weak and wavering.

"I am going insane," he said, laughing harshly. "Fool! To let that woman's memory disturb me. So much for her dire prophecy!" And he snapped his fingers and dropped the letter in the fire.

"What can her curse avail?" he said aloud. "She is gone, turned to ashes like that paper and there is no life after this one. All then is nothing--emptiness--a blank! I need rest. It is this cursed dyspepsia which has made me nervous. Something to compose me, and then to bed!"

In spite of soothing powders, however, he passed a restless night and arose unrefreshed, but ordered his valet to bring one of his lightest suits, and, having dressed, he set a white flower upon his coat, while the servant proceeded to apply various pigments to the wrinkled face, until it took on a mocking semblance to the countenance of a man fifteen years younger. The marquis leered at himself in the pier-glass and assumed a jauntiness of demeanor he was far from feeling.

"I do not look tired or worried, François?"

"Not at all, my lord," replied the obsequious valet. "I never saw you, my lord, appear so young and well."

"Beneath the surface, François, there is age and weakness," answered the marquis in a melancholy tone.

"It is but a passing indisposition, my lord," asserted the servant, soothingly.

"Perhaps. But, François"--peering around--"as I look over my shoulder, do you know what I see?"

The almost hideous expression of the roué's face alarmed the servant.

"No, my lord, what is it?"

"A figure stands there in black and is touching me. It is the spirit of death, François. You can not see it, but there it is--"

"My lord, you speak wildly."

"I have seen some strange things, François. The dead have arisen. And I have received my warning. Soon I shall join those dark specters which once gaily traversed this bright world. A little brandy and soda, François."

The servant brought it to him. The marquis leered awfully over his shoulder once more. "Your health, my guest!" he exclaimed, laughing harshly. "But my hat, François; I have business to perform, important business!"

He ambled out of the room. On the street he was all politeness, removing his hat to a dark brunette who rolled by in her carriage, and pausing to chat with another representative of the sex of the blond type. Then he gaily sauntered on, until reaching the theater he stopped and made a number of inquiries. Who was the manager of Constance Carew? Where was he to be found? "At the St. Charles hotel?" He was obliged to Monsieur, the ticket-seller, and wished him good-day.

Entering the hotel, he sent his card to Barnes, requesting an interview, and the manager, overcome by the honor of such a visit, responded with alacrity. The customary formalities over, the nobleman congratulated Barnes on the performance and led the conversation to the young actress.

"Pardon my curiosity," he said, with apparent carelessness, "but I'm sure I remember an actress of the same name in London--many years ago?"

"Her mother, undoubtedly," replied the manager, proudly.

"She was married, was she not, to--"

"A scoundrel who took her for his wife in one church and repudiated the ties through another denomination!"

"Ah, a French-English marriage!" said the marquis, blandly. "An old device! But what was this lover's name?"

"This husband's, my lord!"

"Lover or husband, I fancy it is all the same to her now," sneered the caller. "She has passed the point where reputation matters."

"Her reputation is my concern, Monsieur le Marquis!"

"You knew her?" asked the nobleman, as though the conversation wearied him. "And she was faithful to his memory? No scandals--none of those little affairs women of her class are prone to? There"--as Barnes started up indignantly--"spare me your reproaches! I'm too feeble to quarrel. Besides, what is it to me? I was only curious about her--that is all! But she never spoke the name of her husband?"

"Not even to her own child!"

"She does not know her father's name?" repeated the marquis. "But I thank you; Mademoiselle Constance is so charming I must needs call to ask if she were related to the London actress! Good-day, Monsieur! You are severe on the lover. Was it not the fashion of the day for the actresses to take lovers, or for the fops to have an opera girl or a comedienne? Did your most popular performers disdain such diversions?" he sneered. "Pardie, the world has suddenly become moral! A gentleman can no longer, it would seem, indulge in gentlemanly follies."

Mumbling about the decadence of fashion, the marquis departed, his manner so strange the manager gazed after him in surprise.

With no thought of direction, his lips moving, talking to himself in adynamic fashion, the nobleman walked mechanically on until he reached the great cathedral. The organ was rolling and voices arose sweet as those of seraphim. He hesitated at the portal and then laughed to himself. "Well has Voltaire said: 'Pleasure has its time; so, too, has wisdom. Make love in thy youth, and in old age, attend to thy salvation.'" He repeated the latter words, but, although he paused at the threshold and listened, he did not enter.

As he stood there, uncertain and trembling, a figure replete with youth and vigor approached, and, glancing at her, an exclamation escaped him that caused her to pause and turn.

"You are not well," she said, solicitously. "Can I help you?"

"It is nothing, nothing!" answered the marquis, ashy pale at the sight of her and the proximity of that face which regarded him with womanly sympathy. "Go away."

"At least, let me assist you. You were going to the cathedral? Come!"

His hand rested upon her strong young arm; he felt himself too weak to resist, so, together--father and daughter!--they entered the cathedral. Side by side they knelt--he to keep up the farce, fearing to undeceive her--while yet only mocking words came to the old man's heart, as the bitterness of the situation overwhelmed him. She was a daughter in whom a prince might have found pride, but he remained there mute, not daring to speak, experiencing all the tortures of remorse and retribution. Of what avail had been ambition? How had it overleaped content and ease of mind! Into what a nest of stings and thorns his loveless marriage had plunged him! And now but the black shadow remained; he walked in the darkness of unending isolation. So he should continue to walk straight to the door of death.

He scarcely heard the organ or the voice of the priest. The high altar, with its many symbols, suggested the thousands that had worshiped there and gone away comforted. Here was abundant testimony of the blessings of divine mercy in the numerous costly gifts and in the discarded crutches, and here faith had manifested itself for generations.

The marquis' throat was hoarse; he could have spoken no words if he had tried. He laughed in his heart at the gifts of the grateful ones; those crosses of ivory and handsome lamps were but symbols of barbarism and superstition. The tablets, with their inscriptions, "Merci" and "Ex voto," were to him absurd, and he gibed at the simple credulity of the people who could thus be misled. All these evidences of thanksgiving were but cumulative testimony that men and women are like little children, who will be pleased over fairy tales or frightened over ghost stories. The promise of paradise, but the fairy tale told by priests to men and women; the threats of punishment, the ghost stories to awe them! A malicious delight crept into his diseased imagination that he alone in the cathedral possessed the extreme divination, enabling him to perceive the emptiness of all these signs and symbols. He labored in a fever of mental excitement and was only recalled to himself as his glance once more rested upon the young girl.

He became dimly conscious that people were moving past them, and he suddenly longed to cry out, "My child!" but he fought down the impulse. There could be no turning back now at the eleventh hour; the marquis was a philosopher, and did not believe that, in a twinkling of an eye, a man may set behind all that has transpired and regard it as naught. Something within held him from speaking to her--perhaps his own inherent sense of the consistency of things; his appreciation of the legitimate finale to a miserable order of circumstances! Even pride forbade departure from long-established habit. But while this train of thought passed through his mind, he realized she was regarding him with clear, compassionate eyes, and he heard her voice:

"Shall we go now? The services are over."

He obeyed without question.

"Over!"

Those moments by her side would never return! They were about to part to meet no more on earth. He leaned heavily upon her arm and his steps were faltering. Out into the warm sunshine they passed, the light revealing more plainly the ravages of time in his face.

"You must take a carriage," she said to the old man.

"Thank you, thank you," he replied. "Leave me here on the bench. I shall soon be myself. I am only a little weak. You are good to an old man. May I not"--asking solely for the pleasure of hearing her speak--"may I not know the name of one who is kind to an old man?"

"My name is Constance Carew."

He shook as with the palsy. "A good name, a good name!" he repeated. "I remember years ago another of that name--an actress in London. A very beautiful woman, and good! But even she had her detractors and none more bitter than the man who wronged her. You--you resemble her! But there, don't let me detain you. I shall do very well here. You are busy, I dare say."

"Yes, I should be at rehearsal," she replied regretfully.

"At rehearsal!" he repeated. "Yes!--yes!--. But the stage is no place for you!" he added, suddenly. "You should leave it--leave it!"

She looked at him wonderingly. "Is there nothing more I can do for you?"

"Nothing! Nothing! Except--no, nothing!"

"You were about to ask something?" she observed with more sympathy.

"If you would not think me presuming--if you would not deem it an offense--you remind me of one I loved and lost--it is so long ago since I felt her kiss for the last time--I am so near the grave--"

With tears in her eyes, she bent her head and her fresh young lips just touched his withered brow.

"Good-by," she said. "I am so sorry for you!" And she was gone, leaving him sitting there motionless as though life had departed.

A rattling cab that clattered noisily past the cabildo and calaboza, and swung around the square, aroused the marquis. He arose, stopped the driver, and entered the rickety vehicle.

"The law office of Marks and Culver," said the marquis.

The man lashed his horse and the attenuated quadruped flew like a winged Pegasus, soon drawing up before the attorneys' office. Fortunately Culver was in, and, although averse to business on any day--thinking more of his court-yard and his fountain than of his law books--this botanist-solicitor made shift to comply with the marquis' instructions and reluctantly earned a modest fee. He even refused to express surprise at my lord's story; one wife in London, another in Paris; why, many a southern gentleman had two families--quadroons being plentiful, why not? Culver unobtrusively yawned, and, with fine courtesy, bowed the marquis out.

Slowly the latter retraced his steps to his home; his feet were heavy as lead; his smile was forced; he glanced frequently over his shoulder, possessed by a strange fantasy.

"I think I will lie down a little," he said to his valet. "In this easy chair; that will do. I am feeling well; only tired. How that mass is repeated in my mind! That is because it is Palestrina, François; not because it is a vehicle to salvation, employed by the gibbering priests. Never let your heart rule your head, boy. Don't mistake anything for reality. 'What have you seen in your travels?' was asked of Sage Evemere. 'Follies!' was the reply. 'Follies, follies everywhere!' We never live; we are always in the expectation of living."

He made an effort to smile which was little more than a grimace.

"A cigar, François!"

"My lord, are you well?--"

The marquis flew into a rage and the valet placed an imported weed in his master's hand.

"A light, François!"

The valet obeyed. For a moment the strong cigar seemed to soothe the old man, although his hand shook like an aspen as he held it.

"Now, bring me my Voltaire," commanded the marquis. "The volume on the table, idiot! Ah! here is what I wish: 'It takes twenty years to bring man from the state of embryo, and from that of a mere criminal, as he is in his first infancy, to the point when his reason begins to dawn. It has taken thirty centuries to know his structure; it would take eternity to know something of the soul; it takes but an instant to kill him.' But an instant; but an instant!" he repeated.

He puffed feebly at the cigar.

"It is cold here, François."

The servant consulted the thermometer.

"It is five degrees warmer than you are accustomed to, my lord," he replied.

"Bring me the thermometer," commanded the old man. "You should not lie, François. It is a bad fault in servants. Leave it to your masters; it is a polite vice. The privilege of the world's potentates, diplomats and great people. Never fall into the rut of lying, François, or you will soon outlive your usefulness as a valet."

"You can see that I speak the truth, my lord," was the response, as calm as ever, for nothing disturbed or ruffled this ideal servant.

He held out the thermometer for the marquis' inspection and the latter examined it carefully. The cigar fell from his fingers to the floor. The attentive valet picked it up and threw it into the grate.

"I believe, François," stammered the marquis, "that the fault lies with me. It is I--I, who am growing cold like death."

"Yes, my lord," answered the calm and imperturbable servant.

"'Yes?' you blockhead!" shrieked the master. "Do you know what you are saying?"

"Well, no, then, my lord," responded the unmoved valet.

"Yes and no!" shouted the marquis in a voice that was wildly discordant. "What do you mean?"

"Whatever my lord pleases," was the quiet response.

"Mon Dieu! I'll discharge you."

The servant only smiled.

"Why did you smile?"

"Oh, my lord--"

"Was it not that you thought it a good joke for a dying man to discharge his servant?"

"My lord is quick to catch the humorous side of anything," returned François.

"Begone, idiot! You are waiting for my death to discharge you. I can see it in your eyes. Yet stay, François, for, if you leave me, I shall be alone. You will not leave me?"

"As my lord desires," was François' response.

"I imagine I should feel better if I had my footbath."

The servant removed the shoes and silken stockings from his master's feet and propped him up in a chair, throwing a blanket over his shoulders and heaping more wood upon the fire in the grate.

"More fire, you idiot!" cried the marquis, peevishly. "Do you not see that I am freezing?"

"It is ten degrees above the temperature my lord always ordered," retorted François, coolly.

"Ten degrees! Oh, you wish to remind me that the end is approaching? You do not dare deny it!" The valet shrugged his shoulders.

"But I am not gone yet." He wagged his head cunningly and began to laugh to himself. His mind apparently rambled, for he started to chant a French love song in a voice that had long since lost its capacity for a sustained tone. The words were distinct, although the melody was broken, and the spectacle was gruesome enough. As he concluded he looked at the valet as if for approbation and began to mumble about his early love affairs.

"Bah, François," he said shrilly, "I'll be up to-morrow as gay as ever. Vive l'amour! vive la joie! It was a merry life we led, eh, François?"

"Merry indeed, my lord."

"It kept you busy, François. There was the little peasant girl on the Rhine. What flaxen hair she had and eyes like the sky! Yet a word of praise--a little flattery--"

"My lord was irresistible," said the valet with mild sarcasm.

"Let me see, François, what became of her?"

"She drowned herself in the river."

"That is true. I had forgotten. Well, life is measured by pleasures, not by years, and I was the prince of coxcombs. Up at ten o'clock; no sooner on account of the complexion; then visits from the tradespeople and a drive in the park to look at the ladies. It was there I used to meet the English actress. 'Twas there, with her, I vowed the park was a garden of Eden! What a scene, when my barrister tried to settle the case! Fortunately a marriage in England was not a marriage in France. I saw her last night, François"--with an insane look--"in the flesh and blood; as life-like as the night before we took the stage for Brighton!" Suddenly he shrieked and a look of terror replaced the vain, simpering expression.

"There, François!" Glancing with awe behind him. And truly there stood a dark shadow; a gruesome presence. His face became distorted and he lapsed into unconsciousness.

The valet gazed at him with indifference. Then he went to an inner room and brought a valise which he began packing carefully and methodically. After he had completed this operation he approached the dressing table and took up a magnificent jeweled watch, which he examined for a moment before thrusting it into his pocket. A snuff box, set with diamonds, and several rings followed. François with the same deliberation opened a drawer and took out a small box which he tried to open, and, failing, forced the lid with the poker. At this, my lord opened his eyes, and, in a weak voice, for his strength had nearly deserted him, demanded:

"What are you doing, François?"

"Robbing you, my lord," was the slow and dignified response.

The marquis' eyes gleamed with rage. He endeavored to call out, but his voice failed him and he fell back, trembling and overcome.

"Thief! Ingrate!" he hissed, hoarsely.

"I beg you not to excite yourself, my lord," said the stately valet. "You are already very weak and it will hasten the end."

"Is this the way you repay me?"

"My lord will not need these things soon."

"Have you no gratitude?" stammered the marquis, whose physical and mental condition was truly pitiable.

"Gratitude for having been called 'idiot,' 'dog,' and 'blockhead' nearly all my life! I am somewhat lacking in that quality, I fear."

"Is there no shame in you?"

"Shame?" repeated François, as he proceeded to ransack another drawer. "There might have been before I went into your service, my lord. Yes; once I felt shame for you. It was years ago, in London, when you deserted your beautiful wife. When I saw how she worshiped you and what a noble woman she was, I confess I felt ashamed that I served one of the greatest blackguards in Europe--"

"Oh, you scoundrel--" exclaimed the marquis, his face becoming a ghastly hue.

"Be calm, my lord. You really are in need of all your energy. For years I have submitted to your shameful service. I have been at the beck and call of one of the greatest roués and villains in France. Years of such association would somewhat soil any nature. Another thing, my lord, I must tell you, since you and I are settling our last accounts. For years I have endured your miserable King Louis Philippe. A king? Bah! He fled from the back door! A coward, who shaved his whiskers for a disguise."

"No more, rascal!"

"Rascal yourself, you worn-out, driveling breath of corruption! It is so pleasant to exercise a gentleman's privilege of invective! Ah, here is the purse. Au revoir, my lord. A pleasant dissolution!"

But by this time the marquis was speechless, and François, taking the valise in hand, deferentially left the room. He locked the door behind him and thrust the key into his pocket.

CHAPTER XII:
IN THE OLD CEMETERY

The engagement at the new St. Charles was both memorable and profitable, The Picayune, before the fifties, an audacious sheet, being especially kind to the players. "This paper," said a writer of the day, "was as full of witticisms as one of Thackeray's dreams after a light supper, and, as for Editors Straws and Phazma, they are poets who eat, talk and think rhyme." The Picayune contained a poem addressed to Miss Carew, written by Straws in a cozy nook in the veranda at the Lake End, with his absinthe before him and the remains of an elaborate repast about him. It was then quite the fashion to write stanzas to actresses; the world was not so prosaic as it is now, and even the president of the United States, John Quincy Adams, penned graceful verses to a fair ward of Thalia.

One noon, a few days after the opening performance, several members of the company were late for rehearsal and Barnes strode impatiently to and fro, glancing at his watch and frowning darkly. To avenge himself for the remissness of the players, he roared at the stage carpenters who were constructing a balcony and to the supers who were shifting flats to the scenery room. The light from an open door at the back of the stage dimly illumined the scene; overhead, in the flies, was intense darkness; while in front, the auditorium yawned like a chasm, in no wise suggestive of the brilliant transformation at night.

"Ugh!" said Susan, standing in one of the entrances. "It is like playing to ghosts! Fancy performing to an audience of specters! Perhaps the phantoms of the past really do assemble in their old places on occasions like this. Only you can't hear them applaud or laugh."

"Are you looking for admirers among ghosts?" remarked Hawkes, ironically.

"Don't," she returned, with a little shiver.

"So, ladies and gentlemen, you are all here at last?" exclaimed Barnes, interrupting this cheerful conversation. "Some of you are late again to-day. It must not happen again. Go to Victor's, Moreau's, or Miguel's, as much as you please. If you have a headache or a heartache in consequence, that is your own affair, but I am not to be kept waiting the next day."

"Victor's, indeed!" retorted the elastic old lady. "As if--"

"No one supposed, Madam, that at your age"--began the manager.

"At my age! If you think--"

"Are you all ready?" interrupted Barnes, hastily, knowing he would be worsted in any argument with this veteran player. "Then clear the stage! Act first!" And the rehearsal began.

If the audience were specters, the performers moved, apparently without rhyme or reason, mere shadows on the dimly lighted stage; enacting some semblance to scenes of mortal life; their jests and gibes, unnatural in that comparatively empty place; their voices, out of the semi-darkness, like those of spirits rehearsing acts of long ago. In the evening it would all become an amusing, bright-colored reality, but now the barrenness of the scenes was forcibly apparent.

"That will do for to-day," said the manager at the conclusion of the last act. "To-morrow, ladies and gentlemen, at the same time. And any one who is late--will be fined!"

"Changing the piece every few nights is all work and no play," complained Susan.

"It will keep you out of mischief, my dear," replied Barnes, gathering up his manuscripts.

"Oh, I don't know about that!" returned Miss Susan, with a defiant toss of the head, as she moved toward the dressing-room where they had left their wraps. It was a small apartment, fairly bright and cheery, with here and there a portrait against the wall. Above the dressing-table hung a mirror, diamond-scratched with hieroglyphic scrawls, among which could be discerned a transfixed heart, spitted like a lark on an arrow, and an etching of Lady Gay Spanker, with cork-screw curls. Taglioni, in pencil caricature, her limbs "divinely slender," gyrated on her toes in reckless abandon above this mute record of names now forgotten.

"What lovely roses, Constance!" exclaimed Susan, as she entered, bending over a large bouquet on one of the chairs. "From the count, I presume?"

"Yes," indifferently answered the young girl, who was adjusting her hat before the mirror.

"How attentive he is!" cooed Susan, her tones floating in a higher register. "Poor man! Enjoy yourself while you may, my dear," she went on. "When youth is gone, what is left? Women should sow their wild oats as well as men. I don't call them wild oats, though, but paradisaical oats. The Elysian fields are strewn with them."

As she spoke, her glance swept her companion searchingly, and, in that brief scrutiny, Susan observed with inward complacency how pale the other was, and how listless her manner! Their common secret, however, made Susan's outward demeanor sweetly solicitous and gently sympathetic. Her mind, passing in rapid review over recent events, dwelt not without certain satisfaction upon results. True, every night she was still forced to witness Constance's success, which of itself was wormwood and gall to Susan, to stand in the wings and listen to the hateful applause; but the conviction that the sweets of popular favor brought not what they were expected to bring, was, in a way, an antidote to Susan's dissatisfaction.

A little knowledge is a dangerous thing and can sometimes be made annoying; in Susan's case it was a weapon sharpened with honeyed phrase and consolatory bearing, for she was not slow to discover nor to avail herself of the irritating power this knowledge gave her. Constance's pride and reticence, however, made it difficult for Susan to discern when her shafts went true. Moreover, although harboring no suspicion of Susan's dissimulation, she instinctively held aloof from her and remained coldly unresponsive. Perhaps in the depths of Susan's past lurked something indefinable which threw its shadow between them, an inscrutable impediment; and her inability to penetrate the young actress' reserve, however she might wound her, awakened Susan's resentment. But she was too world-wise to display her irritation. She even smiled sweetly now, as confidante to confidante, and, turning to her impulsively, said:

"Let me help you on with your cloak, dear?"

Out of the quiet, deserted theater, isolated from external din, to the busy streets, where drays went thundering by, and industry manifested itself in resounding clatter, was a sudden, but not altogether unwelcome, change to Constance. Without waiting for the manager, who paused at the rear entrance to impress his final instructions upon a stolid-looking property-man, she turned quickly into the noisy thoroughfares.

On and on her restlessness led her, conscious of the clangor of vehicles and voices and yet remote from them; past those picturesque suggestions of the one-time Spanish rulers in which the antiquarian could detect evidence of remote Oriental infusion; past the silken seductions of shops, where ladies swarmed and hummed like bees around the luscious hive; past the idlers' resorts, from whence came the rat-a-tat of clinking billiard balls and the louder rumble of falling ten-pins.

In a window of one of these places, a club with a reputation for exclusiveness, a young man was seated, newspaper in hand, a cup of black coffee on a small table before him, and the end of a cigar smoking on the tray where he had placed it. With a yawn, he had just thrown aside the paper and was reaching for the thick, dark beverage--his hand thin and nervous--when, glancing without, he caught sight of the actress in the crowd. Obeying a sudden impulse, he arose, picking up his hat which lay on a chair beside him.

"Yo' order am ready in a moment, Mr. Mauville," said a colored servant, hurrying toward the land baron as the latter was leaving.

"I've changed my mind and don't want it," replied the other curtly.

And sauntering down the steps of the club with ill-concealed impatience, he turned in the direction the young girl had taken, keeping her retreating figure in view; now, so near her in the crowded street, he could almost touch her; then, as they left the devious ways, more distant, but ever with his eyes bent upon her. He had almost spoken, when in the throng he approached within arm's length, but something--he knew not what--restrained him, and a press of people separated them. Only for a moment, and then he continued the questionable pleasure of following her.

Had she turned, she would probably have seen her pursuer, but absorbed in thought, she continued on her way, unconscious of his presence. On and on she hurried, until she reached the tranquil outskirts and lingered before the gate of one of the cemeteries. At the same time the land baron slackened his footsteps, hesitating whether to advance or turn back. After a moment's indecision, she entered the cemetery; her figure, receding in the distance, was becoming more and more indistinct, when he started forward quickly and also passed through the gate.

The annual festival of the dead, following All Saint's day, was being observed in the burial ground. This commemoration of those who have departed in the communion--described by Tertullian in the second century as an "apostolic tradition," so old was the sacrifice!-- was celebrated with much pomp and variety in the Crescent City. In the vicinity of the cemetery gathered many colored marchandes, their heads and shoulders draped in shawls and fichus of bright, diversified hues; before them, perambulating booths with baskets of molasses candy or pain-patate. Women, dressed in mourning, bore to the tomb flowers and plants, trays of images, wreaths, crosses, anchors of dried immortelles and artificial roses. Some were accompanied by priests and acolytes with censers, the former intoning the service:

Fidelium Deus omnium conditor--

A solemn peace fell upon the young girl as she entered and she seemed to leave behind her all disturbing emotions, finding refuge in the supreme tranquillity of this ancient city of the dead. She was surrounded by a resigned grief, a sorrow so dignified that it did not clash with the sweeter influences of nature. The monotonous sound of the words of the priests harmonized with the scene. The tongue of a nation that had been resolved into the elements was fitting in this place, where time and desolation had left their imprint in discolored marble, inscriptions almost effaced, and clambering vines.

--Animabus famulorum--

To many the words so mournfully intoned brought solace and surcease from sorrow. The sisters of charity moved among the throng with grave, pale faces, mere shadows of their earthly selves, as though they had undergone the first stage of the great metamorphosis which is promised. To them, who had already buried health, vitality and passion, was not this chant to the dead, this strange intoning of words, sweeter than the lullaby crooned by a nurse to a child, more stirring than the patriotic hymn to a soldier, and fraught with more fervor than the romantic dream of a lover?

Ut indulgentiam, quam semper optaverunt--

The little orphan children heard and heeded no more than the butterfly which lighted upon the engraven words, "Dust to dust," and poised gracefully, as it bathed in the sunshine, stretching its wings in wantonness of beauty.

Piis supplicationibus consequantur--

Now Constance smiled to see the little ones playing on the steps of a monument. It was the tomb of a great jurist, a man of dignity during his mundane existence, his head crammed with those precepts which are devised for the temporal well-being of that fabric, sometimes termed society, and again, civilization. The poor waifs, with suppressed laughter--they dared not give full vent to their merriment with the black-robed sisters not far away--ran around the steps, unmindful of the inscription which might have been written by a Johnson, and as unconscious of unseemly conduct as the insects that hummed in the grass.

"Hush!" whispered one of the sisters, as a funeral cortège approached.

The children, wide-eyed in awe and wonder, desisted in their play.

"It is an old man who died last night," said a nun in a low voice to Constance, noticing her look of inquiry.

The silver crucifix shone fitfully ahead, while the chanting of the priests, winding in and out after the holy symbol, fell upon the ear. And the young girl gazed with pity as the remains of the Marquis de Ligne, her father, were borne by.

Qui vivis et regnas. Glorificamus te.

CHAPTER XIII:
AN INCONGRUOUS RÔLE

L onger and longer trailed the shadow of a tall tombstone until, as the sun went down, it merged into the general twilight like a life lengthening out and out and finally blending in restful darkness. With that transition came a sudden sense of isolation and loneliness; the little burial ground seemed the world; the sky, its walls and ceiling.

From the neighborhood of the gates had vanished the dusky venders, trundling their booths and stalls citywards. As abruptly had disappeared the bearers of flowers and artificial roses with baskets poised upon their heads, imparting to their figures dignity and erectness. The sad-eyed nuns had wended their way out of the little kingdom of the departed, surrounded by the laughing children and preceded by the priests and acolytes. All the sounds and activities of the day--the merriment of the little ones, the oblations of the priests, the greetings of friends--were followed by inertness and languor. Motionless against the sky spread the branches of the trees, like lines etched there; still were the clambering vines that clasped monolith and column.

But suddenly that death-like lull in nature's animation and unrest was abruptly broken, and an uproarious vociferation dispelled the voiceless peace.

"For Jack ashore's a Croesus, lads, With a Jill for every Jack--"

sang a hoarse voice as its owner came staggering along one of the walks of the cemetery; for all his song, no blue-water sailor-man, but a boisterous denizen of the great river, a raftsman or a keel-boatman, who had somehow found himself in the burial ground and now was beating aimlessly about. How this rollicking waif of the grog shop came to wander so far from the convivial haunts of his kind and to choose this spot for a ramble, can only be explained by the vagaries of inebriety.

"With a Jill in your wake, A fair port you'll make--"

he continued, when his eye fell upon the figure of a woman, some distance ahead, and fairly discernible in the gathering twilight. Immediately the song ceased and he steadied himself, gazing incredulously after the form that had attracted his attention.

"Hello!" he said. "Avast, my dear!" he called out.

Echoing in that still place, his harsh tones produced a startling effect, and the figure before him moved faster and faster, casting a glance behind her at the man from the river, who with snatches of song, started in uncertain but determined pursuit. As the heavy footsteps sounded nearer, she increased her pace, with eyes bent upon the distant gate; darker seemed to grow the way; more menacing the shadows outstretched across the path. Louder crunched the boots on the shell walk; more audible became the words of the song that flowed from his lips, when the sound of a sudden and violent altercation replaced the hoarse-toned cadence, an altercation that was of brief duration, characterized by longshoreman oaths, and followed by silence; and then a figure, not that of the tuneful waterman, sprang to the side of the startled girl.

"Miss Carew!" exclaimed a well-remembered voice.

Bewildered, breathing quickly, she gazed from Edward Mauville, who thus unexpectedly accosted her, to the prostrate form, lying motionless on the road. The rude awakening from her day-dream in the hush of that peaceful place, and the surprising sequence had dazed her senses, and, for the moment, it seemed something tragic must have happened.

"Is he dead?" she asked quickly, unable to withdraw her glance from the immovable figure, stretched out in the dim light on the path.

"No fear!" said Mauville, quietly, almost thoughtfully, although his eyes were yet bright from the encounter. "You can't kill his kind," he added, contemptuously. "Brutes from coal barges, or raftsmen from the head waters! He struck against a stone when he fell, and what with that, and the liquor in him, will rest there awhile. He'll come to without remembering what has happened."

Turning moodily, the land baron walked slowly down the road, away from the gate; she thought he was about to leave her, when he paused, as though looking for something, stooped to the ground, and returned, holding out a garment.

"You dropped your wrap, Miss Carew," he said, awkwardly. "The night is cold and you will need it." She offered no resistance when he placed it over her shoulders; indeed, seemed unconscious of the attention.

"Don't you think we had better go?" he went on. "It won't hurt him"--indicating the motionless body--"to stay here--the brute!"

But as he spoke, with some constraint, her eyes, full of doubts, met his, and he felt a flush mantle his face. The incongruity of his position appealed forcibly to him. Had he not been watching and following her himself? Seeing her helpless, alone, in the silent spot, where she had unconsciously lingered too long, had he not been almost on the point of addressing her? Moved by vague desires, had he not already started impetuously toward her, when the man from the river had come rollicking along and insinuated himself after his fashion in the other's rôle?

And at the sight--the fleeing girl, the drunken, profane waterman!--how his heart had leaped and his body had become steel for the encounter; an excess of vigor for a paltry task! Jack, as he called himself, might have been a fighting-man earlier in the day, but now he had gone down like straw. When the excitement of this brief collision was over, however, the land baron found his position as unexpected as puzzling.

As these thoughts swiftly crossed his mind, he could not forbear a bitter laugh, and she, walking more quickly toward the gate, regarded him with inquiry, not perhaps unmingled with apprehension. A picture of events, gone by, arose before her like a menacing shadow over the present. He interpreted her glance for what it meant, and angry that she doubted him, angry with himself, said roughly:

"Oh, you haven't anything to fear!"

Her answering look was so gentle, so sad, an unwonted feeling of compunction seized him; he repented of his harshness, and added less brusquely:

"Why did you remain so late?"

"I did not realize how late it had become."

"Your thoughts must have been very absorbing!" he exclaimed quickly, his brow once more overcast.

Not difficult was it for him to surmise upon whom her mind had been bent, and involuntarily his jaw set disagreeably, while he looked at her resentfully. In that light he could but dimly discern her face. Her bonnet had fallen from her head; her eyes were bent before her, as though striving to penetrate the gathering darkness. With his sudden spell of jealousy came the temptation to clasp her in his arms in that silent, isolated place, but the figure of the sailor came between him and the desire, while pride, the heritage of the gentleman, fought down the longing. This self-conquest was not accomplished, however, without a sacrifice of temper, for after a pause, he observed:

"There is no accounting for a woman's taste!"

She did not controvert this statement, but the start she gave told him the shaft had sped home.

"An outlaw! An outcast!" exclaimed the patroon, stung beyond endurance by his thoughts.

Still no reply; only more hurried footsteps! Around them sounded a gentle rustling; a lizard scrambled out of their path through the crackling leaves; a bat, or some other winged creature, suddenly whirred before them and vanished. They had now approached the gate, through which they passed and found themselves on the road leading directly to the city, whose lights had already begun to twinkle in the dusk.

The cheering rumble of a carriage and the aspect of the not far-distant town quickened her spirits and imparted elasticity to her footsteps. Upon the land baron they produced an opposite effect, for he was obviously reluctant to abandon the interview, however unsatisfactory it might be. There was nothing to say, and yet he was loath to leave her; there was nothing to accomplish, and yet he wished to remain with her. For this reason, as they drew near the city, his mood became darker, like the night around them. Instinctively, she felt the turbulent passions stirring in his bosom; his sudden silence, his dogged footsteps reawakened her misgivings. Furtively she regarded him, but his eyes were fixed straight before him on the soft luster above the city, the reflection of the lights, and she knew and mistrusted his thoughts. Although she found his silence more menacing than his words, she could think of nothing to say to break the spell, and so they continued to walk mutely side by side. An observer, seeing them beneath the cypress, a lovers' promenade, with its soft, enfolding shadows, would have taken them for a well-matched couple, who had no need for language.

But when they had emerged from that romantic lane and entered the city, the land baron breathed more freely. She was now surrounded by movement and din; the seclusion of the country gave way to the stir of the city; she was no longer dependent on his good offices; his rôle of protector had ended when they left the cypress walk behind them.

His brow cleared; he glanced at her with ill-concealed admiration; he noticed with secret pride the attention she attracted from passers-by, the sidelong looks of approval that followed her through the busy streets. The land baron expanded into his old self; he strode at her side, gratified by the scrutiny she invited; assurance radiated from his eyes like some magnetic heat; he played at possession wilfully, perversely. "Why not," whispered Hope. "A woman's mind is shifting ever. Her fancy--a breath! The other is gone. Why--"

"It was not accident my being in the cemetery, Miss Carew," said Mauville, suddenly covering her with his glance. Meeting her look of surprise unflinchingly, he continued: "I followed you there; through the streets, into the country! My seeing you first was chance; my presence in the burial ground the result of that chance. The inevitable result!" he repeated softly. "As inevitable as life! Life; what is it? Influences which control us; forces which bind us! It is you, or all; you or nothing!"

She did not reply; his voice, vibrating with feeling, touched no answering chord. Nevertheless, a new, inexplicable wave of sorrow moved her. It might be he had cared for her as sincerely as it was possible for his wayward heart to care for any one. Perhaps time would yet soften his faults, and temper his rashness. With that shade of sorrow for him there came compassion as well; compassion that overlooked the past and dwelt on the future.

She raised her steady eyes. "Why should it be 'I or nothing,' as you put it?" she finally answered slowly. "Influences may control us in a measure, but we may also strive for something. We can always strive."

"For what? For what we don't want? That's the philosophy of your moralists, Miss Carew," he exclaimed. "That's your modern ethics of duty. Playing tricks with happiness! The game isn't worth the candle. Or, if you believe in striving," he added, half resentfully, half imploringly, "strive to care for me but a little. But a little!" he said again. "I who once wanted all, and would have nothing but all, am content to ask, to plead, for but a little."

"I see no reason," she replied, wearily, yet not unkindly, "why we should not be friends."

"Friends!" he answered, bitterly. "I do not beg for a loaf, but a crumb. Yet you refuse me that! I will wait! Only a word of encouragement! Will you not give it?"

She turned and looked into his eyes, and, before she spoke, he knew what her answer would be.

"How can I?" she said, simply. "Why should I promise something I can never fulfil?"

He held her glance as though loath to have it leave him.

"May I see you again?" he asked, abruptly.

She shook her head. His gaze fell, seeing no softening in her clear look.

"You are well named," he repeated, more to himself than to her. "Constance! You are constant in your dislikes as well as your likes."

"I have no dislike for you," she replied. "It seems to have been left behind me somewhere."

"Only indifference, then!" he said, dully.

"No; not indifference!"

"You do care what--may become of me?"

"You should do so much--be so much in the world," she answered, thoughtfully.

"Sans peur et sans reproche!" he cried, half-amused, half-cheerlessly. "What a pity I met you--too late!"

They were now at the broad entrance of the brilliantly-lighted hotel. Several loungers, smoking their after-dinner cigars, gazed at the couple curiously.

"Mauville's a lucky dog," said one.

"Yes; he was born with a silver spoon," replied the person addressed.

As he passed through the envious throng, the land baron had regained his self-command, although his face was marked with an unusual pallor. In his mind one thought was paramount--that the walk begun at the burial-ground was drawing to an end; their last walk; the finale of all between them! Yet he could call to mind nothing further to say. His story had been told; the conclusion reached. She, too, had spoken, and he knew she would never speak differently. Bewildered and unable to adjust his new and strange feelings, it dawned upon him he had never understood himself and her; that he had never really known what love was, and he stood abashed, confronted by his own ignorance. Passion, caprice, fancy, he had seen depth in their shallows, but now looked down and discerned the pebbly bottom. All this and much more surged through his brain as he made his way through the crowd, and, entering the corridor of the hotel, took formal leave of the young girl at the stairway.

"Good-night, Miss Carew," he said, gravely.

"Good-night," she replied. And then, on the steps, she turned and looked down at him, extending her hand: "Thank you!"

That half-timid, low "thank you!" he knew was all he would ever receive from her. He hardly felt the hand-clasp; he was hardly conscious when she turned away. A heavier hand fell upon his shoulder.

"You sly dog!" said a thick voice. "Well, a judge of a good horse is a judge of a handsome woman! We're making up a few bets on the horses to-morrow. Colonel Ogelby will ride Dolly D, and I'm to ride my Gladiator. It'll be a gentlemen's race."

"Aren't we gentlemen?" growled a professional turfsman.

"Gad! it's the first time I ever heard a jockey pretend to be one!" chuckled the first speaker. "What do you say, Mauville?"

"What do I say?" repeated the land baron, striving to collect his thoughts. "What--why, I'll make it an even thousand, if you ride your own horse, you'll--"

"Win?" interrupted the proud owner.

"No; fall off before he's at the second quarter!"

"Done!" said the man, immediately.

"Huzza!" shouted the crowd.

"That's the way they bet on a gentlemen's race!" jeered the gleeful jockey.

"Drinks on Gladiator!" exclaimed some one. And as no southern gentleman was ever known to refuse to drink to a horse or a woman, the party carried the discussion to the bar-room.

BOOK III:
THE FINAL CUE

CHAPTER I:
OVERLOOKING THE COURT-YARD

" I n the will of the Marquis de Ligne, probated yesterday, all of the property, real and personal, is left to his daughter, Constance," wrote Straws in his paper shortly after the passing of the French nobleman. "The document states this disposition of property is made as 'an act of atonement and justice to my daughter, whose mother I deserted, taking advantage of the French law to annul my marriage in England.' The legitimacy of the birth of this, his only child, is thereupon fully acknowledged by the marquis after a lapse of many years and long after the heretofore unrecognized wife had died, deserted and forgotten. Thrown on her own resources, the young child, with no other friend than Manager Barnes, battled with the world; now playing in taverns or barns, like the players of interludes, the strollers of old, or 'vagabonds', as the great and mighty Junius, from his lofty plane, termed them. The story of that period of 'vagrant' life adds one more chapter to the annals of strolling players which already include such names as Kemble, Siddons and Kean.

"From the Junius category to a public favorite of New Orleans has been no slight transition, and now, to appear in the rôle of daughter of a marquis and heiress to a considerable estate--truly man--and woman--play many parts in this brief span called life! But in making her sole heir the marquis specifies a condition which will bring regrets to many of the admirers of the actress. He robs her of her birthright from her mother. The will stipulates that the recipient give up her profession, not because it is other than a noble one, but 'that

---

she may the better devote herself to the duties of her new position and by her beneficence and charity remove the stain left upon an honored name by my second wife, the Duchesse D'Argens'."

The marquis' reference to "charity" and "beneficence" was in such ill-accord with his character that it might be suspected an adroit attorney, in drawing up the document, had surreptitiously inserted it. His proud allusion to his honored name and slurring suggestion of the taint put upon it by his second wife demonstrated the marquis was not above the foibles of his kind, overlooking his own light conduct and dwelling on that of his noble helpmate. It was the final taunt, and, as the lady had long since been laid in God's Acre, where there is only silence divine, it received no answer, and the world was welcome to digest and gorge it and make the most of it.

But although the marquis and his lady had no further interest in subsequent events, growing out of their brief sojourn on earth, the contents of the will afforded a theme of gossip for the living and molded the affairs of one in new shape and manner. On the same day this public exposition appeared, Barnes and the young actress were seated in the law office of Marks and Culver, a room overlooking a court-yard, brightened by statues and urns of flowers. A plaster bust of Justinian gazed benignly through the window at a fountain; a steel engraving of Jeremy Bentham watched the butterflies, and Hobbes and John Austin, austere in portraiture, frowned darkly down upon the flowering garden. While the manager and Constance waited for the attorney to appear, they were discussing, not for the first time, the proviso of the will to which Straws had regretfully alluded.

"Yes," said Barnes, folding the newspaper which contained Straws' article and placing it in his pocket; "you should certainly give up the stage. We must think of the disappointments, the possible failure, the slender reward. There was your mother--such an actress!--yet toward the last the people flocked to a younger rival. I have often thought anxiously of your future, for I am old--yes, there is no denying it!--and any day I may leave you, dependent solely upon yourself."

"Do not speak like that," she answered, tenderly. "We shall be together many, many years."

"Always, if I had my way," he returned, heartily.

"But with this legacy you are superior to the fickle public. In fact, you are now a part of the capricious public, my dear," he added in a jocular tone, "and may applaud the 'heavy father,' myself, or prattle about prevailing styles while the buskined tragedian is strutting below your box. Why turn to a blind bargain? Fame is a jade, only caught after our illusions are gone and she seems not half so sweet as when pursuing her in our dreams!"

But as he spoke, with forced lightness, beneath which, however, the young girl could readily detect the vein of anxiety and regret, she was regarding him with the clear eyes of affection. His face, seamed with many lines and bearing the deeply engraved handwriting of time, spoke plainly of declining years; every lineament was eloquent with vicissitudes endured; and as she discerningly read that varied past of which her own brief career had been a part, there entered her mind a brighter picture of a tranquil life for him at last, where in old age he could exchange uncertainty and activity for security and rest. How could she refuse to do as he desired? How often since fate had wrought this change in her life had she asked herself the question?

Her work, it is true, had grown dearer to her than ever; of late she had thrown herself into her task with an ardor and earnestness lifting each portrayal to a higher plane. Is it that only with sorrow comes the fulness of art; that its golden gates are never swung entirely open to the soul bearing no burden?

Closed to ruder buffetings, is it only to the sesame of a sad voice those portals spring magically back? But for his sake she must needs pause on the threshold of attainment, and stifle that ambition which of itself precluded consideration of a calm, uneventful existence. She was young and full of courage, but the pathos of his years smote her heart; something inexplicable had awakened her fears for him; she believed him far from well of late, although he laughed at her apprehensions and protested he had never been better in his life.

Now, reading the anxiety in his face as he watched her, she smiled reassuringly, her glance, full of love, meeting his.

"Everything shall be as you wish," she said, softly. "You know what is best!"

The manager's face lighted perceptibly, but before he could answer, the door opened, and Culver, the attorney, entered. With ruddy countenance and youthful bearing, in antithesis to the hair, silvered with white, he was one of those southern gentlemen who

---

grow old gracefully. The law was his taskmaster; he practised from a sense of duty, but ever held that those who rushed to court were likely to repeat the experience of Voltaire, who had twice been ruined: once when he lost a law suit; the second time, when he won one! Nevertheless, people persisted in coming to Culver wantonly welcoming unknown ills.

"Well, Miss Carew," he now exclaimed, after warmly greeting his visitors, "have you disburdened yourself of prejudice against this estate? Wealth may be a little hardship at first, but soon you won't mind it."

"Not a bit!" spoke up Barnes. "It's as easy to get used to as-- poverty, and we've had plenty of that!"

"You know the other condition?" she said, half-defiantly, half-sadly. "You are to be with me always."

"How can you teach an old dog new tricks?" protested Barnes. "How can you make a fine man about town out of a 'heavy father?'"

"The 'heavy father' is my father. I never knew any other. I am glad I never did."

"Hoity-toity!" he exclaimed scoffingly, but pleased nevertheless.

"You can't put me off that way," she said, decisively, with a sudden flash in her eyes he knew too well to cross. "Either you leave the stage, too, or--"

"Of course, my dear, of course--"

"Then it's all settled you will accept the encumbrance to which you have fallen heir," resumed Culver. "Even if there had been no will in your favor, the State of Louisiana follows the French law, and the testator can under no circumstances alienate more than half his property, if he leave issue or descendants. Had the old will remained, its provisions could not have been legally carried out."

"The old will?" said Barnes. "Then there was another will?"

"One made before he was aware of your existence, Miss Carew, in favor of his ward, Ernest Saint-Prosper."

"Ernest Saint-Prosper!"

Constance's cheeks flamed crimson, and her quick start of surprise did not escape the observant lawyer. Barnes, too, looked amazed over this unexpected intelligence.

"Saint-Prosper was the marquis' ward?" he cried.

The attorney transferred his gaze from the expressive features of his fair client to the open countenance of the manager. "Yes," he said.

"And would have inherited this property but for Constance?"

"Exactly! But you knew him, Mr. Barnes?"

"He was an occupant of the chariot, sir," replied the manager, with some feeling. "We met in the Shadengo Valley; the company was in sore straits, and--and--to make a long story short!--he joined our band and traversed the continent with us. And so he was the marquis' ward! It seems almost incredible!"

"Yes," affirmed Culver; "when General Saint-Prosper, his father, died, Ernest Saint-Prosper, who was then but a boy, became the marquis' ward and a member of his household."

"Well, well, how things do come about!" ruminated Barnes. "To think he should have been the prospective heir, and Constance, the real one!"

"Where is he now?" asked the attorney, thoughtfully.

"He has gone to Mexico; enlisted! But how do you know he--"

"Had expectations? The marquis told me about a quarrel they had had; he was a staunch imperialist; the young man as firm a republican! What would be the natural outcome? They parted in bitter anger."

"And then the marquis made him his heir?" exclaimed the manager, incredulously. "How do you reconcile that?"

The attorney smiled. "Through the oddity of my client! 'Draw up my will,' said the marquis to me one day, 'leaving all my property to this republican young dog. That will cut off the distant relatives who made the sign of the cross behind my back as though I were the evil one. They expect it all; he expects nothing! It will be a rare joke. I leave them my affection--and the privilege of having masses said for my soul.' The marquis was always of a satirical temperament."

"So it seems," commented the manager. "But he changed his mind and his will again?"

"After he met Miss Carew."

"Met me!" exclaimed Constance, aroused from a maze of reflection.

"Near the cathedral! He walked and talked with you."

"That poor old man--"

"And then came here, acknowledged you as his daughter, and drew up the final document."

"That accounts for a call I had from him!" cried Barnes, telling the story of the marquis' visit. "Strange, I did not suspect something of the truth at the time," he concluded, "for his manner was certainly unusual."

A perplexed light shone in the girl's eyes; she clasped and unclasped her hands quickly, turning to the lawyer.

"Their quarrel was only a political difference?" she asked at length.

"Yes," said the other, slowly. "Saint-Prosper refused to support the fugitive king. Throughout the parliamentary government, the restoration under Louis XVIII, and the reign of King Charles X, the marquis had ever a devout faith in the divine right of monarchs. He annulled his marriage in England with your mother to marry the Duchesse D'Argens, a relative of the royal princess. But Charles abdicated and the duchesse died. All this, however, is painful to you, Miss Carew?"

"Only such as relates to my mother," she replied in a clear tone. "I suppose I should feel grateful for this fortune, but I am afraid I do not. Please go on."

Culver leaned back in his chair, his glance bent upon a discolored statue of Psyche in the court-yard. "Had the marquis attended to his garden, like Candide, or your humble servant, and eschewed the company of kings he might have been as care-free as he was wretched. His monarchs were knocked down like nine-pins. Louis XVIII was a man of straw; Charles X, a feather-top, and Louis Philippe, a toy ruler. The marquis' domestic life was as unblest as his political career. The frail duchesse left him a progeny of scandals. These, the only offspring of the iniquitous dame, were piquantly dressed in the journals for public parade. Fancy, then, his delight in disinheriting his wife's relatives, and leaving you, his daughter, his fortune and his name!"

"His name?" she repeated, sadly. With averted face she watched the fountain in the garden. "If he had given it to my mother," she continued, "but now--I do not care for it. Her name is all I want." Her voice trembled and she exclaimed passionately: "I should rather Mr. Saint-Prosper would keep the property and I--my work! After denying my mother and deserting her, how can I accept anything from him?"

"Under the new will," said Culver, "the estate does not revert to Mr. Saint-Prosper in any event. But you might divide it with him?" he added, suddenly.

"How could I do that?" she asked, without looking up.

"Marry him!" laughed the attorney.

But the jest met with scant response, his fair client remaining motionless as a statue, while Barnes gazed at her furtively. Culver's smile gradually faded; uncertain how to proceed, realizing his humor had somehow miscarried, he was not sorry when the manager arose, saying:

"Well, my dear, it is time we were at the theater."

"Won't you accept this nosegay from my garden, Miss Carew?" urged the lawyer in a propitiatory tone as they were leaving.

And the attorney not only accompanied them to the door, but down-stairs to the street, where he stood for a moment watching them drive down the thoroughfare. Then he slowly returned, breathing heavily--invidious contradiction of his youthful assumption!--and shaking his head, as he mounted to his room.

"Culver, you certainly put your foot in it that time!" he muttered. "How she froze at my suggestion! Has there been some passage of arms between them? Apparently! But here am I, pondering over romances with all this legal business staring me in the face!" His glance swept a chaos of declarations, bills, affidavits and claims. "Confound the musty old courthouse and the bustling Yankee lawyers who set such a disturbing pace! There is no longer gentlemanly leisure in New Orleans."

He seated himself with a sigh before a neglected brief. In the distance the towers of the cathedral could be seen, reminding the attorney of the adjacent halls of justice in the scraggy-looking square, with its turmoil, its beggars, and apple women in the lobbies; its ancient, offensive smell, its rickety stairs, its labyrinth of passages and its Babel of tongues. Above him, however, the plaster bust of Justinian, out of those blank, sightless eyes, continued the contemplation of the garden as though turning from the complex jurisprudence of the ancients and moderns to the simple existence of butterflies and flowers.

CHAPTER II:
ONLY A SHADOW

There is an aphorism to the effect that one can not spend and have; also, a saying about the whirlwind, both of which in time came home to the land baron. For several generations the Mauville family, bearing one of the proudest names in Louisiana, had held marked prestige under Spanish and French rule, while extensive plantations indicated the commercial ascendency of the patroon's ancestors. The thrift of his forefathers, however, passed lightly over Edward Mauville. Sent to Paris by his mother, a widow, who could deny him nothing, in the course of a few years he had squandered two plantations and several hundred negroes. Her death placed him in undisputed possession of the residue of the estate, when finding the exacting details of commerce irksome, in a moment of weakness, he was induced to dispose of some of his possessions to Yankee speculators who had come in with the flood of northern energy. Most of the money thus realized he placed in loose investments, while the remainder gradually disappeared in indulging his pleasures.

At this critical stage in his fortunes--or misfortunes--the patroon's legacy had seemed timely, and his trip to the North followed. But from a swarm of creditors, to a nest of anti-renters, was out of the frying-pan into the fire, hastening his return to the Crescent City, where he was soon forced to make an assignment of the remaining property. A score of hungry lawyers hovered around the sinking estate, greedily jealous lest some one of their number should batten too gluttonously at this general collation. It was the one topic of interest in the musty, dusty courthouse until the end appeared with the following announcement in the local papers:

"Annonce! Vente importante de Nègres! Mauville estate in bankruptcy!"

And thereafter were specified the different lots of negroes to be sold.

Coincident with these disasters came news from the North regarding his supposedly immense interests in New York State. A constitutional convention had abolished all feudal tenures and freed the fields from baronial burdens. At a breath--like a house of cards--the northern heritage was swept away and about all that remained of the principality was the worthless ancient deed itself, representing one of the largest colonial grants.

But even the sale of the negroes and his other merchandise and property failed to satisfy his clamorous creditors or to pay his gambling debts. Those obligations at cards it was necessary to meet, so he moved out of his bachelor apartments, turned over his expensive furnishings and bric-à-brac to the gamblers and snapped his fingers at the over-anxious constables and lawyers.

As time went by evidence of his reverses insidiously crept into his personal appearance. He who had been the leader now clung to the tail-ends of style, and it was a novel sensation when one day he noticed a friend scrutinizing his garments much in the same critical manner that he had himself erstwhile affected. This glance rested casually on the hat; strayed carelessly to the waistcoat; wandered absently to the trousers, down one leg and up the other; superciliously jumped over the waistcoat and paused the infinitesimal part of a second on the necktie. Mauville learned in that moment how the eye may wither and humble, without giving any ostensible reason for offense. The attitude of this mincing fribble, as he danced twittingly away, was the first intimation Mauville had received that he would soon be relegated to the ranks of gay adventurers thronging the city. He who had watched his estates vanish with an unruffled countenance now became disconcerted over the width of his trousers and the shape of his hat.

His new home was in the house of an aged quadroon who had been a servant in his family many years ago--how long no one seemed to remember!--and who had been his nurse before she had received her freedom. She enjoyed the distinction of being feared in the neighborhood; her fetishes had a power no other witch's possessed, and many of the negroes would have done anything to have possessed these infallible charms, save crossing her threshold to get them. Mauville, when he found fortune slipping away from him and ruin staring him in the face, had been glad to transfer his abode to this unhallowed place; going into hiding, as it were, until the storm should blow by, when he expected to emerge, confident as ever.

But inaction soon chafed his restless nature, and drove him forth in spite of himself from the streets in that quarter of the town where the roofs of various-colored houses formed strange geometrical figures and the windows were bright with flaring head-dresses, beneath which looked out curious visages of ebony. Returning one day from such a peregrination, he determined to end a routine of existence so humiliating to his pride.

Pausing before a doorway, the land baron looked this way and that, and seeing only the rotating eyes of a pickaninny fastened upon him, hurried through the entrance. Hanging upon the walls were red and green pods and bunches of dried herbs of unquestionable virtue belonging to the old crone's pharmacopoeia. Mauville slowly ascended the dark stairs and reached his retreat, a small apartment, with furniture of cane-work and floor covered with sea-grass; the ceiling low and the windows narrow, opening upon a miniature balcony that offered space for one and no more.

"Is dat yo', honey?" said an adoring voice on the landing.

"Yes, auntie," replied the land baron, as an old crone emerged from an ill-lighted recess and stood before him.

Now the light from the doorway fell upon her, and surely five score years were written on her curiously wrinkled face--five score, or more, for even the negroes did not profess to know how old she was. Her bent figure, watery eyes and high shrill voice bore additional testimony to her age.

"Yo's home earlier dan usual, dearie?" she resumed. "But yo' supper's all ready. Sit down here."

"I'm not hungry, auntie," he returned.

"Not hungry, honey?" she cried, laughing shrilly. "Yo' wait!" And she disappeared into an adjoining room, soon to emerge with a steaming platter, which she set on the snow-white cover of the little table. Removing the lid from the dish, she hobbled back a few steps to regard her guest with triumphant expectation. "Dat make yo' eat."

"What a cook you are, mammy!" he said, lightly. "You would give a longing tooth to satiety."

"De debil blow de fire," she answered, chuckling.

"Then the devil is a chef de cuisine. This sauce is bewitching."

"Yo' like it?" Delighted.

"Tis a spell in itself. Confess, mammy, Old Nick mixed it?"

"No, he only blow de fire," she reiterated, with a grin.

"Any one been to see me, mammy?"

"Only dat Mexican gemmen; dat gemmen been here befo' who take yo' message about de troops; when dey go from New Orleans; how many dey am!"

"You know that, auntie?" he asked quickly. "You know that I--"

"Yes, honey," she answered, shaking her head. "Yo' be berry careful, Mar's'r Edward."

"What did he want?" said the land baron, quickly.

"He gib me dis." And the crone handed her visitor a slip of paper on which a few words were written. "What dat mean?"

"It means I am going away, mammy," pushing back his chair.

"Gwine away!" she repeated. "When's yo' gwine?"

"To-morrow; perhaps to-night even; down the river, auntie!" Rising and surveying himself in a mirror.

"How long yo' gwine away foh?"

"Perhaps forever, auntie!"

"Not foh good, Mar's'r Edward? Not foh good?" He nodded and she broke into loud wailings. "Yo's gwine and yo' old mammy'll see yo' no moh--no moh! I knows why yo's gwine, Mar's'r Edward. I's heard yo' talkin' about her in yo' sleep. But yo' stay and yo' mammy has a love-charm foh yo'; den she's yo's, foh suah."

This offer, coming from one of her uncanny reputation, would have been accepted with implicit faith by most of the dwellers in that locality, superstitious to the last degree, but Mauville laughed carelessly.

"Pshaw, mammy! Do you think I would fly from a woman? Do I look as though I needed a charm?"

"No; she mus' worship yo'!" cried the infatuated crone.

Then a change passed over her puckered face and she lifted her arms despairingly, rocking her body to and fro, while she mumbled unintelligible words which would have caused the negroes to draw away from her with awe, for the spell was on her. But the land baron only regarded her carelessly as she muttered something pertaining to spells and omens.

"Come, auntie," he said impatiently at last, "you know I don't believe in this tom-foolery."

She turned to him vehemently. "Don't go whar yo' thinkin' ob gwine, honey," she implored. "Yo'll nebber come back, foh suah--foh suah! I see yo' lyin' dar, honey, in de dark valley--whar de mists am risin'--and I hears a bugle soundin'--and de tramp of horses. Dey am all gone, honey--and de mists come back--but yo' am dar--lying dar-- de mountains around yo'--yo' am dar fo'ebber and ebber and--" Here she broke into wild sobbing and moaning, tossing her white hair with her trembling withered arms, a moving picture of an inspired dusky sibyl. Mauville shrugged his shoulders.

"We're losing time, mammy," he exclaimed. "Stop this nonsense and go pack a few things for me. I have some letters to write."

The old woman reluctantly obeyed, and the land baron penned a somewhat lengthy epistle to his one-time master in Paris, the Abbé Moneau, whose disapproval of the Anglo-Saxon encroachments-- witness Louisiana!--and zeal for the colonization of the Latin races are matters of history. Having completed his epistle, the land baron placed it in the old crone's hand to mail with: "If that man calls again, tell him I'll meet him to-night," and, leaving the room, shot through the doorway, once more rapidly walking down the shabby thoroughfare. The aged negro woman stumbled out upon the balcony and gazed after the departing figure still moaning softly to herself and shaking her head in anguish.

"Fo'ebber and ebber," she repeated in a wailing tone. Below a colored boy gazed at her in wonderment.

"What debblement am she up to now?" he said to a girl seated in a doorway. "When de old witch am like dat--"

"Come in dar, yo' black imp!" And a vigorous arm pulled the lad abruptly through the opening. "Ef she sees yo', she can strike yo' dead, foh suah!"

The crone could no longer distinguish Mauville--her eyes were nearly sightless--but she continued to look in the direction he had taken, sobbing as before: "Fo'ebber and ebber! Fo'ebber and ebber!"

Once more upon a fashionable thoroughfare, the land baron's footstep relaxed and he relapsed into his languorous, indolent air. The shadows of twilight were darkening the streets and a Caribbee-scented breeze was wafted from the gulf across the city. It swept through the broad avenues and narrow highways, and sighed among the trees of the old garden. Seating himself absently on one of the public benches, Mauville removed his hat to allow the cool air to fan his brow. Presently he moved on; up Canal Street, where the long rows of gas lights now gleamed through the foliage; thence into a side thoroughfare, as dark as the other street was bright, pausing before a doorway, illumined by a single yellow flame that flickered in the draft and threatened to leave the entrance in total obscurity. Mounting two flights of stairs, no better lighted than the hall below, the land baron reached a doorway, where he paused and knocked. In answer to his summons a slide was quickly slipped back, and through the aperture floated an alcoholic breath.

"Who is it?"

"A Knight of the Golden Square," said the caller, impatiently. "Open the door."

The man obeyed and the land baron was admitted to the hall of an organization which had its inception in Texas; a society not unlike the Secret Session Legation of the Civil War, having for its object the overthrow of the government, the carrying of mails and despatches and other like business. Here was gathered a choice aggregation of Mexican sympathizers, a conclave hostile to the North. Composed of many nationalities, the polished continental adventurer rubbed shoulders with the Spanish politicians; the swarthy agents of Santa Anna brushed against the secret enemies of northern aggression. A small bar, unpretentious but convenient, occupied a portion of one end of the room, and a brisk manipulator of juleps presided over this popular corner.

Half-disdainfully, the land baron mingled with the heterogeneous assembly; half-ironically, his eye swept the group at the bar--the paid spy, the needy black-sheep; the patriot, the swashbuckler; men with and without a career. As Mauville stepped forward, a quiet, dark-looking man, obviously a Mexican, not without a certain distinguished carriage, immediately approached the newcomer.

"You have come? Good!" he said, and drew Mauville aside. They conversed in low tones, occasionally glancing about them at the others.

In the hall below the rhythm of a waltz now made itself heard, and the land baron, having received certain papers which committed him to a hazardous service, prepared to leave.

"Here's luck!" said a man on his left, raising his glass. At these words several of the company turned.

"Send it south!" roared a Texan Furioso, emptying his tumbler.

"Send it south!" echoed the others, and "south" the fragrant juleps were "sent," as the land baron unceremoniously tore himself away from the group.

"They say the floods are rising," said the man with whom Mauville had conferred, at the door.

"All the better if the river's running wild!" answered the other. "It will be easier running the guard."

"Yes," returned the Mexican, extending his hand, with a smile; "in this case, there's safety in danger!"

"That's reassuring!" replied the land baron, lightly, as he descended the stairs.

On reaching the floor below he was afforded a view through an open door into a large room, lighted with many lamps, where a quadroon dance, or "society ball," was in progress. After a moment's hesitation he entered and stood in the glare, watching the waltzers. Around the wall were dusky chaperons, guarding their charges with the watchfulness of old dowagers protecting their daughters from the advances of younger sons. Soft eyes flashed invitingly, graceful figures passed, and the revelry momentarily attracted Mauville, as he followed the movements of the waltzers and heard the strains of music. Impulsively he approached a young woman whose complexion was as light as his own and asked her to dance. The next moment they were gliding to the dreamy rhythm around the room.

By a fatal trick of imagination, his thoughts wandered to the dark-haired girl he had met in the Shadengo Valley. If this now were she, the partner he had so unceremoniously summoned to his side. How light were her feet; what poetry of motion was her dancing; what pleasure the abandonment to which she had resigned herself! Involuntarily he clasped more tightly the slender waist, and the dark eyes, moved by that palpable caress, looked not unkindly into his own. But at the glance he experienced a strange repulsion and started, as if awakening from a fevered sleep, abruptly stopping in the dance, his arm falling to his side. The girl looked at him half-shyly, half-boldly, and the very beauty of her eyes--the deep, lustrous orbs of a quadroon--smote him mockingly. He felt as though some light he sought shone far beyond his ken; a light he saw, but could never reach; ever before him, but always receding.

"Monsieur is tired?" said the girl, in a puzzled tone.

"Yes," he answered bluntly, leading her to a seat. "Good-night."

"Good-night," she replied, following his retreating figure with something like regret.

The evening bells, distinct and mysterious, were sounding as he emerged from New Orleans' Mabille, and their crystalline tones, rising and falling on the solemn night, brought to mind his boyhood. Pictures long forgotten passed before him, as his footsteps led him far from the brightly-lighted streets to a sequestered thoroughfare that lay peacefully on the confines of the busy city; a spot inviting rest from the turmoil yonder and in accord with the melancholy vibrations of the bells. He stood, unseen in the shadow of great trees, before a low rambling mansion; not so remote but that the perfume from the garden was wafted to him over the hedge.

"A troubadour!" he said scornfully to himself. "Edward Mauville sighing at a lady's window like some sentimental serenader! There's a light yonder. Now to play my despairing part, I must watch for her image. If I were some one else, I should say my heart beats faster than usual. She comes--the fair lady! Now the curtain's down. All that may be seen is her shadow. So, despairing lover, hug that shadow to your breast!"

He plucked a rose from a bush in her garden, laughing at himself the while for doing so, and as he moved away he repeated with conviction:

"A shadow! That is all she ever could have been to me!"

The Strollers

CHAPTER III:
FROM GARRET TO GARDEN

"Celestina, what do you think this is?" Waving something that crackled in mid air.

"A piece of paper," said Celestina from her place on the hearth.

"Paper!" scoffed Straws. "It's that which Horace calls a handmaid, if you know how to use it; a mistress, if you do not--money! It is-- success, the thing which wrecks more lives than cyclones, fires and floods! We were happy enough before this came, weren't we, Celestina?"

The girl nodded her head, a look of deep anxiety in her eyes.

"Oh, why did the critics so damn the book it fairly leaped to popularity!" went on the bard. "Why did they advise me to learn a trade? to spoil no more reams of paper? To spoil reams of paper and get what--this little bit in return!"

"Is it so very much money?" asked Celestina.

"An enormous amount--one thousand dollars! And the worst of it is, my publishers write there may be more to come."

"Well," said the child, after a long, thoughtful pause, "why don't you give it away?"

"Hum! Your suggestion, my dear--"

"But, perhaps, no one would take it?" interrupted Celestina.

"Perhaps they wouldn't!" agreed Straws, rubbing his hands. "So, under the circumstances, let us consider how we may cultivate some of the vices of the rich. It is a foregone conclusion, set down by the philosophers, that misery assails riches. The philosophers were never rich and therefore they know. Besides, they are unanimous on the subject. It only remains to make the best of it and cultivate the vanities of our class. Where shall I begin? 'Riches betray man into arrogance,' saith Addison. Therefore will I be arrogant; while you, my dear, shall be proud."

"That will be lovely!" assented Celestina, as a matter of habit. She went to the bed and began smoothing the sheets deftly.

"My dear!" expostulated Straws. "You mustn't do that."

"Not make the bed!" she asked, in surprise.

"No."

"Nor bring your charcoal?"

"No."

"Nor wash your dishes?"

"Certainly not!"

Celestina dropped on the floor, a picture of misery.

"Too bad, isn't it?" commented Straws. "But it can't be helped, can it?"

"No," she said, shaking her head, wofully; "it can't be helped! But why--why did you publish it?"

"Just what the critics asked, my dear! Why? Who knows? Who can tell why the gods invented madness? But it's done; for bad, or worse!"

"For bad, or worse!" she repeated, gazing wistfully toward the rumpled bed.

"If somebody tells you fine feathers don't make fine birds, don't believe him," continued the poet. "It's envy that speaks! But what do you suppose I have here?" Producing a slip of paper from his vest pocket. "No; it's not another draft! An advertisement! Listen: 'Mademoiselle de Castiglione's select seminary. Young ladies instructed in the arts of the bon ton. Finesse, repose, literature! Fashions, etiquette, languages! P. S. Polkas a specialty!' Celestina, your destiny lies at Mademoiselle de Castiglione's. They will teach you to float into a drawing room--but you won't forget the garret? They will instruct you how to sit on gilt chairs--you will think sometimes of the box, or the place by the hearth? You will become a mistress of the piano--'By the Coral Strands I Wander,' 'The Sweet Young Bachelor'--but I trust you will not learn to despise altogether the attic pipe?"

"You mean," said Celestina, slowly, her face expressing bewilderment, "I must go away somewhere?"

Straws nodded. "That's it; somewhere!"

The girl's eyes flashed; her little hands clenched. "I won't; I won't!"

"Then that's the end on't!" retorted the bard. "I had bought you some new dresses, a trunk with your name on it, and had made arrangements with Mademoiselle de Castiglione (who had read 'Straws' Strophes'), but perhaps I could give the dresses away to some other little girl who will be glad to drink at the Pierian--I mean, the Castiglione--spring."

Celestina's eyes were an agony of jealousy; not that she was mercenary, or cared for the dresses, but that Straws should give them to another little girl. Her pride, however, held her in check and she drew herself up with composure.

"That would be nice--for the other little girl!" she said.

"The only difficulty is," resumed Straws, "there isn't any other little girl."

At that, Celestina gave a glad cry and flew to him, throwing her arms around his neck.

"Oh, I will go anywhere you want!" she exclaimed.

"Get on your bonnet then--before you change your mind, my dear!"

"And aunt?" asked Celestina, lingering doubtfully on the threshold.

"Your aunt, as you call that shriveled-up shrew, consented at once," answered Straws. "Her parental heart was filled with thanksgiving at the prospect of one less mouth to fill. Go and say good-by, however, to the old harridan; I think she has a few conventional tears to shed. But do not let her prolong her grief inordinately, and meet me at the front door."

A few moments later, Straws and the child, hand-in-hand, started on their way to the Castiglione temple of learning and culture. If Celestina appeared thoughtful, even sad, the poet was never so merry, and sought to entertain the abstracted girl with sparkling chit-chat about the people they met in the crowded streets. A striking little man was a composer of ability, whose operas, "Cosimo," "Les Pontons de Cadiz," and other works had been produced at the Opéra

---

Comique in Paris. He was now director of the French opera in New Orleans and had brought out the charming Mademoiselle Capriccioso and the sublime Signor Staccato. The lady by his side, a dark brunette with features that were still beautiful, was the nimble-footed Madame Feu-de-joie, whose shapely limbs and graceful motions had delighted two generations and were like to appeal to a third. Men who at twenty had thrown Feu-de-joie posies, now bald but young as ever, tossed her roses.

"I don't like that lady," said Celestina, emphatically, when the dancer had passed on, after petting her and kissing her on the cheek.

"Now, it's curious," commented the bard, "but your sex never did."

"Do men like her?" asked the child, with premature penetration.

"They did; they do; they will!" answered Straws, epigrammatically.

"Do you like her?"

"Oh, that's different! Poets, you know, are the exception to any rule."

"Why?"

"Because--Really, my dear, you ask too many questions!"

Although Straws and Celestina had left the house early in the day, it was noon before they reached the attractive garden, wherein was sequestered the "select seminary."

In this charming prison, whose walls were overrun with flowering vines, and whose cells were pretty vestal bowers, entered the bard and the young girl, to be met on the front porch by the wardeness herself, a mite of a woman, with wavy yellow hair, fine complexion and washed-out blue eyes. Sensitive almost to shyness, Mademoiselle de Castiglione appeared more adapted for the seclusion of the veil in the Ursuline Church than for the varied responsibilities of a young ladies' institute. At the approach of the poet, she turned, looked startled, but finally came forward bravely.

"Oh, I've read it again, Mr. Straws!" she exclaimed, impetuously.

"What?" he returned, sternly, pausing at the foot of the steps.

"Your--your lovely Strophes!" she continued, timidly.

The bard frowned. "All great men profess to scowl at flattery," thought Straws. "She will have but a poor opinion of me, if I do not appear an offended Hector!"

"Mademoiselle, I excessively dislike compliments," he began aloud, but having gone thus far, his courage and lack of chivalry failed him in the presence of her dismay; he forgot his greatness, and hastened to add, with an ingratiating smile: "Except when delivered by such a charming person!"

"Oh, Mr. Straws!"

"This, Mademoiselle," resumed the bard, "is the young girl I spoke about. Her mother," he added in a low voice, "was a beautiful quadroon; her father"--here Straws mentioned a name. The wardeness flushed furiously. "Father died; always meant to make it right; didn't; crime of good intentions! Virago of an aunt; regular termagant; hates the girl! Where was a home to be found for her? Where"--gazing around him--"save this--Eden? Where a mother-- save in one whose heart is the tenderest?"

Diplomatic Straws! Impulsively the wardeness crossed to Celestina; her blue eyes beamed with sentiment and friendliness. "I will give her my personal attention," she said. And then to the young girl: "We will be friends, won't we?"

"Yes," replied Celestina, slowly, after a moment's discreet hesitation. She was glad the other did not kiss her like Feu-de-joie.

"I always like," said the wardeness, "to feel my little girls are all my little friends."

"Mademoiselle," exclaimed the bard, "I'll--I'll dedicate my next volume of poems to you!"

"Really, Mr. Straws!"

"For every kindness to her, you shall have a verse," he further declared.

"Then your dedication would be as long as Homer!" she suddenly flashed out, her arm around the child.

Straws looked at her quickly. It was too bad of him! And that borrowed Don Juan smile! Nothing could excuse it.

Castiglione busied herself with Celestina's ribbons. "Whoever did tie that bow-knot?" she observed.

"Good-by, Celestina," said Straws.

Celestina put her arms gravely about his neck and he pressed his lips to her cheek. Then he strode quickly toward the gate. Just before passing out, he looked back. The wardeness had finished adjusting the ribbon and was contemplatively inspecting it. Celestina, as though unconscious of the attention, was gazing after the poet, and when he turned into the road, her glance continued to rest upon the gate.

CHAPTER IV:
"THE BEST OF LIFE"

O n a certain evening about a month later, the tropical rains had flooded the thoroughfares, until St. Charles Street needed but a Rialto and a little imagination to convert it into a watery highway of another Venice, while as for Canal Street, its name was as applicable as though it were spanned by a Bridge of Sighs. In the narrow streets the projecting eaves poured the water from the roof to the sidewalks, deluging the pedestrians. These minor thoroughfares were tributary to the main avenues and gushed their rippling currents into them, as streams supply a river, until the principal streets flowed swiftly with the dirty water that choked their gutters. The rain splashed and spattered on the sidewalks, fairly flooding out the fruit venders and street merchants who withstood the deluge for a time and then were forced to vanish with their portable stores. The cabby, phlegmatic to wind and weather, sat on his box, shedding the moisture from his oil-skin coat and facing a cloud of steam which presumably concealed a horse.

The dark night and the downpour made the cafés look brighter. Umbrellas flitted here and there, skilfully piloted beneath swinging signs and low balconies, evading awning posts and high hats as best they might. There were as many people out as usual, but they were hurrying to their destinations, even the languid creole beauty, all lace and alabaster, moved with the sprightliness of a maid of Gotham.

Straws, editor and rhymster, was seated on the semi-Oriental, semi-French gallery of the little café, called the Veranda, sipping his absinthe, smoking a cheroot and watching the rain drip from the roof of the balcony, spatter on the iron railing and form a shower bath for the pedestrians who ventured from beneath the protecting shelter. Before him was paper, partly covered with well-nigh illegible versification, and a bottle of ink, while a goose-quill, tool of the tuneful Nine, was expectantly poised in mid air.

"Confound it!" he said to himself. "I can't write in the attic any more, since Celestina has gone, and apparently I can't write away from it. Since she left, the dishes haven't been washed; my work has run down at the heels, and everything is going to the dogs generally. And now this last thing has upset me quite. 'In the twinkling of an eye,' says the sacred Book. But I must stop thinking, or I'll never complete this poem. Now to make my mind a blank; a fitting receptacle to receive inspiration!"

The bard's figure swayed uncertainly on the stool. In the lively race through a sonnet, it was often, of late, a matter of doubt with Straws, whether Bacchus or Calliope would prevail at the finish, and to-night the jocund god had had a perceptible start. "Was ever a poet so rhyme-fuddled?" muttered the impatient versifier. "An inebriating trade, this poetizing!"--and he reached for the absinthe. "If I am not careful, these rhymes will put me under the table!"

"Nappy, eh?" said a voice at his elbow, as a dripping figure approached, deposited his hat on one chair and himself in another. The newcomer had a long, Gothic face and a merry-wise expression.

The left hand of the poet waved mechanically, imposing silence; the quill dived suddenly to paper, trailed twice across it, and then was cast aside, as Straws looked up.

"Yes," he replied to the other's interrogation. "It's all on account of Celestina's leaving me. You ought to see my room. Even a poet's soul revolts against it. So what can I do, save make my home amid convivial haunts?" The poet sighed. "And you, Phazma; how are you feeling?"

"Sober as a judge!"

"Then you shall judge of this last couplet," exclaimed Straws quickly. "It has cost me much effort. The editor wanted it. It seemed almost too sad a subject for my halting muse. There are some things which should be sacred even from us, Phazma. But what is to be done when the editor-in-chief commands? 'Ours not to reason why!' The poem is a monody on the tragedy at the theater."

"At the St. Charles?" said Phazma, musingly. "As I passed, it was closed. It seemed early for the performance to be over. Yet the theater was dark; all the lights had gone out."

The Strollers

"More than the lights went out," answered Straws, gravely; "a life went out!"

"I don't exactly--Oh, you refer to Miss Carew's farewell?"

"No; to Barnes'!"

"Barnes'!" exclaimed his surprised listener.

"Yes; he is dead; gone out like the snuff of a candle! Died in harness, before the footlights!"

"During the performance!" cried the wondering Phazma. "Why, only this afternoon I met him, apparently hale and hearty, and now-- you tell me he has paid the debt of nature?"

"As we must all pay it," returned Straws. "He acted as if he were dazed while the play was in progress and I could not but notice it, standing in the wings. The prompter spoke of it to me. 'I don't know what is the matter with Mr. Barnes,' he said, 'I have had to keep throwing him his lines.' Even Miss Carew rallied him gently between acts on his subdued manner.

"'This is our last performance together,' he said absently. She gave him a reproachful look and he added, quickly: 'Do I appear gloomy, my dear? I never felt happier.'

"At the end of the second act he seemed to arouse himself, when she, as Isabella, said: 'I'll fit his mind to death, for his soul's rest.' He gazed at her long and earnestly, his look caressing her wherever she moved. Beginning the prison scene with spirit, he had proceeded to,

"'Reason thus with life; If I do lose thee, I do lose a thing That none but fools would keep--'

"When suddenly he threw up his arms and fell upon the stage, his face toward the audience. With a cry I shall never forget, Miss Carew rushed to him and took his head in her arms, gazing at him wildly, and calling to him piteously. The curtain went down, but nothing could be done, and life quickly ebbed. Once, only, his lips moved: 'Your mother--there!--where the play never ends!' and it was over."

"It is like a romance," said Phazma, finally, at the conclusion of this narration.

"Say, rather, reality! The masque is over! In that final sleep Jack Pudding lies with Roscius; the tragedian does not disdain the mummer, and beautiful Columbine, all silver spangles and lace, is company for the clown. 'Tis the only true republic, Phazma; death's Utopia!"

"But to think he should have died with those words of the poet on his lips?"

"A coincidence!" answered Straws. "No more notable than the death of Edmund Kean, who, when he reached the passage 'Farewell, Othello's occupation's gone!' fell back unconscious; or that of John Palmer, who, after reciting 'There is another and a better world,' passed away without a pang."

A silence fell between the two poets; around them shadows appeared and vanished. Phazma finished his syrup and arose.

"Don't go," said Straws. "My own thoughts are poor company. Recite some of your madrigals, that's a good fellow! What a wretched night! These rain-drops are like the pattering feet of the invisible host. Some simple song, Phazma!"

"As many as you please!" cried his flattered brother-bard. "What shall it be?"

"One of your Rhymes for Children. Your 'Boy's Kingdom,' beginning:

"When I was young, I dreamed of knights And dames with silken trains."

"Thou shalt have it, mon ami!"

And Phazma gaily caught up the refrain, while Straws beat time to the tinkling measures.

* * * * *

The last entry in the date-book, or diary, of Barnes seems curiously significant as indicating a knowledge that his end was near. For the first time in the volume he rambles on in a reminiscent mood about his boyhood days:

"The first bit of good fortune I ever enjoyed was when as a lad in sweeping a crossing in the neighborhood of the Strand I found a bright, shining sovereign. How tightly I grasped it in my little fist that night when I slept in a doorway! I dared not trust it in my pocket. The next night I walked to the ticket-seller at Drury Lane, and demanded a seat down stairs. 'Gallery seats sold around the corner,' said this imposing gentleman with a prodigious frown, and, abashed, I slunk away. My dream of being near the grand people vanished and I climbed once more to my place directly under the roof.

"My next bit of good fortune happened in this wise. Sheridan, the playwright-orator, attracted my attention on Piccadilly one day, and, for the delight of gazing upon him, I followed. When he stopped, I stopped; when he advanced, I did likewise. I felt that I was treading in the footsteps of a king. Suddenly he paused, wheeled about and confronted me, a raw-boned, ragged, awkward lad of fourteen. 'What one of my creditors has set you following me?' he demanded. 'None, sir,' I stammered. 'I only wanted to look at the author of "The Rivals."' He appeared much amused and said: 'Egad! So you are a patron of the drama, my boy?' I muttered something in the affirmative. He regarded my appearance critically. 'I presume you would not be averse to genteel employment, my lad?' he asked. With that he scribbled a moment and handed me a note to the property man of Drury Lane. My heart was too full; I had no words to thank him. The tears were in my eyes, which, noting, he remarked, with an assumption of sternness: 'Are you sure, boy, you are not a bailiff in disguise?' At this I laughed and he left me. The note procured me an engagement as errand boy at the stage-door and later I rose to the dignity of scene-shifter. How truly typical of this man's greatness, to help lift a homeless lad out of the gutters of London town!

"But I am rambling on as though writing an autobiography, to be read when I am gone--"

Here the entry ceases and the rest of the pages in the old date-book are blank.

CHAPTER V:
THE LAWYER'S TIDINGS

The sudden and tragic death of Constance's foster-father--which occurred virtually as narrated by Straws--set a seal of profound sadness on the heart of the young girl. "Good sir, adieu!" she had said in the nunnery scene and the eternal parting had shortly followed. Her affection for the old manager had been that of a loving daughter; the grief she should have experienced over the passing of the marquis was transferred to the memory of one who had been a father through love's kinship. In the far-away past, standing at the bier of her mother, the manager it was who had held her childish hand, consoling her and sharing her affliction, and, in those distant but unforgotten days of trouble, the young girl and the homeless old man became all in all to each other.

Years had rolled by; the child that prattled by his side became the stately girl, but the hand-clasp at that grave had never been relinquished. She could not pretend to mourn the death of the marquis, her own father; had he not ever been dead to her; as dead as the good wife (or bad wife) of that nobleman; as dead as Gross George, and all the other honored and dishonored figures of that misty past? But Barnes' death was the abrupt severing of ties, strengthened by years of tender association, and, when his last summons came, she felt herself truly alone.

In an old cemetery, amid the crumbling bricks, Barnes was buried, his sealed tomb above ground bearing in its inscription the answer to the duke's query: "Thy Best of Life is Sleep." After the manager's death and Constance's retirement from the stage, it naturally followed that the passengers of the chariot became separated. Mrs. Adams continued to play old woman parts throughout the country, remaining springy and buoyant to the last. Susan transferred herself and her talents to another stock company performing in

New Orleans, while Kate procured an engagement with a traveling organization. Adonis followed in her train. It had become like second nature to quarrel with Kate, and at the mere prospect of separation, he forthwith was driven to ask her for her hand, and was accepted-- on probation, thus departing in leading strings. Hawkes, melancholy as of old, drifted into a comic part in a "variety show," acquiring new laurels as a dry comedian of the old school. But he continued to live alone in the world, mournfully sufficient unto himself.

Constance remained in New Orleans. There the old manager had found his final resting place and she had no definite desire to go elsewhere. Adrift in the darkness of the present, the young girl was too perplexed to plan for the future. So she remained in the house Barnes had rented shortly before his death. An elderly gentlewoman of fallen fortunes, to whom this semi-rural establishment belonged, Constance retained as a companion, passing her time quietly, soberly, almost in solitude. This mansion, last remnant of its owner's earthly estate, was roomy and spacious, nestling among the oranges and inviting seclusion with its pretentious wall surrounding the grounds.

The old-fashioned gentlewoman, poor and proud, was a fitting figure in that ancient house, where in former days gay parties had assembled. But now the principal callers at the old house were the little fat priest, with a rosy smile, who looked after the aged lady's soul, of which she was most solicitous in these later days, and the Count de Propriac, who came ostensibly to see the elderly woman and chat about genealogy and extraction, but was obviously not unmindful of the presence of the young girl nor averse to seeking to mitigate her sorrow. Culver, the lawyer, too, came occasionally, to talk about her affairs, but often her mind turned impatiently from figures and markets to the subtle rhythm of Shakespeare. She regretted having left the stage, feeling the loneliness of this simple existence; yet averse to seeking diversion, and shunning rather than inviting society. As the inert hours crept by, she longed for the forced wakefulness and stir of other days--happy days of insecurity; fleeting, joyous days, gone now beyond recall!

But while she was striving to solve these new problems of her life they were all being settled for her by Fate, that arrogant meddler. Calling one morning, Culver, nosegay in hand, was obliged to wait longer than usual and employed the interval in casually examining his surroundings--and, incidentally, himself. First, with the vanity of youngish old gentlemen, he gazed into a tall mirror, framed in the fantastic style of the early Venetians; a glass which had belonged to the marquis and had erstwhile reflected the light beauty of his noble spouse. Pausing about as long as it would have taken a lady to adjust a curl, he peeped into a Dutch cabinet of ebony and mother-of-pearl and was studying a charming creature painted on ivory, whose head like that of Bluebeard's wife was subsequently separated from her lovely shoulders, when a light footstep behind him interrupted his scrutiny. Turning, he greeted the young girl, and, with stately gallantry, presented the nosegay.

"How well you are looking!" he said. "Though there might be a little more color, perhaps, like some of these flowers. If I were a doctor, I should prescribe: Less cloister; more city!"

She took the flowers, meeting his kindly gaze with a faint smile.

"Most patients would like such prescriptions," he went on. "I should soon become a popular society physician."

But although he spoke lightly, his manner was partly forced and he regarded her furtively. Their brief acquaintance had awakened in him an interest, half-paternal, half-curious. Women were an unknown, but beautiful quantity; from the vantage point of a life of single blessedness, he vaguely, but quixotically placed them in the same category with flowers, and his curiosity was no harsher than that of a gardener studying some new variety of bud or blossom. Therefore he hesitated in what he was about to say, shifting in his chair uneasily when they were seated, but finally coming to the point with:

"Have you read the account of the engagement between the Mexican and the American forces at Vera Cruz?"

"No; not yet," she admitted.

"Nor the list of--of casualties?" he continued, hesitatingly.

"The casualties!" she repeated. "Why--"

"Saint-Prosper has no further interest in the marquis' sous," he said quickly.

She gazed straight before her, calm and composed. This absence of any exhibition of feeling reassured the attorney.

"He is--dead?" she asked quietly.

"Yes."

"How did he die?"

"Gallantly," replied the caller, now convinced she had no interest in the matter, save that of a mere acquaintance. "His death is described in half a column. You see he did not live in vain!"

"Was he--killed in battle?"

"In a skirmish. His company was sent to break up a band of guerilla rancheros at Antigua. They ambushed him; he drove them out of the thicket but fell--You have dropped your flowers. Allow me!--at the head of his men."

"At the head of his men!" She drew in her breath.

"There passed the last of an ill-fated line," said the lawyer, reflectively. "Poor fellow! He started with such bright prospects, graduating from the military college with unusual honors. Ambitious, light-hearted, he went to Africa to carve out a name in the army. But fate was against him. The same ship that took him over carried back, to the marquis, the story of his brother's disgrace--"

"His brother's disgrace!" she exclaimed.

Culver nodded. "He sold a French stronghold in Africa, Miss Carew."

Had the attorney been closely observing her he would have noticed the sudden look of bewilderment that crossed her face. She stared at him with her soul in her eyes.

"Ernest Saint-Prosper's--brother?"

The turmoil of her thoughts held her as by a spell; in the disruption of a fixed conclusion her brain was filled with new and poignant reflections. Unconsciously she placed a nervous hand upon his arm.

"Then Ernest Saint-Prosper who was--killed in Mexico was not the traitor?"

"Certainly not!" exclaimed Culver, quickly, "Owing to the disgrace, I am sure, more than to any other reason, he bade farewell to his country--and now lies unmourned in some mountain ravine. It is true the marquis quarreled with him, disliking not a little the young man's republican ideas, but--my dear young lady!--you are ill?"

"No, no!" she returned, hastily, striving to maintain her self-possession. "How--do you know this?"

"Through the marquis, himself," he replied, somewhat uneasy beneath her steady gaze. "He told me the story in order to protect the estate from any possible pretensions on the part of the traitor. The renegade was reported dead, but the marquis, nevertheless remained skeptical. He did not believe in the old saw about the devil being dead. 'Le diable lives always,' he said."

The visitor observed a perceptible change in the young girl, just what he could not define, but to him it seemed mostly to lie in her eyes where something that baffled him looked out and met his glance.

"His brother was an officer in the French army?" she asked, as though forcing herself to speak.

"Yes; ten years older than Ernest Saint-Prosper, he had already made a career for himself. How eagerly, then, must the younger brother have looked forward to meeting him; to serving with one who, in his young eyes, was all that was brave and noble! What a bitter awakening from the dream! It is not those we hate who can injure us most--only those we love can stab us so deeply!"

Mechanically she answered the lawyer, and, when he prepared to leave, the hand, given him at parting, was as cold as ice.

"Remember," he said, admonishingly; "less cloister, more city!"

Some hours later, the old lady, dressed in her heavy silk and brocade and with snow-white hair done up in imposing fashion, rapped on Constance's door, but received no answer. Knocking again, with like result, she entered the room, discovering the young girl on the bed, her cheeks tinted like the rose, her eyes with no gleam of recognition in them, and her lips moving, uttering snatches of old plays. Taking her hand, the old lady found it hot and dry.

"Bless me!" she exclaimed. "She is down with a fever." And at once prepared a simple remedy which soon silenced the babbling lips in slumber, after which she sent for the doctor.

The Strollers

CHAPTER VI:
THE COUNCIL OF WAR

"Adjutant, tell Colonel Saint-Prosper I wish to see him."

The adjutant saluted and turned on his heel, while General Scott bent over the papers before him, studying a number of rough pencil tracings. Absorbed in his task, the light of two candles on the table brought into relief, against the dark shadows, a face of rugged character and marked determination. Save for a slight contraction of the brow, he gave no evidence of the mental concentration he bestowed upon the matter in hand, which was to lead to the culmination of the struggle and to vindicate the wisdom and boldness of his policy.

"You sent for me, General?"

An erect, martial figure stood respectfully at the entrance of the tent.

"Yes," said the General, pushing the papers from him. "I have been studying your drawings of the defensive works at San Antonio Garita and find them entirely comprehensive. A council of officers has been called, and perhaps it will be as well for you to remain."

"At what time shall I be here, General?"

"It is about time now," answered the commander-in-chief, consulting his watch. "You have quite recovered from your wounds?" he added, kindly.

"Yes, thank you, General."

"I see by the newspapers you were reported dead. If your friends read that it will cause them needless anxiety. You had better see that the matter is corrected."

"It is hardly worth while," returned the young man, slowly.

The commanding general glanced at him in some surprise. "A strange fellow!" he thought. "Has he reasons for wishing to be considered dead? However, that is none of my business. At any rate, he is a good soldier." And, after a moment, he continued: "Cerro Gordo was warm work, but there is warmer yet in store for us. Only Providence, not the Mexicans, can stop us. But here are the officers," as General Pillow, Brevet-General Twiggs and a number of other officers entered.

The commander-in-chief proceeded to give such information as he had, touching the approaches to the city. Many of the officers favored operating against San Antonio Garita, others attacking Chapultepec. Saint-Prosper, when called on, stated that the ground before the San Antonio gate was intersected by many irrigating ditches and that much of the approach was under water.

"Then you would prefer storming a fortress to taking a ditch?" said one of the generals, satirically.

"A series of ditches," replied the other.

"Colonel Saint-Prosper is right," exclaimed the commanding general. "I had already made up my mind. Let it be the western gate, then."

And thus was brought to a close one of the most memorable councils of war, for it determined the fate of the City of Mexico.

Saint-Prosper looked older than when seen in New Orleans, as though he had endured much in that brief but hard campaign. His wound had incapacitated him for only a few months, and in spite of the climate and a woful lack of medical attendance and nourishing supplies, his hardy constitution stood him in such stead he was on his feet and in the saddle, while his comrades languished and died in the fierce heat of the temporary hospitals. His fellow-officers knew him as a fearless soldier, but a man reticent about himself, who made a confidant of no one. Liked for his ready, broad military qualities, it was a matter of comment, nevertheless, that no one knew anything about him except that he had served in the French army and was highly esteemed by General Scott as a daring and proficient engineer.

One evening shortly before the skirmish of Antigua, a small Mexican town had been ransacked, where were found cattle, bales of tobacco, pulque and wine. At the rare feast which followed a veteran drank to his wife; a young man toasted his sweetheart, and a third, with moist eyes, sang the praises of his mother. In the heart of the enemy's land, amid the uncertainties of war, remembrance carried them back to their native soil, rugged New England, the hills of Vermont, the prairies of Illinois, the blue grass of Kentucky.

"Saint-Prosper!" they cried, calling on him, when the festivities were at their height.

"To you, gentlemen," he replied, rising, glass in hand. "I drink to your loved ones!"

"To your own!" cried a young man, flushed with the wine.

Saint-Prosper gazed around that rough company, brave hearts softened to tenderness, and, lifting his canteen, said, after a moment's hesitation:

"To a princess on a tattered throne!"

They looked at him in surprise. Who was this adventurer who toasted princesses? The Mexican war had brought many soldiers of fortune and titled gentlemen from Europe to the new world, men who took up the cause more to be fighting than that they cared what the struggle was about. Was the "tattered throne" Louis Philippe's chair of state, torn by the mob in the Tuileries? And what foreign princess was the lady of the throne? But they took up the refrain promptly, good-naturedly, and a chorus rolled out:

"To the princess!"

Little they knew she was but a poor stroller; an "impudent, unwomanish, graceless monster," according to Master Prynne.

After leaving the commanding general's tent, Saint-Prosper retired to rest in that wilderness which had once been a monarch's pleasure grounds. Now overhead the mighty cypresses whispered their tales of ancient glory and faded renown; the wind waved those trailing beards, hoary with age; a gathering of venerable giants, murmuring the days when the Aztec monarch had once held courtly revels under the grateful shadows of their branches. The moaning breeze seemed the wild chant of the Indian priest in honor of the war-god of Anahuac. It told of battles to come and conflicts which would level to the dust the descendants of the conquerors of that ill-starred country. And so the soldier finally fell asleep, with that requiem ringing in his ears.

When daybreak again penetrated the mountain recesses and fell upon the valley, Saint-Prosper arose to shake off a troubled slumber. An unhealthy mist hung over the earth, like a miasma, and the officer shivered as he walked in that depressing and noxious atmosphere. It lay like a deleterious veil before the glades where myrtles mingled with the wild limes. It concealed from view a cross, said to have been planted by Cortez--the cross he worshiped because of its resemblance to the hilt of a sword!--and enveloped the hoary trees that were old when Montezuma was a boy or when Marina was beloved by the mighty free-booter.

The shade resting on the valley appeared that of a mighty, virulent hand. Out of the depths arose a flock of dark-hued birds, soaring toward the morbific fog; not moving like other winged creatures, with harmony of motion, but rising without unity, and filling the vale with discordant sounds. Nowhere could these sable birds have appeared more unearthly than in the "dark valley," as it was called by the natives, where the mists moved capriciously, yet remained persistently within the circumference of this natural cauldron, now falling like a pall and again hovering in mid air. Suddenly the uncanny birds vanished among the trees as quickly as they had arisen, and there was something mysterious about their unwarranted disappearance and the abrupt cessation of clamorous cries.

While viewing this somber scene, Saint-Prosper had made his way to a little adobe house which the natives had built near the trail that led through the valley. As he approached this hut he encountered a dismal but loquacious sentinel, tramping before the partly opened door.

"This is chilly work, guard?" said the young man, pausing.

"Yis, Colonel," replied the soldier, apparently grateful for the interruption; "it's a hot foight I prefer to this cool dooty."

"Whom are you guarding?" continued the officer.

"A spy, taken in the lines a few days ago. He's to be executed this morning at six. But I don't think he will moind that, for it's out of his head he is, with the malaria."

"He should have had medical attendance," observed the officer, stepping to the door.

"Faith, they'll cure him at daybreak," replied the guard. "It's a medicine that niver fails."

Saint-Prosper pushed open the door. The interior was so dim that at first he could not distinguish the occupant, but when his eyes became accustomed to the darkness, he discovered the figure of the prisoner, who was lying with his back toward him on the ground of the little hut with nothing but a thin blanket beneath him. The only light revealing the barren details of this Indian residence sifted through the small doorway or peered timorously down through a narrow aperture in the roof that served for a chimney. As Saint-Prosper gazed at the prostrate man, the latter moved uneasily, and from the parched lips fell a few words:

"Lock the doors, Oly-koeks! Hear the songsters, Mynheer Ten Breecheses! Birds of prey, you Dutch varlet! What do you think of the mistress of the manor? The serenading anti-renters have come for her." Then he repeated more slowly: "The squaw Pewasch! For seventeen and one-half ells of duffels! A rare principality for the scornful minx! Lord! how the birds sing now around the manor--screech owls, cat-birds, bobolinks!"

The soldier started back, vivid memories assailing his mind. Who was this man whose brain, independent of the corporeal shell, played waywardly with scenes, characters and events, indissolubly associated with his own life?

"Do you know, Little Thunder, the Lord only rebuked the Pharisees?" continued the prostrate man. "Though the Pharisee triumphs after all! But it was the stroller I wanted, not the principality."

He stirred quickly, as if suddenly aware of the presence of another in the hut, and, turning, lifted his head in a startled manner, surveying the figure near the doorway with conflicting emotions written on his pallid countenance. Perhaps some fragment of a dream yet lingered in his brain; perhaps he was confused at the sight of a face that met his excited look with one of doubt and bewilderment, but only partial realization of the identity of the intruder came to him in his fevered condition.

Arising deliberately, his body, like a machine, obeying automatically some unconscious power, he confronted the officer, who recognized in him, despite his thin, worn face and eyes, unnaturally bright, the once pretentious land baron, Edward Mauville. Moving toward the door, gazing on Saint-Prosper as though he was one of the figures of a disturbing phantasm, he reached the threshold, and, lifting his hand above his head, the prisoner placed it against one of the supports of the hut and stood leaning there. From the creation of his mind's eye, as he doubtlessly, half-conscious of his weakness, designated the familiar form, he glanced at the sentinel and shook as though abruptly conscious of his situation. Across the valley the soldiers showed signs of bestirring themselves, the smoke of many fires hovering earthward beneath the mist. Drawing his thin frame proudly to its full height, with a gesture of disdain for physical weakness, and setting his keen, wild eyes upon the soldier, Mauville said in a hollow tone:

"Is that really you, Mr. Saint-Prosper? At first I thought you but a trick of the imagination. Well, look your fill upon me! You are my Nemesis come to see the end."

"I am here by chance, Edward Mauville; an officer in the American army!"

"And I, a spy in the Mexican army. So are we authorized foes."

Rubbing his trembling hands together, his eyes shifted from the dark birds to the mists, then from the phantom forests back to the hut, finally resting on his shabby boots of yellow leather. The sunlight penetrating a rift in the mist settled upon him as he moved feebly and uncertainly through the doorway and seated himself upon a stool. This sudden glow brought into relief his ragged, unkempt condition, the sallowness of his face, and his wasted form, and Saint-Prosper could not but contrast pityingly this cheerless object, in the garb of a ranchero, with the prepossessing, sportive heir who had driven through the Shadengo Valley.

Apparently now the sun was grateful to his bent, stricken figure, and, basking in it, he recalled his distress of the previous night:

"This is better. Not long ago I awoke with chattering teeth. 'This,' I said, 'is life; a miasma, cold, discomfort,' Yes, yes; a fever, a miasma, with phantoms fighting you--struggling to choke you--but now"--he paused, and fumbling in his pocket, drew out a cigarette case, which he opened, but found empty. A cigar the other handed him he took mechanically and lighted with scrupulous care. Near at hand the guard, more cheerful under the prospect of speedy relief from his duties, could be heard humming to himself:

"Oh, Teady-foley, you are my darling, You are my looking-glass night and morning--"

Watching the smoker, Saint-Prosper asked himself how came Mauville to be serving against his own country, or why he should have enlisted at all, this pleasure-seeking man of the world, to whom the hardships of a campaign must have been as novel as distasteful.

"Are you satisfied with your trial?" said the soldier at length.

"Yes," returned Mauville, as if breaking from a reverie. "I confess I am the secret agent of Santa Anna and would have carried information from your lines. I am here because there is more of the Latin than the Anglo-Saxon in me. Many of the old families"--with a touch of insane pride--"did not regard the purchase of Louisiana by the United States as a transaction alienating them from other ties. Fealty is not a commercial commodity. But this," he added, scornfully, "is something you can not understand. You soldiers of fortune draw your swords for any master who pays you."

The wind moaned down the mountain side, and the slender trees swayed and bent; only the heavy and ponderous cactus remained motionless, a formidable monarch receiving obeisance from supple courtiers. Like cymbals, the leaves clashed around this armament of power with its thousand spears out-thrust in all directions.

The ash fell from the cigar as Mauville held the weed before his eyes.

"It is an hour-glass," he muttered. "When smoked--Oh, for the power of Jupiter to order four nights in one, the better to pursue his love follies! Love follies," he repeated, and, as a new train of fancy was awakened, he regarded Saint-Prosper venomously.

"Do you know she is the daughter of a marquis?" said Mauville, suddenly.

"Who?" asked the soldier.

"The stroller, of course. You can never win her," he added, contemptuously. "She knows all about that African affair."

Saint-Prosper started violently, but in a moment Mauville's expression changed, and he appeared plunged in thought.

"The last time I saw her," he said, half to himself, "she was dressed in black--her face as noonday--her hair black as midnight--crowning her with languorous allurement!"

He repeated the last word several times like a man in a dream.

"Allurement! allurement!" and again relapsed into a silence that was half-stupor.

By this time the valley, with the growing of the day, began to lose much of its evil aspect, and the eye, tempted through glades and vistas, lingered upon gorgeous forms of inflorescence. The land baron slowly blew a wreath of smoke in the air--a circle, mute reminder of eternity!--and threw the end of the cigar into the bushes. Looking long and earnestly at the surrounding scene, he started involuntarily. "The dark valley--whar de mists am risin'--I see yo' da, honey--fo'ebber and fo'ebber--"

As he surveyed this prospect, with these words ringing in his ears, the brief silence was broken by a bugle call and the trampling of feet.

"The trumpet shall sound and the dead shall arise," said the prisoner, turning and facing the soldiers calmly. "You have come for me?" he asked, quietly.

"Yes," said the officer in command. "General Scott has granted your request in view of certain circumstances, and you will be shot, instead of hanged."

The face of the prisoner lighted wonderfully. He drew himself erect and smiled with some of the assumption of the old insolence, that expression Saint-Prosper so well remembered! His features took on a semblance to the careless, dashing look they had borne when the soldier crossed weapons with him at the Oaks, and he neither asked nor intended to give quarter.

"I thank you," he observed, courteously. "At least, I shall die like a gentleman. I am ready, sir! Do not fasten my hands. A Mauville can die without being tied or bound."

The officer hesitated: "As to that--" he began.

"It is a reasonable request," said Saint-Prosper, in a low tone.

Mauville abruptly wheeled; his face, dark and sinister, was lighted with envenomed malignity; an unnaturally clear perception

---

replaced the stupor of his brain, and, bending toward Saint-Prosper, his eye rested upon him with such rancor and malevolence the soldier involuntarily drew away. But one word fell from the land baron's lips, low, vibrating, full of inexpressible bitterness. "Traitor!"

"Come, come!" interrupted the officer in command of the execution party; "time is up. As I was told not to fasten your hands, you shall have your wish. Confess now, that is accommodating?"

"Thanks," returned Mauville carelessly, relapsing into his old manner. "You are an obliging fellow! I would do as much for you."

"Not much danger of that," growled the other. "But we'll take the will for the deed. Forward, march!"

* * * * *

After the reverberations, carried from rock to rock with menacing reiteration, had ceased, the stillness was absolute. Even the song-bird remained frightened into silence by those awful echoes. Then the sun rested like a benediction on the land and the white cross of Cortez was distinctly outlined against the blue sky. But soon the long roll of drums followed this interval of quiet.

"Fall in!" "Attention; shoulder arms!" And the sleeping spirit of the Aztec war-god floated in the murmur which, increasing in volume, arose to tumultuous shout.

"On to Chapultepec! On to Chapultepec!" came from a thousand throats; arms glistened in the sun, bugles sounded resonant in the air, and the pattering noise of horses' hoofs mingled with the stentorian voices of the rough teamsters and the cracking of the whips. Like an irresistible, all-compelling wave, the troops swept out of the valley to hurl themselves against castle and fortress and to plant their colors in the heart of the capital city.

CHAPTER VII:

A MEETING ON THE MOUNT

Clothed at its base in a misty raiment of purple, the royal hill lifted above the valley an Olympian crest of porphyritic rock into the fathomless blue. Here not Jupiter and his court looked serenely down upon the struggling race, "indifferent from their awful height," but a dark-hued god, in Aztec vestments, gazed beyond the meadows to the floating flower beds, the gardens with their baths, and the sensuous dancing girls. All this, but a panorama between naps, soon faded away; the god yawned, drew his cloak of humming bird feathers more closely about him and sank back to rest. An uproar then disturbed his paleozoic dreams; like fluttering spirits of the garish past, the butterflies arose in the forest glades; and the voices of old seemed to chant the Aztec psalm: "The horrors of the tomb are but the cradle of the sun, and the dark shadows of death the brilliant lights for the stars." Even so they had chanted when the early free-booters burst upon the scene and beheld the valley with its frame-work of mountains and two guardian volcanoes, the Gog and Magog of the table-land.

Now again, from the towering column of Montezuma's cypress, to the city marked by spires, the thunder rolled and echoed onward even to the pine-clad cliffs and snow-crowned summits of the rocky giants. Puffs of smoke dotted the valley beneath the mount, and, as the answering reports reverberated across space, nature's mortars in the inclosure of mountains sent forth threatening wreaths of white in sympathy with the eight-inch howitzers and sixteen-pounders turned upon the crest of the royal hill.

When the trees were yet wet with their bath of dew the booming of artillery and the clattering of small arms dispelled that peace which partook of no harsher discord than the purling of streams and the still, small voices of the forest. Through the groves where the spirit of Donna Marina--the lost love of the marauder--was said to wander, shrieked the round shot, shells and grape. Through tangled shrubberies, bright with flowers and colored berries, pierced the discharge of canister; the air, fragrant at the dawn with orange blossom and starry jessamine, was noisome with suffocating, sulphurous fumes, and, beneath the fetid shroud, figures in a fog heedlessly trampled the lilies, the red roses and "flowers of the heart."

From the castle on the summit--mortal trespass upon the immortal pale of the gods!--the upward shower was answered by an iron downpour, and two storming parties, with ladders, pick-axes and crows, advanced, one on each side of the hill, to the attack. Boom! boom! before one of the parties, climbing and scrambling to the peak, belched the iron missives of destruction from the concealed mouths of heavy guns, followed by the rattling shower from small arms.

Surprised, they paused, panting from the swift ascent, some throwing themselves prone upon the earth, while the grape and canister passed harmlessly over them, others seeking such shelter as rocks, trees and shrubs afforded. Here and there a man fell, but was not suffered to lie long exposed to the fire of the redoubt which, strongly manned, held them in check midway to the summit. Doggedly their comrades rescued the wounded and quickly conveyed them to the rear.

"They've set out their watch-dogs," remarked the general commanding the assault on that side of the hill, to one of his officers, as he critically surveyed the formidable defense through the tangled shrubbery. "Here is a battery we hadn't reckoned on."

"It was to be expected, sir," responded the officer. "They were sure to have some strong point we couldn't locate."

"Yes," grumbled the general; "in such a jumble of foliage and rocks it would take an eagle's eye to pick out all their miserable ambuscades."

"I have no doubt, sir, the men are rested now," ventured the other.

"No doubt they are," chuckled the general, still studying the situation, glancing to the right and the left of the redoubt. "The more fighting they get the more they want. They are not so band-boxy as they were, but remind me of an old, mongrel dog I once owned. He wasn't much to look at--but I'll tell you the story later." A sudden quick decision appearing on his face. Evidently the working of his mind had been foreign to his words.

"Saint-Prosper," he said, "I suppose the boys on the other side are going up all the time? I promised our troops the honor of pulling down that flag. I'm a man of my word; go ahead and take the batteries and"--stroking his long gray goatee--"beat Pillow to the top."

A word; a command; they rushed forward; not a laggard in the ranks; not a man who shirked the leaden shower; not one who failed to offer his breast openly and fearlessly to the red death which to them might come when it would. Unwaveringly over rocks, chasms and mines, they followed the tall figure of their leader; death underfoot, death overhead! What would courage avail against concealed mines? Yet like a pack of hounds that reck naught while the scent is warm, they pressed forward, ever forward; across the level opening, where some dropped out of the race, and over the ramparts! A brief struggle; confusion, turmoil; something fearful occurring that no eye could see in its entirety through the smoke; afterwards, a great shout that announced to the palace on the mount the fate of the intermediary batteries!

But there was sharper and more arduous work to come; this, merely a foretaste of the last, fierce stand of the besieged; a stand in which they knew they were fighting for everything, where defeat meant the second conquest of Mexico! From the batteries the assailants had captured to the foot of the castle seemed but a little way to them in their zeal; no one thought of weariness, or the toil of the ascent. But one determination possessed them--to end it all quickly; to carry everything before them! Their victory at the redoubt gave them such sudden, wild confidence that castles seemed no more than ant-hills--to be trampled on! Instinctively every man felt sure of the day and already experienced the glory of conquering that historic hill; that invincible fortress! Over the great valley, so beautiful in its physical features, so inspiring in its associations, should hang the stars of the North, with the stars of heaven!

The scaling ladders were brought up and planted by the storming party; the first to mount were hurled back, killed or wounded, to the rocks below, but others took their places; a lodgment was effected, and, like the water bursting over a dike, a tide of besiegers found ingress.

Under a galling fire, with shouts that rang above the noise of rifles, they drove the masses of the enemy from their guns; all save one, not a Mexican from his fair skin, who stood confidently beside his piece, an ancient machine, made of copper and strengthened by bands of iron. A handsome face; dead to morality, alive to pleasure; the face of a man past thirty, the expression of immortal one-and-twenty! A figure from the pages of Ovid, metamorphosed to a gunner of Santa Anna! The bright radiance from a cloudless sky, the smoke having drifted westward from the summit, fell upon him and his gun.

With inscrutable calmness, one hand fondling the breech, he regarded the fleeting figures and the hoarse-throated pursuers; then, as if to time the opportunity to the moment, he bent over the gun.

"I wonder if this first-born can still bark!" he muttered.

But an instant's hesitation, friend and foe being fairly intermingled, was fatal to his purpose; the venerable culverin remained silent, and the gunner met hand-to-hand a figure that sprang from the incoming host. Simultaneously the rapid firing of a new wave of besiegers from the other side of the castle threw once more a pall of smoke over the scene, and, beneath its mantle, the two men were like figures struggling in a fog, feeling rather than seeing each other's blade, divining by touch the cut, pass or aggressive thrust.

"Faugh!" laughed the gunner. "They'll kill us with smoke."

The discharge of small arms gradually ceased; the fresh breeze again cleared the crest of the mount, showing the white walls of the structure which had been so obstinately defended; the valley, where the batteries now lay silent, having spoken their thundering prologue, and the alien flag, the regimental colors of the invaders, floating from the upper walls. Below on the road toward the city, a band of white across the table land, successive spots of smoke momentarily appeared and were succeeded, after a considerable interval, by the rub-a-dub of rifles. From the disenchanting distance the charge of a body of men, in the attempt to dislodge a party entrenched in a ditch, lost the tragic aspect of warfare, and the soldiers who fell seemed no larger than the toy figures of a nursery game.

With the brightening of the summit to the light of day, eagerly the two combatants near the copper gun gazed for the first time into each other's eyes, and, at that trenchant glance, a tremor crossed the features of the gunner, and his arm, with its muscles of steel, suddenly became inert, powerless.

"Mon Dieu!--'Tis Ernest--little Ernest!" he exclaimed, wonderingly.

For all that his opponent's sword, ominously red from the fierce first assault at the wall, was at his breast, he made no effort to oppose its threatening point, when a grape-shot, swifter than the blade, fairly struck the gunner. With blood streaming from his shoulder, he swayed from side to side, passing his hand before his eyes as one who questions oracular evidence, and then sank to the earth with an arm thrown over the tube of copper. Above his bronzed face the light curls waved like those of a Viking; though his clothes were dyed with the sanguinary hue and his chest rose and fell with labored breathing, it was with an almost quizzical glance he regarded the other who stood as if turned to stone.

"That was not so easily done, Ernest," he said, not unkindly, "but surprise broke down my guard."

"Before God, it was not I!" cried the soldier, starting from a trance.

"And if it were!" With his free arm he felt his shoulder. "I believe you are right," he observed, coolly. "Swords break no bones."

"I will get a surgeon," said the other, as he turned.

"What for? To shake his head? Get no one, or if--for boyish days!--you want to serve me, lend me your canteen."

Saint-Prosper held it to his lips, and he drank thirstily.

"That was a draught in an oasis. I had the desert in my throat--the desert, the wild desert! What a place to meet! But they caught Abd-el-Kader, and there was nothing for it but to flee! Besides, I am a rolling stone."

To hear him who had betrayed his country and shed the blood of his comrades, characterize himself by no harsher term was an amazing revelation of the man's character.

The space around them had become almost deserted; here and there lay figures on the ground among which might be distinguished a sub-lieutenant and other students of the military college, the castle having been both academy and garrison. Their tuition barely over, so early had they given up their lives beneath the classic walls of their alma mater! The exhilarating cheering and shouting had subsided; the sad after-flavor succeeded the lust of conquest.

"Yes," continued the gunner, though the words came with an effort. "First, it was the desert. What a place to roll and rove! I couldn't help it for the life of me! When I was a boy I ran away from school; a lad, I ran away from college! If I had been a sailor I would have deserted the ship. After they captured the prophet, I deserted the desert. So, hey for Mexico, a hilly place for a rolling stone!"

He gasped, held his hand to his shoulder and brought it away covered with red. But that Saint-Prosper knelt swiftly, sustaining and supporting him, he would have slid to the ground. He smiled--sweetly enough--on the stern soldier and placed his moist and stained hand caressingly on that of his companion. Seeing them thus, it was not difficult to trace a family likeness--a similarity in their very dissimilarity. The older was younger; the younger, older. The gunner's hair was light, his face wild as a gerfalcon beneath; the other's dark, with a countenance, habitually repressed, but now, at the touch of that dishonored hand, grown cold and harsh; yet despite the total difference of expression, the hereditary resemblance could not be stamped out. Even the smile of the wounded man was singularly like that of his brother--a rare transformation that seldom failed to charm.

"That's my story," he said, smiling now, as though all the problems of life and death could be thus dismissed. "As the prophet said: 'I have urged my camel through every desert!' You see I know my Koran well. But how came you here, Ernest? I thought you were in Africa, colonizing--us!"

"It was impossible to stay there long," replied Saint-Prosper, slowly.

"There's that cloud of smoke again," muttered the wounded man, apparently oblivious to the other's response. As he spoke he withdrew his hand from that of his brother. At that moment the tropic sun was bathing him in its light and the white walls shone with luster. "No; it's like the desert; the dark hour before the sand-storm." Upon his brow the perspiration gathered, but his lip curled half-scornfully, half-defiantly. "Turn me toward the valley, Ernest. There's more space; more light!"

The soldier, an automaton in passive compliance, placed him where he commanded the outlook cityward; the open plain, protected by the breast-works of mountains; the distant spires trembling on the horizon; the lakes which once marked the Western Venice, a city of perfume and song. Striking a body of water, the sun converted it into a glowing shield, a silver escutcheon of the land of silver, and, in contrast with this polished splendor, the shadows, trailing on the far-away mountains, were soft, deep and velvety. But the freedom of the outlook afforded the wounded man little comfort.

"The storm!" he said.

A change passed over his face, as of a shadow drawn before it. He groped helplessly with his hand.

"Feel in my burnoose, Ernest. A bag--around my neck--open it!"

Saint-Prosper thrust his hand within the coat, shuddering at the contact with the ebbing life's blood, and drew forth a leather bag which he placed in the other's trembling fingers. With an effort, breathing laboriously, and staring hard, as though striving to penetrate a gathering film, the wounded man finally managed to display the contents of the bag, emptying them in his palm, where they glinted and gleamed in the sun's rays. Sapphires, of delicate blue; emeralds with vitreous luster; opals of brilliant iridescence-- but, above all, a ruby of perfect color and extraordinary size, cut en cabachon, and exhibiting a marvelous star of many rays; the ruby of Abd-el-Kader!

With a venal expression of delight, the gunner regarded the contents of the bag, feeling the gems one by one. "The rarest stone-- from the Sagyin hills, Ernest!" he whispered, as his trembling fingers played with the ruby.

But even as he fondled it, a great pain crossed his breast; he gripped his shoulder tight with his free hand, clutching the precious stones hard in his clenched fist. Thus he remained, how long the other never knew, panting, growing paler, as the veins that carried life to his heart were being slowly emptied.

His head dropped. "How dark!" he murmured. "Like a m'chacha where the hashish-smokers dream!"

The younger brother thought his energy was spent when he looked up sharply.

"The lamp's out, you Devil Jew!" he cried. "The pipe, too--spawn of hell!"

And he dropped back like stone, the gems falling from his hand, which twitched spasmodically on the ground and then was still. Saint-Prosper bent over him, but the heart, famished for nourishment, had ceased to beat; the restless, wayward soul had fled from its tabernacle of dust. Save for the stain on his breast and the fixedness of his eyes, he might have been sleeping.

Mechanically the soldier gathered the sapphires, emeralds and other gems--flashing testimony of that thankless past--and, leaning against the wall, gazed afar to the snow-capped volcanoes. Even as he looked, the vapors arose from the solfataras of the "smoking mountain" and a vast shower of cinders and stones was thrown into the air. Unnoticed passed the eruption before the gaze of Saint-Prosper, whose mind in a torpor swept dully back to youth's roseate season, recalling the homage of the younger for the elder brother, a worship as natural as pagan adoration of the sun. From the sanguine fore-time to the dead present lay a bridge of darkness. With honor within grasp, deliberately he had sought dishonor, little recking of shame and murder, and childishly husbanding green, red and blue pebbles!

Weighing the stones in his hand now, Ernest Saint-Prosper looked at them long and bitterly. For these the honor and pride of an old family had been sold. For these he himself had endured the reflected disgrace; isolation from comradeship; distrust which had blighted his military career at the outset. How different had been the reality from his expectations; the buoyant hopes of youth; the fond anticipation of glory, succeeded by stigma and stain! And, as the miserable, perplexing panorama of these later years pictured itself in his brain he threw, with a sudden gesture, the gems far from him, over the wall, out toward the valley!

Like dancing beams of color, they flashed a moment in mid air; then mingled their hues with the rainbow tints of a falling stream. Lost to sight, they sank in the crystal waters which leaped with a caressing murmur toward the table-land; only the tiny spectrum, vivid reminder of their color, still waved and wavered from rock to rock above a pellucid pool.

"I beg your pardon, Colonel," said a voice at his elbow, breaking in upon his reflections; "are you wounded?"

With drawn features, the officer turned.

"No; I am not wounded."

"The general directs you to take this message to the commanding general," continued the little aide. "I believe I may congratulate you, sir, for you will have the honor of bearing the news of the victory." He handed Saint-Prosper a sealed message. "It's been a glorious day, sir, but"--gazing carelessly around him--"has cost many a brave life!"

"Yes, many a life!" answered the other, placing the message in his breast and steadfastly regarding for the last time the figure beneath the gun.

"We ought to be in the City of Mexico in a day or two, sir," resumed the aide. "Won't it be jolly though, after forced marches and all that sort of thing! Fandangos; tambourines; cymbals! And the pulque! What creatures of the moment we are, sir!" he added, with sudden thoughtfulness. "'Twill be, after all, like dancing over the graves of our dear comrades!"

CHAPTER VIII:

A FAIR PENITENT

The reception to General Zachary Taylor, on his return from Mexico, and the inauguration of the carnival combined to the observance of a dual festival day in the Crescent City. Up the river, past the rice fields, disturbing the ducks and pelicans, ploughed the noisy craft bearing "Old Rough and Ready" to the open port of the merry-making town. When near the barracks, the welcoming cannon boomed, and the affrighted darkies on the remote plantations shook with dire forebodings of a Mexican invasion.

The boat rounded at the Place d'Armes, where, beneath a triumphal arch, General Taylor received the crown and chaplet of the people--popular applause--and a salvo of eloquence from the mayor. With flying colors and nourish of trumpets, a procession of civic and military bodies was then formed, the parade finally halting at the St. Charles, where the fatted calf had been killed and the succulent ox roasted. Sounding a retreat, the veteran commander fell back upon a private parlor to recuperate his forces in anticipation of the forthcoming banquet.

From this stronghold, where, however, not all of the enemy--his friends--could be excluded, there escaped an officer, with: "I'll look around town a little, General."

"Look around!" said the commander at the door. "I should think we had looked around! Well, don't fall foul of too many juleps."

With a laughing response, the young man pushed his way through the jostling crowd near the door, traversed the animated corridor, and soon found himself out on the busy street. Amid the variegated colors and motley throng, he walked, not, however, in King Carnival's gay domains, but in a city of recollections. The tavern he had just left was associated with an unforgotten presence; the stores, the windows, the thoroughfares themselves were fraught with retrospective suggestion of the strollers.

Even now--and he came to an abrupt standstill--he was staring at the bill-board of the theater where she had played, the familiar entrance bedecked with bunting and festival inscriptions. Before its classic portals appeared the black-letter announcement of an act by "Impecunious Jordan, Ethiopian artist, followed by a Tableau of General Scott's Capture of the City of Mexico." Mechanically he stepped within and approached the box office. From the little cupboard, a strange face looked forth; even the ticket vender of old had been swallowed up by the irony of fate, and, instead of the well-remembered blond mustache of the erstwhile seller of seats, a dark-bearded man, with sallow complexion, inquired:

"How many?"

"One," said Saint-Prosper, depositing a Mexican piece on the counter before the cubby-hole.

"We've taken in plenty of this kind of money to-day," remarked the man, holding up the coin. "I reckon you come to town with old Zach?"

"Yes." The soldier was about to turn away, when he changed his mind and observed: "You used to give legitimate drama here."

"That was some time ago," said the man in the box, reflectively. "The soldiers like vaudeville. Ever hear Impecunious Jordan?"

"I never did."

"Then you've got a treat," continued the vender. "He's the best in his line. Hope you'll enjoy it, sir," he concluded, with the courtesy displayed toward one and all of "Old Rough and Ready's" men that day. "It's the best seat left in the house. You come a little late, you know." And as the other moved away:

"How different they look before and after! They went to Mexico fresh as daisies, and come back--those that do--dead beat, done up!"

Passing through the door, Saint-Prosper was ushered to his seat in a renovated auditorium; new curtain, re-decorated stalls, mirrors and gilt in profusion; the old restfulness gone, replaced by glitter and show. Amid changed conditions, the derangement of fixed external form and outline, the sight of a broad face in the orchestra and the aspect of a colossal form riveted his attention. This person was neither stouter nor thinner than before; he perspired neither more nor less; he was neither older nor younger--seemingly; he played on his instrument neither better nor worse. Youth might fade, honors take wing, the face of nature change, but Hans, Gargantuan Hans, appeared but a figure in an eternal present! Gazing at that substantial landmark, the soldier was carried back in thought over the long period of separation to a forest idyl; a face in the firelight; the song of the katydid; the drumming of the woodpecker. Dreams; vain dreams! They had assailed him before, but seldom so sharply as now in a place consecrated to the past.

"Look out for the dandies, Girls, beware; Look out for their blandishments, Dears, take care! For they're always ready--remember this!-- To pilfer from maids an unwilling kiss. Oh, me! Oh, my! There! There!" (Imaginary slaps.)

sang and gesticulated a lady in abbreviated skirts and low-cut dress, winking and blinking in ironical shyness, and concluding with a flaunting of her gown, a toe pointed ceilingward, and a lively "breakdown." Then she vanished with a hop, skip and a bow, reappeared with a ravishing smile and threw a generous assortment of kisses among the audience, and disappeared with another hop, skip and a bow, as Impecunious Jordan burst upon the spectators from the opposite side of the stage.

Even the sight of Hans, a finger-post pointing to ways long since traversed, could not reconcile the soldier to his surroundings; the humor of the burnt-cork artist seemed inappropriate to the place; his grotesque dancing inadmissible in that atmosphere once consecrated to the comedy of manners and the stately march of the classic drama. Where Hamlet had moralized, a loutish clown now beguiled the time with some tom-foolery, his wit so broad, his quips were cannon-balls, and his audience, for the most part soldiers from Mexico, open-mouthed swallowed the entire bombardment. But Saint-Prosper, finding the performance dull, finally rose and went out, not waiting for the thrilling Tableaux of the Entrance into the City of Mexico of a hundred American troops (impersonated by young ladies in tropical attire) and the submission of Santa Anna's forces (more young ladies) by sinking gracefully to their bended knees.

Fun and frolic were now in full swing on the thoroughfares; Democritus, the rollicker, had commanded his subjects to drive dull care away and they obeyed the jovial lord of laughter. Animal spirits ran high; mischief beguiled the time; mummery romped and rioted. Marshaled by disorder, armed with drollery and divers-hued banners, they marched to the Castle of Chaos, where the wise are fools, the old are young and topsy-turvy is the order of the day.

As Saint-Prosper stood watching the versicolored concourse swarm by, a sudden rush of bystanders to view Faith on a golden pedestal, looking more like Coquetry, propelled a dainty figure against the soldier. Involuntarily he put out his arm which girded a slender waist; Faith drove simpering by; the crowd melted like a receding wave, and the lady extricated herself, breathless as one of the maids in Lorenzo de Medici's Songs of the Carnival.

"How awkward!" she murmured. "How--"

The sentence remained unfinished and an exclamation, "Mr. Saint-Prosper!" punctuated a gleam of recognition.

"Miss Duran!" he exclaimed, equally surprised, for he had thought the strollers scattered to the four winds.

"Mrs. Service, if you please!" Demurely; at the same time extending her hand with a faint flush. "Yes; I am really and truly married! But it is so long since we met, I believe I--literally flew to your arms!"

"That was before you recognized me," he returned, in the same tone.

Susan laughed. "But how do you happen to be here? I thought you were dead. No; only wounded? How fortunate! Of course you came with the others. I should hardly know you. I declare you're as thin as a lath and gaunt as a ghost. You look older, too. Remorse, I suppose, for killing so many poor Mexicans!"

"And you"--surveying her face, which had the freshness of morn--"look younger!"

"Of course!" Adjusting some fancied disorder of hair or bonnet. "Marriage is a fountain of youth for"--with a sigh--"old maids. Susan Duran, spinster! Horrible! Do you blame me?"

"For getting married? Not at all. Who is the fortunate man?" asked Saint-Prosper.

"A minister; an orthodox minister; a most orthodox minister!"

"No?" His countenance expressed his sense of the incongruity of the union. Susan one of the elect; the meek and lowly yokemate of-- "How did it happen?" he said.

"In a perverse moment, I--went to church," answered Susan. "There, I met him--I mean, I saw him--no, I mean, I heard him! It was enough. All the women were in love with him. How could I help it?"

"He must have been very persuasive."

"Persuasive! He scolded us every minute. Dress and the devil! I"--casting down her eyes--"interested him from the first. He--he married me to reform me."

"Ah," commented the soldier, gazing doubtfully upon Susan's smart gown, which, with elaborate art, followed the contours of her figure.

"But, of course, one must keep up appearances, you know," she continued. "What's the use of being a minister's wife if you aren't popular with the congregation? At least," she added, "with part of them!" And Susan tapped the pavement with a well-shod boot and showed her white teeth. "If you weren't popular, you couldn't fill the seats--I mean pews," she added, evasively. "But you must come and see me--us, I should say."

"Unfortunately, I am leaving to-morrow."

"To-morrow!" repeated Susan, reflectively. The pupils of her eyes contracted, something they did whenever she was thinking deeply, and her gaze passed quickly over his face, striving to read his impassive features. "So soon? When the carnival is on! That is too bad, to stay only one day, and not call on any of your old friends! Constance, I am sure, would be delighted to see you."

Many women would have looked away under the circumstances, but Susan's eyes were innocently fixed upon his. Half the pleasure of the assurance was in the accompanying glance and the friendly smile that went with it.

But a quiet question, "Miss Carew is living here?" was all the satisfaction she received.

"Yes. Have you not heard? She has a lovely home and an embarrassment of riches. Sweet embarrassment! Health and wealth! What more could one ask? Although I forgot, she was taken ill shortly after you left."

"Ill," he said, starting.

"Quite! But soon recovered!" And Susan launched into a narration of the events that had taken place while he was in Mexico, to which he listened with the composure of a man who, having had his share of the vagaries of fate, is not to be taken aback by new surprises, however singular or tragic. Susan expected an expression of regret--by look or word--over the loss of the marquis' fortune, but either he simulated indifference or passed the matter by with philosophical fortitude.

"Poor Barnes!" was his sole comment.

"Yes; it was very lonely for Constance at first," rattled on Susan. "But I fancy she will find a woman's solace for that ailment," she added meaningly.

"Marriage?" he asked soberly.

"Well, the engagement is not yet announced," said Susan, hesitatingly. "But you know how things get around? And the count has been so attentive! You remember him surely--the Count de Propriac? But I must be off. I have an appointment with my husband and am already half an hour late."

"Don't let me detain you longer, then, I beg."

"Oh, I don't mind. He's so delightfully jealous when I fail to appear on the stroke of the clock! Always imagines I am in some misch--but I mustn't tell tales out of school! So glad to have met you! Come and see me--do!"

And Susan with friendly hand-clasp and lingering look, tore herself away, the carnival lightness in her feet and the carnival laughter in her eyes.

"He is in love with her still," she thought, "or he wouldn't have acted so indifferent!" Her mind reverted to a cold little message she had received from Constance. "And to think he was innocent after all!" she continued, mentally reviewing the contents of the letter in which Constance had related the conversation with the lawyer. "I don't believe he'll call on her now, though, after--Well, why shouldn't I have told him what every one is talking about? Why not, indeed?"

A toss of the head dismissed the matter and any doubts pertaining thereto, while her thoughts flew from past to present, as a fortress on a car, its occupants armed with pellets of festival conflict,

---

drove by amid peals of laughter. Absorbed in this scene of merriment, Susan forgot her haste, and kept her apostolic half waiting at the rendezvous with the patience of a Jacob tarrying for a Rachel. But when she did finally appear, with hat not perfectly poised, her hair in a pretty disarray, she looked so waywardly charming, he forgave her on the spot, and the lamb led the stern shepherd with a crook from Eve's apple tree.

"As thin as a lath and gaunt as a ghost!" repeated Saint-Prosper, as the fair penitent vanished in a whirl of gaiety. "Susan always was frank."

Smiling somewhat bitterly, he paused long enough to light a cigar, but it went out in his fingers as he strolled mechanically toward the wharves, through the gardens of a familiar square, where the wheezing of the distant steamers and the echoes of the cathedral clock marked the hours of pleasure or pain to-day as it had tolled them off yesterday. Beyond the pale of the orange trees with their golden wealth, the drays were rumbling in the streets and there were the same signs of busy traffic--for the carnival had not yet become a legal holiday--that he had observed when the strollers had reached the city and made their way to the St. Charles. He saw her anew, pale and thoughtful, leaning on the rail of the steamer looking toward the city, where events, undreamed of, were to follow thick and fast. He saw her, a slender figure, earnest, self-possessed, enter the city gates, unheralded, unknown. He saw her as he had known her in the wilderness--not as fancy might now depict her, the daughter of a marquis--a strolling player, and as such he loved best to think of her.

Arising out of his physical weakness and the period of inaction following the treaty of peace, he experienced a sudden homesickness for his native land; a desire to re-visit familiar scenes, to breathe the sweet air of the country, where his boyhood had been passed, to listen to the thunder of the boulevards, to watch the endless, sad-joyful processions.

Not far distant from the blossoming, redolent square was the office of the Trans-Atlantic Steamship Company, where a clerk, with a spray of jessamine in his coat, bent cordially toward Saint-Prosper as the latter entered, and, approaching the desk, inquired:

"The Dauphin is advertised to sail to-morrow for France?"

"Yes, sir; at twelve o'clock noon."

"Book me for a berth. Ernest Saint-Prosper," he added, in answer to the other's questioning look.

"Very good, sir. Would you like some labels for your baggage? Where shall we send for it? The St. Charles? Very well, sir. Are you going to the tableaux to-night?" he continued, with hospitable interest in one whom he rightly conceived a stranger in the city. "They say it will be the fashionable event. Good-day." As the prospective passenger paid for and received his ticket. "A pleasant voyage! The Dauphin is a new ship and should cross in three weeks--barring bad weather! Don't forget the tableaux. Everybody will be there."

The soldier did not reply; his heart had given a sudden throb at the clerk's last words. Automatically he placed his ticket in his pocket, and randomly answered the employee's further inquiries for instructions. He was not thinking of the Dauphin or her new engines, the forerunner of the modern quadruple-expansion arrangement, but through his brain rang the assurance: "Everybody will be there." And all the way up the street, it repeated itself again and again.

CHAPTER IX:

"COMUS' MISTICK WITCHERIES"

That elusive, nocturnal company, "The Mistick Krewe of Comus," had appeared--"Comus, deep skilled in all his mother's witcheries"--and the dwellers in Phantasmagoria were joyfully numerous. More plentiful than at a modern spectacular performance, reveled gods, demons and fairies, while the children resembled a flight of masquerading butterflies. The ball at the theater, the Roman Veglioni, succeeded elaborate tableaux, the "Tartarus," of the ancients, and "Paradise Lost," of Milton, in which the "Krewe" impersonated Pluto and Proserpine, the fates, harpies and other characters of the representation. In gallery, dress-circle and parquet, the theater was crowded, the spectacle, one of dazzling toilets, many of them from the ateliers of the Parisian modistes; a wonderful evolution of Proserpine's toga and the mortal robes of the immortal Fates. Picture followed picture: The expulsion from Paradise; the conference of the Gorgons, and the court of pandemonium, where gluttony, drunkenness, avarice and vanity were skilfully set forth in uncompromising colors.

Availing themselves of the open-house of the unknown "Krewe," a composite host that vanished on the stroke of twelve, many of "Old Rough and Ready's" retinue mingled with the gathering, their uniforms, well-worn, even shabby, unlike the spick and span regimentals from the costumier. With bronzed faces and the indubitable air of campaigns endured, they were the objects of lively interest to the fair maskers, nor were themselves indifferent to the complaisance of their entertainers. Hands, burned by the sun, looked blacker that night, against the white gowns of waists they clasped; bearded faces more grim visaged in contrast with delicate complexions; embroidery and brocade whirled around with faded uniforms; and dancing aigrettes waved above frayed epaulets and shoulder straps.

"Loog at 'im!" murmured a fille à la cassette, regarding one of these officers who, however, held aloof from the festivities; a well-built young man, but thin and worn, as though he, like his uniform, had seen service. "If he would only carry my trunk!" she laughed, relapsing into French and alluding to the small chest she bore under her arm.

"Or my little white lamb!" gaily added her companion, a shepherdess.

And they tripped by with sidelong looks and obvious challenge which the quarry of these sprightly huntresses of men either chose to disregard or was unconscious of, as he deliberately surveyed his surroundings with more curiosity than pleasure and absently listened to a mountebank from "The Belle's Strategem."

"Who'll buy my nostrums?" cried the buffoon.

"What are they?" asked Folly, cantering near on a hobby horse.

"Different kinds for different people. Here's a powder for ladies--to dispel the rage for intrigue. Here's a pill for politicians--to settle bad consciences. Here's an eye-water for jealous husbands--it thickens the visual membrane. Here's something for the clergy--it eliminates windy discourses. Here's an infusion for creditors--it creates resignation and teaches patience."

"And what have you for lovers?"

"Nothing," answered the clown; "love like fever and ague must run its course. Nostrums! Who'll buy my nostrums?"

"Oh, I'm so glad I came!" enthusiastically exclaimed a tall, supple girl, laden with a mass of flowers.

"Isn't it too bad, though, you can't polka with some of the military gentlemen?" returned her companion who wore a toga and carried a lantern. "Mademoiselle Castiglione wouldn't let you come, until I promised not to allow you out of my sight."

"It was lovely of you to take me," she said, "and I don't mind about the military gentlemen."

"My dear, if all women were like you, we poor civilians would not be relegated to the background! I wish, though, I had worn some other costume. This--ahem, dress!--has a tendency to get between my legs and disconcert my philosophical dignity. I can understand why Diogenes didn't care about walking abroad. My only wonder is that everybody didn't stay in his tub in those days. Don't talk to me about the 'noble Roman!' Why, he wore skirts!"

"And Monsieur Intaglio lectured to us for an hour to-day about the wonderful drapery of the ancients!" laughed the girl. "The poetry of dress, he called it!"

"Then I prefer prose. Hello!"--pausing and raising his lantern, as they drew near the officer who had fallen under the observation of the fille à la cassette. "Colonel Saint-Prosper, or set me down for an ass--or Plato, which is the same thing!"

"Straws!" said the soldier, as the bard frankly lifted his mask and tilted it back over his forehead.

"Glad to see you!" continued the poet, extending his hand. "I haven't run across you before since the night of the banquet; the début of Barnes' company you remember? You must have left town shortly afterward. Returned this morning, of course! By the way, there's one of your old friends here to-night."

Saint-Prosper felt the color mount to his face, and even Straws noted the change. "Who is that?" asked the soldier, awkwardly.

"Mrs. Service--Miss Duran that was--now one of our most dashing--I should say, charitable, ladies. Plenty of men at Service's church now. She's dressed in Watteau-fashion to-night, so if you see any one skipping around, looking as though she had just stepped from the Embarkation for the Island of Venus, set her down for the minister's pretty wife!"

"And the minister?" asked Saint-Prosper, mechanically.

"He brought her; he compromised on a Roundhead costume, himself! But we must be off. Au revoir; don't be backward; the ladies are all military-mad. It may be a field of arms"--casting his glance over the assemblage of fashionably dressed ladies, with a quizzical smile--"but not hostile arms! Come, Celestina--Nydia, I mean!"

And Straws' arm stole about the waist of his companion, as Saint-Prosper watched them disappearing in the throng of dancers. It was Celestina's first ball, and after her long training at the Castiglione institute, she danced divinely. Evidently, too, she was reconciled to the warden's edict, denying her the freedom of the ball-room, for she showed no disposition to escape from Straws' watchful care. On the contrary, though her glance wandered to the wonders around her, they quickly returned to the philosopher with the lamp, as though she courted the restraint to which she was subjected. Something like a pang shot through the soldier's breast as he followed the pair with his gaze; he seemed looking backward into a world of youth and pleasure, passed beyond recall.

"It is useless to deny it! I knew you when I first saw you!" exclaimed a familiar voice near by, and turning around sharply, the officer observed approaching a masked lady, graceful of figure and lacking nothing in the numerical strength of her escort. It was to her that these words were addressed by an agile man of medium stature who had apparently penetrated her disguise. The lady, who would have attracted attention anywhere by her bearing, wore a pardessus of white gauze, fitting close and bordered with a silver band; the sleeves, short; the skirt of white gauze and very ample, as the fashion of the day required; the feet shod in small white silk "bottines"; the hair in bands, ornamented with wild poppies. Altogether this costume was described by Phazma as "ravishing, the gown adorning the lady, and the lady the gown, her graces set forth against the sheen of voluminous satin folds, like those of some portrait by Sir Joshua or Gainsborough."

"How could you expect any one not to know you?" continued the speaker, as this little coterie drew near, their masks a pretext for mystery. "You may impersonate, but you can not deceive."

"That is a poor compliment, since you take me for an actress," laughed the lady. An hilarious outburst from an ill-assorted cluster of maskers behind them drowned his reply, and the lady and her attendants passed on.

Saint-Prosper drew his breath sharply. "She is here, after all," he said to himself.

"A nostrum for jilted beaux!" called out a mountebank, seeing him standing there, preoccupied, alone, at the same time tendering a pill as large as a plum. A punchinello jarred against him with: "Pardonnez moi, pardie!" On the perfumed air the music swelled rapturously; a waltz, warm with the national life of Vienna; the swan song of Lanner! Softly, sweetly, breathed "Die Schönbrunner;" faster whirled the moving forms. Eyes flashed more brightly; little feet seemed born for dancing; cheeks, pale at midday, were flushed with excitement! Why doesn't he dance, wondered the lady with the white lamb. Carnival comes but once a year; a mad, merry time; when gaiety should sweep all cares out of doors!

"Said Strephon to Chloe: 'For a kiss, I'll give thee the choice of my flock.' Said Chloe to Strephon: 'What bliss, If you'll add to the gift a new smock,'"

hummed the lively nymph, as she tripped by.

"Said Chloe to Strephon: 'For a kiss, I'll return thee the choice of your flock. Said Strephon to Chloe: 'What bliss, With it I'll buy Phyllis a new frock,'"

she concluded, throwing a glance over her shoulder.

A sudden distaste for the festal ferment, the laughter and merriment; a desire to escape from the very exuberance of high spirits and cheer led the soldier to make his way slowly from the ball-room to the balcony, where, although not removed from the echoes of liveliness within, he looked out upon the quietude of the night. Overhead stretched the sky, a measureless ocean, with here and there a silvery star like the light on a distant ship; an unfathomable sea of ether that beat down upon him. Radiant and serene, in the boundless calm of the heavens, the splendent lanterns seemed suspended on stationary craft peacefully rocked at anchor. Longings, suppressed through months of absence, once more found full sway; Susan's words were recalled by the presence of the count.

Suddenly the song of "Die Schönbrunner" ceased within, and, as its pulsations became hushed, many of the dancers, an elate, buoyant throng, sought the balcony. Standing in the shadow near the entrance, aroused from a train of reflections by this abrupt exodus, the soldier saw among the other merry-makers, Constance and the count, who passed through the door, so near he could almost have touched her.

"Here she is," said the count, as they approached an elderly lady, seated near the edge of the balcony. "Ah, Madam," he continued to the latter, "if you would only use your good offices in my behalf! Miss Carew is cruelty itself."

"Why, what has she done?" asked the good gentlewoman.

"Insisted upon deserting the ball-room!"

"In my day," said the elderly ally of the nobleman, "you could not drag the young ladies from cotillion or minuet. And the men would stay till the dawn to toast them!"

"And I've no doubt, Madam, your name was often on their lips," returned the count gallantly, who evidently believed in the Spanish proverb: "Woo the duenna, not the maid; then in love the game's well played!"

The ally in his cause made some laughing response which the soldier did not hear. Himself unseen, Saint-Prosper bent his eyes upon the figure of the young girl, shadowy but obvious in the reflected light of the bright constellations. Even as he gazed, her hand removed the mask, revealing the face he knew so well. In the silence below, the fountain tinkled ever so loudly, as she stood, half-turned toward the garden, a silken head-covering around her shoulders; the head outlined without adornment, save the poppies in her hair.

Her presence recalled scenes of other days: the drive from the races, when her eyes had beamed so softly beneath the starry luster. Did she remember? He dared not hope so; he did not. To him, it brought, also, harsher memories; yet his mind was filled most with her beauty, which appeared to gloss over all else and hold him, a not impassive spectator, to the place where she was standing. She seemed again Juliet--the Juliet of inns and school-house stages--the Juliet he had known before she had come to New Orleans, whose genius had transformed the barren stage into a garden of her own creation.

And yet something made her different; an indefinable new quality appeared to rest upon her. He felt his heart beating faster; he was glad he had come; for the moment he forgot his jealousy in watching her, as with new wealth of perfume, the languid breeze stirred the tresses above her pallid, immovable features. But the expression of confidence with which the count was regarding her, although ostensibly devoting himself to her companion, renewed his inquietude.

Had she allowed herself to be drawn into a promised alliance with that titled roué? Involuntarily the soldier's face grew hard and stern; the count's tactics were so apparent--flattering attention to the elderly gentlewoman and a devoted, but reserved, bearing toward the young girl in which he would rely upon patience and perseverance for the consummation of his wishes. But certainly Constance did not exhibit marked preference for his society; on the contrary, she had hardly spoken to him since they had left the ball-room. Now clasping the iron railing of the balcony, she leaned farther out; the flowers of the vine, clambering up one of the supports, swayed gently around her, and she started at the moist caress on her bare arm.

"It is cold here," she said, drawing back.

"Allow me--your wrap!" exclaimed the count, springing to her side with great solicitude.

But she adjusted the garment without his assistance.

"You must be careful of your health--for the sake of your friends!" Accompanying the words with a significant glance.

"The count is right!" interposed the elderly gentlewoman. "As he usually is!" she added, laughing.

"Oh, Madam!" he said, bowing. "Miss Carew does not agree with you, I am sure?" Turning to the girl.

"I haven't given the matter any thought," she replied, coldly. She shivered slightly, nervously, and looked around.

At that moment the lights were turned on in the garden--another surprise arranged by the Mistick Krewe!--illuminating trees and shrubbery, and casting a sudden glare upon the balcony.

"Bravo!" said the count. "It's like a fête-champêtre! And hear the mandolins! Tra-la-la-la-la! Why, what is it?"

She had given a sudden cry and stood staring toward the right at the back of the balcony. Within, the orchestra once more began to play, and, as the strains of music were wafted to them, a host of masqueraders started toward the ball-room. When the inflow of merry-makers had ceased, bewildered, trembling, she looked with blanched face toward the spot where the soldier had been standing, but he was gone.

At that moment the cathedral clock began to strike--twelve times it sounded, and, at the last stroke, the Mistick Krewe, one by one began to disappear, vanishing as mysteriously as they had come. Pluto, Proserpine, the Fates, fairies and harpies; Satan, Beelzebub; the dwellers in pandemonium; the aids to appetite--all took their quick departure, leaving the musicians and the guests of the evening, including the visiting military, to their own pleasures and devices. The first carnival had come to a close.

CHAPTER X:
CONSTANCE AND THE SOLDIER

"**A**re you the clerk?" A well-modulated voice; a silvery crown of hair leaning over the counter of the St. Charles; blue eyes, lighted with unobtrusive inquiry.

The small, quiet-looking man addressed glanced up. "No," he said; "I am the proprietor. This"--waving his hand to a resplendent-appearing person--"is the clerk."

Whereupon the be-diamonded individual indicated (about whom an entire chapter has been written by an observing English traveler!) came forward leisurely; a Brummell in attire; an Aristarchus for taste! Since his period--or reign--there have been many imitators; but he was the first; indeed, created the office, and is deserving of a permanent place in American annals. "His formality just bordered on stiffness," wrote the interested Briton, as though he were studying some new example of the human species; "his conversation was elegant, but pointed, as he was gifted with a cultured economy of language. He accomplished by inflection what many people can only attain through volubility."

"Yes?" he interrogatively remarked, gazing down at the caller in the present instance.

"Is Colonel Saint-Prosper stopping here?"

"Yes."

"Send this card to his room."

"Yes?" Doubtfully.

"Is there any reason why you shouldn't?"

"There was a military banquet last night," interposed the quiet, little man. "Patriotism bubbled over until morning."

"Ah, yes," commented Culver--for it was he--"fought their battles over again! Some of them in the hospital to-day! Well, well, they suffered in a glorious cause, toasting the president, and the army, and the flag, and the girls they left behind them! I read the account of it in the papers this morning. Grand speech of the bishop; glorious response of 'Old Rough and Ready'! You are right to protect sleeping heroes, but I'm afraid I must run the guard, as my business is urgent."

A few moments later the lawyer, breathing heavily, followed a colored lad down a crimson-carpeted corridor, pausing before a door upon which his guide knocked vigorously and then vanished.

"Colonel Saint-Prosper?" said the lawyer, as he obeyed the voice within and entered the room, where a tall young man in civilian attire was engaged in packing a small trunk. "One moment, pray--let me catch my breath. That lad accomplished the ascent two steps at a time, and, I fear, the spectacle stimulated me to unusual expedition. We're apt to forget we are old and can't keep up with boys and monkeys!"

During this somewhat playful introduction the attorney was studying the occupant of the room with keen, bright gaze; a glance which, without being offensive, was sufficiently penetrating and comprehensive to convey a definite impression of the other's face and figure. The soldier returned his visitor's look deliberately, but with no surprise.

"Won't you sit down?" he said.

Culver availed himself of the invitation. "I am not disturbing you? I have long known of you, although this is our first meeting."

"You have then the advantage of me," returned Saint-Prosper, "for I--"

"You never heard of me?" laughed the lawyer. "Exactly! We attorneys are always getting our fingers in every one's affairs! I am acquainted with you, as it were, from the cradle to the--present!"

"I am unexpectedly honored!" remarked the listener, satirically.

"First, I knew you through the Marquis de Ligne."

Saint-Prosper started and regarded his visitor more closely.

"I was the humble instrument of making a fortune for you; it was also my lot to draw up the papers depriving you of the same!" Culver laughed amiably. "'Oft expectation fails, where most it promises.' Pardon my levity! There were two wills; the first, in your favor; the last, in his daughter's. I presume"--with a sudden, sharp look--"you have no intention of contesting the final disposition? The paternity of the child is established beyond doubt."

Artful Culver was not by any means so sure in his own mind that, if the other were disposed to make trouble, the legal proofs of Constance's identity would be so easily forthcoming. Barnes was dead; her mother had passed away many years before; the child had been born in London--where?--the marquis' rationality, just before his demise, was a debatable question. In fact, since he had learned Saint-Prosper was in the city, the attorney's mind had been soaring among a cloud of vague possibilities, and now, regarding his companion with a most kindly, ingratiating smile, he added:

"Besides, when the marquis took you as a child into his household, there were, I understood, no legal papers drawn!"

"I don't see what your visit portends," said Saint-Prosper, "unless there is some other matter?"

"Just so," returned Culver, his doubts vanishing. "There was a small matter--a slight commission. Miss Carew requested me to hand you this message." The visitor now detected a marked change in the soldier's imperturbable bearing, as the latter took the envelope which the attorney offered him. "The young lady saw you at the Mistick Krewe ball last night, and, recognizing an old friend,"--with a slight accent--"pressed me into her service. And now, having completed my errand, I will wish you good-morning!" And the lawyer briskly departed.

The young man's hand trembled as he tore open the envelope, but he surveyed the contents of the brief message with tolerable firmness.

"COLONEL SAINT-PROSPER: Will you kindly call this morning to see me?

CONSTANCE CAREW."

That was all; nothing more, save the address and the date! How long he remained staring at it with mingled feelings he never knew, but finally with a start, looked at his watch, thoughtfully regarded the half-filled trunk, donned his coat and left the room. Several fellow-officers, the first of the sluggards to appear, spoke to him as he crossed the hall below, but what they said or what he replied he could not afterward remember. Some one detained him at the steps, a gentleman with a longing for juleps, but finally he found himself in a carriage, driving somewhere, presumably to the address given in the letter. How long the drive seemed, and yet when the carriage finally stopped and he had paid his fare, he mentally determined it had been too short! The driver gazed in surprise after the gentleman, who did not wait for his change, but, forbearing injudicious comment, gathered up the reins and drove to the nearest café.

From the carriage the house was some distance, and yet it appeared very near the gate to the soldier, who dimly realized he was passing through a garden where were many flowering plants and where the air was unusually heavy with perfume. Many other details, the construction of the house, the size of the verandas, passed without attracting his notice. Soon, however, he was seated in a great room, an apartment of old-fashioned height and breadth. He felt his heart beating fast. How long did he sit there? No inconsiderable period, surely. He examined everything carefully, without carrying a definite impression of anything to his mind. The large, carved mirror; the quaint decoration of walls and frieze; the soft colors of the rug that covered the floor; the hundred and one odd little things in the cabinet near the chair where he was seated, trifles in ivory, old silver and china; the pictures, a Van Dyke, Claude, and a few modern masters. After this interminable, but confused scrutiny of inanimate things, his heart beat faster still, as a tall figure, robed in white, entered the room!

He rose; they regarded each other with mutual constraint; her face had a bit of color, like the tinge of a rose-leaf; her eyes seemed agitated beneath the sweeping lashes, a sentiment in ill accord with the stateliness of her presence. She gave him her hand; he held it he knew not how long; probably, for the conventional moment. They found themselves, each in a chair; at ease, yet not at ease; he studying her face, furtively, yet eagerly; she turning in her fancy the first strong impression of how gaunt and haggard were his features, bearing the traces of recent illness!

"I am glad you came," she began, their eyes meeting once more.

He bowed. "Mr. Culver brought me your message."

"I heard that you--it was reported you were dead."

"I was wounded; that was all, and soon took to the field again."

The suspense that fell between them was oppressive.

"You should have let your friends--know," she said at length.

He looked at her curiously, vivid memories of their last interview recurring to him. Indecisively she interlaced her fingers, and he, watching them, wondered why she had sent for him. Suddenly she rose, walked to the window, and stood, looking out. He, sitting in the dim light, in a maze of uncertainty, was vaguely conscious of her figure outlined against the brightness without; of the waving, yellow flowers of the vines on the veranda.

"It is long since we have met," he said, awkwardly.

She did not answer. Had she heard? Yet he did not resent her silence. If he had ever felt anger for her it had all vanished now. He was only conscious of regarding her more attentively, as she still remained, gazing out into the sunlit garden.

"Much has happened since I saw you," he continued.

She turned; her eyes were moist; her hand trembled a little against her dress, but she held her head proudly, as she had always done, and it was the aspect of this weakness set against strength that appealed swiftly to him, softening his heart so that he longed to spring to her side.

"Yes, much!" she replied.

Was her voice tremulous, or was it but the thrill of his own heart which made it seem so?

"You have been here long?" she asked, still holding back what was on her mind or blindly endeavoring to approach the subject.

"Only since yesterday."

"And you remain some time?"

"I am leaving to-day--for France."

At that a touch of color left her face, or was it that a darkening shadow fell upon the house and garden, momentarily chastening the outlook?

"For France?" she repeated.

Her lips quivered. Something seemed to still the beating of his heart.

"Constance--what is it?" he half-whispered.

She stepped forward suddenly, her hands outstretched.

"I wronged you!" she cried. "I wronged you. I thought the disgrace was yours. Oh, do not speak!" she added, passionately. "I have suffered for it--and now, would you mind--please--leaving me?"

"You thought the disgrace was mine!" he repeated, slowly. "Not my"--he broke off abruptly. "And you suffered--for it?" he said, wonderingly. "Then you--" He arose quickly and approached her, a new expression transfiguring his bronzed and worn young face.

Swiftly he sought her glance; her eyes gave irrefutable answer. Unresistingly, she abandoned herself to his arms, and he felt her bosom rise and fall with conflicting emotions. Closely he held her, in the surprise and surpassing pleasure of the moment; then, bending, he kissed her lips. A wave of color flooded her face, though her eyes still sought his. But even as he regarded her, the clear, open look gradually changed, replaced by one of half-perplexity, half-reproach.

"That night you went away--why did you not defend yourself?" she asked, finally.

"I never imagined--any mistake. Besides, what had I to offer? Your future was bright; your name, on every one's lips!"

"Did you think you were responsible for another's sins?"

His dark features clouded.

"I suppose I had become accustomed to cold looks. In Africa, by some of my comrades who had an inkling of the story! No matter what I did, I was his brother! And the bitterest part was that I loved him; loved him from my boyhood! He was the handsomest, most joyous fellow! Even when he died in my arms in Mexico my heart could not absolutely turn from him."

She opened her lips as if to speak, but the shadow on his face kept her silent.

"I was weak enough to keep the story from you in the first place--a foolish reticence, for these matters follow a man to the ends of the world."

"Oh," she said, "to think it was I who made you feel this!"

He took her hand; his grasp hurt her fingers; yet she did not shrink.

"You showed me a new world," he answered, quickly. "Not the world I expected to find--where life would hold little of joy or zest-- but a magical world; a beautiful world; yours!"

She half-hung her head. "But then--then--"

"It became a memory; bitter-sweet; yet more sweet than bitter!"

"And now?"

He did not answer immediately.

The figure of the count, as he had seen him the night before, had abruptly entered his mind. Did she understand? She smiled.

"And now?"

At her question he dismissed all thought of jealousy. Looking into her clear, half-laughing eyes, he read of no entangling alliances; without words from her, he understood.

"Shall we go into the garden?" she said, and, opening the window, they stepped out upon the veranda.

In the sky a single large cloud stretched itself in a dreamy torpor, too sluggish, apparently to move, while a brood of little clouds nestled and slept around it. From the window, the count's ally watched them, among the plants and vines, pausing now and then; their interest more in themselves than in the liveliest hues or forms that nature offered. He stood still, regarding his shadow on the path seriously.

"Nearly noon by the soldier's dial!" he said.

She pushed back the hair the wind had blown about her brow.

"My boat sails in an hour," he continued.

"But--you are not--going--now?"

"If I stay, it must be--"

"Forever!" she said. "Forever!"

* * * * *

"Have you heard the news?" said Susan to the count.

"Secular?" drawled the erstwhile emissary. He was in ill-humor, having called three times on Constance, who had been excused on all these occasions.

"Not necessarily," replied she, with the old familiar toss of the head. "Saint-Prosper has come back, and he's going to marry Constance!"

"Eh? What? I don't be--Who told you?" demanded the count, sharply.

"Well, you needn't take my head off! She did, if you want to know."

"Miss Carew?"

"Herself!"

The nobleman lolled back in his chair, a dark look on his face. Here were fine hopes gone a-glimmering!

"Pardie! the creditors will have to wait awhile," he thought. "And I--I have been a dunce, dancing attendance all these days! I had hoped to marry wealth and beauty. What did I come over here for? The demned country's barren of everything!"

"Isn't it delightful they should meet after such a long time?" rattled on Susan, gaily. "So romantic! And then they were exactly suited for each other. Dear me,"--enthusiastically--"I have taken such an interest in them, I almost feel as if I had brought it all about."

THE END